In Development

Rachel Spangler

IN DEVELOPMENT
© 2018 BY RACHEL SPANGLER

THIS TRADE PAPERBACK ORIGINAL IS PUBLISHED BY BRISK PRESS, BRIELLE, NEW JERSEY, 08730

SUBSTANTIVE EDIT BY: LYNDA SANDOVAL
COPY EDIT BY: JONATHAN CROWLEY
COVER DESIGN BY: TREEHOUSE STUDIO
AUTHOR PHOTO BY: WILLIAM BANKS
BOOK LAYOUT AND TYPESETTING BY: KELLY SMITH

FIRST PRINTING: MAY 2018

THIS IS A WORK OF FICTION. NAMES, CHARACTERS, PLACES, AND INCIDENTS ARE THE PRODUCT OF THE AUTHOR'S IMAGINATION OR ARE USED FICTITIOUSLY. ANY RESEMBLANCE TO ACTUAL PERSONS, LIVING OR DEAD, BUSINESS ESTABLISHMENTS, EVENTS, OR LOCALES IS ENTIRELY COINCIDENTAL.

THIS BOOK, OR PARTS THEREOF, MAY NOT BE REPRODUCED IN ANY FORM WITHOUT PERMISSION FROM THE AUTHOR OR THE PUBLISHER.

ISBN-13: 978-0-9987907-2-5

I read that the traditional symbols of the twelfth anniversary are silk and linen to represent luxury and comfort. Susie, you have given me both in exactly the right portions to help me thrive. So, of course, number twelve is all your fault.

Acknowledgments

This book is a love story about two women living in a world most of us can only dream about, and I won't deny part of its appeal draws heavily on our desire to live similar lives of fame and fortune. On a deeper level, however, it relies on my connection to a wonderfully familiar and diverse world filled with female artists. I am inspired every day by women who create and share and spread their knowledge and talents through a myriad of mediums. I have tried to imbue my characters with parts of that artistic passion. Of course, people who are looking will likely see the influence of the more famous figures whose words and experiences helped shape my characters, women like Ellen Page, Taylor Swift, Emma Watson, and my dear friend Diane Gaidry (Diane also deserves a lot of credit for helping me get some of the showbiz terms right.) But along the way, I've also been influenced by and drawn strength from countless other women writers, songstresses, filmmakers, writers, and storytellers. The women of the #MeToo and #Timesup movements have been particularly inspirational over the last few months, but so have many others stretching all the way back to my childhood. I hope as you read you see my admiration for women who face insurmountable odds and risk parts of themselves in order to create art and foster change in a world that is still very much stacked against them.

With that said, I've been blessed to work with some pretty inspiring women on this project as well. The first two of them I need to thank are Susan X. Meagher and Carolyn Norman of Brisk Press. When I first approached them about this book, it was to ask a favor. I wanted to release in the spring, less than a year out, and right between two other books I'd already scheduled with my full-time publisher. It was a time-shortened job, I had no idea what I was doing, and it created a bunch of extra work for them and their imprint, and yet neither of them hesitated. They have both been patient and fun to work with, and I have learned so much along the way.

And while this is a Brisk Press book, I couldn't have done it without the support of my Bywater family. If an author had told most other publishers she wanted to publish a book on six months' notice with a different press, the answer would generally be no, and in some cases lawyers would be called. With the awesome women of Bywater Books, it was more along the lines of "How can we help?" Salem West, Marianne K. Martin, Kelly Smith, and Ann McMan have all been wonderfully understanding. Kelly did the typeset of this book to make sure it was done to her high standards, and as I'm sure you can tell by looking at this amazing cover, it is the handiwork of Ann McMan, famous designer (and author). I've always referred to them as my team because we're working together toward a common goal, but people who work beside you even when they don't have anything to gain, that feels more like a family.

Speaking of family of choice, I am blessed to have a wide and diverse group of people I lean heavily on when trying to make sure everything I publish is the best it can be. I trust them with my work, my ego, my voice, my truth. As always, Barb Dallinger and Toni Whitaker were my first readers, my sounding boards, my cheerleaders who gave me the confidence to plow forward. Lynda Sandoval, editor and friend extraordinaire, helped me fly through new scenes and new insights. For the first time, with this book, I'm working with a new copy editor in Jon Crowley, but Jon is not new to my family of choice. We've known each other since we were both little rainbow Redbird babies, and I was proud to place my new baby into his very capable hands. Another friend from my ISU days, who has become so much more in so many ways, is responsible for my author photo. Thanks for being handy with the camera, Will Banks, aka B. Papi. I also have a wonderful crew of proof readers including, Marcie, Cara, Susan, and Ann who served as my powerful and final line of defense against the horror of typos in the final draft. I thank them all endlessly!

And last but certainly not least are those people whose contributions to my writing are harder to quantify, but whose contributions to my life are boundless. I have the best writing buddies who are also the best distraction buddies, and while those things might appear to be in opposition, they really aren't, because Georgia Beers, Melissa Brayden, Nikki Smalls, and Lynda Sandoval's constant support, humor, and kicks in the pants never let me forget I have the best job in the world. The same goes for every reader who has ever taken the time to read my books and send me feedback. Even on my worst, most insecure days, hearing your words of encouragement reminds me that every day I spend telling stories is a blessing.

And when it comes to blessings, no acknowledgment would be complete without at least attempting to acknowledge that some people mean more to me than all the words in the world could convey. Jackie boy, you are my light, my happy place, and my faith in the future. Susie, you are my rock, my foundation, and my sanctuary, come what may. The two of you make up the two halves of my heart.

Lastly, none of these blessings would be in my life without my loving creator, redeemer and sanctifier. *Soli Deo Gloria.*

Chapter One

The office of Levy and Levy was a whir of human energy vibrating off glass and steel. Everywhere phones rang or buzzed, and there wasn't a surface that didn't glisten or gleam. All the bustle and brightness made Cobie Galloway feel even more out of place than she had outside in Times Square. The lights there were brighter and the noises louder, but at least she'd blended into the crowd. As soon as the elevator doors had opened on the forty-second floor, every eye trained on her. Well, maybe not her so much as her clothes or her hair or perhaps the way she slouched and shuffled up to the desk.

Then again, maybe her demeanor made her stand out more than her low-slung jeans and plain cream waffle-weave shirt. She didn't act like she owned the place, unlike every other sleek, suit-clad person bustling back and forth, talking on a myriad of devices: phones, tablets, Bluetooth earpieces. One guy even seemed to be chatting with his watch. She glanced down at the thick script in her hands and considered trying to have a conversation with it. Instead, she chose the old-fashioned approach and smiled at the receptionist with a severe up-do.

"Hi."

"Yes?" the woman asked, drumming her jet-black fingernails on her frosted glass desk.

"I'm Stan's eleven-thirty appointment."

The receptionist pursed her lips in a way that suggested she highly doubted the truth of the statement but clicked open a document on her iPad. "Mr. Levy has an eleven-thirty appointment with . . ." Her voice trailed off, and she regarded Cobie with a little more interest. Gray eyes flicked over her attire and settled on her face, clearly searching for something to tip the scales of recognition. Cobie decided to make it easier on them both, so she shook her shoulder-length brunette hair from her face, then fluttered her eyelashes a little.

The receptionist's entire demeanor changed. She leaned forward in her chair, showing a startling amount of cleavage, her cheeks flushing pink and her lips curving upward. "Oh, honey, you're much taller than you look in all the movies."

"It's the angles they shoot from," she said frankly. "Jeremy doesn't like anyone to know how short he is."

Her eyebrows shot up. "How short is he?"

Cobie smiled. "Five-seven on a good day. When I'm barefoot, I look him in the eye."

"And is everything else about him . . ." She glanced around like she knew she shouldn't ask but couldn't pass up the chance. "Proportional?"

Cobie shrugged. "I wouldn't know. He uses a body double for love scenes."

The secretary's mouth dropped, and Cobie felt the tiniest bit of guilt. She didn't care a wit about protecting Jeremy's fragile ego, but she didn't want to do anything that might serve as tabloid fodder. She worked hard to protect her own life. She wouldn't want to carelessly subject someone else to that kind of scrutiny, whether she particularly enjoyed their company or not. "That's just between us though, okay?"

The woman pantomimed zipping her lips, locking them, and then depositing the imaginary key in a wastebasket under her translucent desk. The little display made Cobie realize the young woman likely had acting aspirations, which reminded her why she'd stopped by in the first place. "Is Stan in?"

"Oh, yes, of course." The woman rose. "Right this way."

Cobie followed her through a series of hallways reminiscent

of a shiny anthill. She wondered if she should leave breadcrumbs to find her way back, but she was sure one of the starving actresses or musicians waiting in the wings would eat them before her meeting finished.

Finally, the last hallway dead-ended into a massive set of frosted glass doors accented in polished chrome. The receptionist pressed a button Cobie couldn't see and whispered, "Cobie Galloway to see you."

The doors swung open seemingly of their own volition, and the receptionist motioned for her to go inside, even though she didn't cross the threshold herself.

"Thanks," Cobie said, hesitating slightly, as though she'd been summoned by the great and powerful Oz. Then she remembered she'd called this meeting with her manager, who worked for her. Taking a deep breath, she lifted her chin and stepped purposefully inside.

"Hey, Stan."

He smiled at her, holding up one finger and motioning to a cell phone against his ear, and turned to stare out the large windows. "I don't care how much money he thinks the project is going to make. That's a problem for the producers. I only care what my client makes, and if there's not another zero on the next contract I get from you, we'll go shopping."

She should probably be glad he said things like that. Hell, maybe he'd said it for her benefit. He'd likely said it on her behalf several times in the last ten years, and judging from the view of Times Square from his office, he got the answer he wanted more often than not. That's why she stayed with him, she reminded herself. He knew how to get what he wanted, which was what she wanted.

She took a seat in what she assumed was a chair, even though it was made entirely of chrome and angled in a way that kept her feet from touching the ground. Staring down at the script in her lap, she flipped it open and ran her fingers over the title.

Vigilant.

The word stood in bold print. When she closed her eyes, she

could still see it. She'd dreamt about it last night. This was the project she'd waited a decade to be a part of, a project that could make, or rather *remake,* her career into something she could be proud of.

"Cobie." Stan's voice boomed from across the room as he tossed his phone onto the desk. "What a treat to see you in person. What brings you to the city?"

"I heard my manager works here."

"He does. He works very hard here, makes the big deals too, but enough about me." He flashed her a smile, showing teeth too bright not to have been enhanced somehow. "Tell me about you. Surely you didn't fly in just to meet with me. You got a hot date?"

She shook her head. "No, I really wanted to talk to you about my next project."

"Oh, yes. Let me see." He tapped his temple, drawing attention to the fact that his dark, wavy hair had grayed considerably at the sides. "You just wrapped the last Nick Sparks adaptation, right? Hey, how's Jeremy?"

"He's Jeremy," she said with a sigh. "So very . . . Jeremy."

"Ah, I remember you two canoodling outside my office when you were just kids."

She wanted to say she'd never canoodled. Not with Jeremy or anyone else, especially in his office. But she needed to stay focused.

"The time sure does fly, and now you're practically all grown up, both of you."

"Actually, that's what I'm here to talk about," Cobie cut in. "I *have* grown up, and I'm ready for the roles I take on to reflect my maturity."

He stopped abruptly on his stroll down memory lane to look at her seriously for the first time.

"I was looking over the script for *Vigilant* last night."

His eyes went wide, signaling she had his full attention now. "*Vigilant* is a *New York Times* bestseller. Where did you get the script?"

She shook her head, not wanting to go there. She couldn't let the conversation become about her contacts versus his. "That doesn't matter as much as the fact that it's drafted and in my hands to negotiate with."

"Negotiate?" He eyed the document like the Pope might look at a crucifix.

"A full treatment, script, screen writer, and female lead," Cobie said in her most businesslike voice. "It's a package deal. All or nothing."

"Nothing is all or nothing," he mumbled and began to pace. "I heard the author wasn't willing to negotiate, or I'd have beaten down her door myself."

"Yes. But would you have pitched me for the lead?"

"Uh, well." He smoothed his thumb over his eyebrows. "The thing is this will be a very sought-after role."

"So no, then?"

"It's not that I don't think you could handle the acting." He started patronizing, and she gritted her teeth to stay calm long enough to see if he could turn it around. "But since so many people have read the book, they're going to have an image in their heads for the character of Vale."

"And I don't fit the image?"

"No. But do you know who I spoke to last night?"

"Not a clue."

"Christopher Columbus, the director, not the explorer." He chuckled at his own joke.

She rolled her eyes. "I'm sure he's never heard that one before."

"He's doing *Night at the Museum Four*, and there's going to be a love interest for the son this time."

"The son that went to college in the last movie?"

"Yes, that's the one."

"So I'd play a college student?"

"Exactly, but there'll be a few fun action scenes."

She sighed and wiggled her way out of the awkward art chair. "I'm twenty-six years old, and I've never played a character over the age of nineteen."

"Okay, well, Jeremy is in talks for one where he plays a city kid who gets offered a job on a dude ranch for the summer."

"Target audience?" she asked drolly, already knowing the answer.

"Girls, twelve to eighteen."

"I'm too old for teen movies," she said flatly.

"Oh, honey, don't talk about yourself that way. You could easily pass for a high school student. Did you know Olivia Newton-John was twenty-nine when she played the role of Sandy in *Grease*?"

"You've mentioned it before, but the thing is, I don't want to pass for younger than I am."

He opened his mouth but didn't seem to know how to respond to the comment. "Say again?"

"I don't want to be Olivia Newton-John. Don't get me wrong. She killed that role, but I don't want to be America's sweetheart anymore. I don't want to do teen flicks or musicals either for that matter."

"But really you do sing, right?"

"Stan," she said forcefully, "I want to do *Vigilant*."

He shook his head slowly.

"I've got the skills. I've got the build. I'm in great shape."

"All true, but you don't have the image. The character is dark, morally ambiguous, a drinker, a fighter, a lesbian shit-kicker."

"I'm a lesbian shit-kicker."

"Are you?" he asked, his voice a little higher, like someone talking to a puppy or a child.

"Yes," she said emphatically.

"Look." He cut the patronizing tone. "I'm glad you want to branch out, but no one is going to buy you as a lesbian."

"But I *am* a lesbian!"

"Oh, I know. I wrote that press release, but this character is actually going to sleep with women, plural, on screen, and you're just not that kind of lesbian."

"The kind of lesbian who actually sleeps with a lot of women?"

"Exactly," he said, almost triumphantly.

"Excuse me?" she spluttered. "I have slept with women. I mean not in the last few months, but it has happened."

"Good for you. I have a lesbian niece, and I am a sponsor of the big parade in the Village, but—and I mean no offense—to the rest of the world you're still sixteen. And they love that about you. You're a safety gay."

"A safety gay?"

"Like Ellen Degeneres or Ellen Page. Really, it's a shame you're not named Ellen. Hey, that reminds me, how do you feel about a sitcom? We need someone to read for the role of Jane Fonda's granddaughter on that Netflix thing. She's a lesbian, right?"

"No. Lily Tomlin is."

"Really? Since when? Never mind, she's funny! You could be funnier, you know.

"Thanks. And I don't want to play Jane Fonda's granddaughter. Is there an audition for the role of her lover?"

Stanley about choked. "Was that a joke? If so, it was a funny one. If not, then it wasn't funny."

"It wasn't supposed to be funny." She practically exploded. "I want to be challenged. I want a grown-up career. I want a manager who wants to make me happy."

"How about a manager who makes you boatloads of money? Then you can buy whatever makes you happy."

He didn't get it. At least not the way she wanted him to. She would have really liked for him to jump on board with her. His enthusiastic support would have been a boon to her confidence, but ultimately, she didn't need him to share her vision of herself. She did, however, need him to go to bat for her, so she twisted a silver, three-string ring on her right ring finger and played the biggest card left in her hand. "Is your wife in the office today?"

Stanley practically jumped out of his Italian loafers at the comment. "What?"

"Mimi. Is she working today? I haven't seen her in a long time, and I was wondering what she's up to."

"She's very busy. Big meeting on the music side today."

"Do you think she'd make time for me?"

A muscle in his jaw twitched, suggesting he knew she would. They might love each other dearly, but they also loved the job.

They were as competitive with each other as they were with outside agents, maybe more so. She'd long wondered how that kind of competition could work in a marriage, but she understood that's what made them work as business partners. If it also made Stanley work a little harder for her, great. If not, Mimi certainly would.

"Can I see that script for a second?" Stan came around the front of his desk. "I promise I'll give it back."

The change in his tone, from polite to purposeful, told her everything she needed in order to hand the document over.

He scanned the first page, the line of his eyes indicating he'd stopped on the short background sketch of the lead character.

"Dark, tall, brooding, magnetic, sexual, powerful, edgy." He read the adjectives aloud. Then he looked up to study her. "Your hair's too long."

"I can cut it. Dye it, too, if need be."

"Your eyes could be right, especially if you wore some eyeliner."

"Okay."

"You've been working with a trainer?"

"Weights and cardio."

"Double your routine," he said flatly, "like yesterday."

She nodded. She'd gladly push harder for a shot at the role.

He handed her the script and walked around the desk, falling into his chair and leaning back so far he stared at the ceiling. "How bad do you want this, Cobie?"

"I'll do whatever it takes."

"Even something you can't undo?"

She paused, wanting to clarify a little bit, but worried he'd see it as a sign of weakness if she did. "Yes."

"There will be no more teen movies, no more sappy cowgirls or cheerleader roles."

"Good."

"You'll need a complete image overhaul. Six months minimum of your working the press and photo shoots and being seen playing with the big kids."

Her stomach turned. "I can't just go up for the part?"

He frowned. "I can't pitch this with you as you are. Not if you want a major studio and the budget needed to do this right."

"I do. I want everything about this project done to perfection."

"Then you need to make a long-term investment."

She nodded. She wanted long-term. She needed it. "Tell me what to do."

He pushed his palm down his forehead as if trying to smooth out the wrinkles forming there. "Give me twenty-four hours to see what I can come up with. Show up tomorrow, same time, same place, ready to take big steps."

"I will, Stan. I promise I won't let you down."

His smile was faint, showing none of his shark teeth now. "I'll see you then."

Sensing the need to get out while she was ahead, she backed toward the door.

"Tomorrow, eleven-thirty," she repeated, but he'd already picked up the phone. She kept backing away down the hall as she heard him telling someone to clear his schedule. She couldn't believe this was happening, even though the details of what *this* was were kind of shady, very shady actually. Still, it felt big, and she didn't want to do anything to mess up.

She took another step backward and stepped on something hard.

"Ouch," someone said, causing her to jump and bump into a wall, then trip and stumble again.

She might have flailed all the way to the floor if not for two strong hands catching her roughly under her arm and hauling her up.

"What's the matter with you?" a different voice snapped.

She teetered a bit, trying simultaneously to right herself and see the people around her. As she planted her feet firmly back on the ground, she realized she was staring at a massive chest topped off with big shoulders and a sequoia-sized neck. Only when she tilted back farther did she see a strong jaw and deep-set, dark eyes. The African American man was good-looking enough to be an action star, but the set of his features and his crossed arms and his bulging biceps screamed bodyguard.

"Sorry," Cobie said, flustered. "I wasn't watching where I was going."

"Do you know who you just walked into?" someone behind her asked.

She turned to see a much smaller Latino man in maroon skinny jeans and a paisley shirt purse his lips at her.

"You?"

He started to roll his eyes, then stopped abruptly and narrowed them. "Hey, are you the girl from that one movie, with the guy, the one who's got those pecs?"

"Yeah." Cobie didn't need any more description. She was always that girl in that movie.

"Ooh, girl, you look better with the make-up on," he said dramatically.

"Thanks," she muttered and tried to edge past him, but the bodyguard shot out his arm.

"It's fine, Malik," a female voice said from behind him. "I don't think she's a threat to anyone."

He didn't argue, either out of actual agreement or knowing better than to disagree. He simply lowered his arm and stepped to the side.

Cobie's breath caught at the sight of the woman he'd shielded. Honey blonde hair fell to slender shoulders, framing a pale face. Startling blue eyes flashed amusement from under thick lashes, and painted red lips sparked a heated contrast to the otherwise pastel pallet. Cobie actually took a step back at the sight of her. Not that she hadn't seen the face a million times, including the billboard towering several stories high just outside, but she'd never stopped to really notice the perfection of its symmetry and precision. It was almost too flawless to be real, and only after too many seconds of being stupefied did she manage to look away.

Not that lowering her eyes actually did anything to improve her brain function, because that only left her staring at a low-cut, white blouse and a long, flowing black skirt with a slit so far up the side even a gentle breeze would reveal anything underneath. It wasn't a wholly unpleasant prospect. Finally, though, when her eyes reached floor level, she noticed a glaring scuff where the heel of her Doc Martens had clearly tread across the toe of patent leather Manolos.

"I'm so sorry," she said, snapping her head up, "about your toes."

The woman's smile was slow. "They're fine."

"Well, your shoes are scuffed. And probably expensive, so if, um, you want to bill me, you can send an invoice to Stan's office. They can get it to me."

"You're going to buy me new shoes?" she asked, clearly amused by the offer.

"I would," Cobie said earnestly.

"That's adorable," the woman said with the faintest hint of a Southern drawl. Then with a minimal wave of her hand, she turned and walked away.

Cobie stood, bewildered, watching her go, skirt blowing in the breeze she created, entourage trailing dutifully in her wake. She may have even craned her neck a bit as they turned a corner, but when finally left alone in the hallway, all she could manage to think was, "So, that's Lila Wilder."

"Who caused the headache?" Stan asked, tossing back the satin sheets of his king-size bed. Another fourteen-hour day in the books for each of the Levys left them both back where they'd started.

His wife sat on the other side of the mattress, feet dangling daintily off the edge as she plucked three ibuprofen from the nightstand and washed them down with a swig of single-malt scotch. "Take a guess."

He chuckled and adjusted the waistband of his navy blue, silk pajamas. "How long is Lila in town?"

"Forever." Mimi groaned, lying back onto the bed so the dent in her feather pillow created a halo around her perfectly coiffed hair.

Stan climbed in beside her, taking a moment to enjoy the little luxury of silk sliding against silk, but before he got close enough to kiss her, a muscle caught painfully in his shoulder, and he grimaced.

"Oh no, did you tweak it again?" Mimi asked without glancing his way.

"Just a little tense today," he said.

"Who do we have to thank this time?"

He sighed and stared at the ornate crown molding around the room, visually tracing its lines and curves. "Cobie."

Mimi turned to face him. "Not Cobie Galloway?"

"Surprising, right?"

"There really is a first time for everything," Mimi said wistfully. "What does she want? A record deal?"

"I only wish. She wants the lead in *Vigilant*."

Mimi made a strangled noise and reached for her phone.

"Don't bother," Stan said dryly. "They aren't casting. She got her hands on an early draft of the script, and no, she didn't let me see it."

"Cobie hid a script from you?" The shock in her voice mirrored his own sense of bewilderment. He hadn't shaken the unease he'd felt during the meeting, even nearly twelve hours later.

"She didn't hide it so much as refuse to share it, and if you could've seen her, you wouldn't have pushed." He closed his eyes and pictured her as the child she'd been. "God, wasn't she just a little kid yesterday?"

"Weren't we all," Mimi murmured. "You really are lucky it hasn't happened before now."

"Probably," Stan admitted. "I've never known a kid who came up through the business without having a meltdown or a sex tape or a rehab stint or a parental lawsuit. Maybe that's what makes it so shocking. She's always been perfect."

"Does she have the talent for the part?"

"The thing is she's always been more talented than her roles allowed, but *Vigilant* isn't a Disney cruise. It would feel like throwing her to the sharks when I'm not even sure she can swim.

She's always been so self-contained, which saved her from the drama and the pain and the backbiting. I thought she wanted to keep her life quiet. I don't want to expose her to something she can't handle. It would reflect badly on me if I staked my reputation on someone who wilted under the bright lights."

"Reflect badly on you?" Mimi laughed lightly. "She's your baby, you big softy."

"Don't act like you don't have your favorites."

She scoffed. "I remain completely neutral in business situations."

"Sure you do. That's why Lila's been in three times in two weeks."

Mimi smiled. "Neither of them are kids anymore, are they?"

"Lila's been working for a long time to prove otherwise," he said wearily.

"And she's done so successfully."

"Successfully, yes. Gracefully, no."

She rolled her eyes. "Cobie will go too far in the other direction."

"Well she's not going to sleep with every eligible bachelor in Hollywood and a handful of the taken ones."

"Oh, Lila hasn't been *that* bad." Mimi's voice grew a touch defensive, once again reminding him there was a soft spot there. "Though that's actually part of the headache."

"A married man?"

"No. Not enough unmarried ones to keep the news cycle churning between album drops."

"I'm not sure there is a man in the country she could use to shock the paparazzi anymore," he said with a yawn. Even he'd grown bored with the topic of Lila Wilder's love life. "It's all gotten a little dog-bites-man these days, when what she really needs is man-bites-dog."

"Or woman," Mimi said slowly.

"Dog bites woman?" he asked sleepily. "Right. Gender-inclusive language. Woman bites dog."

"Stan," Mimi said, her voice suddenly full of excitement.

"What?" he asked as she threw off the covers and grabbed her phone from the nightstand. "What is it?"

"We're going back to work."

He stared at her for a second before sitting up. After forty years of marriage, he'd come to recognize the wild spark of inspiration in her eyes. The fact that she was willing to share it with the likes of him gave him the same thrill he'd experienced when he kissed her the first time all those years ago.

"Ms. Wilder, it's so nice to see you again."

Lila noted that sometime in the last two years her formal title had changed from Miss to Ms. An acknowledgement of her feminism, prestige, or age? She nodded at the receptionist, who rose and led her down a series of hallways she knew quite well, but this time instead of taking a right out of the central humming hub of the building, they turned left.

Felipe raised an already perfectly arched eyebrow at her. She merely lifted one shoulder in response. He'd get her drift. He always had. Malik, on the other hand, straightened both his shoulders, and the large muscles in his neck tightened. He didn't find change as exciting as she did, or perhaps he did but in a different way, which of course was one of many reasons why she kept him on the payroll.

The receptionist led them into a conference room that, while not as lushly appointed as Mimi's office, still had plenty to gawk at, from the nickel and leather furnishings to the floor-to-ceiling windows providing a magnificent view of snow falling softly over the length of Broadway.

"The Levys will be with you shortly," the receptionist said. "In the meantime, can I get you anything to drink? Coffee? Tea? Mineral water?"

"Water, cold, no ice, please," Lila said from habit. "Latte, Felipe?"

"*Sí, mami,*" he said.

"And coffee, black, Malik?"

He nodded, his eyes still surveying the view as if assessing threats that may lurk forty-two stories above the Great White Way.

"Thank you," Lila said.

As soon as the door closed, Felipe flopped into one of the highback leather conference chairs and twirled it around a few times before stopping himself abruptly. "Girl, what's happening here?"

Lila shook her head slowly. She didn't like not knowing, but she wouldn't let it show. "I told you, Mimi called me."

"Like she should," Felipe said. "Maybe she's got the goods on a new man for you."

"I don't need a manager to get me a man," Lila said dryly. "I pay her to get me publicity."

"You haven't needed her to do that for a while either," Felipe said, only a hint of cattiness in his voice.

She opened her mouth to snap back at him, but the door opened again, and they all stayed stock-still like posed statues.

A young man dressed entirely in black wheeled in a tray with their beverages and asked if he could get them anything else. Felipe smiled as if he'd just thought of a dirty response, but some side-eye from Malik inspired a little restraint. "We're good . . . for now."

The young man ducked out silently.

"They do have all the help trained very well around here," Felipe said, rising and passing Lila her water. He then quickly mixed the coffee and latte before handing one of the now indistinguishable drinks to Malik.

"There are three more glasses," Lila said quietly.

Both men glanced at the tray. Malik frowned, but Felipe's brown eyes sparkled.

"Mimi is one," Lila said, "and the receptionist said the Levys would be in, so another is for Stan."

"Oh, and the third is a mystery." Felipe squirmed in his chair. "A mystery man."

"Maybe, though Mimi didn't seem to have anyone in mind yesterday."

"I know, but maybe it's one of Stan's clients."

A logical conclusion, but if Mimi had found someone overnight, why hadn't she just said so over the phone? Calling another meeting with both agents felt like overkill, and that said a lot coming from her.

Felipe whipped out his cell and said, "Siri, Google Stan Levy's client list."

Not a bad idea. She didn't like surprises, at least not when they concerned her career. Staying one step ahead of the game allowed her to remain cool, detached, independent, and those things combined to keep her safe.

"Who could lucky bachelor number thirty-seven be?" Felipe asked as he swiped his index finger over the screen. "Too old. Too gay. Too much facial hair. Too gay. Oh, could be this one." He held up the screen.

She pursed her lips and inspected the image of a movie poster. There was a truck and some rain and a beefy guy with a woman in his arms. He had her face in his hands, his head angled low, and her chin angled up toward him as if eager for the kiss he was clearly about to give her. She tried to inspect him a little closer. Big arms, short fair hair, chiseled jaw, she noted the features in a disjointed array, but between each entry, her eyes flicked to the woman in his arms.

Her skin was just as sun-kissed as his, her body every bit as firm, without the bulk. Her eyes and hair were darker though. Not black, more like the color of the old mahogany upright piano back home.

She blinked away, startled by the sentimentality of the thought.

"He's . . ." She pursed her lips again, trying to find something to say about a man she couldn't seem to focus on. "Fine."

"He is *fine*." Felipe drew out the word until it had a different meaning from the one she'd intended.

"And the woman," she finally said.

"Ooh, girl, possessive already? She's just an actress. You don't need to get your claws out for another three to four months."

She fought a sigh and waved the screen away. It didn't matter who any of them were. Obviously, she'd rather find someone with a few coherent thoughts in his head and a bit of conversation skill, but she'd worked with all kinds of people, and each one of them brought something to the table. Whatever card she had dealt to her, she'd make it fit into the hand she wanted to play.

Or she wouldn't, because she didn't have to take every offer on the table. She'd earned that right, and she had no trouble reminding anyone who forgot.

The door to the conference room swung open, and this time, the person who entered wasn't an assistant. It wasn't even her agent. It was the woman whom she'd only seconds earlier inspected on a cell-phone screen movie ad.

"Oh, uh, hey. I mean, hi." She stopped a few steps into the room. Her hair fell past her shoulders, and her skin had grown paler since the photo had been shot, but she couldn't be mistaken for anyone else with those big, mocha eyes.

"You're that girl . . ." Felipe said, snapping his fingers

"From the movie with the guy with the arms? Yeah."

"No, from the hallway yesterday, with the tripping and the shoe wrecking."

She blushed an endearing shade of pink. "Right, also true. Sorry to interrupt you again. I was looking for Stan, but I guess I got lost."

She stood there a moment staring at them all, and Lila fought the urge to step in and offer absolution, which would have been fine if not for the fact that she wanted to, badly. The move wouldn't have been magnanimous so much as an opening. To what, she couldn't quite say, and that meant she couldn't quite speak.

"So, yeah, sorry again." She turned to go, but before she could take two steps, Mimi nearly knocked her over.

"Cobie, darling, baby, come here and gimme a hug!" Mimi didn't wait for a response or even a hint of consent before throwing her arms about the woman's waist. Mimi rocked her back and forth wildly a few times while Lila looked on, amused as the blush that had tinted her face seconds before now blossomed to include her neck and ears.

"Good to see you too."

"Unhand her. She's mine," Stan called dramatically as he entered the room with his usual flash and smile, but Lila wasn't sure if he was talking to his wife about his client or vice versa.

He placed a hand on Mimi's shoulder and made a show of prying her off before turning his toothy grin her way. "Lila! So lovely to see you."

"Likewise," she said coolly, her eyes still fixed on the only stranger in the room.

"And this is Cobie Galloway." Stan threw his arm around Cobie's shoulder and squeezed her so tightly his large hand wrinkled the plain, white dress shirt she wore, quite unfortunately, tucked into gray jeans.

"We've met. Sort of informally, and briefly," Cobie said.

"But you made a real impact." Felipe snickered, and Lila shot him a silencing look. She'd set the tone here, just as soon as she decided what she wanted it to be.

"Great," Stan enthused. "Have a seat, Cobie. We'll all want to be comfortable for this one. Water?"

She nodded. "No ice, please."

Felipe's eyebrows shot up as if the request were a secret code, but this time he didn't comment.

Stan handed her a glass and pulled out a chair for her opposite Lila.

"You want me to sit here?"

He laughed. "That's generally what it means when someone pulls out a chair for you."

"Right. It's just when you said we needed to meet, I thought you meant about work."

"I did." Stan nodded to the chair, and Cobie's eyes darted around the room once more before she took the seat.

"I know this is a little unconventional." Mimi closed the door and claimed the chair next to Lila, who noticed none of their usual attendants were present. No staff, no contracts, no

Bluetooth earpieces. Absolutely no fanfare. Just the owners of the agency and what had to be two of their most lucrative clients.

"Ladies, as you know, Stan and I are both dedicated to our own client bases. We generally do not share sources or the details of our communications unless there are extenuating circumstances. But we're not only each other's biggest competition, we're each other's strongest advocates. That balance is what allows us to succeed in business and in life."

Cobie made a face, a sort of polite smile combined with brows knit together at the awkward confusion of being let into someone else's marriage without asking for an invitation. Lila would have laughed at the perfection of the expression if not for her own confusion.

"Each of you came to speak to us yesterday with problems we weren't quite sure how to handle," Stan said.

"And believe you me," Mimi cut in, "that's a pretty rare occurrence these days. We're stuck in our ways, and those ways are pretty damn foolproof."

Lila didn't mind the boast. She appreciated a woman who knew her worth, and Mimi Levy was worth a great deal.

"We ended up talking at length about your respective predicaments."

"I'm not sure I've got a predicament," Cobie said softly.

"You do," Mimi said without a hint of malice. "A big one, stemming from the fact that your image is completely inconsistent with the direction you want your career to take."

"And you," Stan said to Lila, "are on the opposite end of the monkey bars, my dear. Your career is so in line with every decision you've made, you can't surprise anyone anymore."

A muscle in her jaw twitched, but she'd learned to withstand criticism and compliment with the same steely resolve until she had the chance to act definitively.

"Thankfully, you have the two best agents in the business, and we spent all of last night hashing out a plan to help you both get what you want," Mimi continued.

"What you *say* you want," Stan corrected, to his wife's clear annoyance.

"They know what they want, Stan. The question is if they want it bad enough to really go after it."

Cobie leaned forward. "Go after it how?"

Lila looked down at her candy-apple red fingernails. *Wrong answer.*

"You need something shocking, something edgy, something trendy and sexy and grown-up to shift your image," Stan said, then turned to Lila, "and you need something sizzling to recapture the public's attention, only without enough departure from your image to radically change it."

"And you have about six months before Cobie can pitch a new movie. You would both be in a position to help each other."

A movie? Something out of character, something edgy, something sexy, something Cobie would be beholden to Lila for? She liked the sound of that, but she couldn't see what she got out of the deal.

"So, she hangs out with me. We're photographed together at night clubs, she comes to the shows, we party together back stage, I spruce up her wardrobe." Cobie glanced down at her clothes and frowned, but Lila didn't have time to go there right now. "Then we have some big public fights, Twitter snark, I write a song, blah, blah. Bestie break-up girl-fight makes her seem like one of the bad girls of Hollywood."

"Excuse me?" Cobie asked.

"Almost," Mimi said. "You missed one small point."

"Actually, I completely missed the part where I get something out of the deal. Other than a fake friend for a few months."

"Not a friend," Stan corrected. "A girlfriend."

Felipe sucked in a deep breath and squeaked as he struggled to hold in whatever outburst he had bubbling, allowing silence to reign as both managers stared expectantly from one client to the other.

Girlfriend.

The word rattled around Lila's mind and into her chest. Her

20

heart beat faster with an unwarranted excitement, or maybe trepidation. She recognized the yin and the yang of those emotions and their place in her creative process but had a hard time reconciling the mix with the woman across from her now.

"I'm sorry, what?" Cobie finally asked. "I'm a little unclear as to what you're suggesting."

"Of course you are," Mimi said gently. "And that's okay. That's why you have me."

"And me," Stan said drolly.

"Have you for what?" Cobie looked to each of them, then finally across to Lila. "What are we talking about here?"

"It's a fauxmance," Lila said, the exasperation in her voice not at all for show.

"A fauxmance." Cobie tried the word again. "Fauxmance, a fake romance, between me and ... you?"

"Exactly." Mimi slapped the table enthusiastically.

"But, why?"

Lila's eyes went wide. "Are you for real?"

"I'm sorry. I didn't mean to be offensive. You're very beautiful, obviously, but I don't know you."

"I'm Lila Wilder."

"Right." Cobie nodded. "I didn't mean I don't know who you are. I've heard your songs, and some of them are good."

Felipe gasped, and Lila held up a hand. She wasn't offended so much as bemused. No one spoke to her like that, not anymore, at least not to her face. There was always some pretense, some hint of fear or groveling or thinly veiled power-lust. Cobie's demeanor seemed nothing but earnest. And yet she was an actress, clearly a talented one, though her filmography hardly suggested Oscar material. Still, she must be on the brink of something big, or Stan and Mimi wouldn't pull a stunt like this. They saw something in her to pique their finely-honed business sense, and that in turn caught Lila's curiosity. Only, Cobie didn't seem to understand the magnitude of her own power here.

"I think what Cobie means," Stan said smoothly, "is the two of you bring different things to the table. You don't generally run in the same circles. She's more the Hollywood set, while you're more on the recording side."

"Actually, Stan. That's not what she said at all. She doesn't see what I can do for her career. To be frank, I don't think she even really understands what you're suggesting here."

Mimi put a hand over Lila's. "Lila, dear, not everyone is used to your blunt communication style. I'm not sure you meant to sound as dismissive as you did there."

"No, I did."

"And I'm okay with that," Cobie said with a nod of respect. "Since you seem to have a better handle on the situation, why don't you spell it out for me?"

Lila rose gracefully to her full height, accented by the three-inch heel of her fashion boots. "They're proposing that you and I spend some time together, very publically, without making it clear we're trying to be public. We get closer, we get dashingly romantic, probably you move in with me."

"Why don't you move in with me?"

"Don't interrupt right now."

The corner of Cobie's mouth curled in a way that made Lila suspect she wasn't completely befuddled. The subtle shift sparked a deeper interest and pulled her closer. She strode slowly around the table. "I get the increased press that accompanies the shock of a lesbian relationship."

"Bisexual," Mimi corrected. "You see beauty, not gender."

"Bisexuality is really hip right now," Stan added.

She nodded thoughtfully. "I get to double the size of my dating pool. I'm not just a man-eater anymore. We put the whole world on notice. Lila Wilder's within reach, at least hypothetically. And artistically, it's gold. A softer side and a wilder side, infinite possibilities. It's raw, it's hot, but also feminine and passionate. A first love all over again. Getting to the heart, not just the surface. Beauty, not gender. Or better yet, beauty, not body parts."

Mimi snapped her fingers and grabbed a sheet of paper off the credenza behind her. "I like it. I'm writing that down for the press release."

"Yes." Lila closed her eyes and took a deep breath, letting herself settle into the idea. Artistically, creatively, personally, this warmed her muscles and lifted her lungs. This felt exciting and new and thrilling. "Okay, I'm bisexual."

"What?" Cobie laughed. "Just like that?"

Lila opened her eyes and fixed them on Cobie. "Yes."

"I don't think bisexuality is a choice you can just make for yourself."

"No one makes choices for me but me," Lila said flatly.

Cobie pushed her chair back from the table. "What about me? Do I have a choice to make here?"

"You do," Stan said gravely, "and once you make it, there's no going back. You need to think seriously about what you're risking."

"Stan," Mimi warned.

"I have a responsibility to level with her," Stan said. "She doesn't want to be treated like a kid anymore. I'm not going to sugarcoat things. If teenage girls see you having a torrid affair with Lila Wilder, you'll never get another Disney Channel original movie again. You'll never work for the Hallmark Channel again. Jeremy will have his arms around someone else in the next big romcom. America won't line up to see him woo a lesbian."

"They have for years," Cobie said dryly, and Lila stifled a snort. "But that's fine. I'm done with those projects. I'm a serious actress. I want to be known for my craft and substance, but I'm not sure having a fake romance for the sake of paparazzi moves me closer to my goals."

"You want a part, right?" Lila asked.

"Yes."

"A big one?"

Cobie nodded.

"You need directors and producers and viewers to believe you can play a character that's so different from every other character you've ever played, but they can't because you've been typecast. Correct?"

"Exactly."

"You got typecast in the first place by playing those roles so well." Lila walked right up to Cobie's chair and spun it slowly all the way around, then stopped it so they faced each other. "The way to break the mold is by taking a wildly different role."

"That's what I'm trying to do."

"No. You're hoping someone will *offer* you a different role, and that's not how this business works. You have to create your own parts. For the next six months, you need to be a character actress and hone your craft on the most public of stages."

"I'm kind of a private person."

Lila rolled her eyes. "Private means passive. When you let someone else define your narrative, you let them define you."

"I can't control what other people think."

"That's the dumbest thing I've ever heard."

Cobie opened her mouth, but Lila shook her head.

"They're always going to try to pigeonhole us. You can either pretend that isn't true, or you can create the box you want them to put you in and refuse to fit anywhere else."

"You're saying for six months I play the part of some playgirl, it girl, bad girl so I eventually get the role of playgirl, it girl, bad girl on screen?"

"Precisely. You create a part to show you can play the part."

"If I get to create my own show, then why cast you opposite me?"

There were a series of strangled squeaks and gasps behind her, but the boldness of the question and the challenge inherent in it only piqued an interest Lila hadn't felt for a long time.

She extended her hand, and when Cobie took it, she pulled her up to standing. Pushing the chair out of the way, she took a slow walk around her, surveying the canvas she had to work with. Then, without comment, she sprang into action. She yanked Cobie's shirt from the waistband of her jeans and popped open the top button to show more chest, stopping short of actual cleavage. Reaching up, she deftly unclasped the clip from her hair. Sinking her fingers into thick, silky locks before shaking them out, she found them as soft as they looked without the crust and crack of excessive product. She stood back for a second, surveying the progress before deciding something was missing.

She glanced around until her eyes landed on Felipe. She tapped her head and snapped her fingers. His facial expression went from that of a child thrilled to be called on, to one who realized he didn't like the answer he'd been asked to give. Still, he pulled the gray stocking cap off his perfectly highlighted hair and handed it to her. Lila shook it out, then pulled it snugly over Cobie's head until it drooped at a careless slant.

"My, you are a cooperative one," she mused aloud. "I like that. Now turn and face the windows with your hands in your pockets."

"Why?"

"Trust me. I'll make it worth your while."

Cobie shrugged, but she was clearly interested enough to comply, which was another asset Lila desired in someone she would have to spend a great deal of time with.

Once they both faced the plate glass, Cobie jammed her fists into her pockets, and Lila smiled brightly at her reflection before slipping one hand under Cobie's right arm and curling her fingers around the firm biceps. Then she used her other hand to take hold of one of Cobie's belt loops and cocked her hip so it angled toward her. With one final touch, she leaned in and whispered, "Look at us," before placing a feather-light kiss on her cheek.

Cobie's chest rose dramatically as the adorable shade of pink flushed hot under the darker mark left by Lila's lipstick. The phrase "hook, line, and sinker" came to mind as Lila stepped back and marveled at the fact that wooing women didn't seem to require any different skills than wooing men. Any residual concerns she held about her ability to maintain the charade evaporated.

Once she'd broken the contact completely, she turned to face their captivated audience. Every set of eyes had gone wide, even Malik's, which served only as confirmation for what she'd already known. They were sitting on top of a goldmine.

"Can anyone in this room honestly tell me they don't want to see that image on the cover of every magazine in America?"

"I think I speak for all of us when I say that's exactly what we want," Mimi gushed.

"Everyone?" Stan swiveled his chair to look at Cobie, who continued to stare at her reflection, or perhaps past it.

She didn't immediately answer him, and Lila's chest tightened, first with anticipation, then with something approaching dread as the silence stretched on. Startled, she realized she wanted Cobie to say yes. Somehow, somewhere underneath the understanding that this little publicity stunt would likely benefit Cobie every bit as much as, if not more than, her, Lila wanted her to accept with a fervor disproportionate to the amount of press she stood to gain. It had been a long time since she'd let herself want something from someone else and even longer since someone had made her work for the answer she desired. She didn't like being made to do so now, but even as the resentment bubbled up, so did the suspense.

Finally, Cobie turned, her expression blank and her complexion pale. Lila held her breath until the woman before her nodded slowly and said, "Okay. I'll do it."

A collective sigh of relief whooshed through the room, and Lila hoped the others had been too caught up in the gripping plot unfolding before them to notice her own reaction.

"Very well," she said curtly. "Stan, Mimi, work out the timeline and text it to my personal number. I'll have a few outfits sent over to Cobie, labeled with when to wear them."

"Outfits?" Cobie blinked as if waking from a trance.

"We'll have to coordinate somehow, and Lord knows I'm not letting you choose my attire. It'll be best for everyone involved if you just let me do the heavy lifting for a while."

Stan clasped Cobie's shoulder. "She's right."

Cobie hung her head, resignation weighing down her shoulders. "I guess wardrobe is the least of my worries for the next six months, isn't it?"

Felipe's laughter finally got the better of him, and Lila didn't even try to reign it in anymore. Instead, she tossed Cobie a practiced smile and said, "For that, you get to keep his hat."

With a wave of her hand, Felipe fell in beside her and Malik stepped in front as they all moved toward the door in unison.

"Wait," Cobie called. "What do we do now?"

Lila threw a smile over her shoulder and said, "Await my directions, then follow my lead."

"That's all?"

She laughed. "Don't worry. It'll be enough. If you keep your eyes on me, you'll do just fine."

Then she walked away, certain that in spite of minor lapses in judgment or emotion over the last half hour, she'd managed to leave on a high note.

Chapter Two

"She sent me clothes to wear," Cobie said to the dashboard of her Tesla Model 3.

"Are you wearing them? Are they cool? Do you like them?" Emma asked in rapid-fire teenage tone.

"Yes, I guess, and I guess," she said as the car made another self-directed turn. She was more thankful than ever for the autopilot feature because there was no way she could watch Manhattan traffic and the GPS at the same time.

"Cobe, I need more. My sister's going on a date with my favorite singer in the whole world, and she dressed you! Don't make me wait to see it in *People* magazine like everyone else."

"*People*, oy." Cobie pinched the bridge of her nose as the stress of the idea hit her like an icepick to the brain. "She dressed me like Patti Smith, okay. Exactly Patti Smith on the cover of *Horses*."

"What? Who?" Emma asked.

"Patti Smith, black pants, white shirt, skinny tie. Emma, it's iconic. Google it."

Emma giggled. "Okay, but it sounds super gay."

"So gay," Cobie confirmed with a smile, thinking of the note Lila had pinned to the tie telling her to leave it untied. "And she left me written instructions on how to wear it, like I can't figure out how to dress up like a punk-rock goddess. Em, what am I doing?"

"You're being awesome," Emma said with a hint of adoration. "I can't believe she wants to date you. All my friends will die. Hey, can you get me backstage passes?"

"Hey, this phone call is about me," Cobie said dryly.

"Sorry, sorry. I'm fourteen. I'm selfish. It's allowed."

Cobie laughed. "Yeah, I guess. I'm going to hang up on you now, though. I'm a very famous celebrity. It's allowed."

"Totally," Emma agreed. "Send me a selfie, 'kay?"

"Totally," Cobie agreed. "Love you, Em-an-Em."

"Love you, Corn Cobe."

She pushed the disconnect button on the dash and looked around the intersection where the car had stopped. She was definitely in the Village now, the one area of New York City she liked. She used to make it a point to walk by Stonewall every time she came to the city in the early years. At first she was too young to get in, then too closeted. She made the iconic bar her first stop after coming out, but by then she was too recognizable. She got mobbed before she'd really had the chance to reflect on her surroundings. Maybe she'd go back sometime, like on a weeknight, dressed down, when things relaxed.

Her chest tightened as she approached the restaurant and saw the paparazzi waiting in hordes outside. A little voice whispered in her ear saying nothing would ever settle down again. She told it the same thing she had for days. She wanted this. Or she needed it in order to get what she wanted. She wasn't doing anything different than researching a character or working out or dying her hair to get a part. Though as the car pulled to a stop and the cameras swiveled in her direction, it sure felt different.

In an instant, Malik was pulling her door open, and the paparazzi went wild. She'd experienced this kind of flash fest at red carpet premieres and award shows, but never while walking into a restaurant. Her natural instinct to flee took hold. She started to duck back into the car, until Malik put a massive palm on her shoulder and lowered his hulking figure to her ear. "You look great. Now follow me like you own the place, 'cause tonight, you do."

Either the words or the low timbre in which they were delivered calmed her dramatically. She glanced up at him and smiled broadly, realizing it was the first time he'd spoken in her presence. She liked him immediately, but before she could say so, he returned the bodyguard scowl to his face and straightened up.

He was playing a part too. He'd slipped for her benefit, and now he was modeling good behavior by getting back to work.

Work.

The realization hit with sobering accuracy. She was here to play the role of someone hounded by the press. The press had taken their position and waited for her to step onstage. So had Malik. So had Lila. These people were her supporting cast for the next six months. They needed her to buck up and show up ready to play the part she'd agreed to play.

She blew out a heavy breath, rolled her shoulders, and nodded. "Let's do this."

He motioned to the valet and nodded for Cobie to follow him.

Tossing the black jacket Lila had sent over her shoulder, she lifted her chin, fixed a stoic expression, and followed him through the crowd.

Lila was waiting at a table near enough to the front window to be seen from outside. She stood as Cobie approached.

"Nice entrance, stud." She kissed her on each cheek in the European style, then stepped back, but Cobie caught her with a hand lightly on her hip before running her gaze up Lila's body from her tight, black leggings to the oversized olive sweater clasped low enough on her chest to show a delicious hint of collar bone.

"You look lovely," she said. "Cozy, not overdone."

"You sound surprised."

"I just thought maybe since you'd dressed me as a famous rock star, you'd follow suit and dress up like Freddie Mercury or Prince."

Lila threw back her head and laughed loud enough to be heard by everyone in the room, even though there wasn't anyone sitting at the other tables in their immediate vicinity. "I'd think being on a date with an actual famous musician would be enough to hold you over for now."

Cobie smiled and pulled out the chair for Lila. "Well-played."

They sat opposite each other, and immediately a waiter appeared. "Can I get you something to drink?"

"We'll take a bottle of the Renwood Amador and two waters, no ice," Lila said confidently.

As the waiter left, Cobie leaned in and whispered, "I don't really drink a whole lot of alcohol."

"Good." Lila picked up the menu. "Do you eat pizza?"

"Normally, but I'm supposed to be easing off the carbs because my trainer—"

"Your trainer will have to work you harder tomorrow."

"Sure." Cobie smiled. They were already at a trendy Italian restaurant, so she might as well go all in. If the scent of fresh bread baking offered any indication of the quality, she wouldn't regret it. Still, she didn't know if she liked Lila calling all the shots without consulting her. Aside from being a bit intimidating, it also didn't bolster her reputation as a take-charge ass-kicker, which was the whole point. "Will you order for both of us then, or do I get to make a decision at some point?"

"You can order for us, but the decision-making portion is still a maybe," Lila said matter-of-factly. "When the waiter comes back, tell him we'll have the pizze prosciutto arrostito and the pizze boscaiola. Can you handle that?"

"I'm pretty good at learning my lines," Cobie said with a twinge of defensiveness, then tried to lighten up by adding, "I mean, not to brag or anything, but I've got some Teen Choice Awards at home for doing just that."

"Really? Teen Choice? That's a big deal."

"Four of them," Cobie said with fake superiority.

"Huh, four. Well I was about to say we should get your Teen Choice Awards together with my Teen Choice Awards for a play date," Lila said with a frown, "but I have five of them, and I would hate for one of mine to be left out."

"Ouch," Cobie laughed, "zapped again."

The waiter approached the table with a bottle over his arm and two glasses cradled in his palm.

Lila nodded for him to serve them, and he poured a small amount into each glass. Cobie mimicked Lila in swirling it around before sniffing and eventually sipping. The flavor assaulted her tongue immediately as the sweetness blossomed across every taste bud like liquid sugar, but she used every bit of acting talent she had to keep her expression neutral and nod seriously to Lila who said, "It'll do. Thank you."

He poured them each a glass and set the bottle between them. "Are you ready to order?"

"Yes, I'll have the pizze prosciutto arrostito, and Ms. Wilder will have pizze boscaiola," Cobie said clearly, without glancing at the menu.

"Very well, Ms. Galloway," the waiter said and left them alone once again.

"How did I do?" Cobie asked, sitting back.

Lila shrugged. "I'm not sure it was enough to get you another Teen Choice Award, but it should at least put you in the running."

"I'd better have something to show for that performance, because that wine is terrible, and I played it straight."

"You did very well. Not so much as a twitch. And by the by, that's a dessert wine, so it's supposed to be sweet. Also, it's 175 dollars a bottle."

"Then I'm glad I didn't sputter it across the table at you."

"Me too, seeing as how this sweater cost a lot more than the wine."

"But you can afford it," Cobie said.

"And so can you," Lila replied airily.

"And that's what we want to remind people?"

"Never hurts, but mostly we're letting them see us throw caution to the wind," Lila explained. "A nearly 200-dollar bottle of dessert wine ahead of a 15-dollar pizza. Look at us, aren't we whimsical?"

"We are indeed." Cobie raised her glass.

Lila clinked it with her own. "To the whimsy stage of our adventure."

Cobie smiled at the beautiful woman across from her as they both pretended to drink from their glasses and the cameras flashed just outside the window.

"Is this killing you?" Lila asked.

"No," she admitted. "It's odd, but I guess no more awkward than the first day on a movie set."

"How so?"

"Early on, we always do a read-aloud where the cast sits in chairs and we go through the whole script, each of us reading our lines," Cobie explained. "It's like being the new kid at school, trying to figure out what the norms are here, like are you just going to read through and be chill? Or are you going to get into character and really act out your lines?"

"What do most people do?"

"That's the thing. You never know until you get started. So, like, if I start out just reading normal and the person beside me brings it hard, I look lazy and talentless, but if I go all in and open up screaming my head off and everyone else just mumbles through, I look totally overzealous and uncool." Cobie laughed lightly. "Either I underdo it and people think I'm no Meryl Streep, or I sell it hard and everyone is like 'Oh, so now you think you're Meryl fucking Streep.'"

"And that's how you feel tonight?" Lila asked softly.

"A little," she admitted, suddenly feeling the need to fiddle with her napkin.

"Would it shock you if I said I felt the same way?"

"It would," Cobie said quickly, then after a few beats asked, "Do you?"

Lila's smile turned coy. "If I did, no one would ever know."

"Right." Cobie nodded. "I walked right into that one."

"Come on," Lila said. "You're on a date with a famous pop star, drinking expensive wine and eating pizza in a trendy Italian bistro. You're the envy of people the world over. Surely you've had worse jobs."

Cobie smiled in spite of her insecurities. "I worked at an orthopedic shoe store for one summer when I turned sixteen."

Lila grimaced. "Please tell me an evening with me ranks higher than that, or price tag be damned, I *will* throw a glass of wine in your face."

"Well . . ." Cobie drew out the word, pretending to weigh her options. "Yeah, I guess hanging out with a beautiful, talented, famous woman for the next six months has its upsides, but dating you won't offer me an employee discount on bunion pads."

Lila laughed, not a full, head-back, belly laugh, but a genuine, melodic sound of joy as her smile reached her beautiful eyes for the first time. Cobie's breath caught at the sight of something real behind the polished façade and finally said, "Maybe it won't be all bad."

"Can I get you anything for dessert," the waiter asked as he cleared their plates.

"Yes. I'll have the tiramisu, and Ms. Wilder will have a crème brûlée with berries."

Lila tried her best not to look surprised, but as soon as the waiter left, she pursed her lips.

"What, you don't like crème brûlée? 'Cause I can eat both. I'm already down for a double workout tomorrow."

"First of all, you will not touch my dessert. Second of all, you went off script."

"Dessert's always on script," Cobie said casually.

She should probably stand firm. She didn't want to give her date the wrong idea about who was in charge here, but she couldn't find fault with her logic. "I suppose we haven't really been here long enough to make people think we're having a good time, so I'll allow it."

"You'll eat dessert to make people think you're having a good time with me? That's the only reason?"

"It's the primary reason."

"And will that be hard for you? To convince people you enjoy my company?"

Lila thought about the question for a while, mostly to keep Cobie waiting. The conversation had largely centered around neutral topics like mutual acquaintances, schedules for the upcoming months. They hadn't dug too deep, but neither had they struggled to keep the dialogue going. As far as fake first dates went, this one ranked higher on the enjoyment scale than most. Cobie wasn't a riot, but she had a sense of humor and good hygiene, and she didn't seem completely self-absorbed. Still, she played her emotions close to the vest. After an hour together, Lila still wasn't sure how Cobie felt about what they were doing, and she didn't want to be the one to crack first. "I've got a job to do, and as far as jobs go, it's not a bad one."

"I don't know. The schedule Stan sent over looked pretty intense. The middle months look more like a Broadway schedule, five nights a week and Sunday matinees."

"Have you been on Broadway?" Lila asked.

"Yes. A few years ago, just a bit role between films."

"Well that's a first for me," Lila said. "I've dated musicians and screen actors, but never anyone with a theater background."

"I'd have thought being your first female date would've been enough in the notoriety department."

"For some people."

Cobie leaned forward. "What about for you?"

"I can't imagine why pretending to date you would be different from pretending to date a man," Lila said, but her eyes wandered to Cobie's lips. They did appear softer than most. Cobie's hands did too, small, with elegant fingers, and not a hint of callouses. Would everything about her be softer? Smoother? She shook the speculation from her find. "The basic concepts remain the same no matter who your co-star happens to be, right? Some are just better than others."

"You've had bad ones before though?" Cobie asked.

"A few," Lila admitted, running one finger around the rim of her still-full wine glass.

"And what were the cardinal sins of my predecessors?"

Lila raised her eyebrows, surprised at the question. "Are you digging for dirt on my exes?"

"No names," Cobie said quickly. "Just their most grievous offences, so I can avoid repeating them."

She thought for a moment, searching for a way to convey a multitude of grievances without actually sounding too aggrieved. Finally, she shrugged and said, "They forget none of this is ever real."

Cobie sat back. "Well there's the whole crux of the matter. It's sort of like playing Hamlet. You have to convince everyone on stage you're crazy while convincing everyone in the audience you're not."

"And by 'crazy,' you mean 'in love with me?'"

Cobie's cheeks flushed adorably. "I didn't mean it quite that way."

"It's okay. I have a long list of exes who would tell you it's insane to fall for me." She paused while the waiter set their desserts in front of them. Once he'd retreated, she used a spoon to crack the hard sugar shell of her crème brûlée before saying, "So tell me, Cobie, have you ever actually played Hamlet before?"

"Not yet."

"You're about to."

"I'm ready," Cobie said with a hint of defiance. "Are you?"

"It's not my first time on this stage."

"It's your first time here with me."

The little shot of bravado amused her. Cobie seemed to be growing more confident as the evening went on, but she wondered whose benefit the shift was for. Did she view the evening as an audition or the first day on a new job? Was she getting into the role someone else had written or trying to develop her own character? And most importantly, did Lila want to bolster that emerging confidence or keep her off balance? With a man, the choice would've been an easy one. They needed a firmer hand, or at least the ones she'd "dated" certainly did. It required constant work to keep them in their place and not all up in her business. Cobie, by contrast, hadn't yet showed her hand. She seemed to bounce back and forth between going for what she wanted and not quite wanting what she'd gotten. The confusion made it harder for Lila to decide how to react consistently. Then again, consistency might be overrated in situations where they were both out to prove they had new tricks up their sleeves.

She took another bite of her crème brûlée, closing her eyes to savor the sweetness across her tongue before admitting, "I will give you points for the dessert call. This is divine."

"You should try mine."

"I think I will." Lila stuck out her fork toward the tiramisu, and Cobie knocked it away with her own.

"I'm not sure we've reached the dessert-sharing stage of our relationship yet."

Lila's eyes went wide, and her mouth fell open.

"Sorry," Cobie said in a way that made it clear she wasn't. "I'm all for doing a lot of things on the first date, but I'm not the kind of woman to just give up tiramisu right away."

"I'm not used to being told no," Lila said, still not certain if Cobie was serious.

"Shocking." Cobie took another bite.

Lila stared at her a little longer, and the corner of Cobie's mouth curled up.

"You're playing with me, aren't you?"

Cobie lifted another forkful of espresso-drenched goodness to her lips. "If I am, no one will ever know."

Lila's chest tightened at the low timbre of the comment and the sultry slide of Cobie's tongue around the fork as she placed it in her mouth. Both the action and the reaction were so thoroughly unexpected, she needed a second to compose herself.

"Do you really want the tiramisu?" Cobie finally asked.

Lila shook her head. "Why do I suddenly feel like that's a loaded question?"

"Because it totally is."

"You know, it's not too late to split the check and tell the reporters we're just friends out for a girls' night," Lila said without any bite behind the threat.

"Huh." Cobie shrugged. "See, I was just starting to think this might be kind of fun, and we haven't even gotten to the best part yet."

"Are you sure the tiramisu isn't the best part?" Lila asked sarcastically.

"Now that is also a loaded question, but one I'm not afraid to answer," Cobie said, taking one more bite and making a show of savoring it. "As of right now, this tiramisu is the highlight of my evening. It's delicious and satisfying and, most of all, real."

Lila opened her mouth, but before she could speak, Cobie cut her off.

"But I read the schedule Stan sent over, and the biggest act of the night is yet to come. It has the potential to be delicious and satisfying as well."

"But not real," Lila said quickly.

"Well that's up to you."

"No, I think that's up to the contract implicit in our agreement."

"Nothing in the agreement says we have to spend the next six months one-upping each other," Cobie reasoned.

"Says the woman who won't share her dessert."

"To the woman who won't share a single genuine feeling."

Lila rolled her eyes. "One does not need to share feelings to pull off a fauxmance."

"That may be true with dudes, but if we're going to convincingly play-act a lesbian relationship, we're going to need so many feelings, and we'll probably have to process them more times than even most lesbians would consider reasonable."

Lila snorted but didn't dare argue that particular point. "Nothing says those feelings have to be genuine, though."

"Exactly. Just like no one says I have to share my dessert," Cobie said emphatically. "But wouldn't it be better if I did?"

"Oh, I see what you did there," Lila said, running her spoon around the edge of her dessert bowl.

"And?"

==Cobie's dark eyes were soft and tempting as they watched her in a way no one had in a long time. Not with admiration or lust, not with envy or possessiveness. What Lila saw there was nothing more than interest.==

"What do you say? I give you the last bite of tiramisu, and you tell me one honest thing about how you're feeling."

"Do I get to pick the thing or do you?"

"How about you tell me how you're feeling about how we're supposed to end the evening?"

The question wasn't what she expected, and it took her a second to process. "The kiss?"

"Yes."

"It's just a kiss."

Cobie scooped up the tiramisu and swiftly lifted it to her mouth.

"Wait," Lila said quickly. "I told you how I felt."

"Did you?" Cobie asked. "'Cause I didn't hear a feeling statement there. Your first kiss with me, a woman, in front of, like, half the cameras in New York City."

"What, you've never kissed anyone for show before?" Lila asked, not at all liking the emphasis Cobie was putting on the idea of a first time. She didn't want to think of this kiss as anything different than what she'd always done. She certainly didn't want to consider it another lost moment in a long line of opportunities she'd sold.

"Sure. Many times. Every movie I've ever made. In fact, my first kiss ever was a screen kiss."

"Really?" Lila asked, genuinely surprised once again. "Weren't you, like, sixteen in your first movie?"

"Yes. I was a late bloomer. I didn't tell anyone I'd never been kissed before. I tried to tell myself it would be good because it was my character's first kiss, so it'd be like character acting, but really, I was embarrassed. And nervous. And I hated it. Whenever we did interviews for the film and people asked about the kiss, I felt nauseated all over again. I couldn't believe anyone found that scene romantic."

"But they did," Lila said.

"They did." Cobie sounded perplexed, even more than a decade after the fact.

"What about your first kiss with a woman?" Lila asked.

"Now that's a different story." Her dark eyes crinkled at the corners, and her smile grew dreamy. "One you don't get to hear tonight, or maybe ever. Also, you're stalling, and the tiramisu clock is tick-tocking away. You going to spill, or should I eat?"

"Okay, okay." She didn't even really care about the dessert anymore. She just couldn't shake the image of Cobie as a teenager, nervous and embarrassed and being kissed for the first time under bright lights for the whole world to see. She wanted to hear the other story, the one that made Cobie smile, the one that would make Lila feel something other than a genuine connection to her.

"Okay, what? You're ready to tell me how you feel about kissing a woman for the first time, in front of the paparazzi, in less than an hour? And I mean honestly this time or the tiramisu gets it." Cobie opened her mouth wide for effect and lifted the fork once more.

"Fine." Lila sighed in an attempt not to laugh. "I guess I feel mostly curious. Good enough?"

"Elaborate." Cobie moved the fork away but didn't drop it all the way to the plate.

"I've never kissed a woman before, and some of my friends have. And they act like it was a big deal for them. Lord knows the media is going to lose their minds over it or I wouldn't be here. So I guess I'm interested to find out why."

"You really don't know why people will think your kissing me is a thing?" Cobie sounded mildly suspicious.

"You mean other than the fact that we're both rich and famous and beautiful?" Lila tried the flip comment as a diversion, but Cobie only arched her eyebrows. "Well, I guess other than that, no. I'm not sure *why* it would be any different than my kissing a famous, beautiful, rich man. People are people. Some of them are talented, some of them are charismatic, some of them are jerks, some of them smell nice, some of them make me laugh, some of them are jerks."

"You already said 'jerks.'"

"A lot of them are jerks."

Cobie nodded. "True."

"But you seem nice enough. You're polite when you're not holding a dessert for ransom, and you're attractive. I can't figure out why your body parts should affect anything about how you kiss, but people seem to think it'll be a thing, which makes me think it might be a thing. I don't like other people knowing something I don't, so I'm ready to find out for myself."

Cobie smiled broadly and offered the dessert-laden fork across the table. Lila leaned forward and snatched it quickly with her mouth.

Flashbulbs went off in rapid succession outside the window, and Lila smiled around the fork as Cobie withdrew it slowly from her mouth. The bitterness of the espresso and the sweet cream blended together in her mouth, the perfect taste notes to accompany Cobie's expression as the pure joy of her triumph was intruded upon by the hordes of gossip reporters outside.

"I guess that made for a compelling photo op," she finally said.

"Indeed." Lila dabbed her lips with a napkin and laid it on the table. "Papers across the country will spin wild stories about your seductive prowess tomorrow. It's almost a shame none of them will know about the stellar negotiation skills and the hostage tactics you employed to get them the photo."

"It'll be our little secret, along with your complete capitulation to my will."

Lila laughed outright. "Never mind. I take back my earlier curiosity. You're just like the men. Give you an inch, and you take a mile. I think we're ready for the check and the valet."

"How forward of you, Ms. Wilder." Cobie acted scandalized but signaled the waiter. "Are you really so ready for our kiss that you can't wait another second?"

Lila fluttered her eyelashes. "Now you've finally figured me out. I've been waiting my whole life for a staged smooch from Cobie Galloway."

Cobie grinned as she signed the check and added an exorbitant tip. "I get that a lot."

Lila caught Malik's eye. He rose from the table he'd secured next to the front door and whispered something to a restaurant employee, then nodded to her.

"Our signal?" Cobie asked.

"They'll bring your car around for us. Malik will follow in mine."

"Right. You drove here too. So many logistics to consider."

"The only logistic you need to worry about is how you intend to get your lips on mine." Lila rose and slipped into her coat.

"Yeah, actually, I've been thinking about that."

"I'm sure you have."

Cobie smiled but didn't argue. "I think I need to use the restroom before we head out."

"Nervous stomach?"

"Something like that, but women go to the bathroom in packs, so you should come too."

"So many lesbian rules to learn," Lila quipped as she fought a hint of annoyance at being pulled off-schedule once again. She supposed she'd rather follow Cobie to the private area behind the bar than stand awkwardly by the door alone.

Once they were fully out of view of all the other restaurant patrons, however, Cobie stopped abruptly and turned to face her.

"Ladies' room is on the right," Lila said, glancing at her watch.

"I know. I don't really have to go."

"Oh, my God, are you chickening out?"

"No," Cobie said quickly. "Why? Are you?"

"No."

"Good."

"So . . ." Lila drew out the word.

"So I had my first kiss on screen, and it was terrible and stressful and I hated it."

Lila's chest tightened, but she kept her voice cool. "You already told me the story."

"Right," Cobie said, "but I just wanted to make sure you remembered I knew how that felt."

Lila rolled her eyes. "Why?"

"So that someday, when you look back on this moment, you'll know I did it because you deserve better."

"Did what?"

Cobie caught Lila around the waist, pulled her close, and whispered, "This," just before their lips met.

Lila gasped softly in shock, but the sound was smothered by the press of Cobie's mouth against her own. Her initial surprise quickly gave way to the realization Cobie had once again gone off-script, and anger rose fast. She placed both hands flat against Cobie's chest, intending to push her away, but before she did, the next set of sensations overtook her. Softness. Tenderness. The taste of espresso mingled with sweet cream. Despite Cobie's initial boldness, the kiss itself was tentative and gentle, though not quite chaste. A heat burned there, not the kind to scorch or consume, but the kind you wanted to get closer to on a cold winter day. Her shoulders relaxed and her lips parted slightly, but Cobie didn't push for more. She didn't push at all. She merely sank into the sensations enveloping them. Then with one more gentle caress of her lips, she stood back and fluttered her dark eyes open once more.

Lila stared at her, a wave of emotion swirling to the whoosh of her rapid pulse. She struggled to regain her composure while making sense of her feelings of arousal and loss and disbelief and the desire for more. She didn't like being caught off guard. She didn't like surrendering control even for a second. She didn't like the unexpected, and everything about Cobie's kiss had been unexpected. She'd clearly underestimated a great many things about her and this entire situation, and she didn't like that either. And yet she couldn't bring herself to dislike the kiss itself or the woman who'd delivered it, which proved a considerable problem.

"Lila?"

"Yes," she said slowly.

"You okay?"

She nodded.

"Are you sure?"

"Why wouldn't I be?" she asked coolly. "Because you went off script yet again? Because you kissed me without my permission?

Because you assumed you had the right to make a decision for me based on your experiences instead of considering my own?"

"Um, when you put it that way . . . yeah."

She gave an exasperated sigh. "I'm ready to go now."

"Right," Cobie said, a hint of sadness in her voice. "Back to work."

"Back to work," Lila echoed and turned on one high heel before waiting to see if Cobie would follow.

She had to follow her lead. Lila needed her to, and while that made her frustration level rise, she refused to lose her cool. Not over someone like Cobie. Not over a kiss. Not even over the disconcerting tingle of energy still coursing through her.

She was in control.

She would reestablish the power dynamic. She would take the lead next time.

Next time.

She didn't even try to shake the thought away as Malik swung the restaurant door open wide and a burst of cold wind hit her in the face. There would be a next time. There would likely be many of them over the next few months, but none of them would be quite like the first time.

She'd decide later how she felt about that.

They rode in silence through the streets of New York. The car drove itself, but Cobie kept two hands lightly on the wheel and her eyes on the road. She hadn't expected Lila to melt in her arms or even kiss her back, but she hadn't expected the silent treatment afterward either. Then again, she didn't really know what she'd expected. In that moment, she'd just wanted to do something good and thoughtful and sensitive. She knew they weren't on a real date, but she'd enjoyed their time together, or at least parts of it. And she'd listened when Lila expressed her curiosity about kissing a woman. She understood better than most what that kind of exploration could feel like, and she didn't want Lila to be robbed of the experience by a million flashbulbs.

All of her impulses were honest, but apparently, they were also presumptuous, and now all the progress they'd made over dessert had unraveled. For the first time since they'd met, Lila didn't even seem amused by her. Cobie preferred the cat-and-mouse games they'd played early on over Lila's studious disinterest now. Should she apologize? Should she try again to start another conversation about Lila's feelings? Cobie didn't want to push any more than she already had, but the so-called date wasn't over. Lila's comment about her making assumptions echoed through her ears, but would bringing up the kiss to come only force her to face the one that had come before?

The charade suddenly felt like Cobie's real-life experiences with women: intense, confusing, and short-lived. She laughed inadvertently at the thought.

"What's funny?" Lila asked.

"Oh nothing. Sorry."

She glanced over to see Lila's blue eyes boring into her and folded like a cheap tent. "It just struck me as funny that I'm apparently about as good at fake dates as I am at real dates, which is probably why I'm on a fake date instead of a real one."

The corner of Lila's mouth turned up for just a second.

"I guess now you know why I'm single."

Lila didn't respond, and Cobie shifted in her seat to face the road once more. "I'm clearly not as good at this as you are, but I don't think I'm completely hopeless. I can learn to do better."

Still nothing from Lila.

Cobie sighed. "For instance, we're getting close to your place, and I don't want to make any assumptions about how you want to play this next part or, honestly, if you even want to continue down the path we agreed on."

"I'm not the one who likes to break character," Lila said lightly.

"Touché," Cobie said, "so give me the scene. Give me my cues. Help me hit my marks."

"It's supposed to look like you're seducing me," Lila said, her tone all business.

"And we've seen how adept I am at that, so if you're hoping

for something specific, you'd better play the role of director, because if I were really trying to seduce you, I'd walk you to the door and wait for you to unlock it. I'd let you think I was going to leave it at that, but just as you walked through the door, I'd take your hand and pull you back into me. Then I'd kiss you hard and fast, to give you a solid taste of what I had to offer, but break away before you'd gotten your fill. I'd want to leave you wanting more.

"Not my hand," Lila said.

"What?" Cobie asked, a little dazed from her own imaginings.

"Don't hold my hand. Take hold of me around my waist," Lila said matter-of-factly. Cobie felt a twinge of something unsettling as she remembered doing just that moments earlier.

"And if you're facing my front door, the paparazzi will be to your back, so you need to pull me to you in a way that angles our bodies toward them without making it look like you're staging a shot," Lila continued. "You've done that before, right?"

"I've had a little work with camera angles, yes."

This time both sides of Lila's mouth rose a little. "And hold the kiss long enough to let them get the shot, but don't drag on forever. Some of them will have video, and we don't want to give them too much, too fast."

"Just enough to make it clear I'm vying for the role of romantic lead, not supporting actress," Cobie confirmed. "And what's your motivation in this scene?"

"I'm going to pretend the kiss caught me off guard but I liked it."

Cobie thought the last part might be a stretch of Lila's acting abilities, but she was eager to see what that reaction looked like on her. "Then we'll be off. No turning back."

Lila didn't respond. She merely stared out the window, her expression more reflective than resolved now.

The GPS announced their arrival, and Cobie double-parked in front of a row of brownstones before turning to face Lila. "Do I have your permission to kiss you this time?"

Lila nodded. "You do."

"Even though it will be a thing?"

"Only because it will be a thing."

The comment caused her stomach to tighten, but she said, "Okay then. We only get one take."

Cobie unbuckled her seatbelt and reached for the door handle, but Lila grabbed hold of her wrist.

"Wait."

Her heart leaped painfully in her chest at the note of need in Lila's voice. "What?" Was she having second thoughts? Did she feel something, anything, in this moment? Would she call the whole thing off?

"No comment to the press," Lila said.

"Huh?"

"They're going to hound you with questions on the way out of here and anywhere else you go until we see each other again. Don't talk to them."

"The press?" Cobie blinked a few times. Of course. She should have known the pleading in Lila's voice hadn't had anything to do with her. The only thing she needed was to control the story. At least that was one area where Cobie would have no problem complying with her wishes. "Don't worry. I've never talked to them before. I'm not going to start now."

Lila nodded, squared her shoulders, and shifted back into her practiced smile. "Then I'm ready when you are."

Cobie took a deep breath, rolled her shoulders, and swung her car door wide, stepping into the cold winter evening. As she jogged around the front of the car, she mumbled, "Lights, camera, action," then flashed an adoring smile at Lila as she opened her door. Flashbulbs illuminated the night.

Lila accepted her hand and emerged gracefully from the car, her eyes never leaving Cobie's. The mirth she'd seen in the office and earlier in the evening had returned, and Cobie realized she'd missed it.

Malik met them on the sidewalk and pushed open a wrought-iron gate before closing it behind them and staying put at the entrance. He knew his place, Cobie mused. He played his role flawlessly. Maybe he could give her a few pointers sometime. Then again, he mostly just had to look intimidating, whereas she had to look like someone who could sweep a world-famous pop star off her feet.

Totally doable.

The paparazzi hit the gate behind them, their camera bags and bodies clanking dully against the wrought iron that held them at bay, but with Malik there they wouldn't dare try to cross the barrier.

"Cobie. Lila. Lila. Cobie." The shouts were excessive and, quite frankly, worthless. As if either of them could really not know the mob had followed them or what they wanted. "Look over here. Give us a smile. How did you meet? Are you working together? Lila, are you going into movies? Cobie, are you recording an album?"

"It's good to know what the prevailing theories are," Cobie said in a low, cooing voice only Lila was close enough to hear.

"They don't seem to be onto us yet."

"I'm a little hurt actually," Cobie said as she walked casually up the front steps to a hunter-green door set back against the brownstone. "I felt like I made it very clear I was trying to get into your pants tonight."

Lila threw back her head and laughed. "You had high aspirations. They think I'm straight."

"Whatever gave them that idea?" Cobie asked as Lila put the key in the door and opened it before turning back to face her.

"Certainly not you feeding me dessert off your fork." Lila ran one index finger down the length of black tie hanging loosely from Cobie's collar. "Think we should make it a little more clear for them?"

"Yeah, and we've only got one shot, so let's get it right."

Lila's smile turned coy while her eyes held nothing but challenge. "Show me what you've got."

She turned back toward the door, and Cobie's mind went into screen mode. She internally counted the beats, measured the pace, and watched for Lila's cues. The turn, one step, one foot over the threshold, *don't rush it*, one more, let them all see her go. Give them a second to process the ending. The green door started to swing slowly closed, and she shot out her hand to stop it solidly before she reached inside and caught Lila around the waist. With one fluid motion, she pulled her close, letting the momentum of their bodies colliding spin them the half-turn needed to face the clamoring calls of the press.

Holding her close, she cupped Lila's face in her palm and guided her head down until their lips met again. This time she didn't notice the beat of her own heart or the rush of blood it sent roaring through her veins. Here amid the fireworks of flashbulbs and the collective intake of breath, she only counted the seconds to some undetermined number between angelic and over the top. Then, in much the way it had begun, Cobie began her deliberate draw back. She moved fluidly, like a dancer who'd learned the moves enough to add a little flair but never breaking step with the pre-set routine.

First, she loosened her hold on Lila's waist, then she relaxed the pressure of her lips against Lila's. Slowly pulling back only the distance of a breath, she allowed a smile to spread across her face as her eyes fluttered open. She watched as Lila's baby blues came into focus and noted the perfect little circle of surprise formed by her bright red lips. The signs of shock slowly shifted to pleasure, and her heart gave an annoying little twinge of something irrelevant to the scene. She stepped back, her hand lingering only long enough to make sure Lila didn't topple over, a prospect she considered highly unlikely.

"Goodnight, Lila," she whispered.

"See you next weekend, Cobie," Lila murmured as she brought her fingertips to her freshly kissed lips.

Nice touch. She jogged down the stairs with a little added bounce in her step. As she hit the sidewalk, she braced for the onslaught from reporters, silently reminding herself she was supposed to be walking on air right now. She'd just kissed one of the most sought-after women in the Western world. As far as anyone else was concerned, she was a total boss.

Malik swung open the gate and gave her a nod of approval, but she didn't have time to return it before the press pushed in on her.

"Cobie, Cobie, Cobie." The voices shouted out from every direction as they gave her only enough space to take two steps. Cameras flashed and snapped from every angle. "Are you dating Lila Wilder. How long have you been together? Was this your first date? Is Lila gay?"

She kept her sly smile plastered across her face while resisting the urge to grit her teeth at the invasion of her privacy and personal space. *This better be worth it.*

She opened her car door and glanced back up to see Lila still watching her from the top step, her expression of surprise now fully replaced by one of satisfaction. Cobie's heart gave another little leap, and her smile softened to something more genuine as she fired up the Tesla. She'd done her job, and while she'd have to wait for the official reviews to come in, the initial response seemed positive, at least by the standards everyone had set for the evening.

She and Lila hadn't killed each other. No one had made any massive gaffes, unless you counted the first kiss, but the press didn't know about that one. As far as the paparazzi were concerned, she'd just scored the perfect end to the perfect first date, and in a way, she had. They'd both had wildly different goals than she would have had on a real first date, but as far as fake ones went, she'd done pretty well.

As she wound through the streets back to her Times Square hotel, she tried to make sense of her mixed emotions. Part of her remained tense at the multiple sets of headlights following her through the city and at the sense of her privacy slipping away. She'd worked hard to protect herself from the media circus that followed too many of her colleagues. Then again, she'd also worked hard to become a successful actress. The craft of slipping into the heart and mind of another human being was her life's work, and tonight moved her a step closer to where she wanted to be on her career path.

It had also provided her a new challenge as a performer. She didn't love putting her personal life on display, but nothing about what she did with Lila would ever really be personal. It may have felt like that a time or two, but those moments had ended badly, or at least awkwardly. Maybe that was a life lesson for her. She always did better playing someone else than playing herself. That's how she knew she could take on the role of Vale and make it her own, and that's how she would have to play the part of love-interest to Lila. She would stick to the plan, stay in character, harness everything she'd ever learned about acting, and use every opportunity to simultaneously hone her craft and her image. She'd ended the evening with a huge triumph. All she had to do now was stay the course, and really, it wasn't like Lila had given her the opportunity to do anything else. It was simply business. As long as she kept it that way, she'd be fine.

Just then the tech system in the car said, "Incoming message from Lila Wilder."

Cobie touched the button on the dash to read Lila's response to the kiss. It simply said, "Not bad, but the first one was better."

"It's a full-page spread in *Entertainment Herald*," Mimi said excitedly as she climbed back into bed and unfolded the paper.

"Which page?" Stan asked, pulling his reading glasses off his head and onto his nose.

"Front, of course."

"Of course," Stan replied as she skimmed the paper.

"What about the websites?"

"*People*, TMZ, Perez Hilton, they've all got the photos. A few of them have video."

"Same video as last night."

"Pretty much, though I also saw one that starts a few seconds earlier with Cobie opening the car door for Lila."

Mimi put a palm over her heart. "She opened the car door for her? What a sweetheart. You know, she might be just what Lila needs."

"It's not what Cobie needs. The date looked like they were high school sweethearts, not an edgy, out-lesbian dream team," Stan groused. "If she throws away her career for some LGBT afterschool special..."

Mimi laughed. "Lila hasn't done anything PG-rated for at least five years. They'll get to the hot and heavy stuff soon enough."

Stan's brow furrowed, and he worried he might need to bump up his next Botox injection. "What's the paper say?"

"All around It girl, Lila Wilder, was seen out in New York's Greenwich Village Sunday night with teen movie sensation Cobie Galloway. The two had pizza at a small Italian restaurant. It was noted by patrons, who were kept at a distance, that the two often seemed deeply engrossed in heavy conversations, which led some to speculate they might be planning a joint project. Another patron, however, mentioned that Galloway made Wilder laugh on several occasions.

"The first indication that the pair might be more than business associates or casual acquaintances came during the dessert course, when Galloway reportedly shared some of her dessert with Wilder.

"'It just felt tense, like there was something more going on,' said one restaurant employee, who requested to remain anonymous. 'Cobie fed Lila off her own fork, which doesn't seem like something you do at a business meeting.'"

Stan scoffed. "Not any sort of legal business anyway."

Mimi gave him a light slap across the arm. "Focus. Your girl handfed a man-eating lioness. Oh look, there's a picture."

Stan pushed his glasses higher on the bridge of his nose and stared at the grainy photo clearly shot through the restaurant's front window with a super-zoom lens. "Not the best resolution, but they're leaned in, and the eye contact seems good."

"And sexy," Mimi added. "Sweet dessert, shared silverware, lots of focus on lips and tongues."

"Are you editorializing or writing a romance novel?"

"Maybe both," Mimi said. "I wonder if Cobie came up with that on her own or if Lila coached her."

He didn't care to hazard a guess. The press coverage had been good, and the shock value certainly seemed to play across every story he'd encountered, but something still felt off to him. Perhaps it was the millions of dollars in movie deals Cobie had just flushed down the toilet. "Keep reading."

"The pair left the restaurant together and returned to Wilder's West Village brownstone, where Galloway walked her to the door and put to rest any doubts about the nature of their relationship with a whopper of a goodnight kiss."

"It says 'whopper?' Like the burger?" Stan asked, wrinkling his nose.

Mimi pointed to the word in print. "Right there. And it did look like one hell of a kiss. Play the video again."

Stan didn't argue even though they'd both already seen it a hundred times. He clicked the open link on his laptop screen and watched as the camera zoomed in when Cobie pulled Lila to her.

"They really did it." Mimi's voice was filled with awe. "Admit it. Aren't you a little bit proud of her for going all in."

He wasn't sure pride was the emotion he felt, but he did have to admit he didn't just see the shift from a business perspective. Somehow, sometime, Cobie had grown up. She had played last night perfectly, and while he'd always known she had more to her than the simplistic roles she'd played, he also understood the process of transitioning to a different type of stardom would carry a different kind of cost, one he was surprised Cobie had agreed to pay. He worried he might not have made the realities of this risk clear to her. Then again, maybe she was on a mission to make it clear she could handle whatever the industry threw at her.

Mimi reached over and paused the video. "My favorite part is how all the reporters go speechless when Cobie kisses her. It's like you can almost hear the collective air being sucked out of all of them."

Stan nodded. He couldn't deny the drama of that moment, and he couldn't have staged it better himself.

"What's your favorite part?" Mimi asked.

"The part where I get a ten percent commission." He tried to get out of bed, but Mimi caught his arm.

"Nope. Don't pretend you're not invested in this. You're clearly hung up on something the rest of the world isn't getting. Come on. Tell me what you see there."

He rolled his eyes but relented and slid the little video progress bar almost to the end, right as Cobie began to bound down the stairs. "There. How would you describe Cobie's smile?"

"Triumphant. Look how confident she seems right there." She squeezed his arm. "She nailed it, and she knows it."

He nodded, not sharing her exuberance. "Now look at Lila."

Mimi leaned closer to the screen and stared at her own client for a few seconds, "She's . . . she's impressed. Oh, my God, Lila is watching her go like she's a little proud of her too."

He clicked play, and the expression quickly vanished from Lila's face. Her smile grew dreamy as she leaned against the doorjamb.

"She finished on the right note. That dreamy thing, she does it really well. She picked that up in her early music videos."

"I know. I've seen her do it a million times. It's one of her signature moves."

"But the other look, the one she gave right after Cobie broke completely away, wasn't planned or practiced," Mimi added. "That's new."

"A new trick or a new emotion?" Stan asked seriously.

Mimi rubbed her palms together and grinned. "I don't know, but I can't wait to find out."

"Yoo-hoo, Lila."

She looked up from her notepad to see Felipe waving a pair of maroon skinny jeans. "Sorry, for who?"

"Um, you," he said. "Cobie can't pull this off."

"Then yes," Lila said. "I like it. Put them with the caramel short-waisted pea coat."

"And a hat?" Felipe asked. "It'll be cold when you're outside."

"What about a maroon open-knit beret?"

He frowned, and his high, thin eyebrows drew closer together. "Too much."

"Too much maroon or too much, period?"

"Both."

She sighed. "Just pick something."

He hooked the pants hanger back over the rolling rack and joined her on the large, circular ottoman. "Okay, sister, time to spill."

"What are you talking about? You're my stylist. Style me."

He clucked and opened his arms. "Girl, you don't need a stylist. You need a hug."

She laughed and pushed him away. "You're crazy. I'm trying to write."

He made a dramatic show of looking at the wide, blank space on her page. "Yeah, you're killing it."

"I said 'trying.'" Lila tossed the pad to the floor and lay back on the ottoman, running her fingers through the faux fur finish. "Trying fruitlessly is still trying."

"Still searching for the ballad?" Felipe asked.

"I can't start recording until I have one."

He shrugged. "Then write one."

"Did you miss the part where I'm trying? It's not happening."

"'Cause you aren't in love?"

"That's never stopped me before." Lila stared at the ceiling. "I didn't have any trouble writing them for the last four albums, and I wasn't in love then either."

"But you had people who were in love with you at least."

The truth of the statement hit her with unexpected force, causing a little rush of breath to hitch in her throat.

The effects must have shown somehow, because Felipe's mocha skin paled immediately. "I'm sorry. You know what I meant. Tons of people are in love with you, not just one specific one."

"Right," she said dryly.

"Well, I mean, I for one am madly in love with you."

She rolled her eyes just as Malik shuffled into the room in his ginormous bunny slippers and Daffy Duck pajama bottoms.

"Malik is too," Felipe said.

"I'm what?" he asked, setting a carafe of coffee on a small glass table.

"In love with Lila."

"Madly," he said emphatically. "I only sleep with you because she's rebuffed me so many times."

Lila finally laughed and rolled onto her stomach. "You guys are too quick this morning. You're having more sex in my house than I have ever had."

"I'm sorry, baby girl." Felipe stroked her hair.

"Really?"

"I'm sorry that I'm not sorry. Does that count?"

She sat up and shoved him again. "Get off my ottoman. Pour me some coffee."

"Ooh, the rich white lady is being mean to the hired help again."

Malik laughed and shook his head. "She's just lonely. Pimpin' ain't easy."

"Damn right." Lila felt infinitely better than she had moments earlier. Not that she'd solved her writer's block, but it didn't seem as important as it had earlier. "Men are trifling and tiring. I'm building a damn empire. I don't have time to properly torture someone for real, and that's the only way you can truly hold their interest."

"Mhmm, girl. I know that." Felipe snapped his fingers. "I gotta keep that one on a short leash or he's off gallivanting all over town. And now you go and take him down to the gayborhood. Like he wasn't flighty enough before."

Lila giggled as she glanced at Malik's folded arms and steady expression of boredom. "He was very well-behaved last night, honest. I never even saw him talking to one of the male waiters. I kept a close eye on him too."

"Lies!" Felipe screeched. "I watched that video on TMZ like a bazillion times. You were totally engrossed in Little Miss Lesbo."

"I was not."

"You can't fool me. Don't say that girl didn't pique your interest."

"She kissed her," Malik said.

"I know. I just said I watched the video. Keep up, Malik."

"No." He pushed off the wall excitedly. "Before that. I just figured it out. Cobie kissed her behind the bar."

"What?" Felipe whirled around to face her. "Is this true?"

Lila bit her lip.

"Oh, my God, you made your guilty face. Why in the name of all things sacred am I just now hearing this part?" he asked her, then turned on Malik. "You have had, like, fourteen hours to tell me, and you held out."

"We were busy last night."

"Fair," Felipe said. "Your mouth was busy."

"Guys!" Lila said. "Too much."

"He could've told me after," Felipe pouted.

"I didn't put it together until right now when you mentioned keeping your eyes on me. That was the only time of the whole night when I didn't have a direct line of sight on you. I remember because it made me nervous. I was trying to time how long it would take two women to go to the bathroom together."

"And that math was hard for you?" Lila asked.

"I don't know what y'all do in there in groups," he shot back, "but I never actually heard the door open or close, and you were back too soon, and your lipstick was smudged, which I thought you would've noticed when you looked in the mirror."

"It's like a mystery," Felipe proclaimed gleefully. "Was Cobie covered in her lipstick?"

"I didn't see. Lila came back in a hurry, and Cobie came kind of skulking behind her with her head down, but I thought it was just to brace against the press, who went berserk as soon as they saw them. Then we were off again, and I had to work."

"And then your mouth was busy. The end," Felipe said before turning back to Lila. "Now you fill in the blanks, or I swear to both of the Holy Madonnas, I will dress you in polka dots and plaids for the next week."

"Fine," Lila said dismissively. "She kissed me."

"I'm going to need more. Set the scene, and do it right or I'll give you uncomfortable shoes."

She rolled her eyes and thought for a few seconds. How could she explain the kiss to him when she didn't fully understand the situation herself? She didn't even know what emotions to sort through since she'd worked hard all night not to feel anything for fear of what that something might be. Not that she'd phrase her recap to Felipe that way. "She just pulled me behind the bar on the way to the bathroom and said something about my first time kissing a woman. Then she kissed me."

He stared at her as if waiting for more. "And?"

"Then we left."

"She was flushed," Malik said, "and her eyes were like fire."

"Traitor," Lila called.

Malik shrugged. "The truth hurts."

"I was angry she didn't stick to the agreement."

"'Cause she wanted to jump you so bad she couldn't contain herself?" Felipe asked.

Lila shook her head. That would have been the easy explanation and the one she'd give if anyone in the press ever found out, but she knew it wasn't true. Cobie hadn't seemed pushy or overly eager. If anything, she'd come across as almost sad, but the kiss itself wasn't sad so much as sweet, with an almost altruistic undercurrent. "It's hard to explain."

"Try." Felipe pleaded.

"Her kiss caught me off guard. It wasn't rushed or too hard."

"Oh, you rhymed. Maybe you should write a song about Cobie kissing you. Was there tongue?"

"No," Lila said quickly.

"Good, 'cause 'tongue' is hard to rhyme. If she were a guy, you could rhyme it with 'well-hung,' but it doesn't work here."

"I would never use the term 'well-hung' in one of my songs. Can you even imagine all the teenage girls singing along?"

He snickered in a way that suggested he could.

"Besides. The kiss wasn't the stuff of love songs. It was slow and sweet and almost protective. She acted like she was worried about my feelings or my honor or something puritanical. She told some story about her first kiss being in front of an audience, and she said I deserved better."

Felipe and Malik shared a side-eyed glance.

"What?"

Malik let out a low whistle. "Damn."

"You might be in trouble, honey," Felipe added.

"Why?"

"Has it occurred to you that this girl might be for real?"

She scoffed. "She's an actress. None of them are real."

The guys said nothing.

"She signed up for a fauxmance. She wants a movie part. She's not even into me. Trust me, I know when someone's angling to bed me. She's not. She was just being . . ." Lila searched for the right word, but it didn't come. What had Cobie's true motive been? "She was just being . . ."

"Nice?" Felipe asked.

"Genuine?" Malik offered.

"Sincere?"

"Kind?"

"Considerate?"

"Genuine?"

"Stop." She shook her head and stood up. "You said 'genuine' twice. When did you two get such an extensive vocabulary?"

"Probably from listening to you read poetry in sixth grade," Felipe shot back.

Lila tried to pout, but she cracked and giggled just a little. "Low blow, Felipe."

"Come on, you're talking about no one being real. Those poems were all the feels."

She grimaced, remembering not just her early attempts to write in rhyme, but also all the events that had inspired her to seek such an outlet in the first place. She didn't find the connection quite so amusing anymore, but she tried to keep her tone light as she said, "Just for that, you have to take the check to Selena this month."

"No." Felipe immediately backpedaled. "I didn't mean it. Please, can't you mail it?"

"She'll say she didn't get it and ask for another, then cash both," Lila said without a hint of annoyance. "It's got to be done."

"It doesn't have to," Felipe said. "You could cut that cord."

Lila shook her head. The statement might be true, at least in a vacuum, but none of them lived in a vacuum, except Selena, and that could end the minute the money ran out. "Just do it while I'm out with Cobie this weekend, okay?"

Felipe pretended to pout about the chore, but she could tell he did so only to cover his sadness. "Fine. But not because you made me, because I love you and you will owe me your undying gratitude and you will give me all the gossip the minute you come home from your super adorable lesbian hipster date."

"Fair trade. Now you two go canoodle or something. I've got to get back to work."

Malik nudged Felipe, who eyed her for a few seconds before saying, "All right. I need to get Cobie's stuff sent over to her anyway."

Then he wheeled his rack of clothes out the door.

She waited until she could no longer hear them before flopping all the way across the ottoman once more, trying not to marvel at how fast the conversation had shifted from Cobie to Selena. The two were nothing alike. Not in looks, not in temperament, and certainly not in their relationship to her. And yet the lesson of one would undoubtedly shape her interactions with the other. She tried to remind herself that was a good thing. She'd learned her lessons. She'd grown and matured. Maybe if she'd met Cobie at a different time in her life, she would have seen her differently, but she hadn't, and Lila didn't believe in looking back. She couldn't control the past. She could only control the future.

※ ※ ※

"Thanks for coming here today." Cobie extended her hand to her personal trainer, Janna McKinley.

"No problem," Janna said with a toothy smile and an overly tight handshake. "Sometimes it's easier to take an ass kicking in your own home than in a gym."

"I hadn't thought of it that way. I'd only considered what a hassle it'd be for everyone else at the gym for me to go there right now," Cobie said with a grimace. "But I guess the press getting shots of me sweaty and doubled over in pain wouldn't do much to bolster my newfound, suave image either."

"Probably not." Janna grabbed a duffle bag full of aerobic torture devices and tucked a rolled yoga mat under her arm. "But wait until they get a glimpse of your oblique muscles. Every camera in America will zoom in on your midriff."

She found the idea horrifying but managed to smile and nod. She'd perfected the "everything's copacetic" expression over the last week, along with the ability to push past her discomfort and focus on the person in front of her despite the fears swirling around inside her head. "I certainly feel my abs trying to make their presence known." Which was a tactful way of saying her sides felt like Janna had kicked her repeatedly until they developed a self-preservation mechanism that involved never unclenching again.

"You're only at about the midway point of the transformation. It'll get better."

Cobie assumed by "better," Janna meant "harder." It took every ounce of politeness her parents had drilled into her not to tell Janna to fuck off. Instead, she said, "Same time and place tomorrow?"

"Works for me. We'll do more to get your whole ab complex firing together," Janna said, cheerfully oblivious to the murderous fantasies her comments inspired in Cobie.

"See you then."

Just as Janna opened the door, a young man appeared in the hallway outside the suite holding a large black garment bag.

"Your dry cleaning's here," Janna called with undue enthusiasm and then jogged away, because apparently super-fit people must do everything at speeds that intimidate normal people.

"Whoa," the bellboy said. "What did she have in her coffee?"

"Steroids of some sort," Cobie mumbled, then remembered she hadn't sent out any dry cleaning. "Are you sure you've got the right room?"

The boy glanced at the tag on the garment bag and nervously said, "Yes, ma'am."

She frowned. Had she lost track of something in the press-induced chaos of the last few days? "I don't remember sending anything to be laundered."

"I don't think you did." He blushed. "I didn't try to read your stuff or anything, but it just says right here on the tag that it's a gift from Ms. Wilder."

Cobie rolled her eyes before she could stop herself and grabbed the hanger out of his hand. She turned it over and, sure enough, printed right on the front, big enough for the world to see, was a plain white card with a handwritten note saying, "I got you a little something special to wear tonight. XOXO —Lila."

She sighed and fished some bills from the pocket of her track pants. Without looking at how much was there, she handed them to the kid. "Thanks."

"Oh no, thank you," he gushed, staring at the money, then added, "I won't tell anybody."

"Great." She believed him, but she wondered how many other people had handled the delivery over the last hour. Delivery people, drivers, hotel security and staff. Surely one of them would leak, and that's no doubt what Lila wanted.

She carried the bag back through the living room and into her expansive bedroom, tossing it onto the king-sized bed. Part of her wanted to leave it there and go soak in an Epsom-salt bath, but she'd spend the whole time wondering what waited for her inside. She might as well see what she was in for now.

She bent over just enough to reach the zipper and every muscle in her back and shoulders screamed. Wincing, she unsheathed the clothes and stared at the ensemble.

"Really?" she asked aloud despite being alone. Lila had sent over a pair of dark low-cut jeans, a plain black V-neck T-shirt, and a button-down denim shirt, with a pair of Timberland hiking boots. That's what the woman with her own fashion line had come up with? Cobie would look like an emo lumberjack. A butch one. Not that emo lumberjacks ever really presented as femmes, but was Lila playing off some lesbian stereotype manual? She had a flash of annoyance bordering on anger and straightened up abruptly only to double back over as every stabilizer down her sides burned fast and hot.

To add insult to injury, her phone rang from somewhere back across the living room. Not the hotel phone, but her personal cell. She forced herself upright and went to find it. Each ring felt like she was playing the hot-and-cold game until on the fifth ring she managed to locate it between the couch cushions.

Without even looking at the caller ID, she lifted it to her ear and said, "What?"

"Wow, for someone who's sucking face with pop stars, you sure do sound unreasonably tense."

Cobie snorted and sank onto the couch. "Hey, Talia."

"Hey yourself, kid."

She smiled, no longer feeling much like a kid. She tried to remember that's exactly the way she wanted to feel, but the wistfulness in Talia's voice took her back to a time when her youth and innocence hadn't been a burden. "What's up?"

"Nothing much," Talia said lightly. "Just came off a four-day writing bender. I ran to the store to get some toilet paper and ice cream, and while I was there, I also had to pick up about four different tabloids with photos of you sticking your tongue down Lila Wilder's throat."

Cobie snorted. "I love how you buried the lead there."

"I love how I had to see the news on a magazine cover."

"It's not what it looks like."

"So you didn't kiss one of the most egregiously straight women in the world?"

"Well . . ."

"Yeah," Talia said dryly. "So it's exactly what it looks like."

"Maybe, kind of, but not for the reasons it looks like." Cobie struggled to find the words. She'd obviously been sworn to secrecy about the whole charade, but she had to talk to someone, didn't she? And even if she wasn't eager to unload on someone after her shitty week, she couldn't lie to Talia. Not in a friendship sense, because Tal would see through her, and not in a business sense, either, because if anyone needed to know how far she was willing to go to get the part, it was the woman waiting on the other end of the line.

"What reasons? She's stunning and talented and powerful, and her legs go all the way up to her chin," Talia said gleefully. "Not generally your type but a damn good roll in the hay."

"I'm so not angling for a roll in the hay," Cobie said. "She's a piece of work."

"The best ones usually are, but I know the high-profile fling isn't your thing, thank God, so what gives?"

"Well, there's a book I really want to turn into a movie," Cobie said slowly. "The writer's brilliant, and the story is life-changing, and I want to play the main character so much I'd do anything to land the role."

"Uh-huh," Talia said, and Cobie could picture her pressing her tongue to the inside of her cheek. "Go on."

"But the studios aren't going to green light the project with me in the role, at least not the me they know now."

"Uh-huh." Talia made the same noise, but the tone had changed to one of weariness.

"Apparently my image isn't consistent with the image of the character. I'm not edgy enough."

"Cobie, this better not be going where I think it's going."

"Do you think I'm faking a relationship with Lila as a publicity stunt to help get the role I've always dreamed of?"

"I'm starting to."

"Then you are correct." Cobie scrunched up her face and held the phone away from her ear, waiting for the sound of Talia exploding.

Instead she heard a sigh. "I'm sorry."

"What?"

"I never could tell you no."

"I beg to differ," Cobie said. "I can think of a few times when—"

"Not when it mattered. Not when I knew it was really what you wanted."

Cobie's chest ached. "I do want this, Tal."

"I know. And I assume you didn't run your little plan by me first because you knew what I'd say."

"I didn't have a lot of time to make a decision. Believe it or not, Lila's personality is every bit as big as the billboards she's constantly gracing."

"Oh, I believe it," Talia said quickly. "What I don't believe is that you'd jump on board or in bed with someone like her. It's not you, Cobe."

"Maybe it needs to be, for now, for the next few months, until I can get the clout needed to get the movie made the way it deserves to be made."

"Doesn't the writer get a say in how the movie deserves to be made?"

"She does. She said she wanted it done right or she wouldn't sign off on the project."

"She sounds like a real tight-ass."

Cobie laughed as she watched little slivers of outside light shining over her closed curtains. "She really can be, but she's got her reasons, and I respect them."

"God, why do you have to act like such a fucking boi scout when I'm trying to lambast you for being a media slut?"

"Would you rather I actually be a media slut?"

"Sometimes, yes," Talia said matter-of-factly.

"Then let me do this."

"Oh, I don't think there's any 'letting' to it. You didn't ask for my permission, and I haven't heard you ask my forgiveness either. You're a big girl, which seems to be what you're trying to prove here, but I know you. I understand better than anyone what something like this could take out of you. If things go bad . . ." She let her voice trail off, then finished more softly. "I just don't want you to get hurt while making a statement I never asked you to make."

"You're off the hook. You are not responsible for me and my choices." Cobie's voice rose in both pitch and volume. She didn't want to get all emotional about the choices she'd made. She didn't want to think about them too much either, but of all the people she thought she'd have to defend her motivations or capabilities to, she hadn't worried about Talia until right now. "I'm an adult. I'm an actor. I'm every bit as dedicated to my craft as you are."

"Don't get all defensive on me. I've never doubted your dedication or your talent. I'm just looking out for you."

"That's right. You look out for me. It's always been that way. When do I get my chance to repay you?"

"There's nothing to repay. You don't owe me anything."

Talia seemed to believe the statement. Cobie wished she could too. "I have to do this, Tal."

"Not for me."

"For me then. I believe in what you created, and I want to be part of it."

"You really like *Vigilant* that much?"

"Enough to make out with a beautiful woman?" Cobie laughed. "I think it's probably a fair trade."

Talia joined in her laugher. "When you put things that way, is it really a burden hanging out with her?"

Cobie thought about the answer. The publicity stunt came with plenty of burdens. She peeked around the curtains to see a line of paparazzi waiting twenty stories below. "Well, I can't go out of my hotel room without being pelted by intrusive questions, and a small but vocal group of religious conservatives are threatening to boycott my movies for corrupting America's sweetheart."

"Puh-lease, you were much more America's sweetheart than Lila. If anyone's being corrupted, it's you."

"I'm pretty sure that's what the lesbian community is shouting back at them all across the Internet."

"So in other words, it's terrible and you hate it?" Guilt weighed heavy in Talia's voice.

"The trappings, yes," Cobie admitted. "Everything that happens outside of just the two of us alone together is awful, but . . ."

"But?"

"The date part wasn't terrible. I mean, it wasn't like, you know, the best I've ever had."

"Obviously." A hint of bravado laced Talia's tone now.

"But as far as business dinners go, I've had worse."

"A ringing endorsement."

Cobie laughed. "She's hard to read. I haven't made my mind up yet about her as a person, but she keeps me interested, and that's more than I've had going on in a long time."

"At least the next few months won't be boring," Talia said. "You know I expect regular updates, right?"

"Yeah, you and everyone else. Emma hasn't stopped texting me for days."

"I expect you to give me very different information than you share with your little sister. I want all the naughty bits."

Cobie's stomach clenched at the sudden memory of Lila's icy blue eyes after she'd dared to kiss her. She had no desire to crash and burn again. "I'm not sure there'll be any naughty bits."

Talia chuckled knowingly.

"What?"

"Just call me when you get there, okay?"

"Wait, what makes you think I'm going to get there?"

Talia snorted. "Bye, Cobie."

"Bye." Cobie disconnected the phone, sadness once again settling over her as awareness of her aches and pains returned. She wished Talia were here for real. She wished they'd talked longer. She wished she could go for a walk to clear her mind.

Then she shook her head and forced herself to stand up. She didn't have the time or the right to give in to self-pity. No one in the world would feel sorry for her, and she wouldn't either. She'd meant everything she'd said to Tal. She could do whatever it took. She wanted to. She needed to.

Chapter Three

"Skating?" Cobie asked, looking dubious, but her eyes sparkled as Malik pulled into the parking lot at Sky Rink in Chelsea.

"What were you expecting?" Lila asked.

"I don't know. Something more high-end."

"You thought I dressed you like that to go to the Met?"

Cobie glanced down at the outfit, and Lila wondered if she realized how well the casual ensemble suited her. She wasn't the kind of person who needed to be made up. The biggest part of her charm was her comfort in her own skin. It wouldn't be hard to accentuate that quality and bend it enough so Cobie came across as confident or even cocky, but the transition needed to happen slowly to be believable, so she'd started by stripping her look down to the building blocks.

"I thought maybe you were taking me to an Indigo Girls concert."

"I do love them, but no. We need something lighter and fun together. We're still on whimsy, remember?"

Cobie nodded. "So, skating it is."

"Hip, fun, entertaining, and we'll look so very crushy on one another."

"But how will we keep from tripping over all the cameras?"

"I've rented the rink for an hour. It'll be fully staffed: concession stand, skate rental, DJ, and a few attendants."

"And you made sure the press knows we'll be here."

"Of course. But they'll have to stay on the sidelines with the public." She nodded to the plate glass windows on the second level where cameras and bodies jostled for position overhead.

Cobie stared at the cacophony for a few seconds before saying, "You're really good at this."

"It's my job," Lila responded with a dismissive wave, but a little jolt of pride zinged through her. Not many appreciated the skill set. Most never even gave it any thought, and those who did usually looked down on her as conniving or manipulative rather than as socially intelligent.

"So how much is too much tonight?" Cobie asked.

"You just be you. But follow me."

"Sure. That's specific."

"Can you dance?" Lila asked.

"Yes," Cobie said with an amusing hint of defiance. "I'm actually a pretty good dancer."

"I'm going to tuck that little bit of information away for later, but tonight, just pretend we're dancing. I'm the lead, but you know the song as well as I do."

"Got it," Cobie said. "You ready?"

"Just waiting on you."

Cobie rolled her shoulders, lifted her chin, and took a deep breath. Lila watched, captivated by the transition as she shifted from tentative to confident, like someone had flipped a switch. Cobie clearly wasn't a slouch in the acting department. Nodding to Malik in the rearview mirror, she said, "Show time."

Cobie exited the town car, signaling for Malik to stay as she jogged around and opened Lila's door for her. Extending her hand with an exuberant smile Lila almost forgot wasn't real, she said, "May I have this dance?"

In spite of her effort to tamp down any genuine emotions threatening to surface, Lila grinned as she slid her palm along Cobie's. Her hand was every bit as strong as those of the men she'd dated, but so much softer, with graceful fingers that slipped so easily between her own.

Her chest felt unbearably light as Cobie led her up the stairs, where a security officer waved them inside, and Malik set about checking the perimeter. She tried to focus on the steps, the trappings, the parts they each had to play. Everyone had hit their marks so far. Even the cameras flashed from an appropriate distance. But she had to fight to stay aware of them when Cobie's smile shown as brightly as any she'd ever seen her give a leading man on screen.

"What size?" Cobie asked as they approached the rental counter.

"Excuse me?"

"Skate size?"

"Oh, six and a half," Lila said, then added, "figure skate."

Cobie winked. "I figured you for a figure girl."

Lila rolled her eyes good-naturedly. "And you're hockey style."

"Duh," Cobie said playfully, releasing her hand as she turned to the counter.

Lila felt a little chill at the loss of contact, but she blamed it on the sheet of ice next to her. She tried not to think too much about the unexpected flash of feeling Cobie seemed to spark. They were always short-lived and likely steeped in a great deal of theatrical training. Still, she couldn't help but steal little glances at her as she chatted amicably with the young woman behind the rental counter. The girl blushed and laughed as Cobie said something Lila wished she could hear.

"Thanks," Cobie said over her shoulder and headed back toward Lila, skates in hand.

"Were you flirting with the counter girl?" Lila whispered as she kicked off her calf-length boots and set them neatly aside.

"It's a little early in the play for that, isn't it?" Cobie asked as she snugged up her skate laces.

"It is, but I think you made her night."

"Nah, she was just nervous, and I put her at ease."

"That's probably a better skill than flirting."

Cobie's dark brown hair had fallen across her face when she'd leaned forward to tie her skates, but she shook it back to regard Lila seriously. "Yeah?"

Lila ignored the heat of Cobie's inquisitive gaze and finished adjusting her laces. "You disagree?"

"Not at all. I'm just surprised you think so."

"Believe it or not, I didn't get to be rich and famous by treating people poorly."

"I do believe you." Cobie stood. "But that doesn't make any of us less nervous in your presence, and I think you probably don't hate that."

Lila frowned and shrugged. "There's always a power dynamic in any situation. Some people work hard to ignore that fact. I choose to own it. Doing so doesn't make me a bad person."

Cobie shook her head. "I suppose not, but it does beg the question how you manage to always come out on top of that power struggle, but that's a deeper conversation than a second date calls for."

"And what kind of conversations does one have on a second date?" Lila asked, once again impressed with Cobie's ability to assess and shift the tone to fit their needs.

"I think the most pressing question right now," Cobie leaned close and took both her hands, "is can you skate well enough to keep up with me for the next hour?"

Lila laughed and allowed herself to be pulled onto wobbly blades. "I guess we're about to find out. Why don't you show me what you've got?"

"And by 'you' you mean thirty of New York's most morally bankrupt photographers and videographers?"

"Of course," Lila said nonchalantly. "No pressure."

"Don't worry. On my long list of things to feel nervous about tonight, the skating doesn't even break the top ten."

"Go ahead. Take a lap, champ," Lila challenged.

Cobie shrugged, grinning smugly as she opened the door to the rink. As soon as her skates hit the ice, she slipped and shot out her hands. Lila gasped and reached for her, the instinct to protect too fast and strong to be examined, but as Cobie grabbed hold of the side rail, she turned and grinned wickedly. "Gotcha."

"What?"

"I just wanted to see how you'd react before I did this."

"What?" she asked again, her heart still hammering her ribcage from the scare.

Cobie stood up straighter, pushed off with one skate, and did a big, lazy loop to the end of the rink before tucking her body lower at the far end. Crouching with one arm raised, speed-skater style, she shot off across the ice. She gained speed so quickly she was halfway across the rink by the time Lila realized what was happening. She had only a second to be impressed by Cobie's grace and power before the wall rose up in her vision. Cobie didn't seem bothered by the immovable object in her path, though, and took several more rapid strides, each movement strong and fluid in ways Lila wouldn't have imagined possible from her. But she couldn't process her impressive form fully as she was now only feet away from the fiberglass barrier separating them from about fifty camera-wielding reporters. One more push, one more glide, and Lila winced, turning half away from the impending collision while still peeking just enough to see Cobie throw herself sideways, sending a spray of shaved ice ahead of her. It splattered across the sheet of Plexiglass, and every one of the paparazzi who hadn't dived out of the way rewarded her with a rush of shutter clicks Lila could hear all the way across the rink.

As Cobie skated back over at a more casual pace, her grin had changed, now imbued with a shock of confidence she'd only hinted at during earlier encounters. She shook her hair from her dark brown eyes, which danced with a hint of mischief, and her cheeks held a tinge of natural blush more beautiful than any make-up artist could produce. Lila's chest constricted in an unsettling way, and she returned the smile without even meaning to. She could easily see why America had fallen for her. How could anyone not?

The thought jolted her out of her stupor. She was not attracted to Cobie. She could see her finer points and appreciate what she brought to the table. She even enjoyed being amused by her occasionally. But attraction, the genuine physical reaction that had stirred in her, wasn't okay, and not just because of her gender. Man or woman, the rules remained the same. Anything beyond a general sort of mutual respect was dangerous. She shook her head. Those feelings weren't real. She'd merely been taken in momentarily by a good performance from a talented actress.

"What?" Cobie asked. "Not impressed by my athletic prowess?"

"No, I'll cop to that," Lila said slowly, "and showing off your speed and strength to the press won't hurt in your quest for them to see you as an action hero."

"And what about you?" Cobie extended her hand. "Do I seem action hero-worthy to you?"

Lila shrugged, not at all ready to even consider the question seriously. She needed to reassert herself now, if only for her own benefit, so she stepped onto the ice without accepting any help from Cobie. "I wouldn't know. I'm not the kind of girl who ever needs saving."

Cobie couldn't stop smiling, not because she was really all that happy, but because she couldn't figure out how else to stay in character while Lila vacillated between engaged and utterly bored with her. Or at least that's how she seemed to feel, but maybe she was just trying to keep everyone on their toes. If so, then she was great at her job. For a few moments earlier, Cobie had felt like they were on equal footing. After her little skating stunt, she'd almost sworn she saw genuine appreciation in Lila's eyes. Then as quickly as the emotion surfaced, it disappeared again. For the last half hour, Lila had been studiously neutral, keeping the conversation light, but now they'd run out of topics that didn't go any deeper than one would have with a stranger in a check-out line.

Cobie scanned the panoramic view of the Hudson River as they skated by the large windows once again. The water wasn't completely frozen, but only the hardiest commercial ships seemed brave enough to cut through the chunks of ice floating along the surface. Along either shore, piles of snow had begun to gray, making them nearly the same color as the sky and many of the buildings rising to meet it. She wondered how much longer she'd have to stay here.

"What are you thinking about?" Lila asked.

"The city," Cobie said, her voice sounding sadder than she'd intended.

"You're not a fan?"

"It's fine, as far as cities go." She tried not to sound melancholy. "I just prefer more open spaces."

"You were raised in Illinois, right?"

Cobie cocked her head to the side and regarded Lila more closely. "Someone's done their research."

"A good businesswoman always does."

"Well, now I feel like a bad businesswoman," Cobie said, but her tone had grown lighter with the thought of Lila caring enough to read up on her. It also gave her the freedom to ask questions just a hint more personal than the work topics she'd stuck to so far. "What about you? Where does Lila Wilder hail from?"

"Jennings, Florida. Near the Georgia line."

"Sounds . . . nice?"

Lila shook her head and frowned, her blue eyes losing some of their usual focus. "It's not."

Sensing she'd stepped into something unpleasant, Cobie tried to shift. "When did you move to New York?"

"When I was eighteen. I'd done a two-year stint in Nashville before that, but New York suited me better."

"You started out as a country singer."

"It was all I knew at the time," Lila said casually, "but it wasn't long until bigger markets came calling. Markets that didn't restrict me."

"Yeah, you're not the type to tolerate restrictions, are you?"

The corners of her mouth turned up.

"I'm surprised you didn't end up in LA."

"I've got a condo there, but it doesn't have the same creative energy New York does. Plus, I run a fashion line and fragrance line, I produce my own music, and I'm now a tourism ambassador for the city."

Cobie blinked a few times, then nodded. "Is that all?"

"Mostly," Lila said slyly. "No need to brag though."

"Right, very modest."

"I get that a lot." Lila's smile widened a little before she said, "What about you? When did you move to Gotham?"

"I haven't," Cobie said.

Lila stopped skating. "What do you mean? Where do you live?"

"I have a house in the Catskills."

"A vacation home, but where's your primary address?"

"The Catskills house is the primary one. My vacation home is in the woods up by Lake Henry."

"But... but..." Lila's face flushed in frustration. "You're a legit movie star."

The outburst sent Cobie's confidence up a few notches. "Thanks for noticing."

"I thought movie stars had to live in New York or LA."

"And I thought movie stars could live wherever they damn well pleased."

Lila finally laughed. "That might be the smartest thing you've said since I've known you."

"Thanks, I think, but really movies aren't what they used to be. They aren't all shot on sound stages in LA anymore. The last three I worked on were in the Carolinas. One before that was in Toronto and one in St. Louis of all places. My parents loved that."

"What about publicity junkets?"

"They usually involve a couple weeks in LA, but also time in New York and London. It's all travel of some kind, but when I get to go home, I want it to feel like home."

"Home," Lila repeated almost wistfully. "You make it sound like there are actually times when you aren't working."

"That's because there are. Maybe not as often as I'd like, but I always take at least a month off between films."

"What do you do?"

"I hike. I catch up with friends. I have my little sister come visit. I read books. I go to the grocery store and cook my own meals."

"And people let you do that?"

"At home they do. I've never been a big enough deal for the press to follow me two hours into the wilderness, and honestly, the town I'm closest to is full of old Woodstock refugees who have probably never seen my movies," Cobie said with pleasure at the look of astonishment on Lila's face. "The ones who have didn't watch closely enough to recognize me in sweatpants and no make-up. Occasionally, one of their visiting grandchildren spot me, but the most they ever do is shyly mumble hello."

"It sounds like something out of an old-time movie."

Cobie laughed. "I never thought of it like that, but it kind of is. I escape the movie business by going to live in the type of place they try to portray in my movies. Ironic. Everything in my life that people believe is real is fake, but everything people don't believe I can have is real."

Lila frowned. "Right. Which reminds me, we'd better get on with the evening."

Cobie looked around. "I thought that's what we were doing. Date two in full swing."

"No. We've gone around enough times for the press to get bored with us."

"And we'd never want to bore those intrusive fuckers, would we?"

"Wow, language," Lila scolded with laughter in her voice.

"Sorry. I'm just not a fan of them."

"They're means to an end, but I actually happen to agree with you. The press is fickle and intrusive in ways that don't always allow me to control the message. I'd rather cut out the middle-men when possible and go straight to the people."

"How do we do that?"

Lila took her hand and pulled her off the ice. "Just watch."

They took off their skates, and with a nod to Malik, Lila led them over to a booth in the corner of the concession stand. The press clearly couldn't follow them inside, which seemed counter-intuitive if they were about to put on a show like Lila seemed to suggest. She supposed the two nervous-looking teens working behind the counter might surreptitiously be filming them with cell phones, but that seemed like a gamble for someone as in control as Lila.

They had barely sat down when Malik arrived with a tray of cheese fries and two Cokes.

"I love you," Cobie blurted out when he set the fries in front of her.

He broke character long enough to laugh lightly. "You're welcome, Ms. Galloway."

She clasped her hand atop his, noting how tiny and pale it looked by comparison. "Please, call me Cobie."

He paused, his eyes flicking to Lila's, but she gave his giant hand as much of a squeeze as she could, drawing his attention back to her. "Please. It would mean a lot to me, even if only when it's just us, okay?"

He nodded, his eyes softer. "Okay, Cobie, only out of earshot of the press."

"Thank you." She released him and watched him walk away a few yards as the hard set returned to his jaw and shoulders. When she turned back to Lila, she couldn't read the expression on her face. Interest? Curiosity? Skepticism? She shifted a little bit under the intense gaze before finally admitting, "I don't like being waited on."

Lila opened her mouth as if she might say something, then pursed her full, pouty lips and set about rearranging their food. Cobie relaxed a little and snagged a fry, but Lila swatted at her hand.

"Hold on. It's not time to eat yet."

"You want to say grace?" Cobie asked.

"You can if you want, but keep it on the inside. I'm staging." She slid the fries to the corner of the tray and moved the straw from one Coke to the other. "Now slide around next to me."

"Ms. Wilder, are you getting forward with me?" Cobie asked, but she complied, slipping into the Formica-coated bench next to her date.

"Hold this," Lila commanded in full business mode as she lifted the paper Coca-Cola cup with two straws. "Label out."

The phrase immediately contextualized the scene for Cobie. They were shooting an ad, either for Coke or for themselves or most likely both. She'd been here enough times with product placement that her character came easy. She snuggled closer to Lila, wrapping an arm around her shoulder. Lila pulled out her phone and held it at arm's length while taking one of the straws in her million-dollar mouth. Cobie followed suit and pulled a steady stream of soda up into the straw while locking her eyes dreamily on Lila's. She'd used the look hundreds of times in hundreds of takes over the years. It had never been overly challenging for her, but somehow with Lila it came easier than ever.

She never wavered, never blinked as the camera clicked in a rapid burst of photos. Staring into those beautiful eyes didn't take much in the way of coaching or character development. They were certainly nicer than most of the men's—clearer, softer, brighter, not to mention focused on her own instead of working through to the next step, or worse: zoning in on her chest. Even though Lila was also running the shot, she gave back every ounce of energy Cobie put forth between them and somehow managed to stay completely present in the moment right until it ended.

She slowly lowered the camera before leaning back deliberately. Cobie watched her throat constrict slightly as she swallowed, then her lips parted, the tip of her tongue sweeping the last hint of sweetness away. When she blinked, the subtle disconnect snapped the cord of connection that had held them captive.

"Nice work," Lila said as she glanced down at her phone. "I do enjoy how well you take direction."

"I've had practice," Cobie mumbled, still not certain any of her previous roles had fully prepared her to play opposite Lila, but any experience was better than none.

"Golden," Lila mumbled as she swiped her finger across the screen. "Several of these are flawless."

Cobie peeked over her shoulder at the phone to see a perfectly shot frame of them sipping from the same drink while staring longingly at one another. If she hadn't been there, she wouldn't believe for a second that they weren't totally engrossed in each other. Then again, they were. Those seconds spent staring at her had been every bit as compelling as the photo suggested, only seeing the picture being cropped and filtered reminded her they shouldn't have been.

Lila didn't seem to mind though. She appeared genuinely pleased with their work. "You're a good dance partner."

"Yeah, well, you may know more songs than I do, but I like to think I can at least carry a tune."

Lila arched an eyebrow and regarded her for a moment with an unsettling mix of curiosity and challenge before turning back to her artwork. "And now I tag you. And then add our hashtag, which will be Cola."

"Are you trying to get us an endorsement deal with Coke?"

Lila tapped on her phone a few times before looking up and saying, "Now that you mention it, I'll run it by Mimi, but no. Cola is our celebrity couple name."

Cobie frowned. "Our celebrity name?"

"Yes. Cobie blended with Lila is Cola. It'll be trending worldwide in half an hour."

"Sounds like a big deal. Are we sure it's the right fit for us?" She grinned a little. "Maybe you should take top billing since you're running the show. What about Libie? Also works because this whole thing is a lie. Get it? Subtext."

She rolled her eyes but smiled slightly. "Clever, but now I remember why I'm in charge. Cola is sweet and fun, with a dark, sexy undercurrent, just like us."

Cobie shrugged as if she wasn't impressed, but it was a pretty smart call, and she certainly wouldn't have thought of it on her own. Lila had a mind for marketing, and while Cobie still wasn't thrilled with the reality of being a commodity, she might as well be a desirable one.

She glanced up and saw Lila watching her, her blue eyes intent and her body so very close. Cobie's arm still rested casually around her shoulder, and they brushed against one another from hip to knee. Heat radiated off Lila so acutely she wondered why she hadn't noticed before. Then again, maybe the heat wasn't coming off the woman next to her as much as building inside of her. As the intimacy of the pose became too much to bear, she tried nonchalantly to extract herself. She leaned back enough to bring her arm forward, but when she did, her fingers stroked across soft blonde hair. Was there any part of this woman that wasn't perfect?

She tamped down the thought and tried to scoot farther away, but Lila stopped her with a hand on her knee. Giving a little squeeze, she smiled and said, "No you don't. The scene's not over."

Cobie's eyes widened. "No?"

Lila gave a subtle nod to the teens behind the concession counter. Cobie stole a surreptitious glance their way to see both of them had their phones out, doing an inept job of hiding the fact they were shooting either photos or videos. "They'll be the coolest kids at school on Monday."

"No doubt." Lila snagged a cheese fry and held it inches from her lips, giving them time to get the shot, but Cobie, either from sheer hunger or the desire to hold her own, leaned forward and bit the fry right out of Lila's hand.

Lila turned her head with fake incredulity. "You ate my fry!"

"I did."

"We've been around each other, what, three times now?"

"Yes. Four if you count me stepping on your foot."

"Do you want to count that?"

"Not really."

"Still, three times is enough for you to hazard a guess as to how I feel about people taking my things."

Lila was clearly trying to intimidate, but three times was also enough for Cobie to begin seeing little cracks in her armor. From this close, she could also see the little twitches of her smile and the flecks of green blurring into the blue of her eyes. Cobie couldn't contain her grin.

"What?" Lila asked.

"Nothing. I just thought maybe you're right. I've been around you long enough to learn a few things."

"And?"

"If I'm supposed to up my bad-girl cred here, I'd think stealing your fries would be the least of your worries."

Lila pursed her lips but didn't have a quick comeback.

Cobie picked up another fry and held it out to Lila like a cheese-coated peace offering. "Besides, sharing's sexy, and the cameras are still rolling."

Lila snorted softly. "Maybe you can be taught."

With that she took the fry out of Cobie's hand and chewed slowly.

"There, now we're even," Cobie said.

"Are we?" Lila asked as if she didn't quite agree.

"We've both had our moments, balance restored."

Lila smirked. "Then why does only one of us have cheese on her face?"

Cobie sighed heavily, but with Lila looking at her as if she were the most adorable puppy in the world, she had a hard time feeling truly embarrassed. "It's me, isn't it?"

Lila could barely contain her laugher now as she nodded. "Want me to get it?"

"No." Cobie said sarcastically. "I want to own it. I'm a pop culture icon now. It'll be a fashion statement for all the young girls who've always dreamed of cheese lipstick. I'm going to wear it all night."

"You're not."

"Try to stop me."

Lila caught Cobie's face in her hands and kissed her soundly, sweetly, completely, and too quickly. As she pulled away, all the air left Cobie's lungs in a rush, and she realized with sudden certainty that they were in no way on equal footing after all.

"They did it again," Mimi said without looking up as Stan walked into her office. Today, she wore a cream pantsuit à la Hillary Clinton. Fitting, imposing, clean, and competent, the aspect he favored most was the pair of black moon-shaped reading glasses perched low on her nose.

"I just got off the phone with *People*."

"They get nothing. Yet."

He rolled his eyes at the very idea. "Of course not."

"Did they ask about her sexual orientation?"

"They all do."

"Isn't it funny that that's still a thing?" Mimi asked. "Lila is steadfastly refusing to acknowledge that it is. So odd for her to dig her heels in about something that could be sensationalized."

He shrugged and sat down in her chair. Leaning forward, he scanned the multiple photo spreads laid out across her glass and nickel desk. "I like this one."

Mimi picked up the glossy shot of Cobie standing tall and cocky behind a spray of ice, while in the background, Lila stood, eyes wide, hands near her face as if she didn't want to watch but couldn't look away. "That's your girl all right. You know she almost looks like she could play Vale there."

He wouldn't go quite that far, but she had taken a step in the right direction. "Almost."

"And what about this one?" She pointed to a grainier shot, clearly ripped from a cell phone, of Lila kissing Cobie, hands framing her face with perfect affection. "A hundred bucks says that wasn't planned."

He inspected the shot closer. Cobie's eyes were closed but her eyebrows were raised. He could read a hint of surprise in them. Also, her hands were in her own lap instead of on Lila. "I wouldn't take that bet, at least not from Cobie's standpoint. Then again, what Lila has planned and what Cobie has planned could very easily be different things."

"You really think they aren't on the same page yet?"

"I know it's probably not completely fair," he said with resignation in his voice, "but I don't think Cobie is even capable of being on the same page as Lila."

Mimi shook her head but remained quiet, still focusing intently on the papers before her. She shuffled one on top of the others. It featured the two of them in a tacky, rink-side booth, the color of which was not flattering, but the backdrop didn't matter nearly as much as the primary subjects. No one who saw this shot would talk about the bench.

Stan could hardly look at it directly. The intimacy was almost too much, and he had an unreasonably high tolerance for crushing other's right to privacy. Both women stared at each other, eyes soft, lips parted. Neither of their heads was angled even an inch toward the camera, which caught them in profile, the vantage point showing just how close they were to each other. Nothing about the set-up suggested the moment was staged.

"This one could sink us," Mimi said softly.

He nodded, a grim awareness thick in the air around them.

"You're not worried about that, are you?" she asked.

"I worry about everything. It's my job."

She turned to face him, resting the small of her back against the edge of the desk and taking off her glasses. "I love you for that."

He nodded, a familiar flutter in his chest.

"But those are two grown women. They're smart and talented, and deep down they're both good people."

"Do you think they know that?"

She smiled. "Probably not, but we'll just have to make it so clear to the rest of the world that they can't help but see it too."

"You think we can do that?"

She smiled. "I can't speak for you, but I'm a marketing goddess."

He didn't argue. Instead, he clasped a hand on each of her hips and pulled her close enough to kiss. "Did you know I find smart women sexy?"

"Lucky for you, you married one of the smartest around."

He rose and caught her mouth with his own. *Lucky for him indeed.*

Chapter Four

"My sister says we're viral," the text read. "Probably we should get vaccinations."

Lila laughed softly and typed back, "We're very contagious."

"Should we quarantine ourselves?" came Cobie's quick response.

"No, the only cure is more of the cause."

"I'm learning so much. I've never gone viral before."

"I'm glad I could be your first," Lila typed, then biting her lip added, "They say you always remember your first."

"Are you texting Cobie again?" Felipe asked

"Just working out a few details for next weekend." Lila quickly tossed the cell phone into her Versace handbag and stared out the window of the rented town car. They turned north on Broadway, much farther north than the tourists tended to go.

"Is she getting needy already?" There was more than a hint of cattiness in his tone.

Needy? No, she couldn't ever picture Cobie getting needy, and honestly, the thought didn't please her. Lila didn't want a stage five clinger, but she preferred the people in her life to need her more than she needed them. It kept the balance of power tilted in her favor. It also helped her remember that anyone could be replaced. At least anyone in the business. "She's doing fine, just a little green."

"She seemed to hold her own on your date last week, or at least that's what it looked like on *Entertainment Tonight*." He waited for her to bite, and when she didn't, he added, "Because that's where I'm getting my information these days. And you know that's not normal. Something's off here, or you'd be a lot more forthcoming."

She waved him off. "I've told you everything I can tell you. The date went how it needed to."

"But you kissed her this time?"

"It's part of the process."

"A planned part or a spontaneous part?"

She flashed back to the moment, how she'd tried to be annoyed at Cobie's antics, at her eternal optimism, at the playful side Lila found more endearing than she should. She'd made an attempt to scare her with an icy stare, to tamp down her good-natured tenor by reiterating the ground rules. She'd even hoped to reveal some sort of dark underside to Cobie's affability by being sharper than necessary. And when all else had failed, she resorted to the one equalizer that had never failed her: pure sexual prowess.

The move had paid off in the press. The picture of the kiss had been shared almost as many times as the first one, and it had framed well. No one could doubt the moment had been spontaneous and genuine, but looking back, she had a hard time remembering it wasn't. And that bothered her enough to sugarcoat it to Felipe. "It was a little bit of both. She was there, she had cheese on her lip, and the cameras were angled perfectly. I saw an opportunity to sell us, and I took it."

"And that's all it was, seizing a marketing moment?"

"Mostly."

"Ah-ha!" He pointed a perfectly manicured finger at her. "I knew it!"

"There's nothing to know."

"Then why are you blushing?"

"I'm wearing blush," she said dryly but tried to discreetly eye her reflection in the window.

"You wanted to kiss her."

"Maybe, but only because I wanted to put her in her place."

"And her place is on the tip of your tongue?"

"Her place is wherever she'll be most useful to me."

"Oh no, girlfriend, not with me. No you don't." He then gasped and covered his mouth. "Are you gay?"

"I'm bisexual now, remember?"

"Duh, but for real, are you, like, going to start ordering fish tacos?"

"Ordering what?" She asked shrilly, torn between finding the question offensive and hilarious.

"Do you want to become a connoisseur carpet-muncher?"

"I am not going to answer any questions that refer to body parts as seafood or home decor."

"I don't know what you're supposed to call them," he whined. "I don't have them. No one I sleep with has them. I've heard tell of caverns and flower petals and kittens, but it's all hearsay. As far as I know, you could use your down-there parts to spin yarn or whatever fibers they use to make Birkenstock foot beds with."

She laughed outright as they pulled into a covered garage and slowed to a stop outside a set of metal doors labeled Employee Entrance. There was no fanfare, no red carpet, no welcoming committee, and most of all, no press.

"Can we table this discussion until, I don't know, indefinitely? We've got more important things to focus on."

He didn't argue the point, but as she exited the car, he fell in beside her. "Can't you just give me an honest answer to the question of whether or not you find Cobie physically attractive?"

"Of course she's attractive. She's a movie star."

"You know that's not what I meant, and I didn't mean the platonic, everyone-is-beautiful-in-their-own-way bullshit sense either." He held open a large metal door for her.

Lila sighed as they walked straight across the hall and into an elevator. He wasn't going to let up. She might as well give him an answer. She wasn't sure why she hadn't done so already. She could easily tell him she wasn't any more attracted to Cobie than any of the other people she'd dated in the last few years. That wouldn't be saying much, except it probably said a lot. She had dated some of the most desirable men in America, and to put Cobie on par with them would actually put Cobie in rare company. And yet doing so still wouldn't convey quite enough if she wanted to be honest with her best friend. She actually did find Cobie more attractive than any of the others, a fact that disconcerted her on many levels, issues about her sexuality the least among them.

"Never mind," Felipe finally said as the elevator rose through the building. "You're obviously not there yet."

"I'm right where I need to be," she said coolly.

"If you were, you'd be ready to talk about it."

"There's nothing to talk about."

"Being attracted to a woman is kind of important."

"To whom?" she asked quickly. "The press? They were the first to know."

"And I assume you aren't going to tell Cobie?"

She rolled her eyes, catching a glimpse of herself in the brushed metal ceiling. Few people would recognize her dressed down in jeans and a baggy Gap sweatshirt, with her hair pulled back in a ponytail. If her legions of so-called devotees couldn't see past such a subdued disguise, she didn't worry about the likes of Cobie Galloway unearthing any deeply held secrets.

"So you're going to stick with the generic I-see-beauty-everywhere answer?"

"I can't see any reason why anyone would need to hear anything more than that. Who I spend time with matters only to people who stand to make or lose money. It's not worth talking about any other way," Lila said as the elevator doors opened and she stepped out into the pediatric cancer floor of Morgan Stanley Children's Hospital.

The next few hours were a blur of tiny faces and prevention measures. She traded her fashion icon accessories for paper gowns as she entered the rooms where children got their chemo treatments. She wore rubber gloves when she stopped to color a picture for a little girl too weak to hold her own crayons. She kissed the tops of bald heads and signed everything from scrubs to bandages. She kept her phone in her pocket the entire time, never once checking to see if any of the texts she got were more important than the person she was speaking to. She already knew the answer to that question.

She stayed for several hours, stopping in every room the nursing staff had indicated to Felipe ahead of their arrival, but as she quietly slipped out of the last one, a petite woman in Mickey Mouse scrubs caught her arm.

Lila turned abruptly as Felipe shot forward, nearly throwing his body between them, but with one look at the woman's eyes, Lila held up her hand to stop him.

"I'm sorry to bother you, Ms. Wilder." The nurse stepped back and rung her hands together. "I know you're very busy, and you've already spent so much more time here than anyone could expect."

She smiled politely, wondering where she was going with this. The woman had the apologetic mannerisms of someone about to ask a favor. An autograph? A donation?

"But there's one more patient, and I wouldn't mean to keep you very long, it's just . . ."

Her shoulders relaxed. "Of course. I want to see anyone who wants to see me. I thought the list went around earlier today."

"It did. Only this girl, she's not really a typical fan of yours." The nurse's smile suggested she may have used a gross understatement. "But I thought, given recent events, it might do her some good to meet you."

Recent events. Cryptic but intriguing.

"We told Malik we'd meet him ten minutes ago." Felipe offered her an out.

"No, it's okay. What room?"

The woman motioned for her to follow her down a few doors to one that was cracked open only a smidge. The room beyond seemed dark, and Lila worried she might be waking the occupant, until she noticed a faint glow from a television. "Do I need a gown or mask?"

"No. She's nearing the end of her treatment."

Lila's breath caught, and she must have looked horrified, because the nurse's eyes went wide. "No, I didn't mean she—Oh, sorry, I can't tell you anything about her medical information for privacy reasons, but you'll see. Her condition is more complicated than her chart would ever indicate."

Lila nodded, not knowing for sure what she meant but still understanding the sentiment.

"Go on, and don't let her scare you."

"I don't scare easily."

The nurse smiled broadly and squeezed Lila's arm. "Bless you for that."

Then she walked away, leaving Lila to enter the room on her own.

"Knock, knock," she said lightly as she peeked her head inside. The room smelled staler than the others, as if the air didn't move as much and the antiseptic fumes were allowed to stagnate. It took a few seconds for her eyes to adjust enough to see a figure sitting up in bed. She was older than the others, maybe sixteen or seventeen, long and lanky, with a strong jaw and big brown eyes that first widened, then narrowed suspiciously.

"Hi," she whispered. "I'm Lila."

The girl said nothing, and the only movement came from her chest rising and falling slowly, the imprint of a chemo port faintly visible under her thin blue hospital gown.

"Mind if I join you?"

She shrugged and nodded toward a chair beside her bed. Lila sat down, searching her surroundings for any hint as to why the nurse had sent her in, but there were few personal touches to glean information from. Even with the lights off and the curtains drawn, she could make out how sparse the room felt compared to all the others she'd visited. There were no cards, no balloons, no flowers on windowsills, no toys from home, no photographs beside the bed, and most glaringly of all, no family members present.

"I like this cave style of decorating you've got going on here. Very minimalistic chic."

The girl snorted, her smile faint.

"What do you do for fun around here? Hang upside down from the ceiling? Watch the stalagmites form?"

"Sacrifice virgins and make pacts with the devil."

"Now you're talking," Lila said. "Sounds just like signing a record deal."

The girl's smile grew. "I thought you were all sunshine and rainbow shit."

"Hey, that's Ms. Sunshine and Rainbow Shit to you."

"Why are you in here?" the girl asked, not sounding accusatory so much as surprised.

"I'm not sure. What are you doing in here?"

"Killing cancer cells."

"Show off."

The girl smiled again, grudgingly. "I'm Addie."

"Nice to meet you, Addie. You seem like a real smart-ass. I like that in a woman."

Addie's brow furrowed, but she didn't reply, and Lila wondered what she'd said wrong. She looked around, trying to figure out what to say next. She didn't usually have this problem. Kids loved her, everyone loved her, and she never had trouble holding anyone's attention. Not that she didn't have Addie's attention. Those big, dark eyes watched her carefully, seeming to harbor questions Lila couldn't answer any more than Addie could bring herself to ask them. She looked down for a second, trying to gather herself, and noticed a large sketchpad sitting on the floor. She picked it up and raised her eyebrows to Addie. "May I?"

The girl shrugged almost defiantly, causing Lila to smile. She remembered that stage of sharing her work, nervousness blended with a frightening desire for approval, which butted up against the teenage insistence on refusing to care what other people thought.

She flipped open the sketch pad and fought to remain neutral as she thumbed through a series of drawings, from Spanish-style skulls to dismembered angel wings to toys laying broken on stone floors. Each one was stark and compelling, the emotions of the strokes expanding on the technical aspects of the piece. There was a sadness to them, but also a ferocity. As she continued to turn pages, the pictures transitioned from the inanimate to the intimate: a girl in anime style, black and white. She had broad shoulders, big eyes with thick lashes, and long dark hair. Lila stole a glance at Addie lying in the bed. There was no hair on her head, no eyebrows or lashes either, but the eyes were the same, sorrowful and proud.

She turned more pages and another figure appeared, even darker, almost mystical. The character was certainly female, though only her eyes gave her gender away. They were the same eyes as before with thick beautiful lashes, but now the hair was short and shaggy in jagged cuts across her forehead. The rest was covered with a dark hood that blended into a black shirt tucked tightly into dark cargo pants. The ensemble was finished with lace-up combat boots and a knapsack strap slung diagonally across her chest. In an X rising up behind her back stood the handles of either staffs or swords. Who would she fight? There was no enemy on the page, or maybe, from the glint of hardness in those big open eyes, the enemy was meant to be the viewer. Lila's breathing grew shallow at the thought.

Who did Addie have to protect herself from? The cancer? The world at large? Or a more specific threat? She stared over the edge of the pad once more, seeing the same eyes reflecting the same fear and challenge.

"You're really good, Addie," she said softly. "Obviously you're an accomplished artist already, but more than that, I like your vision, your ability to see things as they are and reconstruct them as something deeper."

The girl's face flushed.

"Did you know I design clothes?"

"Nothing I'd wear."

Lila's laugh echoed off the linoleum. "I respect you for saying so."

"Really?" Her eyes brightened.

"Yes, because it was honest. I don't get a lot of that." Her memory flashed to Cobie looking so sweet and earnest, and she quickly blinked away the image. She focused back on the drawing and turned it so Addie could see too. "I also like this ensemble quite a bit."

Addie's eyes narrowed again suspiciously. "I'm not sure it's your style."

"No, probably not, but I know someone it might suit better. I'd like to use this as a concept piece if you'd let me."

The corners of her mouth twitched, but she merely shrugged again. "Sure. Go ahead."

"No," Lila said slowly. "That's not how it works. I need you to sell it to me."

"Oh." Addie's eyes went wide once more. "How much?"

"Well, normally for a fully finished piece I could pay well over twenty thousand dollars."

All the air rushed out of Addie's lungs in an audible exhale.

"But this isn't a fully finished piece," Lila quickly added. "Still, if the person I have in mind uses it to her advantage, it could stand to generate money for her down the road. I'm sure she'd see it as a business investment as well. What would you say to ten thousand up front, followed by another ten if she wears the finished product once, with a plan for residuals if it gets used in any formal business capacity?"

Addie's chalky skin had grown flush, and she bit her already pale lip while she stared at the ceiling.

"You don't have to answer now," Lila said. "In fact, you shouldn't. Talk to a lawyer if you want or, at the very least, your parents. Actually, I probably should too since you're a minor. Are they around?"

Addie shook her head.

"Will they be in after work?"

She shook her head again, and this time Lila noticed tears in her eyes. Leaning forward, she took Addie's hand in her own, feeling the girl's fragility for the first time in the form of thinly covered bone and raised veins. She squeezed gently and whispered, "We can figure it out."

"I'm going through the emancipation process." Addie's voice had grown thick with emotion. "My parents want to send me to conversion therapy after I get out of here."

"Conversion therapy? For, like, an emotional transition?" Lila asked, confused.

Addie shook her head again. "For my soul."

The comment didn't make sense. She would have thought soul therapy might include some sort of meditation or maybe a spa weekend, but Addie' demeanor spoke of something much more sinister.

"They think the cancer was a warning or a wake-up call." The girl grimaced as she swallowed, as if trying to force down something painful. "Or a punishment for being gay."

Lila's jaw tightened as her back teeth ground together. "Can they do that? Do people still do that as, like, a practice?"

The girl nodded. "The facility is full at the moment, so apparently, yeah."

Anger burned hot along the back of her neck, but she stayed deadly still as her mind processed not just the information, but also her options. There were always options when you had money and power. Sadly, people like Addie didn't have enough of either. Memories of that type of helplessness tried to settle across her muscles, freezing her to inaction, but she shook them off. She wouldn't go back. Pain and anger were only productive when properly harnessed. Thankfully, she had a good bit of experience doing so.

"First of all, your work is your creative property. Even as a minor you can secure trademarks and copyrights. No one understands that process better than me. I went through it all when I was your age. I promise your parents will not see a penny of your earnings," she said evenly, choosing to deal with the easier issue first. "A lawyer will visit you in the coming days. She will work for you, on retainer from me. She'll help with the copyright for this design. She will also help with the emancipation filings."

"But I, I couldn't pay you back. I don't even . . ." her voice faded as she hung her head and sobbed one word. "Why?"

"Because you're a fighter, and a lover, and an artist. Because people like us have to stand up for each other. Because you should never apologize for who you are, and anyone who says otherwise doesn't deserve to have any power over you."

"I don't believe them."

Lila raised her eyebrows questioningly.

"About the cancer being a punishment. I don't buy it. Most of the time anyway." She shrugged again, and Lila could read between the lines of doubt. "I just, I'd like to be able to rub it in their faces, you know? Like, if I could be successful, I could prove them wrong. You know?"

She did know, and she smiled at the shot of bravado. She wouldn't undercut it, because Addie would need that mentality to get her through the long road ahead. She wouldn't become a success overnight. She would need support and role models, which Lila finally realized was why she'd been sent in here.

"I get the sense you don't really follow my career."

Addie managed to look chagrined.

"It's okay," Lila said with a hint of laughter. "I don't expect you to start, but it didn't come easy or without its costs. I made choices and sacrifices along the way, but I got to where I am because I never listened to the people who tried to tell me I wasn't good enough or strong enough or pure enough or talented enough, and believe me, I heard those things a lot. I still do. If I listened to them, I'd be waiting tables in Jennings, Florida, right now."

She squeezed Addie's hand again. "There's always going to be someone who tries to make you feel small. And they'll always find their reasons: the way you look, the way you draw, the way you love. They'll lie and cheat and steal if you let them, and sometimes even if you don't, but no one can ever take away who you are, not unless you give them that power. Promise me you won't."

"Okay," Addie said.

"I need more than that, Addie," Lila said, struggling to hold the pleading in her voice to an acceptable level. "I need you to understand that the minute you let someone else tell you who

==you are or how you should feel is the minute you start to lose the best parts of yourself.== Promise me you will fight for your right to define yourself."

She drew in a shaky breath. "I promise."

"Good." Lila released her and smiled. "Then I need to go see to some things, but you and I will talk again soon. Also, if you don't think it will hurt your image too badly to be caught caring about a bubblegum pop star, you might want to have one of the nurses bring you a paper tomorrow, okay?"

"Sure." She shrugged again, but this time she smiled. "Maybe I'll tell them I want to read the obituaries."

Lila laughed. "A woman who knows how to stay in character. You're going to do just fine."

She exited the room to find Felipe leaning against the wall. "Did you catch any of that?"

"Enough that I already got her contact information from the nurse who sent you in there."

"Good. Then make two calls, one to my legal team at Levy and Levy to get her adequate representation."

"On it." He tapped a few notes on his phone. "And the other?"

"Have the press corps outside my house at three o'clock. I'm going to make a statement."

He pressed his lips together and cocked an eyebrow as he tapped the phone a few more times. "Should I have Mimi draft something?"

She shook her head and stared purposefully down the hallway. "No. This one's all me."

Cobie's phone buzzed so much it nearly rattled off the glass-top coffee table.

Janna caught it just before it leapt to its death. "I know you're famous and all, but this is excessive."

"That's not my famous phone. That's my personal number," Cobie said from plank position on the floor.

"Sounds important," Janna said. "How about you give me one

more minute of ab-crushing glory, and I'll let you have a break to check it?"

As sweat beaded her forehead and pain seared through her midsection, she cared nothing about the text messages, but she would have sold a piece of her soul for a break. "Deal."

"All right, you're at four minutes and fifteen seconds now. Let's get you to five."

She tried to take deep, even breaths as the phone buzzed again, and she fantasized about the person on the other line offering the rights to make *Vigilant* with her in the role of Vale. She no longer had a time when some body part didn't ache. Still, the exercises themselves got easier after each session. At least she knew she could do them all now. A few weeks ago, the idea of a five-minute plank would have been laughable. Today it was merely something else to endure.

"Five, four, three, two, one, and down," Janna cued, and Cobie flopped onto the yoga mat.

"How you feeling?" Janna asked.

"Not dead, so I guess I'm ahead of the game."

"You really are, you know? You're keeping an intense pace and holding your own. You earned your phone break."

Cobie flopped over onto her back and extended her hand. Janna placed the phone in her outstretched fingers.

"I'll go grab you some water."

"Thanks," Cobie muttered as she swiped open to her notifications and sat up. Twenty-seven texts during her five-minute plank? She didn't even know twenty-seven people who had this number.

She scrolled through them with one quick swipe and noticed the names of family and friends, including her mom and sister, as well as Stan and Lila, but the one on top happened to be from Talia. It simply read, "Turn on your TV."

She typed back, "Which channel?" while getting up to search for the remote.

A reply pinged before she even found it. "Any of them."

Despite her job, Talia wasn't one to manufacture dramatics, so Cobie decided to forgo the remote and just turn on the TV by hand. The first thing she saw was a CNN feed of Lila atop the stairs to her brownstone, with a bevy of reporters standing silently except for the whir of camera shutters clicking. She wore a red and black plaid coat that went down to her knees, black leggings, and a very serious expression.

Cobie turned up the volume in time to hear Lila say, "I shouldn't have to defend my sexuality to anyone, and I won't, but neither will I hide any part of who I am. Doing so would suggest I'm ashamed when the opposite is true. I'm proud to be a bisexual woman. I'm proud that my capacity to love is not limited by gender. I'm proud that I can recognize beauty in all its forms. I'm proud of who God made me to be. I'm a woman, an artist, a friend, and a girlfriend. I also happen to be queer. I have my own set of talents, quirks, and passions. Without any one piece, the puzzle wouldn't be complete. We all have qualities that set us apart and make us unique. I believe those are the parts of ourselves most worthy of celebration. I love all of who I am, and I believe that in loving myself, I am more open to loving others."

"Are you doing this for Cobie Galloway?" a reporter yelled.

Lila held up a hand. "I'm speaking my mind for every young person who's been taught to hide who they are or told they aren't good enough or that they don't deserve love. I'm doing this for every person who's been made to feel ashamed of something they can't control and should never have been asked to. I'm speaking out to show the world that you can love who you love and love yourself, and no one has any right to try to convince you otherwise."

Cobie's phone buzzed the long, low hum of a call instead of a text. She accepted the call and lifted the phone to hear ear without saying a word.

"Is she doing this off the cuff?" Janna whispered from behind her.

Cobie scanned the TV screen for notes or a teleprompter but found none. "I guess so."

"Is this your official coming out?" another reporter called on screen.

"I think of it more as an affirmation, but you can certainly call it a coming out statement, because I'm also coming out in opposition to the damaging practice of conversion therapy, especially when used on minors. I'm joining with the Center for Lesbian Rights in their hashtag bornperfect campaign to ban conversion therapy in all fifty states. Please visit their website and stay tuned to my social media outlets for further information on how you can help me prove to all our young people we're born perfect and love is never wrong. Thank you."

Then Lila turned and went back inside, leaving Malik to hold back the crowd as he silently faced a barrage of questions.

"Was that planned?" Janna finally asked.

"If it was, I wasn't privy to it."

"Wow," Janna said, then shifted awkwardly from one foot to the other as Cobie's phone started to buzz again. "I think I'm going to head out now. You can go through your cool down when you're ready."

She should argue. She should drop the phone and get back to work. That's what Lila had done, kept on working. She didn't give any thought to what Cobie had planned for the day or what she might feel about learning of an announcement like that on television with the rest of the viewing public. Why should Cobie give a second thought to someone who clearly didn't give the same to her?

Instead she nodded and mumbled, "Thank you," while pressing the little call icon next to Lila's contact information.

"Hello." The familiar voice answered on the second ring, which suggested Lila had expected this call.

"So my workout got interrupted by some breaking news, and then my trainer abandoned ship because, apparently, she got the strange idea that my girlfriend just told the world she was bisexual without my help or support, which she seemed to find super awkward, though I can't imagine where she'd get an idea like that."

Lila laughed lightly, and Cobie waited for her to speak, to offer some explanation or even an apology. As silence took over the connection, it became increasingly clear none of the above were forthcoming.

"Lila?"

"I thought maybe you were calling to congratulate me."

"For what? You just showed me up on national TV."

"Don't be silly. I made a statement, about me, on my own. It had nothing to do with you."

"Are you insane? You and I have been on multiple dates. As far as the press is concerned, I brought you out."

Lila laughed again. "I think very few people outside the religious right would find that to be a believable storyline."

"Then what *is* the damn storyline, because from where I'm sitting, it seems to keep changing." Cobie paced around the living room of her expansive suite. "You're the one who has been adamant about following the script, following the rules, following some master plan for rehabbing my career and—"

"That's right," Lila cut in, a little edge to her voice now. "Your career. The rules are for you. They don't apply to my time or my business. Do you understand that? The two key words are *my* and *business*. I control my storyline at all times, whether it's intersecting with yours or not, so unless you have something to say right now that's going to add to my brand or my projects moving forward, I'd rather you stick to our scheduled interactions."

"Lila, you can't just—"

"I've got another call."

And with that she was gone. Cobie stared at the "Call Ended" notification until it faded from her screen.

What the hell had just happened? She could easily replay the sequence over again, but doing so wouldn't do a damn thing to help her make sense of any of it.

Thankfully, she was saved from the prospect of rehashing the basics by another buzz, this one accompanied by the name of the only person she'd even consider trying to hold a conversation with in her current disorientation.

"Hi, Tal."

"Hey, you. What's new?"

Cobie snorted. "Oh, you know, my fake girlfriend, who won't even allow me to have a fucking French fry without asking for her permission, came out, and she didn't even mention her big gay press conference to me until I saw it on TV." Cobie sank onto the couch. "And now even my physical trainer thinks I am the worst girlfriend ever because I didn't go to an event I wasn't invited to."

"And if you were? If she'd told you ahead of time and asked you to support her, what would you have done?" Talia asked. "Gone and held her hand through her touching speech?"

Cobie hung her head as she mentally replayed Lila's passionate plea to celebrate queer youth. Somehow those details had gotten lost in her initial shock. "It was a pretty good speech. It will probably help a lot of kids. She's got a mammoth following with the youth market."

"Duh," Talia said. "She's their supreme leader. Most of them will no doubt follow her into battle."

"I guarantee you hashtag bornperfect is already lighting up Twitter and Instagram."

"So this is a good thing then, right?"

Cobie sighed. "Probably."

"Why don't you sound thrilled?"

"I don't know. I mean the words were all right, and she seemed sincere. I think in her own way, she meant it."

"What do you mean 'in her own way'? She said she's bisexual. That means the same thing in all the ways, doesn't it?"

"Lila makes her own meanings, or at least bends them to her own will."

"So you don't think she's queer? You think that whole thing was just a publicity stunt?" Talia asked, frustration rising in her normally soothing voice. "She just took your essence, a huge part of who you are, and used it to get attention without you?"

"I don't think Lila does anything if she didn't have something to gain. She says she's bi, which is a legit identity, but in Lila's case, it's a damn convenient one. She's only ever dated men before me, and she's not really that fond of me. If she was genuinely interested in women, she could have found one she actually liked. I thought dating me would just be a short stunt for her. I didn't expect her to get political."

"But it's good that she's raising awareness."

"Yeah." Cobie rubbed her eyes. "But what happens to all those queer youth she cares so much about when she goes back to dating men exclusively and stops speaking to them? I don't think her image-conscious boy-toys will want her to keep reminding the media they are playing second fiddle to me, or even worse, will she act like I was just some momentary lapse in judgment for her?"

"She won't do any good for queer kids if she treats her sexuality as a choice she can turn on and off at will. But is that really what's happening here?"

"What do you mean? Is she making a choice who to be attracted to?"

"No. I mean is she actually attracted to you, at least physically, if not emotionally?"

"Oh." The question made Cobie's chest tighten. "I don't know."

"Really?"

She sighed. She did know. "No. I don't think she is. I mean there's been a moment or two, but . . ."

"But?" Talia pushed gently.

"But she's adamant she's in this thing to generate press, and she just did that very well. I guess we long-suffering queers should just be thankful she deigned to share some of her limelight with us. I'm sure that's what she would have said if she hadn't hung up on me."

"Ouch."

"Yeah, she said the rules don't apply to her, she had to take care of her business, and honestly, I think she believes herself. She's raising awareness for an important cause. Why does it matter if she actually cares or not?"

"I guess it doesn't matter when we're talking about a cause, but it matters quite a bit when we're talking about my best friend."

Cobie smiled sadly. "We're not talking about me. Not really. As far as this one goes, I'm merely a prop on the great stage of Lila Wilder's life."

"So you don't think there's any chance she's going through some sort of genuine awakening?"

Cobie started to say no, then she remembered their kiss at the ice rink. It had been so unexpected, so confusing. It was tender and playful but also hot. For a woman who'd gotten angry about Cobie going off script, she didn't seem to have any trouble doing so herself. Had the kiss been a whim or an impulse? Did that make it genuine or was it merely a power play? The latter seemed most likely given everything she'd learned about Lila. "Every now and then I sense something beyond the façade, but honestly, it's probably wishful thinking on my part. I want to see something deeper in her."

"You want her to be gay or bi or what?"

"Maybe. Honestly? I'd settle for anything I could point to without a doubt and say, 'That's the real Lila.' If there was some sort of genuine attraction or hint of personal connection to me, I'd be thrilled, but in order to feel some sort of connection to a community or person, she'd have to care about something other than herself for a little while, and I have a hard time believing she's capable of that."

"Wow, Cobie."

"What?"

"That didn't sound like you at all. I've seen you take hold of some pretty shallow characters and find something human in them, something worth drawing out. And Lila's not even a flat character sketch. She's a living person."

Cobie closed her eyes and felt Lila's lips on hers once more. She would not deny Lila was real flesh and bone, but physically real and emotionally real were two very different things. "It's easy to be attracted to her physically. She's stunning and she knows it. She carries this confidence that's easy to believe in. She's strong and talented and smart. On that level, she's the total package, the dream woman, but I don't think I could ever really trust her."

"And that's a deal-breaker."

"It is," Cobie admitted, feeling sadder than she had in a while. She hadn't told Talia anything she didn't already know deep down, but somehow saying the words out loud made the facts harder to ignore.

"Have I mentioned before how much I dislike you're going through with the fauxmance?" Talia asked softly.

Guilt bubbled up through her sadness. She should have known Talia would think she bore responsibility for putting her in that position, no matter how much she tried to convince her otherwise. "Look, it's not a big a deal. Maybe it would be if I were actually trying to romance this woman, but I'm not. She's not terrible to be around. I've honestly had some fun on occasion, and I'm learning a lot about social media marketing, which will come in handy if I get the green light to make *Vigilant*."

"If you don't get the green light after all of this, we're both running away to the mountains to forsake consumerism and live off the land."

Cobie laughed. "You killed every plant in your garden last year."

"Right, well, here's a better plan B. You use all the energy you're spending trying to keep up with the whims of Ms. Wilder and spend it learning to grow edible plants, then we escape society."

"Or . . ." Cobie offered, "let me stick to plan A. It's only been a month. Who knows? Lila and I might be on the verge of a breakthrough."

"You really think that's possible?"

She didn't, but she wouldn't say so to Talia. "For better or for worse, anything's possible with Lila."

"Especially since you're about to spend a long weekend in Vegas with her."

Cobie stifled a groan and forced a little lightness into her voice as she said, "Yeah, a weekend in Sin City with a beautiful woman. What could go wrong?"

Talia laughed. "I don't know, but I look forward to hearing the answer as soon as you get home."

"We've got access to the high rollers area of the casino," Lila called from her uncomfortable spot atop an overly firm leather couch. "The staff there have instructions to allow the press a good view of us while keeping them out of our way. No one's going to be in our faces tonight, but there won't be a moment when the cameras aren't watching."

"You're saying I shouldn't pick my nose or anything. Is that it?" Cobie asked through the doorway between her bedroom and the living area of the sky loft.

"Obviously. Also, don't look at other women or roll your eyes at me behind my back."

"I wouldn't dare," Cobie said while adjusting her cufflinks. "Why would anyone do anything but gaze lovingly at you, dear?"

Lila rolled her eyes, thankful Cobie couldn't see her do what she'd just warned against. Then again, there were no cameras in the loft. The only other people within earshot were Felipe and Malik, who had claimed the second-floor bedroom.

"I promise to be on my best behavior tonight," Cobie said. "I'm feeling all swanky, like some member of the artistic avant-garde."

"Not too preppy though," she said as she flipped through an informational guide on the MGM Grand's various properties.

"Says the woman who dressed me in a tux." Her voice sounded much closer and slightly more intimate, which made Lila glance up. When her eyes landed on Cobie standing rakishly with one shoulder leaned against the doorjamb and the other hand stuffed lightly in the pocket of the tuxedo pants, her breath caught. She'd pulled her hair back away from her face, and her only make-up was a subdued hint of black eyeliner. The little touch drew attention to her eyes, making them seem bigger and darker than usual. Lila looked away from their intensity.

She inspected the jacket, trying to move her mind into designer mode. It fit perfectly across her shoulders and cut in ever so slightly to showcase her slender waist. Lila would have commended herself on choosing it, but even she hadn't been prepared for how well Cobie wore it. God, this woman's body was built for luxury, and she made a mental note to show that off more often. Or maybe not, because she needed to be seen as gritty. But she wouldn't mind playing woman du jour to Cobie's Jane Bond style in a few photographs along the way.

"Can you help me with these cufflinks?" Cobie asked, seeming oblivious to the images floating through Lila's mind.

She pushed off the couch as gracefully as she could in her skin-tight black dress that came to an abrupt stop just shy of mid-thigh. "You can't do your own cufflinks?"

"Shockingly, they don't teach young girls to use them much while growing up in central Illinois," Cobie said with a half grin. "I'm sure I could do it on my own eventually, but I'm kind of nervous about taking longer to get ready than you did."

"Don't worry. Not everyone can look this good with so little effort," Lila said, taking Cobie's sleeve in her hands and threading the silver clasp through the buttonholes.

"Yeah, I'm sure you just rolled out of bed, right into those heels."

Lila smiled and snapped a cufflink into place before reaching for the other one.

"Do they still count as high heels when they're that tall? Or at some point do they become stilts?"

"It's not the tool. It's how you use it."

"Oh, right, like 'guns don't kill people, people kill people,' or people with legs like yours kill people."

"Why, Miss Galloway, I'm surprised you even noticed my legs. I thought you were being studiously disinterested in me since Malik picked you up in New York. You barely said ten words to me on the plane."

"You weren't wearing that dress on the plane."

She bit her lip, trying not to feel too pleased with the compliment, but she knew better than to be distracted by flattery. Something had been bothering Cobie all day or, rather, since the press conference. For some reason, instead of being pleased with Lila's announcement, Cobie had been frustrated and maybe even a little hurt. That realization sparked a mix of emotions that put Lila on the defensive, and she'd resorted to falling back on the things she could predict and control. She'd expected Cobie to do the same, and when their interactions earlier in the day had remained distant, she'd spent more time than she should have trying to decide whether or not Cobie's displeasure mattered to her and how much. But seeing a flash of something more amiable in her now, she realized she'd missed that easy connection. Of course, now she had to decide how she felt about that too. She didn't want to give her too much power, and admitting Cobie's moods affected her would do that, but she also didn't like not knowing where she stood. It also hadn't escaped her notice that for better or worse Cobie hadn't mentioned her press conference again either.

"So," Cobie said when Lila snapped the second cufflink into place, "I know we're gambling, and then we're dancing. Then we're going to get handsy in the VIP room. We're living the lifestyles of the rich and famous. I assume Robin Leach will narrate the footage as it airs on Entertainment TV?"

"I've already got him on retainer."

"Then all I need now is my motivation. You're the director of this play. Who am I playing?"

"You're in the tux to look like a winner, but don't get too preppy or stiff. You're rolling the dice with one arm around my waist. You're young Marlon Brando in *Guys and Dolls*, and you're lucky because I'm your lady tonight."

Cobie blew out a breath, rolled her shoulders, and crooked her arm for Lila to take. "All right, baby. Let's roll."

Lila let fly a little whistle, and Malik appeared at the top of the stairs, dressed in a black suit with a black t-shirt underneath. The only bright thing on his body was his massive smile when he saw them.

"Damn," he said. "I'd say you don't need me 'cause no one's gonna mess with you with Cobie looking so fly, but then you go and look like sex on stilts, so maybe I'll have to beat the boys off with a stick."

"I made the stilt joke too," Cobie said, sounding pleased.

He thundered down the stairs like a St. Bernard who thought himself a lap dog. "Whatever part you guys been playing at, you're about to take it up a notch tonight."

Lila checked her bright red lips in a mirror by the door on the way out. "That's the plan."

※ ※ ※

"Another seven for Ms. Galloway," the dealer said as applause faded. The stickman corralled the dice, then pushed them back toward Cobie.

She cupped them in her right hand and gave them a little shake. She enjoyed the weight of them and the little clicks they made as they knocked against each other. With an arcing loft, she sent them tumbling through the air once more. They flipped, then plummeted, bouncing off the table and down to the far bank before spinning to a stop, six and five on top. The gathered crowd went wild again.

"Eleven. Yo, eleven," the dealer called.

A few furrowed brows from the dealers and a nod from the box man made Cobie grin. She turned, putting her back to the table as the casino crew rotated for the second time in ten minutes. She looped an arm around Lila's waist and pulled her close until their hips were flush. Cupping her face, she pulled her lower so she could whisper in her ear, "How did you manage to load the dice?"

Lila threw back her head and laughed heartily. Leaning close once more, she nipped at Cobie's earlobe before whispering, "I didn't."

Reaching past her so their bodies pressed tightly together for a moment, Lila grabbed the dice the dealer had pushed across the table and handed them to her. "Roll again, rock star."

Cobie hoped her smile came across as something cocky. She didn't know what to make of her luck being genuine tonight, at least where the dice were concerned. Everything else had been carefully orchestrated by Lila. The crowd around their table was filled with beautiful people who had clearly been instructed not to intrude on them with more than applause or the occasional high five. The photographers were kept far enough away to blend in, and the staff had by and large acted like they would with any high-end client, or so she assumed. She'd never actually been a high-end casino client before. And she had to admit, she was enjoying the experience. Even as someone who fully understood the magic of the movies, Cobie could still get lost in a carefully created illusion for long stretches at a time.

She tossed the dice again, this time to a more subdued response as they came up one and four. More chips were thrown out, and Cobie set down a small stack of high-denomination chips for the dealer to place on the six and eight. She turned back to Lila and said, "I'm betting that I'll roll a six or eight before I roll another five or bust."

"I know," Lila said evenly.

She raised an eyebrow.

"Surprised?"

"No. I suppose you wouldn't have put us in a game you didn't know how to win."

Her brightly painted lips curled up.

"I just thought maybe you'd let me play the role of teacher tonight."

"Don't get greedy. I'm willing to let you get away with a lot tonight, but I don't play dumb for anyone," she said, a flash of fire in her eyes reminding Cobie of the way she looked during her press conference. Cobie had forgotten to be mad at her for the last few hours, but before her irritation could return, Lila's tone lightened again. "Besides, I'm already letting you play the role of rock star."

"How's that working for you?"

"So far, so good, but I reserve the right to change my mind."

"A woman's prerogative," Cobie said as she threw a six and collected her winnings. "But that works both ways. I'm a woman too, remember?"

She glanced over her shoulder in time to catch Lila's eyes rake across her backside, but instead of looking embarrassed, she simply said, "How could I forget?"

The words, or maybe the coy way she delivered them with a hint of sensuality, sent a shiver up her spine. She tossed the dice once more and came up with an eight before pulling another stack of chips off the table and handing them to Lila. "Here, why don't you hold onto these for later?"

Lila smiled in that practiced way she always did when up to no good. She slipped her hand inside Cobie's tuxedo jacket and dropped a few chips into the inside pocket before saying just loud enough for those nearest to hear, "I don't pay for anything here, stud, but if you don't take me dancing soon, you might need that."

Cobie sighed dramatically, then turned to the table and said, "I think I'm going to have to call it soon, folks."

"No," everyone protested in unison.

"Sorry, we've got plans."

One guy with particularly spiky hair leaned over the table and called, "What plans could be better than this?"

She smiled and quirked an eyebrow at Lila, who took hold of her lapels, pulled her close, and kissed her hotly on the mouth. God, she was good at that. Cobie's hips rolled forward of their own accord, as if seeking contact that wouldn't be at all appropriate on a casino floor. As quickly as it had begun, Lila cut off contact, leaving Cobie kiss-drunk and a little wobbly on her knees. She had to clutch the edge of the table with her free hand to steady herself, but she managed an I-told-you-so smile to all the astonished faces circled around.

Then she rolled a seven and busted every one of them.

No one seemed too upset with her as she settled up. Maybe they were grateful for the massive amounts of cash she'd made them over the last run, or maybe they just couldn't blame her for leaving the party early since they no doubt expected her to be headed for a better one. Still, she handed the waitress enough chips to buy everyone a round and generously tipped the table crew before extending her arm to Lila. "You ready to heat up the dance floor?"

Lila fanned herself with her hand. "I don't know. I think you might have burned the place down already."

"Me?" Cobie asked as they strolled through the VIP area toward the flashing strobe lights and heavy bass beat that could only indicate a dance floor nearby. "What about you, playing tonsil hockey at the craps table."

"Tonsil hockey?" Lila smacked her in the stomach lightly. "As if. I didn't even use tongue."

"That's not what *People* magazine is going to report tomorrow," Cobie said playfully.

"And how do you know?"

"Because while you were kissing me, I did this." Cobie stuck her tongue firmly in her cheek and wiggled it around so it could be seen from the outside.

Lila's eyes went wide and her face flushed. "You did not!"

Cobie shrugged. "You said you wanted to take things up a notch."

"Please tell me you're joking. Please, please, please, Cobie."

"Okay, I'm kidding, but if I'd known it would get you to beg my name, I would've tried it sooner."

Lila rolled her eyes. "I'm not sure I like you as well when you're playing young Marlon Brando. I might have actually preferred the doe-eyed ingénue who stepped on my suede shoes."

Cobie's heart gave a twinge at the desire to have that statement be true, but it wasn't, or maybe it was, but not for the reasons she would have liked. "She was probably easier to control."

"Indeed," Lila said, then after a heavy pause added, "though maybe a little too susceptible to bad influences."

"And now?" Cobie asked as they approached a darkened doorway and had a velvet rope pulled back for them.

"Tonight you seem just as likely to do the corrupting as allow yourself to be corrupted."

Another chill ran through Cobie, along with the realization that while she wasn't sure if the statement was true, part of her desperately wanted it to be.

Cobie's body brushed against hers, the silky cool of her tuxedo pants against Lila's bare legs in direct contrast to the heat of her hands on her hips. The bass beat pumped through them as the lights pulsed in time overhead. Every eye in the club was on them, and a slew of cell phone cameras as well, but Cobie never once let them down. Lila would have never admitted to being worried about Cobie's moves, but she silently wondered how long the Midwestern-girl-made-good could last on the dance floor with someone who had music flowing through her veins. Those fears were apparently unfounded. Cobie not only followed beautifully, she also managed to lead a time or two.

Suddenly the song changed from a standard techno thrum and throb to an excessive mechanical overlay of a familiar melody. A celebratory cheer went up from the gyrating masses around them. Lila smiled and gave a nod of acknowledgment to the DJ as her own voice rattled through the sound system.

"Are you going to sing for them?" Cobie asked.

"Why? It'll sound exactly like what he's playing. No need to get redundant."

"Oh no, you'd never want to seem overexposed," Cobie said with mock seriousness.

Lila laughed lightly. "You're on point tonight."

"You're welcome."

Lila shook her head, but Cobie pulled her closer, one arm passively around her waist as their hips rocked together. Their eyes stayed trained on one another, and Lila would have been completely captivated by the tantalizing hint of mischief she saw in Cobie if not for the distraction of her lips. A little redder than they had been at the start of the evening, they were also moving. It took a few seconds for full understanding to sink in, but when it did, her eyebrows shot up. "Why, Cobie Galloway, are you singing along with one of my songs?"

Cobie pushed her away long enough to give her a little twirl before reeling her back in. "Would it surprise you if I were?"

"A little."

"Good," Cobie whispered, then she began to really sing along. Her voice was rich and low. What it lacked in power and refinement, it made up for in raw timbre. Lila's heart beat a little faster as her own words washed over her in the sultry sound of a voice both familiar and fascinating.

She struggled to keep her breath even, but it took a minute to compose her thoughts enough to say, "You've been holding out on me."

"Maybe," Cobie said, still moving close and fluid. "I get the feeling that doesn't happen to you very often."

"It doesn't," Lila admitted, though she wouldn't give away how impressed she was that Cobie managed to keep a few secrets.

"Well, now you've found me out, I guess I can cop to my master plan. I never wanted to play Vale. It was all an elaborate ruse to become one of your back-up singers and go-go dancers."

Lila laughed immediately, picturing Cobie on stage with her, bumping and grinding while teenage girls screamed in glee. "I'd have to see you in one of the costumes before I could make a job offer. I'm thinking short skirt, lots of beadwork, tons of silver sequins."

"I would kill in that get up, and you know it."

"I might have one on the plane, though I'm not sure I can wait that long. Maybe I should call Felipe and have him fetch it." She raised her hand as if intending to signal for Malik, but Cobie caught it and brought it lightly to her lips.

"Maybe later."

"Getting cold feet?"

"Some of the best things in life are worth waiting for."

"So they tell me," Lila pouted, "but I've never found that to be true."

"Maybe you just haven't found the right things yet," Cobie said, turning serious.

"And you think you're the one to show me?"

"That would be awfully presumptuous of me."

Lila smiled, noting that Cobie hadn't exactly denied the charge, but as much as she enjoyed the little cat-and-mouse conversation, it had gone on too long to be useful. As her song came to a close with a smattering of applause, she waved to the crowd with one hand and clasped Cobie's with the other, leading them to a VIP booth in the back of the club.

Lush leather seats ringed a table that seemed to ooze an

eerie blue light. All around the circle hung thick heavy curtains, creating a cave of cloth that protected them from the flashing strobe and clashing subwoofers. It also had the added benefit of allowing them to control who saw what.

Lila pulled Cobie inside, staring at her like something she intended to devour, and tugged the rope holding the curtains apart, letting them fall shut with a soft rush.

"And scene," Cobie said, flopping onto the couch. "Nice dramatic flair there at the end. Anyone watching you undress me with your eyes has no doubt you're ripping my clothes off right now."

"We'll make sure you're properly ruffled before they see you again," Lila said, sitting down beside her and rubbing her tired ankles. "Your tie will be undone. I'll get some lipstick on your collar, untuck your shirt, maybe mismatch a couple buttons."

"Whoa," Cobie said, her complexion paling slightly. "So we're to assume you got to second base."

"And you might've gotten to third."

Cobie swallowed hard enough to make the knot of her white tie bob ever so slightly. "Before we get on any bases, would it be possible to maybe take a fully-clothed and completely nonsexual selfie?"

Lila frowned. "I'm not sure that helps us any at this point. I'm glad you're getting into the social media scene, but we have to be careful about the narrative we're constructing. You shouldn't share platonic photos with the press tonight, or probably for a while actually."

"It's not for the press." The color rushed back to Cobie's cheeks. "It's, um, for my little sister."

"You want a picture with me to send to your sister?" Amusement filled Lila's voice.

Cobie's blush deepened. "I know it's a working weekend, and I'm supposed to be focused, but I don't get to see her much, so we text at least once a day. When I promised to stay in touch, she asked for pictures."

"Does she know we're not really dating?"

Cobie shook her head and stared down at her hands.

"And you hate that?"

Cobie nodded and sighed. "She knows not to talk to the press, not that she would. We're a quiet family, but I didn't want to put her in a position where she felt like she had to lie for me. Or maybe like she would think of me as a liar."

Lila's heart gave a disconcerting thud at the realization that Cobie actually cared. She cared about being honest with her sister, she cared about protecting her, and she cared about being a hero in a young girl's eyes. "You're doing your job, Cobie."

She shrugged. "Yeah, well, I'm not sure I'd go that far, but I've made my choices. I'm a big girl. She's just a kid, and I want to keep her that way as long as I can."

Her chest tightened again at the protectiveness in Cobie's voice. That kind of concern didn't win her any fans or make her any money. It simply existed somewhere deep inside her.

"So, selfie?"

She forced a smile and scooted close to her on the couch. "Of course."

Cobie held her phone at arm's length and framed the shot. They both smiled brightly as she pressed the shutter button. "Thanks."

"Anytime. How old is she?"

"Fourteen," Cobie said.

"She's right in my wheelhouse."

"Yeah, I'd like to say you're her second favorite celebrity, but she doesn't have any posters of me on her wall."

Lila laughed. "You should bring her to one of my shows next month. It'll earn you big sister points."

"Oh, my God, her birthday's in March." Her excitement was immediate and too exuberant to be anything but real. "I would win big sister of the year! Are you sure it wouldn't cramp your fauxmance game?"

"I have no intention of making out with you on stage, if that's what you mean."

"You never know. You might find me so irresistible when you see how awesome I am with my sister," Cobie boasted. "I am superhero sibling material. I mean, you might have sisters or brothers that you think are cool, but—"

"I don't," Lila said abruptly, her throat suddenly hot and dry.

Cobie blinked. "You don't what?"

"Have any siblings I think are cool." The whiplash from Cobie's genuineness to the topic of her own family left her vision blurry around the edges. She picked up her phone and opened a text to Malik, desperate for a distraction.

"Oh, I'm sorry. I just really like my sister a lot. I guess that's kind of nerdy."

"It doesn't matter. She can come to the show." She waved her hand as if she could somehow wipe away the topic and all the conflicting emotions it inspired. "I need a drink. You want something?"

"Um, yeah, sure. Water?"

Lila nodded and texted Malik with instructions on the drinks and on the final act of their little play. She was ready to get back to work. She was aware enough to realize a simple conversation about siblings shouldn't be nearly as fraught as the thought of making out with a woman in a club for publicity's sake, but she didn't particularly care about what she should feel. She only cared about what she did feel, and right now that was the need to reassert control.

"We've got two minutes before Malik gets here. He's going to open the curtain all the way. We need to look like he interrupted something. Then he's going to leave the curtain open just enough to offer a few minutes of tantalizing view."

"Then I lead you out of here all sexily disheveled and possessive," Cobie finished. "Got it."

"Good." Lila nodded resolutely, her pulse returning to normal. "Anything off limits?"

"Your hands stay over my clothes from the belt down."

"Of course."

"And you?"

"Same. All exposed skin is fair game. Don't expose anything else."

Cobie's eyes raked over her legs, but her expression remained neutral. "And if I do anything you don't like or feel uncomfortable with at any point, pinch me on the side or the arm, and I'll stop."

"Oh, that's a handy trick. Did you learn that in the movies?"

Cobie smiled. "I've never explicitly stated that rule to anyone before, but I've had to use it a time or two myself."

Lila frowned at the idea of some man taking that kind of liberty with Cobie's body against her will, and her chest filled with those pesky emotions again at the thought of Cobie making accommodations so she wouldn't have to face the same sort of discomfort. It reminded her of their first kiss, the real one, the feel of Cobie's lips so soft and the concern evident in those dark eyes, both then and now.

She quickly reached up and tugged the loose end of Cobie's white tie until it fell splayed across her collar.

"Oh, we're going now," Cobie muttered as she popped open the top few buttons on her collar. "Okay then."

Lila unclasped Cobie's hair, sinking her fingers into the lush strands and shaking them out so they fell across her shoulders. "Lose the jacket."

She complied, tossing it onto the back of the booth, and tilted her head to the side, exposing her neck. "Lipstick ready?"

"Right. Let me reapply." Lila grabbed her clutch and pulled out her make-up, using a bold shade to coat her lips before blotting just the lower one on the crease of Cobie's starched collar.

Cobie watched, giving her the thumbs up. "Looks smashing on both you and on me."

"Then I guess it's time for you to smear it."

Cobie did her usual shoulder roll that signified her getting back into character, but this time, her pupils expanded as she turned to face her fully. She slipped her arm around Lila's back, scooting firmly against her and planting a dramatic kiss on her lips.

The scene flowed effortlessly from there. Lila caught a fistful of her shirt and twisted it until another button popped open. Cobie pressed forward, taking control of Lila's mouth in ways she hadn't before. The tentative softness of the first kiss had been replaced by the command of a woman who knew what she was doing. Her lips moved with confidence and skill matched only by her hands. Cobie sank her fingers into the hair at the base of Lila's neck, using the grip to urge her back until she lay flat on the leather bench. Lying half on top of her, she cupped her ass and slipped her arm down along her leg, urging it up as she went. Lila had no trouble following her direction. It was as if Cobie knew what her body wanted to do on its own and merely gave it the freedom to do so.

Lila hooked one high heel onto the bench and a leg around Cobie's thigh until they were tangled together beautifully. The position couldn't have been more erotic if she had staged it herself, and it suddenly occurred to her that she hadn't.

Somewhere between setting the parameters for the scene and actually playing it out, Cobie had taken over, and she'd done so with such adept skill Lila hadn't noticed. Maybe it was the easy way she moved, or simply her ability to take direction and make it work for her, but part of her also suspected Cobie was simply a very good kisser. Certainly better than the men, but maybe even better than Lila, who only managed to return, not exceed, what she'd been given.

Her breath came hot and sharp at both the contact between them, and also the growing awareness that her response was not contrived. Her pulse quickened, much the way it had when Cobie turned sincere, and the same fear rushed behind it. Everything felt real, and while it should always look that way to the outside eye, letting those feelings seep inside her was dangerous on so many levels.

The curtains were pulled wide around them. Bass and light assaulted their senses, and they both shot up off the bench. Malik had hit his mark perfectly, standing to the side with two drinks in hand and plenty of space for photographers, both amateur and pro, to get their shot of them. If the flashes were any indication, they did so with fervor. She blinked and straightened her dress, not quite playacting at disorientation. Cobie held up a hand to shield her face, either from the onslaught of light or the photos, but she also reached for Lila's hand and found it almost as if by instinct. She leaned toward the contact, putting her own body between the invasion and Lila. The move wasn't great from a publicity standpoint, but once again, Lila suspected the protectiveness came naturally to Cobie. Unfortunately, she didn't share that compulsion.

Lila didn't need to be sheltered or cared for. She didn't really need anything from anybody. She was a strong, independent woman who set her own scenes. She made all her own choices, and chivalry was dead.

"Come on." She squeezed Cobie's hand and pulled her up. "We're leaving."

"I thought we were going to—"

"I thought you were going to take direction," she snapped through a smile contrived for the cameras.

"Anything you say, dear." Cobie's voice didn't sound certain or even compliant so much as resigned.

She swept out of the VIP area, dragging Cobie behind her. She assumed Malik set down the drinks and rushed to follow them. He was a professional. He could roll with the punches. So could Cobie. She had already rebounded and had her arm around Lila's waist and her tuxedo jacket slung over her shoulder as they made a break for the exit. The crowd on the dance floor parted to let them through, and even they kept their cameras rolling. Everyone on this stage played their part to perfection. Not one of them missed a beat or broke character. They never faltered. They never cracked. Everyone did exactly as she ordered.

Everyone but her.

Chapter Five

"Nice place." Cobie set her suitcase down in the entryway of the large brownstone.

"We like it," Felipe said as he eyed her suspiciously.

"You live here too?"

"In the servants' quarters. She don't let the hired help use the front entrance. Brown folks might bring down the property values."

"Oh, I'm . . ." She didn't even know what to say. She felt indignant on his behalf, and embarrassed, which only amplified the urge to flee this next step in their charade. Finally, she managed to blurt, "I'm so sorry."

He threw back his head and cackled. "I'm just messing with you, *chica*. Damn, your face was priceless. I didn't think you could get any whiter. This is going to be fun!"

She stared at him in disbelief. "What?"

"You need to relax, girl, or I'm going to run roughshod over you for the next two months. Come on. Let me show you around."

"Sure," she said, still wary. "So just to clarify, you do live here?"

"Technically, Malik and I live next door. Lila bought the brownstones on either side of this one to give her a bubble of privacy."

"Oh, well, that's smart and . . . extravagant."

He laughed as he led her through the wood-paneled entryway, past a large staircase and formal study into a more open living area. "That's our girl, smart and extravagant."

"She does seem to have her way with things." Cobie took in her surroundings from the ornate marble fireplace to the high ceilings with delicately carved crown molding. Impressed, she noted that while the space was grandiose and lavishly furnished in all white, nothing constituted over the top or garish. Lila knew style. Hell, she embodied it. "Is the lady of the house home?"

He turned to her. "Well, I like to think of myself as the lady of the house, but if you mean Lila, she's in her studio on the third floor. I already let her know you're here."

But Lila hadn't come down to welcome her. Too lost in her work? Too important to care? Or perhaps making a deliberate choice to keep Cobie in her place.

"This is the formal living room. We use it for entertaining. It's sort of the public space of the house. Interviews, photo shoots, dignitaries, et cetera. We're never in here when it's just us."

"Just us," she repeated softly, wondering if that now included her.

"And this is the chef's kitchen." He walked her through another doorway to a huge kitchen with a white marble-topped bar and stainless steel appliances. "It's fully stocked. If you leave a list of what you like on the chalkboard by the fridge, it will magically appear in a day or two."

"Convenient."

"People cook for us when folks come over, but there's not a chef on staff full-time. Malik does make grilled cheeses on command, my command mostly, but if you're nice to me, I'll put in a good word for you."

"Good to know." She smiled. "Where do I sleep?"

He turned slowly, his eyes serious. "In Ms. Wilder's bed, I presume."

"Oh, right, I mean, of course I sleep with Ms. Wilder when other people ask, but . . ." Her face burned. "Oh, God, really?"

He laughed again. "You are so easy. How have you survived so long in Hollywood without getting eaten alive?"

She rolled her eyes. "Felipe! Are you trying to give me a heart attack?"

"Maybe." He shrugged. "But you'll sleep in the same wing as Lila for convenience sake. It's actually in the next brownstone over. We can get there through the dining room, but since you'll be on the second floor, it'll be easier to go up the front steps."

She followed, carry-on suitcase in hand, as he led her back the way they'd come and up a flight of stairs. They went past a few open doors along the way, guest rooms, an office, and a sewing room, as well as several closed-off spaces that left her wondering what one person could do with so much room. As they cut through a less formal living space, she noticed French doors at the far side, in what she assumed was once the outer edge of the house. Felipe flung them wide with a dramatic flourish as he said, "This is your domain."

Cobie was taken aback. The boxy broken-up spaces and hallways vanished in a single open room with lavish carpets, overstuffed chairs, and bright airy windows. Guitar cases lay open on the floor, and notes spilled off an enormous ottoman the size of a coffee table. In one corner near the windows stood a white baby grand piano draped in lush scarlet fabric samples. "Wow."

"Right?" Felipe practically squealed. "Not a bad place to hole up for a while."

"No, it's so . . . so . . . Lila."

"Oooh, you say her name so dreamy and romantic." Felipe practically swooned.

Cobie wanted to say, "Did not," but she got the sense that Felipe could sense drama like a shark could smell blood in the water. Not that there was any drama between her and Lila. They'd had virtually no contact since leaving Las Vegas last weekend. Even when they'd been in Sin City, they'd mostly stayed in their own corners ever since their abrupt departure from the club.

Cobie frowned, thinking of that moment for the hundredth time. It had only been a slight change in plans, nothing worth obsessing about, and the press hadn't seemed to notice anything awry. The pictures of them from that night were still splashed across every major magazine and gossip site. She'd spent the entire next day in interviews with celebrity news outlets, while Lila had made the rounds at a radio DJ convention. The two of them had barely seen each other all day, but they'd talked of nothing else with anyone else.

By all accounts, the trip had been wildly successful. They'd accomplished everything they'd set out to and then some. Even Cobie had been impressed with the glossy images of them together. She looked good, suave and in charge, despite not feeling like any of those things at the time. Even knowing what she did about their power dynamic, she had a hard time seeing reports of them together without believing she had been the one to sweep Lila off her feet. Maybe that was the problem. There were a few moments throughout the course of the evening when she believed in the illusion too much. Those instances were few and fleeting, but they probably shouldn't have happened at all.

"So, um . . ." Cobie shook her head slightly, aware that Felipe was still watching her closely. "Bedroom? Mine, not hers."

He pointed to a door across the room. "That one's all yours for a while. Go ahead and make yourself comfy."

"Thanks," she said, grateful he didn't intend to follow her inside. She'd need a sanctuary to get through this experience. She pushed open the door slowly, and some of the tension from her shoulders relaxed. The space wasn't ostentatious but rather oozed comfort, from the four-poster bed loaded with a cream-colored down comforter to the lush maroon drapes to deep mahogany dressers and night stands.

"You can do this," she whispered to herself as she tossed her suitcase on the bed and forced herself not to wonder how many others had stayed here before her.

She unzipped the carry-on and pulled back a sweater to reveal two framed photographs. One showed her parents, smiling and happy, the other framed her and Emma laughing at something silly. She couldn't remember the joke, but she could still recall the feeling it sparked, and that's what she wanted to hold onto. She set both pictures on a nightstand next to the bed and stood back.

Now this place was at least as good as the hotels she'd spent too much time in. She could do this. She could cohabitate with a woman in order to make her dreams come true.

She laughed in spite of her remaining unease. Under other circumstances, living with a bright, talented, beautiful woman would have *been* a dream come true in and of itself. Maybe she needed to be a little more specific in her wishful thinking.

She resisted the urge to crawl into bed and stay there all day. She would not complain or cave to self-pity. She had a job to do, and no one would feel sorry for her because she had to live in a fully appointed mansion for a while. And this place had a kitchen, which made it infinitely better than her last hotel. Maybe she could go get a grilled cheese lesson from Malik.

She headed back through Lila's living room, as she already thought of it, and into the hallway, but when she reached the stairs, something stopped her. She inclined her ear and realized she heard the faintest strains of music coming from somewhere above. The melody was unfamiliar but intriguing, and without thinking, she climbed the stairs to get closer to the sound.

The first door she came to was closed but not latched. A small sliver of space allowed the rich chords to waft out and over her. At first she couldn't tell what she was listening to as two distinct sounds met her ears, but after a second, she understood someone was playing a guitar and a harmonica. She started to back away, realizing someone else was in there with Lila, but the person playing the harmonica let fly a long soulful riff, and something in Cobie's chest soared. She didn't know whether to dance or cry. If she closed her eyes, she could have been on Bourbon Street instead of in a New York brownstone.

She moved toward the music like a mosquito toward a blue bug-zapper, and for a moment the result might have been the same as well, because as soon as Lila's intense eyes landed on her, the music stopped with a low hum of electricity still buzzing in the air.

"Hello, Cobie," she said, in a low dangerous tone. "Welcome to my home. This room is by invitation only."

"Sorry." She said the only word she could think of as she took in the full picture of Lila perched on a plain wooden stool with a beautiful black Les Paul guitar across her bare knees and a shiny copper harmonica hanging from a metal holder around her neck. "I'm sorry I interrupted. Sorry you stopped. I'm sorry I underestimated you."

One of Lila's eyebrows arched, and then she pursed her lips.

She was clearly treading a dangerous path, but the music still coursed through her, calling her to either bravery or insanity. "What were you playing?"

"Nothing important."

She nodded absently. "Play it again?"

Lila shook her head slowly.

"Please."

Lila's eyes flashed and her mouth opened, but instead of tearing into her, she brought the harmonica to her lips, and her fingers twitched into action. For the next three minutes, Cobie stood transfixed as her heartbeat provided a solid drum component to the riffs and wails burning up her consciousness. Her mind floated from dark alleys to humid bayous and out across soggy deltas.

The tune faded, and Lila stilled as the last low hum hung in the air. Cobie opened her eyes and smiled slowly. "Thank you."

Lila removed the harmonica holder and set it atop a piano before pulling the guitar off her lap. "This can't become a habit, Cobie."

"Why?"

"Because my home studio has to be a safe space for me."

"I meant why don't you play music like that anywhere but in here?"

She laughed and rose, cradling the guitar in its stand. "It's not part of the plan."

Cobie cocked her head to the side and waited for more, but as Lila began to gather a few notes, she realized she wasn't going to offer any more explanation. "What plan?"

"The plan to rule the world," Lila said lightly.

"Right." She drew out the word, still not sure what she'd stepped into.

Lila finally sighed. "You know I got my start in country music, right?"

She nodded. She hadn't given any thought to the fact before now, but she did indeed remember Lila breaking onto the scene in sundresses and cowgirl boots. "But then you grew out of the genre? Or did your tastes change?"

"Both. Neither. I can't be limited by labels someone else has defined. I'm bigger than a genre," Lila said matter-of-factly. "I still love country music. If I were only playing in this room, I'd probably sound more like June Carter or Reba McEntire, but playing in this room doesn't make me money, and playing those songs won't build me an empire."

"I don't know. June and Reba seemed to do just fine for themselves."

"But I want to go farther. I want to have my finger on the pulse of America for decades, and to do that I need to be on the cutting edge, never ahead of it, never behind it. Ten to twelve years ago, country music saw a boom, and it offered the best outlet for a sixteen-year-old girl to sell records about first crushes and loyal friendship."

"Sounds about right," Cobie admitted. "Just like I got my start in teen movies."

"Exactly, but just like you're not seventeen anymore, neither am I. The girls who listened to country music when I started are now in their twenties. They're making their own way in the world. They have entry-level jobs and lovers and drama. They want to be taken seriously, and they want to think they are on the road to someplace better. I want to give them a voice."

"So those are the songs you sing them?"

"Those are also the songs I sell them," Lila said. "I sell them snapshots of where they are, their hopes and dreams and their fears, but I also sell them glimpses of where they want to be, where they believe they should be. I sell glamour, power, love, a sense of connection amid the disjointed isolation of their lives."

"What will you do when they reach their mid-thirties?"

"I'll sing power ballads and love lyrics about finding the one. I'll write the songs people will play at their weddings. I'll sing about not having enough time and thinking we'd have gone farther by now," Lila explained evenly. "And when we're forty, I'll break out retrospectives and nostalgia and break-up songs about feeling betrayed by the world and people who promised to be there forever. And always feminism."

"Feminism?"

"Songs to women in power, women who take charge, women who know what they want and never settle for less, because those songs will resonate with women across generations. They deserve those songs. They deserve those messages. They deserve to be reminded every day that they don't have to compromise or apologize for who they are."

"You seem to do that very well," Cobie said with a hint of a smile.

"But?" Lila asked.

"But nothing," she admitted, impressed that Lila actually cared so much about her message to plot it out long-term. "You're good at your job. I should probably be more like you."

"But?" Lila prodded again.

She shrugged. "I just thought it could all be organic, you know? Like I would grow up and my audience would grow with me, and we could make and watch what we wanted in any given moment because we shouldn't answer to the market. The market should answer to us. Like I could just be a good actress and make good movies, and we'd all get judged on our merits."

"That's not how it works," Lila said softly. "Unless you want to be a starving artist or a hobby artist, you have to have a market, and to have a market you have two choices: you can find one or you can create one."

"You do both."

Lila smiled proudly. "I do. That's why you're here. It's time for my career to move onto a new stage, one where I spread the message that all options are open and no one gets to define me but me."

126

"It's working," Cobie said. "You've impressed the press. Your fans are tweeting out against conversion therapy. You're ushering in a new era of lesbian chic."

"I'm also building a sense of anticipation for my next album. If I'm this unpredictable in my love life, just imagine what I'll do in the recording studio."

"But you won't produce any zydeco or bayou blues?"

She laughed. "Not that unpredictable, but I may be darker or angrier or softer or more wistful. No one knows."

"No one except you."

Lila's smile grew tight. "Either way, we've gotten off topic. The point is what happens in this room isn't for sale until I say so. Here I play for me, off market. It's my space. No expectations, no explanations."

"For love, for craft, for fun." Cobie got it. She understood the need to get back to the joy of her work. She hadn't had enough of that lately. "I'm sorry if I interrupted your creative time. I just really liked what I heard. And maybe I'm a little envious that you have that kind of outlet."

"You could too."

Cobie laughed. "I guess I could go ahead and play Hamlet aloud in my bedroom by myself, but it doesn't seem quite the same."

"Maybe not, but you want to play Vale, right?"

"That's why I'm here."

Lila frowned so briefly Cobie almost missed it, but before the thought could fully register, Lila began to circle. Blue eyes raked over her until the corners of Lila's mouth curled slowly up once more.

"Uh-oh," Cobie said. "I'm starting to recognize that look, and I don't usually like what follows."

"You want your chance to play for a captive audience. Now you've got one. You can play powerful or seductive or brooding or captivating, and we'll all play along while you hold us spellbound."

Her eyes narrowed. It sounded too good to be true. "How?"

"Tomorrow we're going to play 'what would Vale do.' You can

practice your character study on us, and we can help you hone your power."

"Why tomorrow?" Cobie asked, though she meant "Why can't we start right now?"

Lila's smile widened. "Because today you're busy getting a makeover."

"Wait. What? No." What had happened to honing power and holding people spellbound? "I'm not sure what you think lesbians do when we move in together, but it's generally not a hair and make-up type of slumber party."

"Nice try." Lila shook her head, then with a sure hand ran her fingers tantalizingly through Cobie's hair. "Humor can't save you now. You're my captive."

The words were all wrong, but the unexpected touch sent a shiver of pleasure along her spine. Lila was so close, the heat of her body raised Cobie's own temperature. What had she just said? Something about captive? When had the conversation shifted into Lila's domain, and shouldn't she do something to turn it back around? Instead of protesting, Cobie closed her eyes and muttered, "Um, okay."

Not her best or strongest answer ever, but there was something about being in Lila's space, under the spell of her fingers, with the promise of power hanging in the air that made her forget everything but what she wanted right then and there. And in this moment, she wanted whatever Lila wanted.

"God, your hair is amazingly soft," Lila gushed in a moment of pure admiration. She ran her fingers through the long luscious strands as warm water cascaded over Cobie's head.

"Yeah, I keep it that way by not dumping a bunch of toxic chemicals on it."

"The dye is only toxic if you drink it." Lila squeezed some shampoo into her hand and began to work it into Cobie's hair. The suds were rich and aromatic as they multiplied.

"Oh, then I'm glad you're only putting it on my scalp," Cobie said. Her forehead relaxed as she leaned back, her neck cradled on a rolled-up towel over the sink. "You know, the scalp that covers my brain."

"Yes, it'd be a shame if it leached into your brain and ruined your shot at the Ivy league, 'cause that happens all the time," Lila said lightly as she turned the water up and began to rinse out the soap. "Honestly, I'm surprised you've been in Hollywood as long as you have without dyeing it."

"Me too, actually," Cobie admitted. "I've always played characters close enough to my own image that I haven't had to change anything about myself. I guess it's a reminder of how little I've challenged myself."

"Telling, no?" Lila asked as she watched Cobie's serene features more than her own hands. She really was striking. There was no use trying to deny her appeal. Everything about her was flawless, from her smooth skin to her perfectly arched eyebrows to the slight upturn of her mouth. She could easily understand why America had claimed her as one of their sweethearts, but there was more to her than a pretty face and a pliable nature. As if to illustrate that point, Cobie's dark eyes flashed opened, revealing a reserve of depth that caused Lila to falter in her work.

"I never thought of it that way until now," Cobie said pensively. "I always kind of thought not changing my looks all the time kept me real, or genuine, but maybe I've been a little too real, you know? I mean, I'm an actor. I'm supposed to slip into someone else's skin. I like to think that it's all about my craft, my talent for conveying emotions, but if I really inhabit my characters, Cobie Galloway shouldn't even be recognizable on screen, right?"

"Like when you watch Meryl Streep play a role, and you know it's Meryl Streep, but you only see a witch or Julia Child."

"Right?" Cobie laughed, looking up at her with her sincere eyes. "Thank you, Lila. I was kind of dreading this part, but you're good at helping me see things differently."

"It's nothing." She tried to ignore the twist of emotion in her stomach. "I'm bored today, and besides, the darker and more mysterious you get, the edgier I seem by association."

"Yeah, I love how much the press thinks I'm corrupting you. The religious right is having a conniption fit," Cobie said as Lila set about drying her hair. "What with my gambling and clubbing and making out in dark booths and . . ." Cobie's voice trailed off when Lila's hands stilled with the memory.

She willed the sudden heat in her cheeks to cool but feared her shallow breathing might have given her away. She glanced down to find Cobie's face as red as hers felt, and it only took a second to process why. As Lila had leaned over, towel in hand, to dry the longest of her dark locks, she'd practically cradled Cobie's head between her breasts. The position that had started out as purely utilitarian now seemed glaringly intimate, if not outright erotic.

"Lila," Cobie finally whispered.

"Yes?" The word sounded a little strangled.

"I think I can probably dry my own hair."

"Yeah," she managed, leaning back slowly and looking anywhere but at Cobie. "I, um, I think I'll go tell Felipe we're ready for him to help us with the dye."

She didn't wait for a response before exiting the bathroom and walking purposefully through Cobie's bedroom.

Not the guestroom. Cobie's bedroom. With her photos on the nightstand and her jeans tossed casually on the bed. The bed where she would sleep. She sighed. Why did everything sound so personal now?

She swung open the door to the living room. "Felipe, give me a hand with her."

Both Felipe and Malik jumped. They shared a look, all wide eyes and raised eyebrows.

"Don't," she commanded.

"Oh, girl, what happened?" Felipe asked excitedly.

"Nothing. What do you mean? It's time to style and dye Cobie's hair like that drawing I showed you. You're my stylist. Get to work."

"Did you ever notice how bossy she gets when she has feelings?" he asked Malik.

"It's a coping mechanism, Boo," Malik said patiently. "She's scared."

"I am not," Lila snapped. Reining in her tone, she said, "I've got a job to do. I want to get it done."

"As quickly as possible?" Felipe asked.

"Yes."

"So you don't have to be alone in a room with a woman who makes you feel things you don't want to?"

"Yes," she said quickly, then processed the question further. "Wait, no. I mean, she doesn't make me feel feelings. She makes me feel different things than feelings."

They exchanged another look, this one oozing amusement.

"Guys." She sighed. "I put my breasts in her face. On accident. But she was talking about Vegas and making out, and I got distracted and I—"

"Put your boobs in her face," Felipe supplied. "Makes total sense, honey."

She sank onto the couch. "In what world?"

"In the world where you like her more than you want to," Malik offered.

"Ugh. This is not okay. I am not into her. She is not my type."

"Because she's a woman?" Malik asked.

"No. Why does everyone get hung up on the woman part? It's not 1950 anymore. I can like women, just not this one. She's too damn, I don't know, earnest?"

"True," Felipe agreed.

"She's not going to play games," Malik added.

"I don't want to play games."

Felipe scoffed. "But you're so good at them."

She rolled her eyes but didn't disagree. "We have to work together."

"And live together," Felipe added enthusiastically. "This is going to be so much fun."

"Felipe!" They both scolded him in unison.

"What? Come on. You've had a steady parade of earth's hottest bachelors and playboys through here for years now. They have been the best of the best, the quickest, prettiest, wittiest, and most shallow human beings in the world. And every one of them fell for you, only to be rebuffed, every flipping flopping one. Despite the fact that they're all supposedly exactly your type and well-matched in every way." His eyes sparkled with sheer giddiness. "Now you try to fake it with a woman who's your complete stripes-and-polka-dots-type opposite, and she's the one who actually trips your trigger. That's glorious."

"That's karma," Malik added.

She shot him a look. "Traitor."

"Sorry, girl, you got yourself a little of what-goes-around-comes-around here." He headed for the door. "I'm going to go make some popcorn."

"Make me some too," Felipe said, taking Lila's hand and pulling her back toward the bedroom. "Then come join us while I make Cobie even hotter than she already is."

Lila dug in her heels, literally and figuratively, pulling him up short. "Maybe the makeover wasn't the best idea."

"Please, when is a makeover a bad idea?" Felipe tugged harder, but he must have seen something telling in her expression, because he allowed their joined arms to go slack. "Hey, there's nothing wrong with being genuinely interested in someone."

"I'm not sure I am," she said defensively. "And even if I were, how would I know? I've pretended so many times, it all gets so muddled."

"And you don't like muddled."

She shook her head. She didn't like not knowing things. She didn't like feeling uncertain. Uncertainty didn't build empires. It made her weak. She had a plan, not just for today or even for the next five years. She had a plan to keep herself safe and steady and secure. And it wasn't like she thought she and Cobie could ride off into the sunset, because clearly that was absurd. If she did feel something for Cobie, it was a momentary lapse, a spark of interest or attraction that would fade like every other moment in her life. Nothing lasted forever. She couldn't put herself in a position to threaten everything she'd fought for by indulging a disconcerting twinge of attraction that probably wouldn't, and shouldn't, ever be reciprocated.

She set her jaw and dug her nails into Felipe's soft hands. "This can't be a thing."

"Whoa, girl."

"I mean it," she reiterated. "I don't care how funny it is or how cute she gets. No one is as hot as my future right now."

He grimaced, then smiled. "When you put it that way, yeah. You're on fire."

"And did I get there by chasing whims or losing my head to my emotions?"

"You did not."

"Then stay the course."

He nodded solemnly. "Okay, but can't I tease you just a little bit?"

She finally smiled. "As long as we're all clear about how this ends, cattiness may commence at will."

He threw an arm around her shoulder and dropped a kiss on her cheek. "This is why we work: a perfect balance of business and pleasure."

She felt a little steadier as they headed back toward Cobie. Balance between business and pleasure—she could live with that.

Cobie yawned and took a second to orient herself. She'd had plenty of practice waking up in hotel rooms, so finding herself in Lila's brownstone shouldn't have felt any different. And yet she could hear music overhead. The distance made it impossible to pick out a tune, but the notes that wafted down the stairs were slow and languid.

She sat up, clutching the sheets tight to her bare chest when she spotted a stranger opposite the bed.

"Shit." She was looking at her reflection in the large mirror over the dresser. She tossed off the down comforter and padded across the room to get a better look. She'd seen the haircut the night before. It was short and shaggy, layered so she could still

133

tuck a few of the front strands behind her ears, but instead of hanging straight down, they curled and stuck out at jagged intervals. The color added to the edge, offering a jarring contrast to her pale complexion. Jet black and lustrous, it set off her eyes, making them seem almost as dark as the dye. She barely looked like the woman who'd arrived in this room yesterday, and yet she still looked like herself, albeit an older, more mysterious version, maybe even a better, more interesting one.

She smiled at the mirror and noticed that even her expression seemed a little cockier than usual. Relief gave way to a new kind of energy, and the need to move buzzed through her. She threw open her closet door and grabbed a pair of black low-rise jeans. Pulling them on, she flipped through her shirt options. She wanted a sassy T-shirt, but Old Man Winter hadn't quite released New York City, so she perused her way through heartier options until she landed on a black waffle-weave Henley. Turning back to the mirror, she liked the way the snug fit of the ensemble showed off her recently enhanced oblique and biceps muscles, but it was a lot of black. She wasn't going to a funeral, so she fished through her duffle bag for a small, red box. Smiling wistfully, she opened it, pulled out a silver labrys charm, and fastened it around her neck with a polished silver chain. It went well with her standard silver three-cord ring.

Grabbing her phone off the nightstand, she cocked an eyebrow playfully at the mirror and snapped a photo. There was only one person she'd ever send it to, so she sent it quickly before she had the chance to second-guess herself.

"What in all the fucks?" Talia texted back.

"My new look. You approve?"

"I almost didn't notice the style. Too busy being traumatized by the idea of you taking mirror selfies."

"Ha." Cobie shot back as her mood faltered. Her first mirror selfie. Was she seriously that person now? No, Lila was that person, and yet Lila wasn't here. She was in her studio being a serious musician. Cobie couldn't blame her frivolity on anyone but herself.

134

Her phone buzzed again. "Honestly, I'd bust you pretty hard for this one if I wasn't afraid you'd come through the phone and kick my ass in that super fierce get-up."

"No worries. I don't start training with the martial arts team until Wednesday. Speak freely."

"In that case . . ."

Cobie's heart hung on those three little dots. She shifted from one foot to the other as she waited for more. Finally, a notification popped up telling her Talia was typing. When the message appeared, it read, "You look fan-fucking-tastic."

She gave a little first pump.

"Do you love it?" Talia asked.

Love might have been a bit strong, but the seed of something pleasurable was certainly being nurtured in her now. "I don't hate it."

"What a Vale thing to say," Talia shot back. "Go break some hearts."

Cobie tapped back a quick message. "I'm on it."

Bolstered by the fact that not even her best friend could manage to bust her chops this morning, she practically charged into the upstairs living room, only to find it empty. The notes coming from above gave her momentary pause, but she'd learned her lesson about barging into Lila's studio uninvited, so instead she turned downstairs hoping to find Malik and Felipe, or at least some coffee. The room was cold and empty. She barely gave the high-end espresso machine a glance, not wanting to break her win streak by doing battle with a monster like that. Snapping her fingers as an idea came to her, she headed for the door.

The number of reporters outside had seriously decreased from the night before, but what they lacked in numbers, they made up for with enthusiasm.

"Cobie, Cobie, Cobie," they shouted as if she didn't know her own name.

She flipped down a pair of dark sunglasses and walked straight for them like a pedestrian game of chicken. When she was two steps away, they parted, and she breezed through, not even trying to suppress her victory grin. Now she was onto the important business at hand. She needed bagels. Good ones.

Thankfully, she did not have to go too far to find such treasures in Manhattan. She strutted down the sidewalk like she owned the dirty gray concrete, and as the reporters called her name and trailed in her wake, it felt like she did.

She reached the bagel shop two blocks down and held the door for a beautiful young Latina in a pantsuit carrying two trays of coffee and who did a double take on her way out. Then she closed the door behind her, keeping the press on the outside.

"Good morning," she said to the teenage girl working the counter.

"What can I get for . . ." Her voice trailed off and her eyes narrowed.

Cobie lifted the glasses and winked.

The girl's jaw dropped.

"I'll take two whole grain, two everything, two sesame, and two plain bagels," Cobie continued as if she couldn't knock the kid over with a feather. "Oh, and four dark roast coffees, black with room."

She nodded and rushed to the back like she needed moral support to complete the order. As the time ticked on, Cobie wondered if she'd perhaps passed out. Surely she wasn't the only one working.

After about five minutes of leaning against the counter, resisting the urge to make faces at the paparazzi waiting outside, the girl came out of the back with four other teenage girls and slid a bag across the counter to Cobie. Another one offered a cardboard coffee carrier like a wise man offering frankincense to the Holy Child.

Feeling like a total badass, she tossed a hundred-dollar bill on the counter. "Have a great day, guys."

Just as she reached the door, one of them shouted, "I love your new haircut."

She threw a smile over her shoulder. "Thanks."

The press once again parted Red-Sea-style to let her through, and if she had to guess, a few more reporters had joined the herd as they fired a barrage of inappropriate questions.

"Did you spend the night with Lila Wilder?"

"Are you two living together?"

"Why did you dye your hair?"

"Did you turn Lila gay?"

"Are you getting butcher for her?"

"Do you care about how many men she's slept with?"

Even the last once couldn't break her stride this morning. She honestly didn't care how many men had been in this position before her. Nothing she felt right now had anything to do with them. This morning was all hers, and she was slaying it. For the first time, she felt like she could handle whatever anyone threw at her, on the street or on the screen. She had what it took to be a legit player. She'd only needed to see it herself, and everyone else would too.

She left the trail of flashbulbs at the front gate and jogged up the stairs, but before she could even shift the bag of bagels to her free hand, the front door opened. Malik's hulking frame filled the entire entryway.

"Hey," she said, tilting her head back to see his frowning face. "You're up. I got bagels."

"Did you perhaps also get some roses or jewelry?" he asked, tugging her inside.

"Well that's a little forward of you. I didn't think we'd reached that stage of our relationship yet, and what would Felipe think?"

He rolled his eyes so far back she could only see the whites of them. "Don't say I didn't try to warn you."

"Warn me about what?" she asked as she breezed past him toward the kitchen, but as she turned the corner and saw Lila sitting at the marble island, she knew the answer.

"Where the hell have you been?" She wore yoga pants, an oversized sweatshirt, and a look of sheer fury.

Cobie's high crashed instantly, and she held up her purchases as a peace offering. "I got bagels."

"Bagels?"

"And coffee. Maybe you should have some right away."

"You seriously left my house first thing in the morning, just waltzed out the front door without telling anyone or taking anyone with you, for bagels."

She thought about pointing out that ten o'clock wasn't exactly first thing in the morning, but since everything else happened to be true, she didn't figure it would help. "Yes."

"What were you thinking?"

"I was thinking, and try hard to follow this logic, that I wanted some bagels."

She threw her hands in the air. "After everything we've done and built and orchestrated, you went off over some fucking bagels."

"Give me a break, Lila," she said sternly. "I didn't run naked down the street or cozy up to any reporters."

"How am I supposed to know what you did or said or to whom? You went rogue."

"Rogue?" She laughed, though it didn't actually feel funny. "Are you serious? Getting breakfast is not an act of treason. Why are you losing your shit over this?"

"Because you don't seem to understand that what you did was a massive risk."

"A risk? I didn't go skydiving or text while driving."

Lila slapped her hand on the countertop. "Either of those things would have been more consistent with the tone we're trying to set here. Your running out to get me breakfast makes it look like we're super-duper cute and doting."

"The press thinks I just shacked up with you, then I step outside the next morning with an entirely new look to buy four black coffees and a bag of bread." Cobie circled around the island, getting closer to make her point. "As far as they're concerned, I'm on a caffeine and carb bender to replenish me after the life-changing fuckfest we've had for the last twenty-four hours."

"That's kind of a spin job," Lila said as her cheeks turned pink.

"This whole thing is a spin job," Cobie shot back. "And I've been cool about that. I've played lap dog to the rich and powerful like a boss. Every time you've asked me to jump, I've asked how high? I let you pick all the dates, all the times, all the places. I've let you dress me like butch Barbie and parade me around like a show pony. I've done it all because that's part of the deal, but the deal changes now."

Lila stepped into her personal space, her chest rising and falling dramatically. "You don't have the right to change the deal."

"Oh, I do, because we're playing in my domain now. You promised today would be 'what would Vale do?' day, and Vale would take charge," Cobie said, her confidence growing as she stepped more fully into the role. "You got to be the boss during the sickening sweet stage. You got to make everyone swoon because that's what you do, but now we're in phase two. You got your lesbian love story to tantalize the public. Now I'm getting my swagger on hardcore."

"By buying bagels?" Lila scoffed. "That's so badass."

"By doing what I want."

"You're still in my house."

"No," she shouted. "For the next six weeks, it's *our* house. I am not your prisoner or your plaything, and I will not be treated like one. I will come and go as I please. I will eat what I want and talk to who I want."

"Even the press?"

"If I think it will serve my cause, yes," Cobie said resolutely.

Lila shook her head and pursed her lips.

"I'm not going to sink you in the process. I'm a team player, but this . . ." Cobie motioned back and forth in the small space between them. "Us? We need to start functioning more like a team and less like a hostage situation."

"For someone who doesn't want a hostage situation, you're sure making a lot of demands."

"I'm making up for lost time. Consider me a temperamental starlet if you have to."

Lila's lips curled up briefly.

"But I'm a professional. I'm here to develop a character who matters much more to me than she does to you. I'm not going to throw that away or miss opportunities while you tinker in your studio. I'm not sitting around for two months waiting for you to come to terms on a script."

"I thought I had."

"Oh, you have, many times, but the rules always change. I'm done being micromanaged if you're going to abandon ship mid-stream."

"I don't—"

"Don't bullshit me." Cobie cut her off. "You do it all the time. You kissed me without warning at the ice rink, you walked out on me at the club in Vegas, and yesterday you ordered a makeover, then left me with my head in the sink for ten minutes before dumping me off on Felipe."

Lila's face flushed crimson, but she apparently had no defense to offer, so Cobie plowed forward. "The scene always shifts unexpectedly, or the rules only apply to me, and that's got to end now or I'm going to keep going rogue."

"Is that a threat?"

"Nope, just the way it has to be. I tried to make this as easy as possible. I'd hoped you and I could be friends, but if we're just going to be colleagues, then I have to demand a bit of professional courtesy from now on."

Lila opened her mouth, then closed it again and stepped back. "Fine."

"Fine?" The shock radiated through Cobie.

"You're right," Lila said slowly, as if she had a hard time getting the words out. "At least partly."

"Which part?" Cobie asked suspiciously.

"You're doing a job here. Name your conditions."

"Oh." Cobie had done better when angry. She didn't know what to make of Lila's surrender. She'd never been in this position before. Still, she couldn't give up ground she'd only just won. "From now on, if you feel it important to plan something out, we will both agree to the terms and stick to them, but barring a mutual agreement, I'm going to do my own thing."

Lila shook her head slowly, then shrugged. "Sure. We can coordinate schedules daily. You'll let me know if yours changes, and I'll do the same."

"Deal," Cobie said emphatically, but as the tension faded from her body, she became increasingly aware of her proximity to Lila, with her flushed cheeks and red lips. Awkwardness rushed in to fill the void anger had left, and she blurted, "So you want a bagel?"

Lila rolled her eyes and walked away. "Bye, Cobie."

Cobie shrugged, trying not to let the dismissal bother her. She'd just stood up to Lila for the first time, and she'd won. She would trade the bagels for badassery every time.

Lila sighed and grabbed the lined paper off her Steinway. Snatching up a pencil, she set to work erasing the entire chord sequence she'd spent the last half hour constructing. She'd been holed up all day in the studio working.

Working.

Not hiding.

Maybe hiding a little bit, but dwelling on that would make her angry all over again, so she didn't. Instead she'd chalked her lack of progress up to needing a change in scenery. Her move from the studio to the living room, however, hadn't done much to stir her musical mojo. Then again, maybe she didn't have any mojo of any kind. She'd certainly let Cobie steamroll her this morning. Her face flamed at the embarrassment associated with the memory. She lost complete control in the face of Cobie's defiance. Hell, she'd lost it the minute she heard the front door open and realized Cobie had left without telling anyone. Fear gave way to frustration as old memories threatened, which, in turn, sparked the anger. By the time Cobie waltzed back in with the stupid bagels and her sexy new haircut and that cocky smile and—the pencil cracked in her grip, and she set it back down gently.

Turning to the piano, she played a few keys in haphazard order. She may as well chicken-peck at random than keep up the trends of the day. She closed her eyes and started hitting notes aimlessly. They didn't grow any more coherent as she went, but they did get louder until she hammered the keys with enough force to make the whole piano vibrate under her fingers. The exercise wasn't productive, but the release felt cathartic, so she kept it up for a few minutes before someone cleared their voice.

"Shit," she muttered as she opened her eyes and saw Cobie leaning up against the doorjamb across the room. She still wore all black, a choice that would have seemed maudlin on anyone else, but with a twinge of irritation, Lila had to concede it worked. Maybe that bothered her a little bit too. Cobie hadn't needed her help today. Not with the clothes, not with the press, and not with locating her backbone.

Lila ignored her and turned back to her notes. She had half a verse and the start of a chorus. Maybe if she finished the lyrics, the music would follow.

Cobie didn't seem to get the message that she didn't want her there, or perhaps she did but didn't care. Wasn't that the point of their argument? Cobie was going to do what Cobie wanted to do, and apparently right now Cobie wanted to hover over her.

She leaned against the piano and glanced over the discarded drafts before walking around to see the one Lila currently had propped up on the music stand. Lila felt like a child being graded on her work, and she lashed out in kind.

"Are you here to apologize for earlier?"

Cobie laughed lightly. "No. I stand by my statements."

"Then what are you doing?"

"I thought maybe my statements could use a little clarification."

"I think you made your feelings clear."

Cobie smiled again, maddeningly. "Good, but now I thought I could tell you it's not because I don't appreciate your help or your input. I do, but I also believe I know Vale's character better than almost anyone in the world. I know her intimately."

She arched an eyebrow. "Intimately?"

Cobie's cheeks flushed. "I mean in depth."

Lila turned back to her piano keys, softly tapping a few, not sure she believed her.

"I'm dedicated to my craft, Lila. And I'm dedicated to what we're doing together to further my career. I know it may not seem so all the time, because it's harder for me, but I'm every bit as invested as you are. Maybe more so."

She pressed her lips tightly together.

"I didn't mean that as a cut down," Cobie quickly amended. "I only meant you've done this sort of thing before. I'm one of many chances you get to play the part you want, but I might have only one shot at this character. I have to stick the landing right here, right now."

"Why?"

"Because if I don't, they might give the part to someone else, or they might not make the movie at all."

Lila finally looked up, noticing a hint of pleading in Cobie's eyes. "No, I mean why this movie? There will be other films. What's the end game? What are you going to do with your newfound fame, or does this character matter more than the rest?"

Cobie's jaw twitched and she looked away. "It's hard to explain."

"Try."

"It's just, I can't." She shook her head. "It's personal, okay."

Curiosity tried to claw its way through Lila's determination to stay distant, but she refused to beg her for information. Doing so would give Cobie the upper hand in the conversation. Perhaps more importantly, if she pushed too hard she might actually get her answer. The hard set of Cobie's jaw and the far-away look in her eyes suggested she'd stepped into something deeper than pure ambition, and she didn't really want to unearth anything that might make her feel too much. She'd already come too close to doing so earlier that day, and she hadn't enjoyed it. Raw emotions could undermine both her resolve and her self-preservation tactics. Not to mention Cobie's newfound confidence didn't do anything to help her stay focused on being angry. It was maddeningly attractive.

She gave the piano keys her full attention once more, hoping that even if she couldn't compose a song right now, the distraction could at least help her compose herself. Cobie didn't take the hint and instead sat down on the bench beside her. Lila immediately scooted over, not wanting to be close enough to feel the heat radiating off her or smell the familiar fragrance of her own shampoo on Cobie's hair. Then she realized that making room for Cobie might have seemed like a welcoming gesture.

Damn it. Why was she second-guessing everything? She hardly even recognized herself.

"Are you stuck?" Cobie whispered.

"No," she snapped, but as Cobie waited patiently for her to elaborate, she wavered. "Maybe."

"What's the song about?"

"It's a female empowerment anthem."

Cobie nodded. "You're good at those."

She smiled slightly, enjoying the compliment more than she should. She didn't need anyone else's affirmation, which was kind of the point of the song.

"Play me up to the last line you have?"

The mix between statement and question kept her from completely rebelling and pushing Cobie off the bench, but she still took a deep breath to calm herself before playing through the opening and giving voice to the first verse. "We all play the same game, even though we're all dealt different hands. It doesn't mean we can't work together . . ." The words and the music both faded out.

Cobie's brow furrowed, and she frowned for a second before snapping her fingers and saying, "Take a better stand?"

Lila raised her eyebrows but knew better than to argue during the creative process. She played the line again, this time adding in Corey's contribution. "Not terrible."

"I'll take that as compliment coming from such an accomplished songstress."

"Might be beginner's luck," Lila said, but the grudgingness

she'd meant to put in her voice didn't quite come through. "Try another?"

Cobie nodded, her dark eyes serious. "Sure."

"No one else gets to judge, it doesn't matter how they rate, because you're the one and that's all I have," Lila sang.

Cobie laughed this time. "Tough one. Play it again, please?"

She obliged without a second thought this time.

"That's kind of hard. I have a word that works with the rhyme, but not the line leading into it."

"Lay it on me, I'm writing in pencil here."

"You could pair 'rate' with 'validate.' It rhymes and it fits the theme, but—"

"No, that's not hard to rework." She grabbed her cracked pencil and made a few corrections. "No one else gets to judge, because it doesn't matter how you rate. You only need you to validate."

"Sounds like you've found your way again."

"Actually, I think *you* found my title."

"Yeah?"

Lila scrawled across the top of the page in a strong bold script and held it up for Cobie to see. It simply read, "Validate."

"Well, look at me making a contribution. I guess I'm not a total waste of air in this household."

Lila sighed. "You're not. You're already earning your keep, but now I guess you also earned a songwriting credit."

"Oh no." She shook her head. "I didn't do anything but piggyback off what you started, and you started in a very good place."

"Doesn't matter. That's how collaboration works. We don't all have to start in the same place, we just have to work toward the same goal."

"Sounds like the song you're writing. Do you really believe it?"

"I do," Lila said quickly. "I never write or record a song I don't believe in. I sing the truth. Always."

Cobie nodded as if trying to process the statement.

"You don't believe me?"

"I'm trying to. I'm running through your songs I know in my mind. I guess it's true."

"You guess?" Lila asked, getting defensive again.

"I'm sorry. I didn't mean to imply you were lying. You just caught me off guard after all your talk about marketing and working a career plan to get what you want. I sort of assumed you just did what the trends dictated."

"Just because I'm acutely aware of my career goals doesn't mean I sacrificed my soul for them," she said sharply. "I like a variety of music. I write a variety of music. I'm not someone who is defined by genres or labels. There are lots of good true parts of myself, and yes, I emphasize certain parts at different times and to different audiences, but that doesn't make the feeling behind them any less real."

Cobie held up her hand in surrender, but Lila was on a roll now, finally feeling the stability she'd lacked earlier this morning. "No one would ever say that because you took a different kind of movie role you had fundamentally changed who you are. No one accused you of being straight because you kissed some boy on screen after coming out."

"No, they didn't," Cobie agreed.

"Hell, you could play a murderer on TV, and no one would actually think you're a killer. They would say you did your job, and I'm sure they'd think you were doing it well if you could adapt to changing characters and still maintain a high level of craft. I can take meaningful lyrics and powerful messages and put them into a medium that will get them to a wide audience of people who really need to hear them."

"Lila," Cobie whispered.

"Why is it that when you change your look and your style and your public image to better do your job, you're dedicated, and when I do the musical equivalent, I'm a sell-out?"

"Lila," Cobie said louder.

"What?" she practically shouted.

"I said, I agree with you."

She shook her head, but Cobie reached up, tenderly taking Lila's face in her soft hands. "Look at me."

She didn't really have a choice. She'd frozen at the touch.

"I'm not arguing with you. I agree. You're smart and talented and business savvy. You should write the songs you feel compelled to write, any way you see fit to write them."

"I do," she whispered.

"And you do it well. I didn't mean to imply otherwise. It's just hard for me sometimes to tell what you're really thinking or feeling."

"Why does it matter?"

"Professionally, it doesn't," Cobie admitted, letting one hand fall away, but she used the other to stroke a thumb along her cheek in the most heartwrenchingly intimate way. "But on a more personal level, I want to know."

"Why?" She hated the quaver in her voice, but she couldn't seem to control any part of her reaction right now.

"Maybe I'm a glutton for punishment. Or maybe I'm just a softy who can't stand to have a beautiful woman mad at me." She smiled broadly. "Or maybe, like it or not, I actually care about you."

She shook her head. "You shouldn't."

"Probably not, but honestly, we've already done a lot of things we shouldn't. I shouldn't be pretending to date someone I'm not. I shouldn't manipulate the public to advance my career. I shouldn't have lied to friends and family. Hell, I probably shouldn't be touching you right now. There's a whole lot of shouldn'ts in my life at the moment. What's one more really going to matter?"

Lila kissed her.

She didn't think about why beforehand, and once she got started, she didn't care about her reasons. Cobie's mouth became reason enough, soft and firm all at once because her shock never had a chance against her instincts. They had gone through the motions so many times. Their bodies held a familiarity that felt discordant with the sense of newness, of awakening, of exhilaration surging through her now as their lips parted, offering access previously denied.

For her part, Cobie didn't merely keep pace with the changes occurring between them. She pushed forward, her tentativeness from earlier encounters nowhere to be found as she worked her fingers in the hair at the back of Lila's head. She urged her forward and encouraged exploration neither of them had dared to seek before. Tongues tangled and breath traded hotly between them. Was it all the talk of doing what they wanted, what they believed best, or was it merely their heightened sense of passion that gave them the freedom to greedily reach for more? Lila couldn't give the question more than a fleeting thought, because Cobie's other hand was at her side now, playing a teasing set of feather touches across her ribs, the way Lila might coax the sounds she sought from the piano.

God, had Cobie always been this good? Could she have felt like this all along? Had Lila merely overlooked these skills the way she'd underestimated her in so many ways, or was sexuality just another of the many areas where Cobie had come into her own lately? Either way, she had never kissed her this way in the past. Maybe no one had ever kissed Lila this way.

Cobie slipped her hand down Lila's back, urging her forward until their chests brushed together with each ragged intake of breath. She ran her tongue along Lila's lower lip, then followed the sensual caress with a possessive nip of her teeth.

Nope, no maybe about it, she had definitely never been kissed like this before. The thought both terrified and thrilled her. She didn't want to stay, but she didn't want to run away either, which left only one choice. She charged forward.

Taking the hem of Cobie's shirt blindly between her fingers, she pulled it roughly up and off. They broke the kiss long enough for Lila to discard the barrier. Cobie never spoke a word, but her dark eyes opened wide, filled with questions Lila had never seen in a lover before. There was pleading laced with desire even as it sought permission. Lila tore herself away from the intensity of her stare and let her own gaze rake over the bare skin of Cobie's beautiful form, from the soft swells of her breasts encased in a simple black bra to the hard ridges of her abs and the subtle curves of uniquely feminine strength along her waist and hips.

"I want..." Lila started the sentence before she'd thought what would follow. What did she want? To touch Cobie? To be touched by her? Did she want some declaration? Some affirmation? Some sign she wasn't the only one burning with this mind-melting desire? Or simply to surrender to it all?

"Yes," Cobie finally whispered.

"What?" She blinked, trying to clear the red tinge of lust from her vision.

Cobie cupped her face once more. "It doesn't matter what the question is. My answer is yes."

Lila closed her eyes and kissed her again, searingly, as if she'd picked up where they'd left off, then cranked the volume up several more notches. Every remaining doubt faded, or was at least overcome by a more pressing pulse, one that started in her chest and pounded out through her limbs. Cobie deftly unbuttoned her shirt, and Lila reveled in the heat of her hands through the thin fabric, the urgency building between them until the last one fell open.

Cobie tore her mouth away to kiss a line down her neck and across her shoulder, pushing away the shirt as she went until it slipped down her arms and to the floor. Then Cobie kissed her way along her collarbone. She took her time, painting Lila's skin with her lips, imprinting it with the stamp of her mouth. She never wanted her to move, and yet she wanted her everywhere. Her senses burned with the need to be claimed and consumed, ravaged and ravished.

Cobie unlatched Lila's bra, once again looking up, her dark eyes seeking permission before she lowered another defense.

Lila nodded, almost frantic to have the heat of Cobie's mouth there. "Please."

Cobie complied and let the barrier fall, but before replacing it with her mouth as Lila so desperately craved, she instead took her hand and urged her up.

"You're beautiful," Cobie whispered. Kissing her briefly again, she added, "But you know that."

Lila smiled, feeling something akin to shyness. "I didn't know you'd noticed."

"I have," Cobie said seriously. "I want you very much right now, but I need to know you feel the same. I need to know you want this too."

"Really?" Lila asked, both amused and mystified. No one had ever stopped this far in to ask such a thing of her.

"Yes," Cobie said.

She caught hold of a belt loop on Cobie's pants and pulled it forward. "I thought I'd made myself clear."

Cobie nipped her ear lobe. "I want you, Lila. I want to make love to you until you can't see, can't move, can't think."

A shudder raced through her body as the words washed over her.

"But I won't take something that's not being offered."

She nodded.

Cobie sucked hard on her neck and practically growled. "Say it."

"I want you," she said in a rush of heat as she clawed her fingernails across her flat stomach. "God, Cobie, I want you so much I can't stand it. Don't make me wait."

It was as if giving voice to the desire brought it more fully to life, but no matter what had conjured the need, Cobie was the one to fill it. No, she exceeded it.

With one arm around Lila's waist, she guided her steadily while they kissed until the back of her knees hit the large soft ottoman. If not for Cobie's commanding hold on her body, she would have toppled over. As it was, she stayed upright only long enough for Cobie to peel her jeans over her hips, then she laid her down gently before stripping them all the way off. She kissed her way up Lila's leg until she reached the final silk barrier between them. Hooking a finger in the waistband, she waited for Lila to arch up so she could pull them away.

Her hips rocked forward of their own will, but even as she felt the cool rush of air against the heat building at her center, Lila was seized with an impulse she rarely felt. ==Perhaps physical vulnerability at Cobie's hands inspired a willingness for emotional vulnerability, or maybe Cobie had just wrecked her==

==usual defenses enough to allow for a disconcerting bout of openness==, but she whispered. "Cobie, I've never been with a woman before."

Cobie smiled, sexy and taut as she crawled up along her body. "It's okay. I have."

The shot of bravado should have annoyed her. Instead, she caught hold of Cobie's hips and pulled her down hard. "Show me."

Cobie lowered her head and set to work doing the most amazing things with her mouth, down her neck, across her breasts, along her rib cage. Lila's skin burned everywhere she kissed, and she writhed beneath her, desperate for more, until the moment Cobie's lips closed around her need.

She bucked up hard as the sensations overwhelmed her, twisting through her body and incinerating her mind. She was both covered and filled with Cobie, who played and coaxed with each press of her fingers or stroke of her tongue. She called out, but the words blurred together like her vision, as though need of this magnitude had no coherent language. She sank one hand into the plush fabric of the ottoman, trying to hold herself anchored, while the other clutched tightly at the back of Cobie's head, urging her to send them both toppling over the edge. The two instincts warred within her, the one to hold tight and the one to let go.

Cobie apparently had no such conflict. She remained relentless in her pursuit of Lila's pleasure through the proof of her own skill. In her fevered thoughts, Lila fervently vowed to herself and any higher powers who might listen she would never underestimate this woman again if only she'd keep doing whatever amazing thing she was doing with her mouth. Then, as if her prayer had been answered or the ante upped, Cobie pushed inside her, and another of the cords tethering her to reality snapped.

A million lights flashed behind her eyes as every muscle coiled and pulsed. Her hips, legs, and back all arched off the ottoman, and air fled her lungs in the most exquisite rush. Then everything crashed back into a thrumming tangle of limbs and nerve endings. Aftershocks raced along her spine, contracting and shattering every connected muscle group. Still, Cobie refused to stop until she'd pulled every last bit of energy she had, leaving Lila completely spent beneath her.

Crawling up beside her, Cobie curled into the crook of her neck and kissed Lila softly on the cheek before whispering, "Thank you."

Lila had the wherewithal only to wonder what Cobie could possibly be thanking her for when it seemed like the opposite was much more warranted. Cobie had been kind, attentive, respectful, skilled, and a million other delicious things that left her mind and body whirring. She should say so, or at least offer something in return, and she intended to as soon as she closed her eyes for just a moment to gather her wits and her strength once more.

Chapter Six

Two questions cycled repeatedly through her mind as she stood over the beautiful sleeping body curled up so serenely in her bed. The first was what the hell did we do, and the second was when can we do it again? There probably should have been a third, something along the lines of how can we undo this or what the hell can I do to mitigate this disaster, but ==Lila was too stunning in the early morning light to allow the darkness of regret to take hold.== Cobie surrendered to her own reckless will one more time and kissed her lightly on the temple.

Lila's eyelids fluttered at the contact but didn't open, and Cobie didn't know if she should be relieved or disappointed. She would have liked to have seen those baby blues fixed on her as they blinked away a night of contented sleep, but then again, she worried how they might shift as Lila realized she'd woken in Cobie's bed. Would she be grateful? Happy? Dreamy? Or would she distance herself? Perhaps she'd lash out or, worse, accuse Cobie of misreading or even taking advantage of the situation. She'd never know, at least not about Lila's initial reaction. By the time she got back from her meeting, the moment would have passed, and she didn't doubt she'd come back to find Lila fully dressed, fully poised, and in full defense mode.

She straightened up and quickly left the room before she freaked out at the prospect of Lila turning on her. She'd have to have her mini-meltdown on the way to work.

Malik waited for her in the front entryway, and a surge of guilt shot through her. Why? Because she'd slept with his friend? Because he didn't know? Or maybe he did, because Malik seemed to know a lot more than he ever said aloud. Did he judge her? Had he seen this happen before? Had he hoped for better? Probably not. She was likely pinning her own emotions on him because doing so was easier to deal with than turning the mirror on herself.

"Ready?" He finally asked as he held out a stainless steel go-cup, which from the smell held a strong serving of coffee.

She nodded. "Thank you."

He didn't speak any more as he led her out the door. There were no paparazzi as they got into the car this morning. Perhaps her staying there had become old news after only two days, or more likely, they didn't expect anyone to be up so early. Funny how her going to get bagels the day before had been downright scandalous, but sneaking out on the sleeping star in her bed didn't attract any attention. That was probably a good metaphor for her and Lila's entire relationship. Everything that tantalized the public interest was safe, and every mundane moment carried an underlying current of danger. Every scripted encounter dripping with sexual innuendo left her distant and disconnected, while a quiet evening off the clock ended with them having sex.

Cobie groaned, and Malik's eyes flicked to the rearview mirror, but he said nothing, leaving her twisting in her own thoughts. She had slept with Lila Wilder. No, even the idea of sleeping together left her off the hook. She'd had sex with Lila. And Lila had willingly come along for the ride. She didn't know which fact she found harder to believe.

At least Cobie was a lesbian. She'd clearly been the one to understand what was happening at all times last night. She'd done most of the driving, and why shouldn't she? She was physically attracted to Lila. Even now she felt the pull in her gut begging her to turn back toward the naked body in her bed, to kiss, to drink, to dive deeper into pleasure she'd denied herself for too long. But she couldn't be that person. She couldn't just take what her baser instincts demanded. Maybe in a full and equal relationship she would have kept Lila writhing beneath her for days, but what they shared had never been full or equal.

And yet, last night she had not been alone, and she did not suffer any power dynamic Lila maintained, which was probably why she found Lila's participation in the encounter so surprising. Perhaps participation was too clinical a word. Lila hadn't just come along as a passenger. She'd kissed Cobie first. She'd removed the first article of clothing. She'd practically begged for release. Lila Wilder did not beg for anything, and yet she had. For Cobie.

A surge of pride stirred in her, but she quickly tamped it down. She could not and would not see Lila as a conquest or something she'd used for the purpose of bolstering her confidence. Despite the new haircut and wardrobe, she wasn't Vale, some devil-may-care, morally ambiguous womanizer. She'd never done anything like this before. She was in uncharted territory, which wouldn't bother her so much if she felt like Lila could say the same. She didn't begrudge Lila any of her past lovers, but it did bother her to think that Lila would once again have the upper hand in their power dynamic because of her experience in similar situations.

She shook her head. She couldn't believe she was sitting in a town car with a bodyguard, obsessing over the power dynamics of a business deal because she'd slept with a woman she was fiercely attracted to. Those things shouldn't go together. Maybe they did for Lila, but not for her. She couldn't sleep with someone and pretend it didn't mean anything or, even worse, pretend it meant something it didn't. Her body, her emotions, they weren't about getting power plays or getting a movie role. Her sexuality wasn't for sale, not for Lila, not for Stan, not even for Talia. She'd compromised her morals as far as she could for this charade, but she couldn't have sex with someone to get ahead in her career.

It all seemed so simple when she put it that way, and yet last night hadn't been about work or the movie or even the charade. If it were about those things, at least then she'd know what to do, but she'd slept with Lila out of pure desire to do so. Desire was trickier, more complex, and less morally certain. Did what they'd done make a fake relationship a real one? Not exactly. Parts of it were still definitely for show, other parts were too real to be trusted, but now the two parts had intertwined in ways she couldn't always decipher. If she took Lila's hand in public, would it be because she wanted to or because the press wanted her to or because Lila wanted her to? And why would Lila want her to? Because she desired it or because she desired some benefit that might come from it later on? Could she ever know the answers to those questions? Could she live with herself if she went forward anyway?

"Would you like me to park in the garage or let you out at the front door?"

She jumped at the sound of Malik's voice. Looking around frantically, she realized they'd arrived in Times Square. How the hell had she missed Times Square?

"No," she whispered.

"Excuse me?" Malik asked.

She jumped again. She had to pull herself together. He'd asked her a question, one that needed more than a yes-or-no answer. "Sorry. You can just drop me here."

He pulled to the side, blocking traffic as horns blared around them. "Text me when you're done, and don't come out of the building until you see me pull up, okay?"

She didn't argue. His protectiveness was the least of her concerns right now. "Thank you."

She walked quickly through the lobby, refusing to make eye contact with anyone as she went. She couldn't handle small talk or autograph seekers right now. She had a meeting with her manager. A business meeting she needed to handle like a professional. Like the professional she'd felt like yesterday morning. A professional who was committed to giving her fauxmance with Lila everything she had in her. Her mind flashed to the memory of Lila, spread naked and open across the ottoman. Her stomach tightened and her face burned. Perhaps giving everything she had was a bit too much, and yet if the situation arose again, she didn't trust herself not to react the same way.

Thankfully, she was in the right place to put a stop to it. As she rode the elevator up to Levy and Levy, she realized she was once again on solid footing. Stan didn't care about her feelings. Stan didn't even know she had feelings. Stan knew business. Stan made deals happen. He also knew how to make them go away. She didn't know how, but that's what she paid him for. He found a way to get her into this mess. He could find a way to get her out.

She thought of Lila again, curled up in her bed, features serene and soft and vulnerable, but as the elevator doors opened, the rush of people and glint of glass jarred her back to reality. She and Lila weren't a couple. They were a business agreement.

The receptionist recognized her quickly this time and sprang from her desk. "Ms. Galloway, we've been expecting you."

Cobie followed her through the maze of hallways, feeling a sense of purpose growing in her as she settled on her plan to call the whole thing off. This was the right call. She would end the turmoil. She would protect her heart and her integrity. She would live with whatever fallout she needed to because it was the right thing to do.

"Cobie!" Stan boomed before she'd even gotten her foot in the door. "There's my girl. Sorry, I should say, 'There's the young woman of the hour,' because you're clearly not a kid anymore."

She froze at the threshold. Who was this man, and who did he think she was to greet her in such a way?

"What can we get you? Tea? Coffee? Coke? The drink or the drug." He laughed. "Just kidding, of course. We can do that now, right?"

"Sure." She nodded skeptically, then added, "More coffee, please."

The receptionist smiled brightly. "Of course, Ms. Galloway."

"You look fantastic by the way." Stan continued his lavish praise. "I can't even believe you're the same person who was in here a month ago."

"Yeah about that . . ." Cobie started, but his effusiveness had knocked her off-kilter.

"And the press. It's been phenomenal." He smoothed his eyebrows with his index fingers. "Even I'm impressed, and that's not easy to do. Can I tell you something honestly, just grown-up to grown-up here?"

She nodded again, not sure she liked the emphasis on the grown-up part. What did that even mean?

"I had my doubts, Cobie." He walked around the desk and leaned against the front of it. "I'm ashamed to admit, but even though I knew you had the acting talent, I didn't know if you had it in you to pull off a press push of this magnitude."

"Yeah, I sort of got that from you."

He hung his head so his chin touched the silken knot of his paisley print tie. "I'm sorry. Part of me still saw you as a kid, and I wanted to protect you. I hated the thought of you getting hurt. Part of me even worried you wouldn't be able to separate your personal feelings from your career goals."

She made a strangled little noise in the back of her throat, but he only laughed.

"I know, I know, I'm old-fashioned sometimes in ways Mimi isn't. I should've trusted you. You're smart. You think things through. You know what you want. I shouldn't have doubted your commitment or your ability to follow through."

She swallowed a ball of emotions. "Yeah, so about the career stuff."

He smiled broadly. "Okay, okay, I didn't mean to make you uncomfortable. We can stick to business from here on out, but I just wanted you to know I'm sorry for underestimating you. I promise things will be different from now on. If you can stay the course on this, you can chart your own course anywhere, and I'll let you make those decisions for yourself."

Holy hell, he was killing her here. How could she admit she'd fucked up after a speech like that? And still, she had fucked up. She hadn't stayed the course at all. She'd taken the ship and rammed it into the rocks. Maybe she did need a handler. The thought made her grimace. She didn't want to undo the progress she'd just made with him. Still, none of it would amount to anything if she fell apart. She could still get out. If she continued down this path, God only knew what would happen, but if she called it off now before there was real damage to any of their careers, only her ego would suffer.

"Stan, I need to talk to you seriously about where this is headed."

"Of course, of course. Less talk, more action. Which is why I asked you to come in today. You've got an offer on the table."

"A what?"

"It's not a leading role, which I know is probably disappointing, and it's not as dark as *Vigilant*, but it's a major leap in the right direction."

Her interest momentarily overwhelmed her initial intent. "What's the part?"

"It's a hero film, not one of the big ones, but it has a sizable budget and the possibility of a spin-off."

"You said I'd be supporting?"

"Yes, they want you for the role of the villain's sidekick. You'd get to kick people and shoot guns and make a lot of sarcastic comments."

"Like Robin, but evil?"

"Yes!"

Her heart beat faster. God, that sounded fun.

"It's a big step for you, maybe not as big as you'd hoped, but—"

"No, I get it," Cobie agreed. "It's a major shift. I appreciate your seeking it out for me."

He grinned like a giddy kid. "I'd love to take credit, but they came to me. They don't even want you to read. It's an offer."

Cobie sank into one of his uncomfortable chairs. "They asked for me just straight up?"

"Well, not straight up. I think the high-profile lesbian relationship helped with your appeal."

Her stomach roiled. "Right." Of course it did. Of course today had to be the first morning where she saw tangible benefits from what she and Lila had done. Then again, she'd seen significant physical evidence of what she and Lila had built together last night. Why did those two things have to be in opposition?

"They had another actress slated for the role, but she had to go to rehab. It's a short shoot, and your character would only be in a handful of scenes, so you can catch up. I don't think you'd be on location for more than two weeks. The shoot is in New York, by the way."

She nodded. Everything was perfect, everything was easy, everything pointed to this being the right call. She'd be lying to herself if she said she didn't care about being wanted and having strong, fun, creative roles thrown into her lap. And yet that didn't happen by accident, and it didn't happen because of who she was as an actress. She'd gotten the opportunity to play someone shady only by becoming someone shady.

"I don't want to push you," Stan said, concern now creeping into his voice. "I'm just not sure why you wouldn't jump at this role."

"No, you're right. I should. It's everything I've worked for."

"But?"

"But nothing." She stood quickly. "It sounds like a good job."

"It is," he assured her, "and I know you're up for whatever they throw at you."

She appreciated the vote of confidence, at least intellectually. She'd waited a long time to hear something like that from him. Only, for the first time ever, she wasn't sure she deserved it. She couldn't shake the sick feeling in the pit of her stomach that said she would let him down, that she'd let them all down if she hadn't already, but bailing today wasn't an option. She might not want to deal with what she wrought last night, but Stan was right about one thing, she was a grown-up now. She couldn't pawn her decisions off on anyone else.

"Make the deal," she finally said. "I'll be in touch about the details later."

"That's it?" He sounded like he'd expected more of a fight, or perhaps more direction. "No money conditions or contract riders?"

She shrugged. "I trust you to do your job the same way you trust me to do mine. That's how this works from now on."

"Thank you, Cobie," he said so sincerely she had to at least attempt to return his smile. "That means a lot to me."

Someday it would probably mean a lot to her too. Hell, today it probably meant a great many things she'd have to sort out on the way back to Lila's, but for right now, all it really meant was she had to figure out what to say to the woman in her bed.

Lila sighed dreamily and reached out for Cobie before she even opened her eyes, but her fingertips sank into cool sheets. Her sleepy muscles tightened. Cobie wasn't there and hadn't been for some time. She blinked against the harsh morning light streaming through the windows and moved through a set of rapid observations from big to small. Cobie wasn't in the room, her watch and rings were gone from the bed stand, her shoes were no longer on the floor. She hadn't just gone downstairs, she'd gone. Lila's heart rate spiked as bile rose in her throat. Cobie had sneaked out on her. She'd gotten whatever she wanted—the fame, the conquest, the bragging rights—and then left without so much as telling her. She'd pretended she cared, then left her just like—

She stopped the thought before it even fully formed. No, this was nothing like that. No betrayal could compare to Selena. She wouldn't let it. She'd allowed Cobie to get close, but not that close. Still, the realization of how much she wanted her to be different, how much she'd believed her to be different, caused her head to spin.

She fought the urge to flop back onto the bed and pull the covers over her head. Throwing back the blankets, she looked around for something to put on, suddenly hyperaware of her nakedness. She didn't have to search long. Cobie had neatly folded her clothes and placed them on the end of the bed. She supposed she should be grateful for that level of consideration, but it only made her angrier because Cobie had stopped to think about what she was doing and continued to do it.

She pulled on the outfit Cobie had taken off her hours earlier and threw open the bedroom door, then screamed as she came face to face with Felipe.

"Ah ha!" he shouted. "You did sleep with her!"

She tried desperately to cover his mouth, but he jerked away, shouting, "Ew, God, yuck, did you wash your hands after you touched whatever you touch during girl sex?"

"Shut up," she whispered harshly.

"Calm down." He laughed. "We're the only ones in the house."

She stopped. "What? Where's Malik?"

Felipe rolled his eyes. "Was the sex so good it made you lose your memory? Cobie had some big meeting with Stan this morning, and you didn't want her to leave the house alone, so . . ."

A rush of relief surged through her and she sank onto the nearest couch.

"What?" Felipe asked, genuine concern seeping into his voice. "What's wrong?"

"Cobie had a meeting. A meeting I knew about. A meeting she'll come back from."

"And?"

"She didn't just run out on me."

"Oh, honey." He sat down beside her, pulling her close and kissing the top of her head. "I'm sorry. I didn't think you'd even worry about that."

"I shouldn't have," Lila said flatly.

"Because Cobie's not that person."

"No, because I'm not that person." She sighed. "Or at least I shouldn't be."

"There's nothing wrong with wanting the person you slept with to stick around in the morning."

"No, there's nothing wrong with wanting it, but there's a lot wrong with getting upset if it doesn't happen. There's a lot wrong with letting my emotions get invested, there's a lot wrong with giving her that kind of power just because we had great sex."

His eyes went wide with excitement once more. "O-M-G, so the sex was great?"

Lila sagged back against the couch and let the tingle of arousal race through her once more. "Amazing sex. Fantastic, earth shaking, all the things."

"All the things!" Felipe cheered.

"She's got skills," Lila admitted. "One very specific one involves using her tongue to—"

"Nope!" He covered his ears. "Too much. I like my lesbian sex to be vaguely titillating so I don't have to think about the details."

She laughed. "But the details were so good. The details are where Cobie set herself apart from her competition."

"Can she really do things a man can't do?"

She thought about the answer. "I suppose men could learn those skills, but in my experience, none of them have mastered them the way she has."

"So do you think this is, like, some lesbian awakening for you? Are you going to go full-on lezzer now, or are you just totally hot for Cobie specifically?"

She thought about the question for a moment, because it was a pretty big one with widespread implications. "I've never disliked sleeping with men. There've been some instances in which I quite enjoyed it."

He grinned wickedly. "I know, right?"

"You're not helping."

"Fine. Did you like sleeping with Cobie more than any of the men?"

"Yes," she answered without hesitation.

He raised his eyebrows. "Okay, well that's kind of a big deal."

"But what if I liked all women more than all men?"

"Are you attracted to any other women?"

"Sure, I can tell which ones are beautiful and which ones aren't for me."

He rolled his eyes. "I didn't ask if you were blind. I asked if you were, like, legit physically itching to go muff-diving with other women."

"I suppose I wouldn't rule it out, but I've never had any strong urges to before."

"No, honey, then the answer is no," he said seriously. "This isn't some random woman you happened to fall face first into. You have a thing for Cobie."

"I do have a thing for Cobie," she admitted. Saying the words aloud after so much time lying to herself and others felt like a heavy rock she hadn't realized was on her chest finally lifted. "She's just got something about her. A mix of power and vulnerability, and she cares, like legitimately cares about things, me included. And she's got this quiet competency. She doesn't need anyone else to tell her what she knows or what she's good at, and she's quite good at so many things."

He nudged her gently with his elbow. "Things like sex?"

"I meant things like dancing and singing and songwriting and reading people and, yes, kissing and sex too."

"And you haven't been able to break her down, which means she's strong-willed."

"I didn't think so at first, but I misread her. And she's only getting stronger. Her confidence last night was what did me in. I tried to push her away, and she didn't really push back, but she stood her ground." Lila shuddered at the memory of Cobie's dark eyes on her, at the heat of her body so close, at the silent certainty. "She doesn't need to stomp her feet and yell. She just holds steady."

"You haven't had a lot of steady in your life," he said softly, then playfully added, "other than me, of course."

"Yeah, you're a Rock of Gibraltar," she teased. "But I'm not sure I want steady."

"Because steady scares you?"

"No," she snapped, then shook her head. "Because steady isn't good for a career, not for a pop star. Steady equates to static, and static equals outdated."

"And outdated means dead."

"Exactly. My image isn't that of someone who settles down with the dependable Midwestern girl next door. That's the opposite of what I wanted to accomplish here. I want to be edgy and unpredictable and on the go at all times."

"But you're drawn to her. You had amazing sex with her, and she's an above-average human being, plus you have all the things sexually. That's kind of a big deal."

"I do like her in all the ways, and last night I acted on that. I'm not ashamed, and I don't regret it."

"Because you want what you want and you take it because feminism."

She laughed again. "Something like that, and it was a great moment. But I cannot make long-term decisions based on moments that will inevitably end."

"Is an ending inevitable?"

"Of course it is." She didn't even take time to consider any other possibility. "Everything that doesn't adapt ends. The only thing I can count on to last is me, myself, my dreams, and in order for that to happen, I have to stay in control."

"Yeah, so that's one take on it," he admitted.

"What's another take?"

"It's not really your career you're worried about hurting. It's your heart."

She scoffed. "You've been watching too many Hallmark movies."

"I like them. Don't take my joy, and don't change the subject, because you, of all people, can make your career work any way you want to. You don't follow the market. You shape it. You have all the control there. You don't have all the control with Cobie, and that's a lot harder for you to deal with."

"You're reading too much into this," she said, steadfastly refusing to acknowledge the ache in her chest. "I had great sex with someone I like. I've done so before without losing my head or throwing my livelihood away."

"But this sex was better, and quite frankly, the person is better too."

She threw up her hands. "I'm not sure the degree to which any of those things are true really matters, when—" She stopped short at the sound of the front door opening.

"Hello," Cobie called, her footsteps falling heavy on the front stairs. "Anyone up and about?"

"We're in the living room," Felipe called out casually.

"Which one?"

"Marco."

Cobie laughed. "Polo."

"Marco," Felipe said again.

"Polo," Cobie answered as she put her head through the doorway. "Oh hello."

"Good morning, Ms. Galloway," Felipe said with put-on formality. "I was just going to make some breakfast, and by that, I mean I intend to make Malik make breakfast. Would you like anything?"

"Maybe later," Cobie said, "thank you."

"Don't mention it." He rose and headed for the door. "Malik and I will be downstairs if you need us."

Lila turned to him, wide-eyed. He was leaving her? Alone with Cobie? After the conversation they'd just had? How uncharacteristically respectful of him. What was the point of living with a nosey drama queen if he left her alone when things actually got dramatic.

"Hi," Cobie said once he was out of earshot.

"Good morning," she said more calmly than she felt.

"Is it?" Cobie asked, almost shyly. "A good morning for you? 'Cause I really hoped it would be, but I had to leave before I could check in on that front. I kind of hoped I'd be back in time to do that properly."

"Is that why you didn't wake me before you left?"

"Yes," Cobie said quickly. "Also, you were sleeping really peacefully, and I didn't know if today would be kind of hard in the peaceful department, so I wanted to give you as much time as I could."

She nodded slowly, trying not to let the sweetness of the gesture weaken her resolve. "That was very considerate of you."

"Yeah, well." Cobie smiled. "Also, I'm kind of a big chicken, and I worried you might have some regrets this morning, and I didn't know how to deal with that."

Lila laughed at the unexpected bout of honesty. "Do you have regrets?"

"I probably should," Cobie said, "but I don't. Concerns, yes, so many of those. But regrets, not so much."

"I concur," Lila said, grateful for the opening. "I don't regret anything we did last night, but I also don't think it's a good idea to repeat it."

Cobie exhaled and sat down across from her. "I'm really glad to hear you say so."

"I enjoyed myself. I also enjoyed you quite a bit." She blushed at a slew of memories before pushing on. "But we've got a job to do together, and getting too emotional isn't wise."

"I agree," Cobie said earnestly.

"We're both at important crossroads careerwise. We really can't lose track of who we are right now, either as individuals or as public figures. That doesn't mean what we had wasn't amazing, because it was."

"Absolutely."

"I don't want to hurt your feelings or act like last night didn't mean anything, but it has to be a one-time thing."

"I'm totally with you."

Lila's eyes narrowed. "You are?"

"Yeah," Cobie said, relief evident in her voice. "Clearly I'm attracted to you. You're beautiful and smart and talented and passionate, but you're also a colleague. We're co-stars on our little publicity tour, and I don't sleep with co-stars."

Lila blinked a few times, trying to piece the picture back together. She'd been so certain she had to convince Cobie they couldn't be a real couple, she hadn't taken any time to consider Cobie might not want to be one. The realization stung more than it should have. Every logical part of her should have been relieved things wouldn't get messy or heartbreaking, but a little voice whispered maybe Cobie didn't want her as badly as it had seemed. What if she hadn't enjoyed last night as much as Lila, or what if she'd gotten what she'd wanted and lost interest?

"Lila, I'm sorry if I overstepped my bounds or pressured you in any way."

She waved off that concern quickly. "You didn't. I wanted everything that happened. I enjoyed everything immensely. It should go without saying, but I'll say it anyway: I am every bit as attracted to you as you are to me."

"That's pretty attracted," Cobie said with a smile that made Lila's heart kick-start again. "But we're also professionals, right?"

"Yes. We can admit to these feelings without acting on them. We have work to do, and we have to put our careers first."

"Good." Cobie placed a hand on each knee and pushed herself to standing. "Because I got offered a movie part today, and I think I have you to thank for that. Apparently, my new image overhaul is working. I want to stay focused."

"Of course," Lila said, noticing the shift away from personal to business. It's what she wanted, what she could depend on. Nothing else was meant to last. "Eyes on the prize. Congratulations."

"Thank you. For everything."

She forced a smile and nodded. "You're welcome."

"You coming down for breakfast?"

"Actually, will you have Felipe send mine to the studio? I've got a lot of work to do today."

"Sure," Cobie said, "busy day of songwriting ahead."

She took a second to process the comment. The work she'd alluded to wasn't so much musical as emotional. "Right, gotta get back to what I know."

Chapter Seven

"Am I really going to meet her tonight?" Emma squealed as Malik pulled off the expressway toward Toronto's entertainment district.

"No, sorry. I forgot to mention that you have to stay in the hotel by yourself while I go to the show, 'cause I'm super famous and you're not."

"Shut up," Emma said with laugher in her voice. "Malik, can you put my sister in the trunk and move my luggage up front? My luggage is nicer."

Malik smiled but didn't reply.

"Really, when do I get to meet Lila?"

"She had a meet-and-greet this afternoon." Cobie glanced at her watch. "Then she has a radio thing, but she might come back to the hotel room for a few minutes in between to say hi, but if you're super nice to me, I think I might score us two tickets to the after-party."

"The after-party," Emma said dreamily. "It sounds so glamorous. When did you get so glamorous?"

"What? I was born glamorous. I used up the whole glamour part of the gene pool before you came along. "

"Yeah right. Everyone knows Lila raised your stock like a million points. She's rubbing off on you."

Cobie laughed again but didn't argue. Lila had rubbed off on her in a myriad of ways. Some she liked, some she didn't, but the results couldn't be ignored. She'd signed the contract to play supervillain sidekick last week, and as word of the deal had leaked, more offers had come pouring in. Stan fielded calls about her playing an unwed teenage mother, a crime scene investigator, and a cop. None of them were high-profile lead roles, but the shift was on now, and she had to make sure she kept moving in the right direction. "I like to think I'm rubbing off on Lila. Just wait until tonight. I bet she puts on a great show, and I don't want to say I taught her everything she knows, but yeah, most of it."

"Stop with your lies." Emma laughed. "I want to know the real story. You've been dodging me on the phone for months. I'm going to meet her in, like, ten minutes. Give me a warning. What's she really like?"

Cobie shrugged. "She's just Lila. You read the news. You know."

"I only know what she's like on TV and Twitter."

"So there you go."

"You're nothing like you are in movies or on Twitter."

It was a fair point and one she was really glad Emma could make. Being able to recognize that what happened in the media wasn't always real would help her fight off some of the issues that often plagued teenage girls. Selfishly, she hoped it might also help her process the emotions when everything between Lila and Cobie came crashing down. And it would come crashing down, so she had to walk a fine line this weekend.

"We're here," Malik said as he pulled up behind the Renaissance Hotel attached to the Rogers Centre. Emma and Cobie hopped out and hustled toward a side entrance, successfully dodging the press.

"Please," Emma pleaded as they slipped into a staff elevator. "I've heard so many things, good and bad, about what Lila's really like in private. I want to know which is true so I can brace myself."

Cobie sighed. The truth was a sticky subject when it came to Lila. She still wasn't sure she herself understood what was real and what was for show, and she'd seen it all up close. "Everything you've heard is probably true. Or at least partly true."

"How can it all be true?"

"Because Lila's a complex woman. She's not some flat character no matter how much the press or advertisers or even she tries to pretend otherwise. She's smart and talented and powerful," Cobie said, trying to measure her words carefully, for Emma and for herself. "But she's also ambitious and controlling and has little tolerance for disagreement."

"Is she moody?"

Cobie smiled at the understatement. "At times, but she's also passionate and independent, and she's never mean for the sake of being mean. She's just sometimes driven to the point where she's blinded to other things. And those aren't bad qualities in a woman, no matter what some men may tell you. Those qualities made her who she is even if they don't always make her easy to live with."

Emma stopped and put her hand on Cobie's arm as they exited the elevator onto their executive floor. "But you're happy, right?"

Cobie's throat clogged with emotions she didn't realize she'd held at bay. How could she answer Emma honestly when she wasn't even sure she was being honest with herself? She wasn't unhappy with Lila, especially over the last two weeks. They'd fallen into a comfortably distant routine. They made regular outings to Tribeca and Hell's Kitchen to be seen as super sexy together and ultra-cool in general. At the house, they largely kept to their separate spaces, with Cobie rehearsing and Lila in her studio. Any meals or evening activities they shared also included Felipe and Malik. They were never alone together. And she was grateful for that, most of the time.

"Cobie." Emma's eyes started to water. "What's wrong?"

"Nothing." She shook her head and forced a smile.

"If you can't say you're happy with a woman you're living with, there's something wrong."

Her heart clenched at the concern in her little sister's voice.

She was supposed to worry about Emma, not the other way around. She opened the door to their suite. "It's fine. I'm happy. It's just a lot to juggle, and I worry about what you see in the press."

"I know not to read the tabloids."

"Good." She put a hand on her sister's brunette hair, the same color hers used to be. "But I know you're on Twitter and Insta, and you need to know those aren't always real either."

Emma shook off her hand. "Are you trying to tell me you don't really like her?"

"No," Cobie said quickly, partially out of preservation for the work she'd done and partially in honest defense of Lila. "I like Lila a lot, and more than that, I respect her. I want to be more like her in a lot of ways. She's been a true partner to me, especially over the last few weeks. She's taught me to be strong and to better advocate for what I want."

"Plus, she's hot," Emma said, bumping Cobie's shoulder with her own.

"So hot," Cobie said, then laughed. "Off the charts hot."

"Then what's the problem?"

"No problem," she said quickly. "I just don't want you to get too attached and start planning weddings or naming our unborn children, because . . . because . . . well we're . . ."

"Friends with benefits?"

Her face flamed. "No. Why do you even know that term? God, aren't you, like, seven?"

Emma rolled her eyes in a way that made it clear she was very much a teenager. "I know how these things work."

"How? How could you possibly?" She didn't even know herself.

"You guys are like a legit celebrity couple. You go out, you have fun, you get your picture taken, and—oh, my God, are we staying in a hotel room that overlooks the concert?"

Cobie laughed as she watched her sister take in the floor-to-ceiling windows that did, in fact, offer a panoramic view inside the Rogers Centre. "Yeah, see what I mean about her rubbing off on me."

Emma turned to her again, the wonder in her eyes tempered by a sisterly softness. "I love you, Corn Cobe. You know I don't care about all the other stuff, right? I just want you to be happy."

Cobie pulled her into a hug. "When did you get so grown-up, Goober?"

"Like forever ago."

Just then the main door opened and Lila strolled in several steps before halting as her eyes fell on their embrace. A shadow fell over her expression just a second before she forced a smile and exclaimed, "You must be Emma!"

Emma twirled out of her arms, eyes wide, mouth open, but she only managed to squeak out, "Hi."

"Hi," Lila returned, her smile melting from the practiced version to the genuine one that crinkled her blue eyes. "I've heard so much about you."

"And we were just talking about you," Cobie said. "Emma wanted to know if you were everything the press made you out to be, and I told her yes, one hundred percent true."

Lila laughed. "I'm afraid so. At least the most juicy bits."

"That's not exactly what we were talking about," Emma mumbled, her cheeks pink. "Cobie teases me."

"It's what big sisters do," Cobie said. "Right?"

Lila's expression tightened for the second time in one minute. Cobie had learned not to put much stock in her mood swings, but there was obviously something going on just below the surface. Emma didn't seem to notice though.

"My sister says she really likes you because you're smart and passionate and super hot."

Now it was Cobie's turn to blush, but Emma smiled innocently.

"Also all true," Lila agreed. "What else has your sister said about me?"

"Well," Emma took a deep breath as if preparing to unload, but Cobie covered her mouth.

"I said you were talented and important and very busy and had a show to get ready for."

"Oh, right. I'm sorry. I didn't mean to interrupt. I'm really excited about the show and going to the after-party." Emma said *after-party* as if she loved to hear the words roll out of her mouth, and Cobie relaxed again.

"I do need to go get changed, but I definitely want to make sure we get back to this conversation later," Lila said with a wink. "I also want to hear all the embarrassing stories about Cobie growing up, okay?"

Emma frowned slightly. "I'm not supposed to talk to people about family stuff. Cobie likes to keep her private life private."

"That I already know about her," Lila said, then with a hint more emotion added, "I think it's awesome you honor that. You're a good person, Emma, just like your sister."

"Do you really care about her?" Emma asked, all teenage star-struck wonder gone from her voice.

"Emma," Cobie whispered in gentle rebuke, but Lila waved her off.

"It's a good question. One I'm proud of you for asking, because it means you care about your sister more than you care about your own interests." Lila took Emma's hand in both of her own and for a second looked as if she might cry. Then she smiled and said, "Your sister is one of the finest people I've met in maybe ever. She knows who she is and who she wants to be, and she doesn't lose sight of that amid all the glitz and glitter. She respects herself, she treats other people with respect, and she commands their respect in return. She's kind and giving and compassionate. She always tries to take care of me even when I haven't given her credit. I don't make her life easy, Emma."

Emma smiled. "She mentioned that."

"I bet she did." Lila laughed. "And that's okay. I know I've put her through a lot. She hasn't made my life a cake-walk either at times, but she's made me happy plenty of times too, more than anyone else I've ever been with. So while I can't promise she and I will live happily ever after, I can honestly say I do care about your sister. I care about her very much, and nothing will change that, no matter what happens."

Emma threw her arms around Lila's neck and gushed, "I'm really happy to meet you."

Lila wrapped her arms around Emma a little less enthusiastically and rested her chin on the girl's shoulder, but her eyes stayed on Cobie, who stood frozen and heartsick. Either Lila had just lied to her little sister, in which case she was a much better actress than Cobie, or she'd meant every word she'd said. And while the intent mattered a great deal, it clearly didn't change the sense of sadness hovering around both of them at the thought of what was still to come.

"This was the best night of my whole life!" Emma exclaimed as they exited the elevator and Malik did a quick walkthrough of the area before letting them into the bi-level suite.

"I'm glad to hear that," Lila said, and she wasn't merely being polite. She liked having Emma there. She was a like a younger, more open version of Cobie. She didn't play her feelings as close to the vest, and she didn't have a well-developed internal filter, but she was kind, happy, and well-adjusted for a teenage girl. Though to be fair, she also seemed to take her cues from Cobie, who modeled good behavior. They had both been endlessly patient as Lila worked a room full of fans and radio execs all night. Even more, Cobie had managed to perfectly balance her roles as doting sister, infatuated girlfriend, and superstar on the rise, shifting easily between personas depending on who was nearby.

She shouldn't have been surprised, and maybe she wasn't really. Perhaps impressed was a better word. No matter what she threw at her in public, Cobie always managed to assess the situation quickly and adjust accordingly. Lila wondered if Emma would ever understand how hard her sister had to work to keep all the plates spinning this weekend. She sort of hoped she didn't. She liked having someone around who wasn't a cynic, or even a realist. Emma still had pyrotechnics from the show shining in her eyes as she surveyed the massive picture-windows overlooking the stadium.

"I can't believe you were just on that stage a few hours ago."

Lila nodded as she walked over to stand beside her. "Sometimes I can't believe it either."

"I do," Cobie said, joining them as they stared down at the roadies who were already busily breaking down the elaborate set. "It was so you. I don't know what I really expected, maybe that I'd feel disconnected from superstar you, but you were still like you are at home, even with thousands of people screaming for you."

She turned to Emma. "She's kidding. I don't strut around the house in sequined skirts and five-inch heels. I don't randomly burst into song either."

"Sometimes you sing when you're distracted," Cobie said, a hint of the teasing she'd lavished on Emma still evident in her voice. "But that's not what I meant. It's more subtle, like your smile or your gestures or the way you purse your lips when you're pretending to pout. I could still see *you*. I kept having these flashes of awareness, where I was like, 'Yeah, that's my girlfriend.'"

Lila eyed her over the top of Emma's head. It was the first time Cobie had used the term, at least in her presence, and while she hadn't expected it, she didn't hate it either. The pride in Cobie's voice didn't hurt. Just because Lila didn't need her affirmation didn't mean she didn't enjoy having it.

"That's the first time you've seen her perform?" Emma asked, sounding confused.

"Yeah, well, pop concerts aren't usually my scene, but I only made an exception for you."

"Yeah right," Emma scoffed. "I heard you singing along. You knew the songs, like, more than a few of them."

Lila threw back her head and laughed. "Busted."

Cobie feigned dismay. "How many times you gonna throw me under the bus tonight, Em-n-Em?"

"As many as it takes, Corn Cobe."

"Corn Cobe?" Lila was laughing so hard her cheeks hurt.

"Oh yeah, and Corn-a-cobia and Cobra and Co-Jack cheese."

"Lila, will you excuse us while I go smother my sister with a pillow?"

Emma ducked behind Lila, who put out her arms to create a human wall. "This kid is worth her weight in gold to me right now. Don't make me scream for Malik."

Cobie folded her arms across her chest and gave her the villainous stare she'd been practicing as of late. The smolder in her eyes was enough to cause a disconcerting flame to spark in Lila's core, but she stood her ground. She'd gotten very good at hiding her physical reactions to Cobie's more sultry expressions, even if she hadn't been able to completely forget the sight of her naked body hard and attentive above her own.

"Fine," Cobie finally said dramatically. "I'll let her live, but only until she gets her first boyfriend so I can embarrass her the same way."

Lila glanced over her shoulder and noticed Emma's cheeks had gone a bright shade of pink. "Cobie, something tells me you won't have to wait as long as you think."

"No, I've got a couple years at least," Cobie said, then faltered. "Em?"

Emma's blush deepened. "I wanted to tell you in person."

"Tell me what?"

"Remember how I went to the Christmas dance with Tommy Martin?"

"I remember how you said you went with a friend."

"Well, now we're more than friends."

"Since when?"

"Since we went to the movies two weeks ago and he held my hand."

"And?"

"And last weekend we went out for pizza and he kissed me goodnight."

All the color drained from Cobie's face, and Lila stepped closer, momentarily afraid she'd have to catch her when she passed out. "Hey, I think this is a couch conversation."

"Yeah," Cobie agreed as she slowly lowered herself down to the cushioned surface.

"Are you mad?" Emma asked.

"No," Cobie answered. "Of course not. I'm just surprised this happened as early as it did."

"I'm almost fifteen."

"Yeah, I'm surprised that happened as fast as it did too," Cobie admitted. "And I'm sad I wasn't there for you when you got home. I'm sad I didn't get to wait up for you and meet him at the door and give him my new villain's-apprentice stare. Mostly, though, I'm sad I didn't get to hear about it until a week later. You know you can always call me anytime you have something to talk about."

"I know. It's just not the same as talking in person," Emma said, sitting down beside her. "And I knew I was going to see you this weekend. And I'm here now. And I told you. It's not like it's earth-shattering."

"A first kiss is a big deal."

Something about the way Cobie said the words, so soft and caring, made Lila's heart twist. The memory of Cobie's lips on hers the first time caused her to lift her hand to her mouth. She hadn't understood then, or maybe she hadn't wanted to, but the look on Emma's face, her dreaminess in her eyes, the blush in her cheeks, the memory she'd cherish forever, that's what Cobie had offered her in the restaurant. Something tender, something thoughtful, something so much like Cobie herself that Lila couldn't even believe such a thing had existed then. Perhaps because she hadn't understood people like Cobie truly existed then.

"He's a nice guy," Emma said. "He didn't pressure me. He was sweet. So was the kiss."

"Good," Cobie said firmly, "'cause I have friends in high places and a lot of money to burn. If he ever so much as says a cross word to you, or about you—"

"Cobie!" Emma grabbed a pillow off the couch and used it as its name suggested by throwing it at her sister.

"I mean it, Em," Cobie said, her tone a little lighter. "I want the best for you, and I know it probably sounds corny, but you're special. You deserve to be around people who never let you forget that. Your first love is a big deal, but it's really easy for things to

178

get away from you. You do one thing to please him, then another and another, and they're all little things, but before you know it, you can lose track of what's for him and what's for you. From there it's not a long way to losing track of who you are."

Emma turned to Lila. "Do you see? Do you see why I didn't want to have this conversation on the phone?"

Lila laughed. "I'm starting to."

"Oh, come on." Cobie cut back in, but even she was laughing now. "You can't gang up on me. Especially you, Ms. Wilder. You're like teenage role-model extraordinaire. How many songs did you sing tonight about staying true to yourself?"

"A few," Lila admitted.

"And how many songs did you sing about loss and regret and boys."

"A few."

"And what about the time between songs when you told the girls in the audience never to settle for less than they deserved. That was a very good speech. I got goose bumps."

"You did?" Lila asked, surprised. She wouldn't have expected Cobie to take her so seriously, not after everything they'd done over the last few months. She would have thought Cobie considered her a fraud. And she supposed in some ways she was. She'd spent the last two weeks doing exactly what she'd told her audience not to do. She'd passed up a shot at something genuine, something exciting, affirming, and wonderful to appease some expectation she let the market set for her.

"I did too," Emma said.

"Wait. Why is it inspirational when Lila says those things and silly when I do?"

Emma laughed. "Because she's her. She's dated, like, everybody, and I haven't even met any of your girlfriends since Tal."

Cobie made a little squeak in her throat, and all the color drained from her complexion once more. Emma looked quickly from her sister to Lila and back again. What had she missed? The name? Tal? It didn't mean anything to Lila, but it clearly meant something to the two of them. Cobie looked like she might vomit, and Emma's expression suggested she might have accidently killed a puppy. Lila's curiosity was overshadowed by her need to soothe them both, and thankfully, she'd learned to dodge unpleasant topics like a pro. Playing oblivious was always a valid choice for a pretty blond.

"I think your sister is probably a much better relationship model than I am," Lila said. "I've kissed a lot of frogs and very few princes, and while I've never lost my head over any of them, I do have my fair share of regrets. How do you think I managed to write all those ballads?"

Emma's mouth quirked up a little like she wasn't sure if she was supposed to smile or not. The move reminded her of Cobie, and the kid worked her way a little deeper into Lila's heart. "The first time I met your sister, I thought she was a massive dweeb. Honestly, you should've seen what she was wearing, and she literally fell all over me."

"Did you?" Emma asked Cobie.

"I'm not sure I'd phrase it that way," she said warily, "but I suppose the fact was I did trip over her. Was there a point to this story?"

"The point is," Lila said, "your sister might not seem very cool at first glance, but she manages to be her own person, a good person, in a business that works hard to break women down and turn them into someone else. And that's actually really cool, so maybe you should listen to her."

"She might have a few good ideas about standing up to pressure. I guess I have to give her that, but I think she's punked you a little bit if you think she's cool."

Lila laughed. "Maybe I've just grown immune to her dorkiness after being around her for so long."

"Like if you have chicken pox you can't get them again because the virus is already in you."

"All right." Cobie grabbed Emma and pulled her into a headlock. "I'm sitting right here! No comparing me to viruses."

Emma squirmed away, her laugher once again light and easy. "Fine, you win, not on the cool part, but you're still my sister, so

I guess we have to have each other's backs no matter what. Sisters are forever."

The final words struck Lila like a lance to the chest. She had to steady herself against the back of the couch and stifled a gasp by faking a yawn.

"Oh, jeez," Emma said, looking over and seeming to notice her shaken state. "You look like you're about to crash."

Lila nodded. It's all she could do as she turned from one sister to the other.

"I bet the shows take a lot out of you," Emma said kindly, "and then all the people afterward."

"It's part of the job," Lila answered, and after making sure her voice didn't convey too much of her inner turmoil added, "but it does catch up to me eventually. Would you mind terribly if I went to bed?"

"Not at all," Emma said quickly. "You guys go ahead."

"You guys?" Cobie squeaked. "I'm going to stay in the room next door, with you."

"No, you're not. You're going to sleep with your girlfriend."

Both Lila and Cobie froze. Only their eyes moved back and forth from each other to Emma in a silent sort of questioning.

Emma finally laughed. "Do you guys think I'm a little kid or a prude?"

"No," they both answered.

"We get the gossip news in Illinois."

"Em, you're not supposed to watch that stuff."

"I don't, but you two are everywhere. The magazines are in the airport, at the doctor's office, the hair salon. I know you're living together. You really think I believe you sleep in separate rooms?"

Lila frowned. They did sleep in separate rooms, with only one exception, but of course no one would believe that, which was sort of the point. But she'd never stopped to consider that everyone included people like Emma. Real people with real emotions and real investments. She didn't have people like that in her life, and she hadn't stopped to consider the fact that Cobie did.

"Guys," Emma pleaded, "please don't treat me like a little kid."

Lila met Cobie's eyes, seeing the questions and concerns roiling there. How could they get out of this without hurting Emma's feelings or furthering the betrayal they'd already spent months perpetrating? Would telling her the truth now hurt her any less? If she believed that to be true, she'd do it without hesitation, but then everything else they'd said to her tonight would also feel like a lie, and it wasn't. She thought back to earlier, when Emma told her Cobie really liked her and she replied in kind. That was the truth. It might not be the whole truth, but it was their truth. She cared about Cobie, and Cobie cared about Emma. They couldn't undo what they'd done. They could only move forward with as much thought and caring as they could muster.

"She's right," Lila finally said. Cobie's head snapped up, her eyes wide and her mouth open as if she intended to protest. Lila didn't give her the chance. "She's respected us. We need to show her the same respect. She's not a child, and neither are we."

"Yeah, but—"

Lila held up her hand and turned to Emma. "We're three strong responsible women who care about each other very much." She turned to Cobie, looked her straight in the eye, and said, "There's nothing to be ashamed of or to apologize for when two people who respect each other want the same thing. Teaching her otherwise doesn't help anyone."

A muscle in Cobie's jaw twitched, but she nodded. "Okay, you're right. As usual."

"This sister of yours is very smart," Lila said to Emma exaggeratedly. "Or at least she knows when she's beat, and that's a kind of smarts too."

Cobie snorted. "A kind of smarts Lila hasn't developed yet."

"It's one I haven't had any chance to practice."

Emma rolled her eyes. "Yeah, and you two thought I wouldn't know you're sleeping together. Go bicker in your room so I can get some rest in mine."

"Are you sure you don't want to hang out more?" Cobie tried one more time.

"Goodnight, Cobie," Emma said resolutely and headed in one

direction while Lila took her cue and walked off in the other, with Cobie following reluctantly.

Lila shut the bedroom door, and the two of them stared awkwardly at each other.

"I'm sorry," Cobie finally said.

"There's nothing to apologize for."

"I wasn't prepared," Cobie said sadly. "In my mind, she's still a little kid who skins her knees on her bike and watches cartoons on TV. It all happened so fast. I didn't think things through."

Lila got the sense that Cobie wasn't only talking about tonight. She could hear the doubt in her voice, and after witnessing the close bond they shared, she suspected those concerns went deep. She wished she could help more. She didn't want to see Cobie suffer, and she didn't want to hurt Emma, but she didn't have answers for them. She didn't have any experience with the kind of relationship they had, at least not any experiences she'd want them to emulate, and she didn't have the emotional energy left in those areas to offer a cautionary tale. She could only say what she knew to be true. "Emma's a good kid, and you're a good sister. You'll be fine. Let's try to get some sleep."

"Right," Cobie said. "If you can spare a pillow, I can curl up on the floor."

"Don't be silly," Lila said. "It's a huge bed. We're both fully clothed adults, and we're both exhausted. I think we can be trusted to resist temptation for one night."

The corners of Cobie's mouth quirked up. "I don't know. I'm pretty irresistible."

Lila raked her tired gaze over Cobie, seeing not only her dark jeans and tight shirt, but also the memories of what lay beneath them. Thinking of Emma sleeping in the other bedroom, she gave a shudder. She had more than the physical enticing her. She also had powerful forces holding her back. She suspected it would be the latter that proved strongest.

⊗ ⊗ ⊗

Cobie must have fallen asleep. She didn't think she would with Lila's body so soft, warm, and tantalizing just across the sea of sheets, but as she stirred in the darkness, she found that sometime in the night the vast space between them had shrunk. Or, rather, disappeared.

Her eyes had yet to adjust to the darkness, but the warmth of Lila's breath caressed her cheek as the scent of orchids and amber filled her nose. Lila was dangerously close and restless. The sheets stirred with erratic movement, and fingers clutched at Cobie's sleeve.

"You can't." Murmured words floated through the night, followed by a string of incoherent mumblings.

"You said you wouldn't." Lila's voice grew louder. "You said. You promised."

Cobie sat up. "What?"

"You promised, Selena!"

"Promised Selena what?" Cobie was fully awake now, and the lights coming from the stadium were enough to illuminate Lila's pale form on the bed beside her. Her face contorted, full lips pressed thin.

"I can't," Lila whimpered, and Cobie realized she was dreaming. Lila's beautiful eyes were closed tightly against something she didn't want to see, but her effort was fruitless, as whatever phantom tortured her clearly lived on the inside.

The urge to protect was strong and swift. Cobie lay a hand on Lila's arm and whispered, "Shh, I'm right here."

"No," Lila begged. "Don't go."

"I'm not going anywhere," Cobie said a little more firmly. "I promise."

"Selena, I can't do it alone."

Selena? A friend? A lover? Whoever she was, Cobie hated her for whatever she'd done to cause such a strong woman to shiver and shake.

"Lila," Cobie said. She remembered reading once that you weren't supposed to wake people from nightmares. Supposedly doing so could cause something bad to happen, but something bad was already happening inside Lila, and the thought of watching her suffer was too much to bear. "You're dreaming. Wake up."

Lila jerked, her eyelids fluttering but not coming all the way open. "Selena?"

"No. It's Cobie."

Lila's chin quivered, and two big tears glistened along her white cheeks, reflecting in the dim light. The sight shattered Cobie's heart. She sank to the bed once more, only this time she didn't seek the distance she'd so adamantly imposed before. Wrapping an arm around Lila's waist, she pulled her close so their bodies spooned together tightly.

Lila's shoulders shook as she shed silent tears, and a piece of Cobie's heart dissolved with each one. She didn't know why Lila was hurting, but she was, and that's all the mattered in the moment. The desire to soothe her overrode every curiosity or instinct for self-preservation. She held Lila tightly to her, stroking her hair and kissing the top of her head while she whispered soft reassurances. "I've got you. You're safe. No one's going to hurt you now. I'm here."

After a long time the shudders subsided, and short shallow breaths gave way to a steadier rise and fall of her chest. For several moments, Cobie suspected Lila had fallen back into dreamless sleep, but she couldn't bring herself to let go. Something still didn't feel right. This clearly hadn't been a random night terror. Lila hadn't merely trembled. She'd called out a name. A woman's name. A million thoughts swirled through her, but she fought to slam the door on all of them. Tonight, for better or worse, she was the only woman in Lila's life. She was the woman in Lila's bed. She was the woman holding Lila in her arms. She kissed her shoulder lightly and snuggled closer.

"Cobie?" The sound of her name in the darkness would have startled her if Lila's voice hadn't sounded so small and raw.

"I'm right here."

Lila turned slowly in her embrace until they shared a single breath.

Cobie's body responded against her better instincts, but fighting her own heartbeat was useless. She gave into the urge to fall into Lila's shimmering eyes and imprint the memory of her body so supple and languid against her own.

"Thank you," Lila whispered.

She smiled. "My pleasure."

"You'd throw everything away right now if you could to protect Emma, wouldn't you?"

The question was so simple and yet so unexpected it hurt her heart. All she could do was nod.

"You won't have to," Lila said. "I promise."

The conversation felt surreal, the topic so disconnected from the press of their bodies. "I don't know what you're talking about."

"It's okay," Lila said. "I do."

Cobie didn't understand her, but she believed her. "You aren't alone."

Another tear escaped the corner of Lila's eye, and Cobie used her thumb to wipe it away, but as she drew back her hand, Lila caught it in her own. She brought the palm to her lips and kissed it. Cobie drew a heavy breath as a mix of emotions and sensations raced through her, each one trying to top the others. The urge to soothe battled with the urge to consume. She chose the better angel and shifted so her lips weren't so perilously close to Lila's. Placing a chaste kiss on her forehead, Cobie closed her eyes to the temptation stirring in her core. Lila, however, didn't share her fortitude, or perhaps she rejected the notion that she needed to be protected from the new tension building between them. Cupping Cobie's face in her hand, she tilted her chin until their lips were once again level and pressed forward.

The kiss was feather light and soft as a spring breeze. There could be no danger in anything so tender, or at least that's what Cobie told herself as she surrendered. Their mouths moved against each other slowly, exploring in ways they hadn't had the time or inclination to do before. Lila's lips were soft and searching, yielding and enticing. And soft. Had she already marveled at their softness? It was worth enjoying more than once. Lila's kiss was no longer that of a woman with something to prove or someone surrendered to reckless abandon. She kissed Cobie like a woman who wanted nothing more than to be right here, right now. She kissed her squarely on the mouth, then along the corners that tried to flex up in a smile. She kissed her lower lip, bringing it gently between her own, and then moved up to kiss the tip of her nose, her cheek, her eyebrow. She started a slow arc around her hairline to her temple to her earlobe, pausing there to whisper, "You feel so good."

"You," Cobie muttered against the smooth skin of Lila's cheek.

"I want you," Lila said, her voice low.

"I'm right here."

"I want you everywhere."

Cobie groaned and pressed her lips more fully to Lila, her muscles coiled tightly, ready to spring into action, to take, to meet, to fill every need until her tongue flicked across her own lips and the taste of salt brought her up short.

Tears.

Lila was still crying.

Slowly, softly, silently, but still hurting. All the lust drained from her veins, and the energy that had coursed through her seconds before disappeared with it. She couldn't do this.

"Lila." She breathed the name as if it were as essential to her as the air carrying it. "We can't."

"What?" Lila searched her eyes. "Why?"

"Because you're hurting, and I don't know why."

"You don't need to."

"You're right. I don't need to know. Not if I want to hold you. Not if I want to comfort you. Not if I want to protect you. I can do all those things right now, and I will, gladly. I promise I'll be here through tonight and as many nights as you want without ever knowing anything more than the fact that I care about you," Cobie explained, her voice trembling from the weight of the truth it carried. "But I can't make love to you without knowing it's for the right reasons."

Lila stiffened and started to sit up, struggling against Cobie's arms around her waist. "Who gets to decide what reasons are right?"

"You get to decide for you, but I get to decide for me. And I don't want to be a numbing agent or a moment of weakness. I don't want to be a regret."

She expected a fight, or at least a cold shoulder. She got the sense that no one told Lila Wilder no, especially in bed. Lila's eyes went wide, the pain now clearly visible there, but instead of wrenching away, she crumbled back onto the mattress, and resting her head on Cobie's chest, she began to sob.

Cobie held her tightly once more, rocking her lightly and kissing her hair. She didn't understand this pain. If she could have broken open her own chest and allowed Lila to crawl inside, she would have gladly borne her anguish, but she couldn't control it or even combat it. She could only stand witness while it poured itself out, shaking them both and soaking her shirt. She held her as close to her heart as she could, for as long as she could, knowing that even after the storm passed and Lila pulled away, a part of her would always remain imprinted there.

Chapter Eight

"So, she didn't sleep with you?" Malik asked softly as they drove through the streets of New York City. She sat beside him today, though she didn't know why, and he hadn't asked. He never did. Maybe that's why she found herself telling him things she didn't tell anyone else.

"She slept with me, but that's it. I mean that's not it. She held me all night. She kissed me. She promised she'd be there for me."

"That's a lot."

She sighed. "But it didn't lead to sex."

"Does it have to?"

"It always has in the past," Lila admitted. "I mean, not the whole crying thing. That was new, but the holding and tenderness and the empty promises."

"Why do you assume her promises are empty?"

"All the others' have been."

"But they always led to sex too."

She understood his point, but she didn't like it. Cobie wasn't like all the others. Somewhere deep inside she'd known that for a long time, maybe even from the beginning, but then again, she'd known that in the past too. She'd been so sure. She'd felt it with every fiber of her being only to be proven wrong. Nothing lasts forever.

"What did you tell her in the morning?"

"Nothing," Lila said, shame pricking her chest.

"Nothing?"

"I snuck out of bed. I couldn't face her. She was so perfect and strong and pure, and I wasn't any of those things. I was a coward. I hid behind Emma."

He didn't respond. He kept his eyes firmly on the road ahead, and she could feel his disappointment as keenly as her own. She knew Cobie deserved better. She'd known it even then as she'd ordered a lavish meal from room service and kept the conversation light, never allowing the two of them to be alone. Not that morning and not after they'd returned to New York. In the week since, she'd used Felipe and work and even the press as a buffer. Not that Cobie had pushed. Cobie never pushed. She just stood there, always present, always steady. Lila would have almost preferred an outburst or, at the least, the petty arguments they'd had before. She would have preferred bickering to the quiet reminders of her own cowardice.

"I think having Emma there set me off."

He nodded.

"I really haven't had the dreams for a long time."

He nodded again.

"I think it's just because Emma's at that age."

He didn't nod.

She sighed. "You think it's because of Cobie, don't you?"

"I didn't say that."

"She's different. I see it. You think the contrast should mean something to me?" she asked, then didn't wait for him to speak. He wouldn't. "Just because she's a good sister doesn't guarantee she'd be the same in a relationship."

"No."

"And just because she didn't want to sleep with me doesn't mean she's some sort of self-sacrificing saint."

"No."

"She's a very good actress."

He nodded again.

"Good sister, good person, good actress, I can't trust any of it.

I mean I could, but I don't have to. I don't want to. I'm doing fine, Malik. And Cobie, it's just . . . damn it."

He smiled, but not his big one. This one was more subdued, more sympathetic. "You're going to have to deal with Selena."

"I deal with Selena just fine, thank you. I deal with her to the tune of several thousand dollars a month."

"You know that's not what I mean." He pulled the car into the parking garage and put it in park.

She folded her arms across her chest and stared out the side window. Of course she knew.

"Girl, you go after what you want in every other area of your life. You bend the whole world to your will when it comes to your career. You build empires and topple kings. You call every shot in every area but this one." He laid his big palm softly on her shoulder and gave a gentle squeeze until she turned to face him. "If you let her keep you from trusting again, whether that's trusting yourself or trusting someone else, you're still beholden to her."

"I'm not. She's nothing but a bad memory."

"Then why can't you go after what you want with Cobie the way you go after everything else in your life?"

"I'm not sure what I want with Cobie."

His dark eyes regarded her sadly, so much like the ones she tried not to remember. "That's something only you can figure out. It's your choice, but until you make peace with where you've been, you're going to keep pulling her in and pushing her away, and you deserve better than momentary brushes with real connection."

"You mean she deserves better."

"That too."

She sighed and shook off his hand, then reaching for the door, swung it open.

"Lila," Malik said softly. "You got a lot of love in you. Sometimes denying that hurts worse than losing it."

Emotion clogged her throat to the point she couldn't speak. She merely gave him a curt nod and walked away.

She stalked through the halls of the hospital, ball cap tugged low, and ducked into the staff elevator. Pushing the button she wanted a little harder than necessary, she rubbed her hand and willed herself to settle down. She shouldn't be angry at Malik. She wasn't really. Maybe frustrated was a better term. He hadn't given her anything she hadn't asked for. And she'd opened that door because he was polite and insightful and sensitive. She shouldn't be frustrated with him for being exactly what she loved about him.

Love.

Why had he used that word? She hadn't said it herself. She didn't even feel it. Not toward Cobie, not toward Selena, not toward anyone. Sure, she cared. She had interests and passions. She was also deeply attracted to Cobie, and not just on a physical level.

The elevator opened, and she kept her head down as she strode through the hall, avoiding eye contact with patients and nurses alike. No one paid her any attention anyway. Their problems dwarfed any inner turmoil roiling through her now. Coming to a stop outside an open door, she peeked quietly inside to see a young woman sitting on the bed, frail and alone as she stared out the window, a single suitcase next to her on the bed.

"Addie?"

The girl turned slowly, her smile tired and wary but resilient. Her eyes sunken but shining. Her body beaten but not broken.

Lila's heart constricted in her chest as a rush of protective instinct clattered up against a wall of helplessness. Was that what love felt like? If so, then Malik was correct. She did have a lot of it in her, but she also had plenty of safer outlets for it than Cobie Galloway.

"Come on," Lila said. "Let's get you out of here."

Cobie rose from the massive glass conference table at Levy and Levy as the opaque glass door swung open to allow Malik to enter. She smiled at him, but he was in full work mode, noting her presence the same way he would a potted plant. Once his intense gaze had swept the room, he stepped aside for Lila to breeze in, followed by Felipe.

"Hey," Cobie said. "Where did you run off to before breakfast this morning?"

"I had some things to attend to." Lila sat beside her, crossing her legs in a way that made her already-tight maroon pants seem like a second skin.

"Things to attend to?" Cobie raised an eyebrow. "Vague."

"I told you I'd meet you here."

She glanced at her watch but didn't mention the fact that their agreed-upon meeting time had passed twenty minutes ago. Lila didn't usually do fashionably late when it came to business meetings, so one time wasn't worth fighting over. Then again, not much felt worth fighting over after Cobie had held her while she sobbed. Ever since then, their interactions had been limited to the short and tentative, and they never occurred in private. She'd considered pushing for more of an explanation or simply trying to check in on more than a surface level several times, but Lila had worked hard to never give her the chance.

Maybe that wasn't completely true. Lila had been evasive, and Cobie had willingly accepted the message. She didn't want to hurt her or embarrass her, and she certainly didn't want to go back to them bickering all the time, but if she'd wanted to, she could have tried a little harder to knock down the walls between them. The truth was she wasn't just worried about making Lila mad or triggering some unpleasant memories. She had concerns about her own emotional fortitude as well. It had been hard enough to resist Lila when their attraction had been purely physical. If she started feeling the need to protect her or comfort her or hold her through those long nights, she wasn't sure she could survive. So while she didn't really love being avoided, if the choice was polite distance or complete abandon, she supposed Lila had done her a favor by pulling away. Sure, she would have loved some middle ground, but when it came to Lila, there didn't seem to be any chance of doing anything halfway.

"Ladies," Stan called as he burst through the door with Mimi in tow. They were both dressed in pinstripes today. He wore classic navy with red accents, hers was cream and fuschia. "What a joy to have you both here at the same time."

"Come here," Mimi called as she skipped, her high heels giving happy little clicks across the floor as she went. "Can I hug you? I'm going to hug you. Both of you. Group hug!"

Cobie had barely gotten to her feet when Mimi caught her by the scruff of her shirt and pulled her in. She wrapped her arms around them both and did a happy dance, causing everyone to rock back and forth. Cobie sighed and extended her arms in resignation, which triggered a fleeting connection with the subtle curve of Lila's waist where her soft sweater had ridden up. Her fingers brushed along smooth skin, and the images that flashed though her mind sent Cobie stumbling back. She might have gone all the way to the ground if Stan hadn't caught her.

"Oh, that martial arts training hasn't completely entrenched any catlike reflexes yet, has it?" he asked, his smile big and artificially white as he steadied her.

"I guess not." Cobie took her seat again quickly in the hopes that no one would notice her blush. "But I had my initial read-through, and it went really well."

"Oh, right," Lila said as if remembering some important detail. "I forgot to ask. Did you read or act?"

Cobie grinned. "I acted the shit out of it."

"Way to own it, Meryl," Lila said with the broadest smile Cobie had seen from her in weeks.

Mimi and Stan exchanged a look of amusement, or was that concern? It was hard to tell with all the Botox they'd had injected into their brows and foreheads.

"You two are playing beautifully together," Stan said. "I already told Cobie, but it bears repeating, we're impressed with both of you. You've been consummate pros, and the press's reactions have gone beyond my wildest expectations."

"Hear hear." Mimi slapped a heavily jeweled hand on the glass tabletop with a metallic plink. "You've both upped your profile in what could've been really dry months for you. And Lila, you've cut your downtime between records in half. You're ready to start recording?"

"Mostly," Lila said, Cobie recognizing her show smile. "The major tracks can roll any day. Just working on the last song now."

"The love song?" Mimi asked with a frown. "We could pull in a different writer."

"No, no need." Lila's voice carried a forced casualness. "It's almost there. So much love, a hit for sure."

Cobie suspected Lila was lying but didn't know if she'd fibbed for Mimi's sake or her own. She didn't have long to ponder the question though, because Stan cut back in.

"How'd the costume fitting go last week, Cobie?"

"Great. I mean I can't eat for the next two weeks because everything's skin-tight leather, but the director seemed pleasantly surprised with the muscle tone I've built over the last few months."

"So I keep hearing," Stan said, "and yet I only see pictures of you in baggy pants and sweatshirts."

"That's my doing," Lila said. "We're still gunning for the Vale look, dark and ominous rather than sex kitten, but I can vouch for the muscle tone. It's there, and it's impressive."

Mimi and Stan's eyebrows shot up so far they managed to even wrinkle their plastic foreheads this time, but Cobie couldn't summon any more embarrassment through the wash of pleasure at Lila's unexpectedly sexual compliment. She found her muscles impressive? That little bit of information would have her walking on air all day.

Stan cleared his throat. "Sounds like everything is right on track for where we need it to be."

"Need it to be for what?" Cobie asked.

"We're halfway through the charade," Mimi said, pulling out her iPhone and tapping a few buttons. "It's time for your big number, the climax if you will."

Felipe snickered from the corner, but Cobie refused to look at him for fear she'd give too much away. "Climax?"

"The big show," Stan said. "Your most public appearance as a couple before we start to unravel the whole thing."

"Unravel. Right," Cobie said uneasily. Somehow, she'd gotten so focused on keeping everything together for the last few months, she hadn't let herself think about how they'd gleefully blow all their hard work to bits.

"We've got a plan," Mimi said, "and of course it's up to you, but we think it's a good one."

Lila didn't seem nearly as eager as she had in the first meeting. She sat back in her chair and quietly nodded, her eyes dull and tired. It hadn't escaped Cobie's notice that she seemed more content than ever to let Mimi and Stan drive this bus.

"We think you need to have a party, an exclusive bash," Mimi said.

"A costume party. Lots of famous friends, all of them dressed as their favorite literary character. Cobie, you obviously go as Vale and let everyone and their dog take selfies with you," Stan said. Turning to Lila, he added, "The highlight of the evening will be an intimate performance of one of your new songs."

"It'll be the event of the season," Mimi practically squealed. "Picture beautiful people, so much talent, lavish everything, and flashbulbs going off all over the place. You two will be super dramatic. You can even work up some tense dialogue and make sure you let people accidently overhear."

She put accidently in air quotes as if Cobie hadn't already understood the implications. She was supposed to invite a bunch of sharks into the pool with her, and then make sure she shed a little blood.

"Isn't it perfect?" Mimi asked in a tone that made it clear she expected the answer to be yes.

Lila nodded slowly. "Make it a fundraiser. Childhood literacy, LGBT library, elementary school funding. Something for kids or education to make the book costumes feel less contrived."

"And because raising money for kids is always a good idea," Cobie added.

"Of course," Stan said, making a few notes. "I'll research reputable organizations. But other than that, it's perfect, right?"

Lila turned to Cobie, clearly deferring to her, which, in its own way, was weird enough without taking into account that having a bunch of famous people and photographers all up in her personal business was generally Lila's bag and Cobie's complete nightmare.

And yet, she had no real argument. The plan was genius. She'd get to step into character for the whole world to see without ever having to sign any contracts. She could show everyone exactly what she wanted them to see, and she'd get to do so with Lila by her side. The last part probably shouldn't have mattered nearly as much as it did, but somewhere along the way, Lila had become as big a part of her character development process as anything else. It wouldn't feel right to debut Vale without her there. So sitting back, feeling more relaxed than she would have thought possible a few months ago, she said, "Yeah. Sure. Let's do this."

Chapter Nine

Lila switched off the sewing machine and held up her handiwork. It hadn't been easy to get the thick black canvas of the hood attached evenly to the stiff leather of the motorcycle jacket, but the end result had made the effort worthwhile. She wanted to be the one to make this happen. She wrote it off as being a control freak, but her sense of responsibility to Addie and her debt of gratitude to Cobie also played a role. Still, she chose to focus on the fun parts of getting to dress Cobie up like her own little hooded punk Barbie for a party.

Then there would be the hefty check for Addie, because Cobie wearing her design to the party would no doubt count as a business event. Lila had already set her up in a small apartment in a safe neighborhood and arranged for a transitional guardian to help her finish the emancipation process. The money she'd made off the concept would cover her share of the rent and feed her long enough to get her on her feet. The bonus of Cobie wearing the piece would keep her stable long enough to finish high school via the state online curriculum. If the party went as well as Stan and Mimi hoped, the outfit could even become a concept piece for a major blockbuster. Then Addie would have all kinds of doors open to her. She was getting a little ahead of herself, but she liked where the idea was headed.

"Hey, what you up to?"

Lila jumped so hard she hit her knee on the sewing table and dropped the jacket to the floor.

"Sorry. I didn't mean to scare you. I made noise coming up the stairs, and the door was open."

"You're fine," Lila said quickly. "I was just lost in thought. I didn't hear you."

"What are you working on that has you so engrossed?" Cobie bent over as if intending to pick up the jacket from the floor, but Lila kicked it out of the way and scooted her chair over to block it.

"Sorry." Cobie stepped back, brow furrowed. "I didn't mean to barge in."

"No, you didn't. It's nothing."

"Whatever you say." Cobie frowned and started to back away. "I just hadn't ever seen you in here before. I didn't even know you could sew."

"I learned as a kid."

"Oh yeah? Who taught you?"

"No one." Lila grimaced at her sharp tone but couldn't rein it in as quickly as usual. "I just picked it up."

"Right," Cobie said, sounding completely unconvinced. "I'll let you get back to whatever it is you don't want to tell me about."

"Have a good night," Lila managed to mumble to Cobie's back as she walked away.

God, what was wrong with her? She picked up the jacket and held it up. She fingered the leather, which was contoured enough to give a subtle hint of Cobie's feminine waist but firm enough to keep from being scintillating. She'd added a few scuffed-up skater-style plates down one arm from the shoulder to the elbow. She circled each one with her fingertips, enjoying the contrast between their rigidity and the supple give of the sleeves. Why hadn't she shown it to Cobie? She'd been right there. She'd wanted to talk. She'd reached out, again, like she'd tried to do so many times over the last two weeks. Cobie seemed so good about making the first overture. Why couldn't Lila accept gentle offers of simple connection?

Maybe because that's all Cobie offered. The first overture, the simple conversation, the initial contact, but what about the next step? Cobie never seemed to follow up anymore. She retreated at the slightest hesitation or pushback from Lila. The steadiness Lila had been drawn to had all but vanished, leaving her to wonder if Cobie really did want to connect or if she was merely being polite. Clearly, they'd crossed that line in the past. Maybe Cobie was afraid of doing so again. Perhaps that's why she ran anytime Lila offered her an excuse to do so.

The thought disappointed her. Cobie had seemed so strong as she held her. She hadn't taken the easy way that night. She hadn't accepted Lila's attempt to lead them both into physical oblivion. She had done and said all the right things, but what if she hadn't meant them? She'd promised to be there, to hold her, to protect her. Now she couldn't even trust her to stand firm in the face of a few socially awkward exchanges.

She shook her head and folded the jacket, setting it neatly on top of a pair of layered and patched cargo pants. She knew she wasn't being fair to Cobie, but she also knew better than to trust promises made in the moment. Everyone's first instinct was to offer soothing words or fleeting vows of solidarity, but when things got dark and hard and dangerous, people always chose their own self-interest. She did. How could she blame Cobie for feeling any different? She hadn't asked for anything other than a publicity boost, and honestly, she hadn't even really asked for that. She had no obligation to stand by Lila as she cried out in the night. Selena, at least, had legitimate reasons to stay—genuine connections, a past, a history—and none of them had meant anything in the end.

Selena.

How had she ended up there again? The dream? Her conversation with Malik? Or something deeper? Lila didn't like the way those memories had become intertwined with her and Cobie's current disconnect. She remembered Malik saying something about making peace and moving on. Maybe that's what she needed to do. At least the moving on part sounded good. The peace part did too when she thought about it. Peace didn't have to mean surrender. It could just mean coming to terms, right?

Right. She answered her own question with a fleeting thought for her own sanity as she snatched up the costume and padded down the hall.

She rapped lightly on Cobie's bedroom door, and it swung slowly open. "Hello? Cobie?"

She didn't get an answer, so she peeked her head inside just to be sure. The room was empty, the bed made, with a few items of clothing strewn across the comforter. She smiled, glad to see Cobie wasn't perfectly ordered all the time. She crept into the room and set the folded pants and jacket on the pillow, which still held the imprint of Cobie's head. She patted the gift lightly, smiling at the thought of Cobie finding it there later, and turned to go. She had her hand on the doorknob when Cobie's voice called her back.

She stopped. No, Cobie hadn't called out to her. She'd sung. A soft muffled sound at first, but it pulled Lila through the room to the bathroom door. Cobie's voice lifted in a familiar melody, accentuated by the beat of water against tile. Lila smiled as she leaned against the wall next to the door.

Cobie was singing in the shower. And not just any song either, one of Lila's. *Passions uncaged, fires burning, flame to the page.* She'd heard her lyrics covered by others before, but never had anyone made her own words sound so sexy. Cobie's voice thrummed low and raw, unpolished and yet compelling, or maybe that was Lila's own bias for the singer filtering in. The heat spread through her body as Cobie reached the chorus. Lila could picture the cloud of steam surrounding her as hot water sluiced over hard muscles. She shuddered at the mental image of Cobie's slick glistening skin, so taut and—God, what was she doing? Standing outside a bathroom door fantasizing about the naked woman inside? Who had she become?

She couldn't go down this path again. She had to regain her composure. She had to find some way to compartmentalize what she was feeling. She should leave, but where would she go? To her own room and obsess about Cobie and the feelings she didn't want her to inspire? It was too much. Cobie was too much. She could burn Lila up, just like the flames to the page she sang about. God, she'd never fully felt her own lyrics until she heard them against the drumbeat of water cascading over a perfect body.

No. She couldn't think of her as some temptation too close to resist. Cobie had to be a colleague. She had to get her the part. She had to think of her as a job. But God, if the producers only knew what they'd missed in this woman, Lila wouldn't be the only one drooling over her. Cobie offered the total package: smart, hot, talented. She was a fucking artistic goldmine. Why didn't anyone but Lila see that?

An idea struck quickly, and she clung to it with the desperation of a drowning woman to a life preserver. She pulled her phone from her pocket and opened a video recorder just as Cobie reached the chorus again. She filmed the bathroom door, which wasn't a compelling visual to accompany the sultry sounds of Cobie's voice, but if her followers' imaginations could fill in the blanks half as well as Lila's, Cobie would be an Internet sex symbol by morning. She would move up another notch in the celebrity food chain, which would put her one rung closer to her dream job, which would be the end of her and Lila's need to work together.

Her heart thudded dully in her chest at the thought of Cobie being done with her, but that was all the more reason to hurry the process along. She was so close to making it out of this charade relatively unscathed, she had to finish the job.

Taking a deep breath, she screwed up all her courage and pressed "Share," then quickly walked away.

※ ※ ※

Cobie could hear her phone rattling even from inside the shower. One buzz, then another, until the vibrations and pings became a near steady whir of alerts.

"What in all the fucks?" She'd had a hard day on set, taking a literal ass-kicking at times, and all she'd wanted to do was have a long, hot, relaxing shower to loosen her tight and bruised muscles. Why did one hundred people suddenly decide now was the time to chat or tweet or email or whatever the hell they were doing to her phone.

Sighing heavily, she turned off the water and grabbed a towel. The phone continued to buzz while she tried to dry off and finally stepped, still dripping from her legs, onto the lush bathmat. She'd grown used to these little bursts over the last few months. They always came at random times. Maybe this one was about her movie. She shook her head. These blasts usually had to do with Lila. Someone ran a new photo of her and Lila, or Lila tagged her in a tweet, or Lila made an announcement that had nothing to do with her but she got wrapped up in it by virtue of social proximity.

She swiped open the notification center on her phone and saw over one hundred items from social to personal. All of them had video in the tagline. She rolled her eyes. Someone had shared a video of her. She didn't doubt who. She'd learned to roll with it and was just about to toss the phone back on the counter when a text came through from Emma. "Wow, surprised you let her post that. You must really like her."

Cobie frowned. What was that supposed to mean? Before she could ponder more, a text from Talia popped up. "Please tell me you knew about this beforehand."

"What?" She asked both aloud and in text.

A link came back immediately as if Talia had anticipated the question, followed by another message that said, "I'm going to take that as a no."

Cobie walked to the bed, still clad in only a damp towel, but she worried she might need to sit down as she clicked on the link.

At first, she didn't know what she was watching. Just a grainy dimly lit video of a door? Then she glanced up. It was her door. Her bathroom door. She thumbed up the volume button in time to hear her own voice, and her stomach turned nauseatingly. How? Why? Who?

Lila.

Grabbing her dirty shirt from the floor, she pulled it on and charged out of the bedroom. "Lila!"

The sense of betrayal ripped through her veins as she tore upstairs. Lila wasn't in the sewing room or the living room, so Cobie pounded on her bedroom door. "Lila, open up!"

When the door finally opened, Cobie didn't wait for an answer before shoving her phone screen in Lila's face. "What the fuck?"

Lila took a step back, either from Cobie's proximity or the force in her voice. "Cobie."

"Don't 'Cobie' me. You videoed me in the shower?"

"No!"

"Then how did this bullshit end up on your feed?"

"I shot the video, but I didn't get you in the shower. The door's closed."

"Do you think anyone has any doubt what's happening here?"

Lila shook her head. "You can't see anything."

"That's not the point. You snuck into my room and videotaped me during what I thought was a private moment, then posted it on the Internet."

Lila snatched the phone out of her hand and turned it back around to face Cobie. "And in case you hadn't noticed, the world is in love with it."

"That's not the point," Cobie snapped.

"What is the point?" Lila shouted back. The initial shock of Cobie's anger had clearly worn off, and she'd found a little spitfire of her own.

"You invaded my privacy."

"Oh, now I see. I'd think the point was that this video is promotional gold. Have you seen the comments?"

"No."

Lila turned the phone back around and ran her finger through what Cobie could only assume were viewer responses as she read, "Wow, that's hot." "Did anyone else know she could sing?" "Is it just me, or did Cobie Galloway just get way sexier?" "I'm kind of questioning my sexuality here, guys." "Why isn't this woman in all the movies?" "Why isn't this woman in all the showers?"

She tossed the phone back to Cobie, who caught it awkwardly. "You don't get it, do you?"

"Get why you're standing in front of me in a wet shirt and a precariously placed towel, acting morally indignant? No. I don't, but it's a good look for you. I'm tempted to take a picture of this . . ." Lila drew an air circle around Cobie with her index finger. "And post it all over the Internet too."

"I want to say you wouldn't dare, but why not, right? What's next? Would you sneak into my room and get pictures of me sleeping? Want to snip a lock of my hair and sell it on eBay? Oh, how about I draw you a vial of blood? Would you like that?"

"Yeah," Lila said defiantly, "if it would help bump up our image, yes I would. I'd work hard, and I'd sell hard, because guess what? That's my job! I take my job seriously. The bigger question is why don't you?"

"How dare you! I take my job every bit as seriously as you do."

"Do you?" Lila asked with mockery in her voice, "because if you did, your head would explode with gratitude for that video. In thirty seconds, it raised your mass-market sexual appeal like three levels. You don't want to be seen as a teen star anymore? Then grow up."

"Adulthood doesn't mean tramping myself up for the World Wide Web."

"No, but it does mean making tough choices between what you want and what you need."

"Yeah, and it's also about making those choices for myself." Cobie refused to back down. "I didn't get to make this choice, Lila. You made it for me."

"If I'd shown you the video, you would have deleted it."

"Maybe, maybe not, but my body, my career, my choice. We agreed on that."

"We also agreed to get back to being professionals. We agreed to focus on work, and I know I contributed to getting off track, but can't you see I'm trying to fix that? Why can't you let me get back to what I know?"

The anguish in the last question cut through Cobie's wall of self-righteousness. "What are you talking about?"

"I'm trying, Cobie." Lila's voice caught, and she looked away. "I'm trying to right the ship. I'm trying to do what we set out to do."

Cobie blinked away the remaining red tinge of anger from her gaze, and for the first time, she noticed how pale and tired Lila looked. Something in her chest tightened as the memories of Toronto came rushing back. "Are you okay?"

"Yes, damn it, I'm fine. I know you saw me in a moment of awful weakness, but I'm not shattered or broken."

"Lila, no. I don't think of you that way."

"Well, I do," she snapped, "and I'll own that. My slip, my fault, but I'm also going to take responsibility for pulling us back on track. Just because I had a rough night doesn't change anything about my drive to succeed, to win."

"I never thought it did," Cobie said, reaching out to soothe her, but Lila took a step back.

"You didn't? Because you've sure backed off lately. You're handling me with kid gloves, and that's nice, but it's not how business works. You either go all out for the win, or you're not really playing at all," Lila said matter-of-factly. "And we're running out of time."

Cobie's jaw twitched as she ground her teeth together. Had she really backed off? She knew she had, but not because she saw Lila as weak. If anything, she'd been frightened by the strength of the emotions she'd seen in her, and the ones she experienced in herself, but how could she explain that to Lila? Being angry was so much easier than being afraid.

"So, which is it, Cobie?" Lila pressed, her blue eyes sharp and focused once more. "Are you sitting in the stands, or are you in the game to win?"

Cobie opened her mouth, intending to say nothing felt like a game to her anymore. She wanted to grab Lila and shake her, to beg her to tell her something, anything real, but she knew better. Lila had made it clear from their first date that the cardinal sin was forgetting nothing was ever real. If she fell apart and broke the fourth wall now, she'd only reveal herself to be the same kind of fool as all the others who'd come before her. Trying to appeal to Lila on some emotional level, or even a personal one, was about as useful as trying to remove a viral video from the Internet at this point. At least they could agree on one thing though: Their days together were numbered, and Lila would walk away a winner. Cobie could either join her or get left in the dust. She didn't like the choice, but she clearly knew which was the better option.

"Yes." She rubbed her face. "I'm still in the game to win."

"Really?" Lila pushed, the challenge gone from her voice as her pretty features twisted in a frown.

"Sure." Cobie shrugged. "If it's all just a game, might as well win."

Lila pursed her lips for a second, then nodded resolutely. "Fine. Then we've both got a lot of work left to do."

She abruptly shut the door in Cobie's face.

Dismissed, Cobie walked back to her room, trying not to think about the emotions that had flashed fast and jumbled across Lila's features in the seconds between Cobie's answer and Lila's response. Surprise? Disappointment? Sadness? Or resignation? Cobie would never understand this woman, and she needed to stop exerting so much energy while trying to.

She closed the door softly behind her and was just about to flop on the bed when she noticed a bundle of black clothes on her pillow. She approached them tentatively, as though they might explode in her face, but as she got closer, she recognized the top layer as the piece she'd seen Lila working on earlier. All the questions faded as she held up the jacket.

"Vale," she whispered. Running her fingers over the leather, she sighed again. The costume was perfect. She had no other word for it. The concept, the design, the detail work, was all flawless. Cobie doubted even Talia could have brought this vision to life so seamlessly. How long had Lila worked on this? How much time and energy and forethought had she spent? Cobie had just screamed at her for being thoughtless and careless and self-centered. And yet she was those things too. She was so many things all at once, and Cobie never could tell which attributes were genuine and which ones were carefully calculated. Or were they all contrived? Then again, could they all be genuine?

She'd drive herself crazy with those questions, and she'd never have her answer. All she had was a few more weeks with a woman who would keep her head spinning, and she could only take every moment as it came. Now if only she could sort out her own feelings, she might make it out unscathed. But as she sat back on the bed holding the jacket to her chest, she doubted her ability to know her own heart when it came to Lila Wilder.

Chapter Ten

"Whoa," Cobie said, and Lila turned to see her decked out in full costume.

"Whoa indeed." Her eyes raked over Cobie's body in the ensemble. It almost didn't look like a costume but a piece Cobie was born to wear. The pants were made of ripped leather over black denim and tucked into black lace-up Doc Marten boots. The cut wasn't tight, but the ragged lines hinted at a strength in her legs Lila wished she didn't have firsthand knowledge of. The jacket, on the other hand, fit more snugly, with a subtle curve at Cobie's narrow waist arcing gracefully up to broad shoulders. She'd darkened her facial features as well by wearing the hood up so it cast shadows over her big dark eyes ringed in black eyeliner. Lila had seen the look in all its various stages, but no amount of peeking behind the curtain prepared her for the thrill of seeing the final product. Raw, powerful, commanding, sexy. "You're Vale."

"Huh?" Cobie asked, her mouth hanging slightly open.

"The part. You nailed it. Cobie, you're her. No one is ever again going to say you don't have the look for the role. You are the role."

Cobie blushed slightly.

"What?" Lila asked.

"Your dress."

Lila glanced down at the little red-sequined flapper get-up. "I'm Daisy Buchanan from *The Great Gatsby*."

"Yeah you are. You'll drive more than a few men toward bootleg liquor and jazz tonight."

"Thank you," Lila said politely, but she knew which of them people would be talking about tomorrow, and she didn't blame them. Cobie was a showstopper. She didn't just wear the costume. She inhabited it in a way that sent Lila's senses into overdrive.

"Can I help with anything?" Cobie asked. "Food? Drinks? Help with the waiters? What do you need from me?"

A kiss? A ravishing? To be thrown up against the wall and taken before the guests arrived? She shook the haze of arousal from her mind and glanced out across the room. "I'm good, thanks."

"You look better than good. You're stunning."

Lila turned in time to catch her eyes take a path over her body that she wished Cobie would follow with her hands.

She had to stop thinking like that if she was ever going to get through tonight, much less the trials to follow. She had to focus.

"Ms. Wilder?" A young woman in a navy suit and a headset peeked in the door. "Your guests are arriving."

"Thank you," she said. "Keep them on the main floor with the drinks flowing until Ms. Galloway and I make our entrance, then open up the rest of the museum, including the terrace. Circulate the waiters indoors only."

"Yes, ma'am." The woman ducked out again, and Cobie gave a low whistle.

"You're super commanding in work mode."

"Anything worth doing is worth doing well," Lila said, hoping some of her confidence would return soon. She'd been on edge all week since her fight with Cobie, and while they'd both doubled down on their resolve to make the most of their remaining time together, things at home had remained tense. Cobie had avoided her, or maybe it had been the other way around. They'd both been busy, with Cobie shooting day and night, and Lila absorbed in finer points of party planning. Mimi had hired a top-notch event planner, and Lila had insisted on triple checking everything from the menu to the guest list in a vain attempt to exert control over at least one area of her life, but she worried in doing so she'd allowed the chasm between her and Cobie to become uncrossable. Now, standing there, warmed by the familiar smolder in Cobie's eyes, she suspected that bridge hadn't burned completely.

Maybe it should have though, because she suddenly wanted to chuck all her carefully laid plans off the balcony and into the Hudson River, then follow this woman wherever she led.

"You want to run through the plans one more time before we go down?"

"Yes!" she exclaimed, entirely too excitedly. "I mean, yes, the plan is good. The plan is important. Let's stick to it, okay?"

The corners of Cobie's mouth quirked up. "I intend to."

"Good," Lila said quickly. "So, we go down together—down the stairs, I mean. Make a glamorous entrance."

"It'd be hard to not be glamorous during an exclusive evening at the Whitney with you on my arm."

Not helpful, Cobie. Sexy, but not helpful. "Then we'll make the rounds and greet the guests. You don't have to mingle with everyone though. You're an aloof celebrity tonight, not a Midwestern farmer's daughter."

"Technically I'm both."

"You're at an audition tonight, a job interview, not a *Good Housekeeping* hostess convention."

"I know," Cobie said, a low thrum of confidence in her voice that made Lila believe her. "I'll own the room."

"With me. We stick close early on. I dote on you."

"And I show you off."

"Yes, you're proud, but also possessive. You keep your hands on me." Lila realized she'd added the last statement for her own benefit, but Cobie didn't argue. "Until you introduce me at the piano."

Cobie glanced at the white baby grand set atop a small riser behind them. "Piano, third floor, new album, you in all your glory. Consider it done."

"Then the real show begins."

"Then after you play, we play?"

Lila nodded solemnly. "Do you need a script?"

Cobie shook her head. "You play you. I'll play me. Sparks will undoubtedly fly."

Lila didn't doubt the truth of the statement. "Just make sure they fly in front of some cameras."

Cobie took a deep breath in through her nose and out through her mouth, then rolled her shoulders, signifying her personality swap. Then extending her elbow for Lila to take hold, she flashed her one of the dashing smiles Lila always fell for even though she knew it wasn't really for her. "Break a leg."

Lila sighed and threaded her arm through Cobie's, wrapping her fingers around a muscle that made its presence known even under the thick case of leather, and they headed for the stairs. Still, she couldn't quite bring herself to echo Cobie's call to action, because she feared that if anything got broken tonight, it would be hearts rather than legs.

She still felt slightly off balance and unexpectedly wary as she and Cobie continued to make the rounds almost an hour later. Nothing had gone wrong. On the contrary, early reports seemed to suggest this would be one of the highlights of New York's spring social season. Drinks flowed freely at the bar, and waiters in black ties wove nimbly through a mixed crowd of celebrities. Matthew Broderick and Sarah Jessica Parker were dressed as Romeo and Juliet as they talked to Justin Bieber and his girl *du jour*, who'd come as Peta and Katniss. Across the room, Adele wore a Scarlett O'Hara dress in a fun contrast to Cobie's usual costar, Jeremy, who'd chosen to come as a beefed-up version of the Cat in the Hat.

"Do you think he's vying for a roll in some sort of animated feature?" Lila had asked when he walked in with the drawn-on whiskers and cat suit cut so low it showed a little bit of his chest hair.

"No," Cobie said, failing to stifle a laugh. "He probably just hasn't read any books since kindergarten."

"It's fun to see who shows up as what and try to infer their reading levels from there."

"If we're extrapolating, I'd say the Broadway set is a lot smarter than the Hollywood bunch. No surprises there."

"Oh, cattiness about other actresses?" Lila squeezed Cobie's arm. "I like it."

"Yeah, well, it's not like musicians aren't a mixed bag. Jay-Z showed up as Odysseus, but Katy Perry is some sort of sexy Winnie the Pooh."

"And Cordelia Esme . . ." Lila drew out the name as she tried to process and then compartmentalize her surprise, "just walked in wearing wizard robes?"

Cobie's eyes scanned the crowd, then lit up as they fell on a woman with honey and amber locks spilling over onto a dark cloak. "Her? She's Hermione Granger!"

"She's Cordelia Esme," Lila said flatly.

"She's a pop singer, right?"

"Sort of, I suppose, but she's very folksy, sort of sultry. She doesn't have a wide market, and she's terrible with the press."

Cobie eyed her suspiciously. "So not a contemporary of yours?"

"Hardly. I wouldn't say she's B-list. She's got talent and a certain kind of appeal, but she keeps a low profile. I'm kind of shocked she's here."

"Introduce me?"

"To her?" Lila asked, trying to sound bored despite the nervous clench of her stomach.

"Sure, why not? I love Harry Potter."

"You know she's not actually from Hogwarts, right?" Lila stalled.

Cobie placed her hand on Lila's back, brushing her fingers against bare skin from the low-cut dress. "Come on."

Lila shivered from the touch, breaking her pout and melting easily to Cobie's will. They crossed the room side-by-side, turning more than a few heads as they went.

"Cordelia," Lila called cheerfully, "what a wonderful surprise."

"Lila." Cordelia smiled as they approached, then leaned in to kiss Lila lightly on each cheek. She smelled of honey and sandalwood, and Lila fleetingly wondered if Cobie would like the combination. "I know I don't get out as much as you do, but I just couldn't resist a book event."

Lila stepped back, "Have you met—"

"Vale Ortanos!" Cordelia called enthusiastically.

"Actually, this is Cobie Galloway."

Cordelia blushed. "Right, sorry. I knew that, but I'm such a fan of *Vigilant*. Vale is one of the best female characters I've read in ages, and you're her. I mean not her, but you nailed the image. Oh, my God, are you going to play Vale in the movie?"

Cobie laughed a deep, rich laugh that wasn't at all consistent with the brooding character she'd played all night. "Cordelia Esme, right? Or should I call you Ms. Granger?"

"Oh, I do like the sound of that so much better than what my friends call me."

"What's that?"

She blushed again, and Lila rolled her eyes. No one was seriously that modest. "Dilly."

"Dilly." Cobie smiled and nodded. "Cute."

"Right, cute, but you, you're so dark and ominous. Like people can't tell if they'd hate to meet you in a dark alley or if they'd go in there looking for you. But I guess that's the whole appeal of the character. Did I mention I loved *Vigilant*? I did, didn't I?"

"You did," Lila confirmed.

"Which is cool." Cobie cut back in. "I'm a huge fan of Talia Stamos's work."

"She's a genius. Have you met her?"

"I have," Cobie said, a blush of her own creeping into her palely powdered cheeks.

Lila needed to get her out of there before she blew her character completely, but she was too transfixed by the dreamy look in her eyes.

"Oh, God, what a dolt," Cordelia said. "I forgot she did the script for one of your movies, or not the script, but the book it was based on, right?"

Cobie's blush turned crimson. "I'd rather not remember that movie, and I know she feels the same."

Cordelia grimaced. "I wasn't going to mention that the book was better."

"No worries. I know it. You know it. Tal certainly knows it."

Tal? The name set off alarms in Lila's brain, or maybe the tone in which it had been said, drenched in nostalgia and delivered with affection.

"*Vigilant* will be so much better if I have my way," Cobie said, a hint of steel to her voice.

Cordelia put her hand on Cobie's shoulder and looked her earnestly in the eye. "I don't doubt it. None of us are who we were ten years ago."

What the hell was that supposed to mean? Lila would have laughed if not for the heavy sigh that shook Cobie's shoulders. "Thank you, Cordelia. I really appreciate that."

"Yes, and we both appreciate your being here," Lila said quickly, "but we've got to make the rounds before I warm up."

"Of course," Cordelia said with a wholesome smile. "I'm so looking forward to hearing your new work."

"It was nice to meet you," Cobie managed as Lila pulled her away.

She wove back through the lobby, past the bar, and up to the stairs.

"You okay?" Cobie finally asked as they were out of earshot of the general crowd.

"Fine."

Cobie watched her out of the corner of her eye as their footsteps fell in tandem up the stairs, the dull thud of Cobie's boots providing a baseline to the high click of Lila's heels.

"You sure?"

"Just getting into work mode."

"Right," Cobie said. "Are you nervous about debuting a new song in front of so many famous people?"

She started to nod but then pursed her lips. Nervous? Is that what she felt? Not quite. There was a tightness in her stomach instead of butterflies, and while her mind did flit quickly from one topic to another, it didn't ever land on her upcoming performance. Instead, her erratic thoughts all raced around Cobie's interaction with Cordelia. Their easy connection over books, their shared geekdom, the complete lack of pretense, they'd all left Lila feeling like an outsider. And the talk about Talia, or Tal. Cobie knew the author of *Vigilant*. They had worked together, and from the wistful way Cobie called her Tal, they'd shared more than a script. A memory floated into the front of her mind. Emma had said she hadn't met any of Cobie's girlfriends since Tal.

Her footsteps faltered, and she ground to a stop. Cobie came up short next to her. "What is it?"

She stared at her, searching the eyes she'd stared at so many times, never once wondering what secrets lay behind their dark reflective surface. Cobie and Talia had been lovers. Why hadn't she realized that? They'd spent months together working toward *Vigilant*. Why had she never examined Cobie's drive in that area when she'd passively accepted so much else in her life and career? And perhaps more importantly, how had Cordelia uncovered in five minutes what Lila had missed for months?

"It's nothing," she said, then resumed climbing the stairs more slowly. "Just a little winded."

It wasn't a complete lie. She was having a hard time getting a deep breath. Cobie and Cordelia. Cobie and Talia. Why hadn't Cobie told her? She hadn't exactly asked the questions Cordelia had, but Cobie had never opened up to her as easily as she did to Cordelia either. Why Cordelia? Why Talia?

Why not Lila?

"Lila?" Cobie asked again, "are you sure you're okay?"

"Yes. I'm fine, I'm just . . . I'm just . . ." She pursed her lips as the unpleasant end of that sentence struck her.

Jealous.

"Ladies and gentlemen," Cobie said, raising a champagne flute. "Thank you all for joining us tonight to benefit such a worthy cause. Whether you were a kid who loved to read or an adult who loves to write or you're just a human being who understands we are all better off when the general population is literate, I think we can agree that reading education benefits us all."

A few people applauded lightly.

"Words matter. Words help us define who we are as artists and as people. As actors, singers, writers, or poets, we depend on the written and spoken word to help us convey everything we love, everything we feel, everything we need the world to know." Cobie sought Lila's eyes in the crowd, locking her own gaze with those stunning blues. "With that, I would like to welcome to the stage a songstress and wordsmith who has a better grasp on the language and music that invoke the fullness of our human connections than anyone I've ever met. She also happens to be stunning and funny, and she knows how to throw one hell of a party. Please welcome our host, Lila Wilder."

The audience parted to grant a path, and Cobie did an admirable job of keeping her jaw off the floor as the beadwork of Lila's dress shimmied and shook on her way to the stage. Cobie had been standing impossibly close to her all night and had yet to find an unflattering aspect to the flapper get-up. Low cut at the top and high cut at the bottom, it shivered with Lila's every breath, flashing as red as her pouty kissable lips. What she wouldn't give to slip the spaghetti straps off those proud shoulders.

A cold sweat broke out across the back of her neck. She was never going to see that dress on the floor. She would never again see the beautiful body beneath it. She couldn't, and she knew all the reasons why, but knowing something and making peace with it were two different things. She extended her hand to Lila and watched red-tipped fingers slide slowly across her palm, but instead of merely helping her onto the stage, Cobie gave a gentle tug and pulled her into her arms. Without waiting for the surprise to fully register, she kissed her, a quick but sensual kiss full of heat, longing, and a desire for something she couldn't claim as her own. Lila kissed her back. There was no question, no hesitation, no subtle rebuke for going off-script.

The combination left her dizzy as she steadied Lila with a firm hand passively on her hip, then she stepped back. The famous faces of the crowd came slowly back into focus, but they all seemed dull and distant compared to Lila's satisfied smile. Cobie didn't know what exactly had just passed between them, but she liked it more than she should have, and from the look on her face, Lila did too.

Still, they had a job to do, so she backed off the stage to a few catcalls and several nods of respect as Lila took her seat at the piano and adjusted the microphone.

"Thank you, Cobie. That was too generous. And the introduction was nice too."

Laughter rippled through the room.

"She's something else, isn't she ladies and gentlemen? Smart, talented, and sexy as all get out."

A smattering of applause prompted Cobie to take a little bow.

"I've already bought about thirty tickets to her new supervillain movie, and it's not even out until next Christmas," Lila continued, "but in the meantime, I wanted to share a little something we worked on together."

Someone gave a high-pitched whistle, and Lila laughed. "Not that kind of something. I'm going to play you a number that will appear on the album I started laying tracks for this week. Cobie has a songwriter's credit on this one, and I'm pretty proud of it. I hope she is too."

Cobie forced a smile as Lila's fingers came to rest on the opening chords of "Validate."

Her voice came in soft but strong, and Cobie was glad for her long sleeves to cover the goosebumps rising on her arms.

"We all play the same game, though we're all dealt different hands. It doesn't mean we can't work together to take a better stand. You can play your way, and I can play mine. Still we can help each other on the uphill climbs."

Lila closed her eyes and sang with a soulfulness Cobie had heard before, but never on something they shared.

"We all make choices the best that we can, you be you, and I'll be who I am. I'll stand beside you through day and night. I'll always defend your right to fight. Because no one else gets to judge, it doesn't matter how you rate, you only need you to validate."

A tingle went up her spine each time Lila sang the chorus, and though she mostly felt mystified to hear her words, she did share some of Lila's pride. This song would stand for the rest of her career as something to look back on fondly. No matter what happened from here, they would always share something lasting, something good, something real.

She looked around the room as beautiful people nodded or swayed to the music. Lights twinkled overhead and reflected on the floor-to-ceiling glass walls while their song held everyone's rapt attention. She was a part of this. All of it. If everything ended tonight, at least they went out on a high note.

The thought did little to soothe the ache in her chest as she finally faced the fact that this was the last hurrah. Starting in a matter of minutes, they would pull the plug that would send everything spinning down the drain. She shook off the thought.

Not yet.

She didn't want to go there yet. Closing her eyes, everything else faded. She let Lila's voice wash over her in an attempt to hold onto this moment a little longer. Just the two of them, their words, their emotions, their legacy.

As applause thundered through the cavernous space, a terrifying jolt of awareness hit Cobie squarely in the chest. She was alone. She wasn't with Lila. Everything about this moment was based on a lie, one she'd willingly told everyone in the room. Why did she feel nostalgic for that? Why did she want to drag out the charade? Why get emotional about ending her time as a professional liar? Had she gotten so used to lying it felt normal?

She sighed, and after checking to make sure Lila was completely surrounded by her adoring public, she slipped out onto the terrace.

Had she made peace with lying about her feelings for Lila because somewhere along the way she'd stopped lying? Or had she started believing the lie? She didn't know which, but she couldn't deny that she'd kissed Lila tonight because she'd wanted to. And that scared the crap out of her. Despite all her best efforts to hide behind professionalism or ambition, she'd developed genuine feelings for Lila. But did they justify anything? Could she make herself less of a liar by becoming more of a fool? Those feelings didn't absolve the lie, and they weren't mutual. It took two people to make a relationship.

She leaned against the terrace railing and stared out at the dark shimmering waters of the Hudson. Who had she become?

"That was quite a show," a woman said as she stepped out of the shadows, her dark robes rippling softly on the cool breeze.

Startled, Cobie stepped back and then smiled as she recognized Cordelia Esme's kind expression.

"Yeah, Lila's quite the performer."

"Just Lila?" Cordelia asked. "You seemed pretty adept in the limelight yourself."

Cobie shook her head. "That's just her influence rubbing off on me."

"So you're not a fan of the high life?"

Cobie shook her head, which felt just a little clearer. "If you're referring to the flashing cameras and throngs of reporters following me around all the time, no."

"It's exhausting, right?" Cordelia said conspiratorially. "What's wrong with those people? Don't they have lives of their own?"

Cobie chuckled. "I guess they're just doing their jobs, but

really, why does anyone want to know where and what I ate last Friday? I'm not that interesting."

"Oh, I wouldn't go that far."

"I would," Cobie said. "If it were up to me, I'd be at home in sweatpants watching reruns of *The West Wing*."

Cordelia eyed her suspiciously. "Who told you?"

"Told me what?"

"That *The West Wing* is my favorite show of all time."

"No, it's my favorite show." Cobie laughed. "I called it. I'm going to snuggle up with CJ Craig all day tomorrow to recover from tonight."

"Is there any way we can just do that now?" Cordelia asked.

"You can, but if I sneak out now, there'll be all kinds of hell to pay."

"Oh, right," Cordelia said. "You're sort of in charge here tonight."

"Oh, I haven't been in charge of anything for months," Cobie said. Then her face burned, and she rushed to pull her foot out of her mouth. "That sounded bad. I'm so sorry. Please don't take it the wrong way. The last few months have been amazing and wonderful and—"

"Don't worry," Cordelia said quickly. "You've been busy. That's not a reflection on anyone. It's easy to let life run away with you. It's just the nature of the business."

"Yeah?" Cobie asked, wishing that were the case. "You been there?"

"Maybe not quite at the level you have. I do have to keep a really tight rein on things like my press and events and appearances, but my line of work lends itself to periods of quiet withdrawal more than yours does. Everyone sort of expects folk singers to disappear into the woods alone a couple times a year."

"God, that sounds nice," Cobie said. "I have a log cabin in the Catskills. Cute, cozy, quiet. Actually, just about a mile from Talia's."

"Sounds amazing."

"It is, or at least it was last time I was there."

"When?"

"Christmas," Cobie said miserably.

Cordelia edged a little closer along on the rail. "It doesn't have to be that way, you know."

Cobie shrugged. She did know, but she also knew she'd made her choices and had to live with them.

"I'm not trying to brag, and I wouldn't say this to anyone but you right now, but I've made plenty of money to live really well. I could never record another thing and be fine. I don't need the fame or the fans or the contracts anymore, and knowing that, really being okay with what I have, has given me a tremendous amount of freedom and peace and contentedness."

Cobie nodded. She got the point. She had enough. She had more than she needed. She didn't have to do anything she didn't want to do. And yet here she was, afraid to go, afraid to stay, afraid to lose something she'd never have. The things that seemed so important a few months ago were within her grasp now. She could be done. Life could be so easy, so simple again. Just her and her work and her little house in the woods.

"I didn't mean to get heavy on you," Cordelia finally said as she stepped away. "I don't know you. I only know Lila in passing. Who am I to tell you how to live your life? You live in a foreign world by my standards."

Cobie turned and rested her back against the rail, cold metal radiating through the thick skin of her jacket. "Then why are you here tonight?"

"What?"

"You don't know me or Lila. You're not a fan of glitz and glamour. You're not trying to get noticed by the press. If you like the quiet life, why wade into all of this tonight?"

"If we're on the record, if there are any members of the press lurking around," she said in a stage voice, "I'd say I'm here because I care about childhood literacy. Words matter, stories matter, equal access for all voices matters, and like you said, I want to live in an educated society."

"And if there weren't any reporters lurking around, would you give me an honest answer?"

Cordelia's smile turned sweet. "My formal answer is ninety percent of the truth."

Cobie stepped closer. "What if I wanted the other ten percent of the truth? Would you tell me?"

"Probably. I've never been good at pretense," Cordelia said. "The other ten percent of the truth is that I just really wanted to meet you."

A soft gasp escaped Cobie's lips before she could stifle the reaction. "Me?"

"Now I've said the wrong thing," Cordelia said with a grimace. "I know you're with Lila. I'm not trying to stir any drama. Please don't think I'm throwing myself at you. I meant what I said. I wanted to *meet* you."

"But there are so many more famous and interesting people here tonight. Why me?"

Cordelia's smile turned bashful again. "Because you seem like a major movie star who also manages to be really real. Like someone I could sit on a porch with and talk to about whatever was weighing on my mind."

Cobie looked around. If you substituted terrace for porch, that's exactly what they were doing. "Well I guess that's true enough."

"And you're steady. You don't change who you are all the time to chase trends. You don't let the pressure make you into something you're not."

Until recently, Cobie thought.

"And you're gay."

Cobie laughed. "Truest statement you've made all night."

"When you came out, I was so happy because you weren't teasing us or toying with the idea to see if it was advantageous from a career standpoint. You just stood up and said, 'This is who I am.'"

"It hadn't occurred to me to do it any other way."

Cordelia gave her shoulder a little shove. "And *that's* what I like about you. Also, you look really good as Vale. Really good. And now I'm gushing again. I should have quit while I was ahead, if I ever was ahead, which I'm not totally sure of."

Cobie laughed a little harder this time. "You were, and you still are. Honestly, this is the most enjoyable conversation I've had in weeks. I don't get many people saying they like the things about me you claim to like."

"Except for Lila."

Cobie frowned. "Lila. Right."

"She obviously likes you a lot."

Cobie turned to look back out over the river. "Yeah. That's true."

Sometimes it did feel like Lila liked her a lot, but usually those times came directly on the heels of a massive argument when it seemed like Lila couldn't stand her or, worse, couldn't care one way or another about her presence, or her feelings. The worst part, though, was not knowing which Lila to believe.

This moment with Cordelia was the first real one she'd had in ages. Maybe that's why she didn't want to go back inside, even though she should walk away before she said anything else. She had a job to do, and flirting with one of Lila's contemporaries wasn't on the schedule for the evening. Not that Lila would care. The longer the two of them talked, the more likely people were to notice, and the more people who noticed, the more drama they'd stir. And Lila loved drama. Hell, she'd probably give them her blessing.

And yet it still didn't feel right. Maybe because flirting with Cordelia wouldn't be for the press. Cordelia was too close to the type of person she could really fall for. She had all the talent, fame, and money in the world, but she didn't need to prove anything to anyone. She remained laid back and honest amidst everything she'd accomplished. She clearly didn't have experience playing games, and she admired all the sides of Cobie she used to like about herself. All signs pointed to her being the kind of person Cobie would like to spend time with. And that's exactly why she should walk away.

Cordelia reminded her of who she was, who she could be again, and that person didn't flirt with other women while her girlfriend waited inside. Of course, Lila wasn't really her girlfriend, but she felt a loyalty to follow through with what they'd started, no matter what they may have morphed into along the way. And even if that devotion wasn't a two-way street, she wouldn't break her end of the bargain. They all deserved better.

Her phone buzzed, and she fished it out of her pocket to check the notification on the screen. Lila asked, "Where are you?"

She hung her head. "I'm sorry. I have to go. It's not that I don't want to talk to you, but it's complicated."

"Hey." Cordelia laid one hand softly on Cobie's. "It's okay."

Cobie gave a mirthless laugh. How could she possibly understand?

"Trust me," Cordelia said and slipped the phone from Cobie's hand. She tapped the screen a few times and handed it back to her. "I know you're fully committed to Lila, and that makes me respect you even more. But if you ever need someone to remind you that you're a pretty great catch yourself, you've got my number."

Cobie glanced at her contact screen and noticed a new entry entitled Dilly's Porch.

She smiled broadly. "Thank you."

"You're welcome. Now you'd better get back to work."

Work. She nodded. Yes, that's what she needed now, even if it's not what she wanted.

Lila ground her teeth together at the sight of Cordelia's hand on Cobie's. As she stood near the window to the terrace, she couldn't make out what they were saying, but she didn't like it. The intimate set of their bodies, close enough to share a whisper, made her stomach twist. And their casual, comfortable touches spoke of an easiness that made her pulse throb at her temples. Whatever they were saying wasn't small talk, or business talk either.

Lila recognized what genuine interest looked like on Cobie. She'd had it directed at herself more than a few times, but she'd never leaned into it the way Cordelia was.

A set of new emotions churned through her. Jealousy was back with its sickening taste in her mouth, but something deeper flowed below its acidic surface, a feeling she hadn't encountered in a long time, except in her dreams.

Betrayal.

It burned and chilled at the same time, like a fever that sweats even while shivering. Cobie had kissed her. So proud, so strong. She'd taken her in her arms in front of the world, made her feel for a second that she really belonged there. Is that how Cordelia felt right now? Seen, cared for, appreciated? She'd always known Cobie had the ability to make a person feel like the only woman in the room, and she knew that skill was as dangerous as it was powerful. What she hadn't realized was how awful it would feel to see her put that talent to use with someone else.

Suddenly Cobie turned and walked back toward the large glass wall. Lila straightened her tight shoulders and lifted her chin in a show of defiance largely for her own benefit. Then she strode purposefully toward the door, meeting Cobie before she'd even gotten one foot fully inside.

"Did you have a nice little break?"

Cobie leaned back. "Um, yeah. Got some air."

"Air," Lila repeated in a harsh whisper. "Oh, is that all? Because it sort of looked like you got a phone number."

The rush of color to Cobie's face confirmed her suspicions.

"Lila, it's not what you—"

"Never mind." Lila turned quickly on one spiked heel, but Cobie caught her arm and tugged her back, reeling her in like a fish strung helplessly on a line.

"Don't pull away from me, please," she pleaded softly. "You always pull away. I never get a chance to talk to you."

"But you can talk to Cordelia, is that it?"

Cobie's eyes went wide and then narrowed, as though searching Lila's. As though suddenly remembering they weren't alone, she glanced around the room. Several people turned to stare, and more than one of them had cellphones out. They all quickly focused on their screens as if finding something infinitely more interesting than the conversation they were clearly eavesdropping on.

"Oh," Cobie said, "right."

"What?"

Cobie rolled her shoulders and blew out a heavy breath. Work mode. All the genuineness faded from her expression, and even in her hyperemotional state, Lila reacted to the transformation. With a few subtle shifts of her face and posture, Cobie changed from caring and concerned to hard and aloof. With the flip of some internal switch, she was completely in control once again. Lila had seen her make the shift plenty of times, but never had she understood the full magnitude of the talent until just then.

"I just went outside for a few minutes. Gimme a break. You're suffocating me."

"I'm suffocating you?" Lila shot back in a terse voice. Okay, not her most brilliant comeback.

"You're all up in my business all the time. I can't even talk to someone without you getting jealous and judgmental."

Lila tried to make scoffing sounds, but it came out sort of like a squeak. She wasn't giving Cobie anything tangible to work with here, but the stage fighting felt too close to the real fights they'd already had, and she desperately didn't want to go back to those.

"Oh sure, now you don't have anything to say?" Cobie called her out from a different angle. "What, you don't want all your fancy friends to hear there's trouble in paradise? Wouldn't want anyone to see the cracks in your glittery armor?"

Now that she could work with. "Just stop, Cobie."

"Stop what? Telling the truth?"

"Stop making a scene," she stage-whispered. "There are people around."

"I thought you liked having people around."

Lila scanned their immediate vicinity and noted many of the onlookers weren't even trying to hide their interest anymore.

They'd accomplished what they needed to, and she didn't want things to escalate into a full-blown fight, for fear of what other truth bombs Cobie would manage to drop in the process. "Can we table this until we get home?"

Cobie's shoulders slumped on a heavy exhale, and she rubbed her face with both hands. "Yeah. Sure. Whatever you say, dear."

Lila forced a smile, wondering if the resignation in her voice was part of the act or a genuine reaction to tabling the topic. "Do you want me to have Malik bring the car around?"

Cobie shrugged. "Whatever you want."

Lila raised a hand and caught Malik's eye. She wanted so many things right now, but none of them could be found in this room. The evening had at least accomplished what they came for, and perhaps much more. On the surface, it seemed she'd gotten everything she'd wanted. And yet now she had to face whether she actually wanted what she got.

Chapter Eleven

"Holy crap," Cobie said as she crashed onto the couch outside her bedroom door. "I don't know how you manage to do this kind of thing on a regular basis."

"It's my job," Lila responded coolly.

"You do it well," Cobie said, fumbling with the laces on her boots. "Tonight was a success on all counts."

"We'll see."

Cobie glanced up at her. Lila had taken a seat at the piano, but she didn't look interested in playing. Her eyes focused on something much farther away than the music stand. "We raised a lot of money. Had a great turnout. Took many a dashing photograph."

"Time and the press will decide what to make of all that."

"Everyone I talked to loved the Vale costume. Gushing would not be too strong a word for their reactions. Have I said thank you enough for that?"

"You have, but I've actually been meaning to tell you, a friend of mine designed the concept."

"Oh yeah?" Cobie sat up at the tentativeness she heard in Lila's voice.

"I want you to credit her with the design, not me."

"But you made the costume."

"But a young woman named Addie Hammels gave me the concept drawing for the piece."

"So you share joint credit."

"I don't want the credit," Lila snapped.

Cobie frowned. What had caused that little outburst? Lila had been tense and quiet the whole way home from the party, but she'd just assumed she was tired or facing a little come-down from their fake fight. Now she wondered if there wasn't more to her mood, or the fight. "You don't want people to know you made a costume for me?"

"Not really, no."

"Oh, I see."

"I doubt you do."

"Then explain it to me."

"It doesn't matter." Lila rose off the bench, the beads on her dress swaying in a crimson wave, but as she passed by the couch, Cobie caught hold of her hand, turning the long graceful fingers against her palm.

"Obviously it does matter," Cobie said, "or you wouldn't be so worked up."

"I'm not worked up."

"You are," Cobie said calmly. "What's bothering you?"

"Nothing."

Cobie laughed.

"What's so funny?"

"I used to worry you might be a better actor than me, but now I don't think so."

"What's that supposed to mean?"

"You're obviously upset about something. This Addie woman?" Her chest tightened at the thought, but she pushed on. "Who is she?"

"That's not really any of your business."

"Well, if I'm wearing her clothes and getting snapped at about it, I think that makes her very much my business."

"I didn't snap at you about her." Lila tried to pull away, but Cobie intertwined their fingers to hold her a little tighter. "I'm fine."

"Look, that might work with the guys you fake date, but I'm a woman. I know how deadly the word 'fine' can be when delivered in that tone. Something's obviously upset you. Why don't you tell me what?"

"We don't have that kind of a relationship," Lila said, ice in her voice, but the fire in her eyes gave her away. "I don't owe you any explanation for my moods or my decisions, and you don't owe me any explanation about your past or other women."

Cobie winced. "Other women?"

Lila rolled her eyes and jerked her hand free. "You don't owe any answers to me, but I'd appreciate it if you didn't treat me like an idiot. I saw you with Cordelia tonight."

Cobie frowned and hoped the heat in her face didn't show. "Nothing happened between me and Cordelia. We talked. Nothing more. I wouldn't do that to you."

"It's fine. She's your type. It doesn't bother me."

"Obviously it does or you wouldn't be angry."

"Don't tell me how I feel," Lila shouted.

"Oh, my God, are you insane? You're literally yelling at me about how you aren't mad. That's a bit hypocritical, even for you, Lila." Cobie got to her feet so they stood nearly eye-to-eye. "And that's what's driving you crazy, isn't it? You're mad that you're mad about this. You don't want to care about me and other women. You don't have any right to be upset, but you are, and you can't admit it."

"Now you're an armchair psychologist?" Lila said, but she looked away, a sure tell Cobie had hit her mark.

Instead of feeling victorious, the realization made her feel guilty. She'd hurt Lila's feelings. She hadn't ever stopped to think about Lila's feelings for her. Sure, she'd had glimpses of them, but Lila worked so hard to hide anything real, Cobie never knew where the lines were. Still, that didn't mean she'd wanted to cross them. "Nothing happened with Cordelia."

"What about with Talia?"

Cobie gasped as the force of the memories rushed back to her. The redirect caught her off guard, and it stung.

"You and Talia were lovers." It wasn't a question.

"My past isn't on the table for you."

"But it was for Cordelia?"

"No."

Lila snorted. "You told her in two minutes what you didn't manage to tell me in months. You and Talia have a history. That's why *Vigilant* matters so much. It's because *she* matters to you."

"Talia isn't relevant to you."

"Really? The fact that you slept with the scriptwriter for the movie deal our entire relationship is based on isn't relevant?" Lila exploded. "What about the fact that I had to find that out in a room full of people while listening to you flirt with some other woman?"

"I wasn't flirting with her." The comeback was off point, but it was all she had.

"Who's the hypocrite now?"

"You are," Cobie shot back. "You keep everything from me. You do what you want, when you want, with whoever you want. You keep me on a strictly need-to-know basis, and, honestly, even less than that because you change the rules all the damn time. I never know anything until it happens, and even after the fact, I don't know what was real and what was for show and what was some damn trap for your own amusement. Everything is fair game for you, but the minute I try to protect something meaningful to me, something private and personal, you lose your shit."

"It's not private and personal if you talk about it with another woman in front of me."

"What about you? Do the same rules apply?"

"What?"

"You spent a night sobbing in my arms over someone named Selena, and you never told me a damn thing about who she is or how she broke your heart. You just pretended like nothing happened and expect me to do the same."

"That's different."

"Because the rules don't apply to you? Because you're a hypocrite?"

"Shut up, Cobie."

"No. I want an answer." Cobie pushed. She'd already pissed Lila off. Why not have it out? At least then she'd know where they stood. "Why do you have a right to know about my exes when I don't have a right to know about yours?"

"Because Selena's not my ex. She's my sister."

"Oh." That took the wind out of Cobie's lungs. Images of Emma flashed through her mind, and the protective instincts took hold. Is that why Lila hadn't talked to her, some sort of ingrained protectiveness? Lila's body language was rigid as she folded her arms across her chest. Something still didn't add up. Clearly Cobie had made a pretty dumb assumption, but how the hell was she supposed to know that if Lila wouldn't talk to her? "I didn't know you had a sister."

"You don't know anything about me."

"And whose fault is that?" Cobie asked a little more softly. "I'm sorry your sister . . ." What? Hurt her, left her, died? She had no idea what a sister could do to cause the grief she'd witnessed in Lila.

"Don't talk about her," Lila said dismissively.

"Fine." Cobie sighed. If that's how it had to be, she could at least demand the same for herself. "Then don't talk about Talia."

"Fine."

"Fine," Cobie repeated. "While we're at it, let's not talk about your jealousy over Cordelia either."

"Sure. Let's also avoid talking about the kiss tonight."

"Good. I didn't want to talk about that anyway."

"Then why'd you bring it up?" Lila snapped.

"I didn't. You did."

Lila opened her mouth and then faltered as if trying to remember if that were true or not.

Cobie snorted. "Yeah, little Freudian slip there?"

"That's cute coming from the woman who slipped her tongue into my mouth. Was that an accident or part of those acting skills you're so fond of?"

Why did she have to have a comeback for everything? "Are you complaining?"

"What? About the fact that you kissed me or the fact that you still had my lipstick on you when you exchanged phone numbers with Cordelia?"

"Yeah, actually," Cobie said, honestly curious. "Which one of those things bothered you more? Or did the latter only bother you because of the former?"

"Why do you care?"

"Because if you're just pissed that I kissed you, I'd say, 'Too damn bad.' You told me to get into character. You said you'd follow my lead. I did my job, and I don't regret it."

Lila golf clapped. "Do you think they'll give you an Oscar for that performance?"

"But if you aren't mad about the kiss," Cobie continued, "if you're mad I got a woman's phone number shortly after kissing you, then I do have to apologize, because I clearly missed a memo somewhere."

"What memo?"

"The one where you like me enough to be jealous. The one where our kisses are more than business transactions. The one where you actually care about what I do and who I do it with, and not just for the sake of the press."

"Don't flatter yourself."

"What about you? Should I flatter you?"

"I'm going to bed now." Lila turned toward the door.

"Why? You don't want to hear the truth?" Cobie asked, stepping into her path. "Does it complicate your tightly controlled world to know that I kissed you on a whim? Because I wanted to, and I didn't care who was watching? Because I found you too beautiful and enigmatic to resist? Because I didn't know how many more chances I'd have and the thought of missing out on even one of them scared me more than the fear of incurring your wrath, which is actually a pretty legit fear for me in case you're wondering."

"Get out of my way."

"Tell me why," Cobie pleaded. "Why can't we talk about this?"

"Because if I have to stand here looking at you, listening to you, for one second longer, I'll . . ."

"What, Lila? What will you do?"

Lila wrapped her hand around the back of Cobie's neck and pulled her closer until their lips connected in a passionate rush of heat.

There. She'd done it. She'd kissed Cobie the way she'd ached to all night, or all week, or since the last time she'd done it. The thought terrified her. Every second of the night, every part of her had longed to feel those lips pressed against her own. And now she had her fix, her drug, her secret desire. Would it be enough? She almost laughed at the absurdity of that question, but nothing was funny about Cobie's strong arm around her waist, pinning Lila to her hard body.

She almost couldn't stand the heat burning between them, and yet she didn't have it in her to resist the flame either. At this point, she would have crawled toward it even while incinerating. She fumbled with the single zipper down the front of Cobie's jacket and pulled downward in one steady tug. Then sliding her hands back up under the leather, she pushed it off those tightly muscled shoulders. She ran her fingers over the soft skin there, tracing the ridges before tearing her mouth away from Cobie's and replacing her hands with her teeth.

She bit harder than she meant to, but the knot of tension where shoulder met neck was hers, and she would mark it as such. She'd caused that tension. She was likely still causing it, but from the way Cobie's head lolled back in surrender, she had no more power to stop this than Lila.

"Bed," Lila commanded.

"Which one?" Cobie asked, all argument drained from her voice.

Lila couldn't answer, her mouth occupied with the important task of kissing Cobie once more. Instead, she pressed both hands flat against the tight black tank top, just above the subtle swell of her breasts, and pushed her toward the bedroom. The door swung open at the first bump from Cobie's back, and Lila kicked it shut as she went by.

They made out all the way across the room, until Cobie collided with the bed and began to fumble with her own belt. Lila helped as best she could with her mouth and mind still fully engaged in other activities, but the buckles needed more attention than she could give them while intoxicated by Cobie's skillful lips. With a little groan, she pulled away and focused her eyes on the belt. "When I made this thing, I didn't give any thought to how hard it'd be to rip off you."

Cobie laughed. "I can do it."

"No." She kissed her again quickly before sinking to her knees on the lush carpet. "Let me."

Cobie's breath sounded strangled as she stared down at her, and Lila thrilled at the knowledge that she wasn't the only one struggling to function through the haze of lust surrounding them. She flipped open the belt buckles and pulled back the studded leather to reveal the button and zipper of the pants, then looking up long enough to lock eyes with Cobie, she undid them both quickly.

"Lila," Cobie managed in a raspy whisper.

"Yes." She hooked her fingers in the waistband, denim and leather both bending to her will as she pulled them down to reveal solid black boxer briefs.

"Come here." Cobie slipped a hand gently under Lila's chin and urged her up. "I need this dress off."

Turning her around, Cobie wrapped an arm around Lila's waist, flattening her splayed fingers across her stomach until Lila's ass ground back against her. Cobie's breath flared hot against her neck as she lowered the straps of her dress and followed them down her arms and over her hips until it fell to the floor.

Brushing her hair aside, Cobie kissed the nape of her neck and cupped Lila's breasts in each of her hands. Massaging softly, she kissed her way up to Lila's jaw before moving on to her earlobe. She sucked for a second as Lila rolled her head back, giving her better access until Cobie whispered, "This is what I was thinking about when I kissed you earlier. I was out of my mind with desire to see your dress on the floor and feel your naked body pressed against mine."

"We're not there yet," Lila said, turning in her embrace. Clutching the scruff of Cobie's tank top, she pulled it over her head before Cobie had a chance to catch up and help shed the briefs. Then both their hands were on Lila's red lace thong, pushing and peeling until it fell on top of the dress. Turning around one more time, Lila bent nearly in half to unfasten her matching high heels.

Cobie clasped her hands on Lila's hips and pulled her back fully into her, before growling, "Now you're just teasing me."

Lila laughed. "Maybe a little. Is it working?"

"Is it working?" Cobie asked. She answered by scooping Lila up, one strong arm behind her back, the other in the bend of her legs. "Let me show you how well it's working."

She laid Lila on the bed and settled her body over her, kissing a hot path between her breasts, over her stomach, and down one of her legs. Cradling Lila's ankle in one hand, she used the other to unclasp the shoe before tossing it over her shoulder. She then did the same with the other stiletto, smiling down at her. "Better, Cinderella?"

"Infinitely," Lila practically purred. "Now come back up here."

"Yes, ma'am," Cobie said without releasing Lila's foot. She kissed the arch, the ankle, the calf, and then every few inches on her way back up.

"Now who's teasing?" Lila asked as she reached her lips again.

"Not me," Cobie said between kisses. "I'm very serious."

"Yeah?"

Cobie stopped and stared down at her, those endless brown eyes full of questions. "I am serious. I want you, and not just right now. I've wanted you so much longer than I should have, and in so many more ways than I should."

Lila nodded, completely understanding the sentiment even though it terrified her. Still, even the fear attempting to bubble up in her chest felt small and insignificant with Cobie holding her. It was as if Cobie's bravery and better angels had summoned

Lila's. "I want you too. I want you so much I can't think of anything else."

"You don't have to." Cobie punctuated her words with a soft kiss. "Tell me what you want, and it's yours."

Lila didn't have to think about that answer. "I want to make love to you."

Cobie's hips rocked forward as though her body needed to confirm what her mind hadn't yet found the words for.

Lila used the momentary lapse to roll Cobie to her back. Trailing her fingers from collarbone to sternum, she circled one small, firm breast then the other in a lazy figure eight. "You're so beautiful, so soft and strong at the same time."

"Just like you," Cobie murmured.

"I don't know how you like to be touched, but I want to learn. I want to know how to do the things to you that you've done to me," Lila said. She wanted to learn *everything* about Cobie. The thought should have been jarring, but she couldn't process anything other than the amazing body before her.

"I like to be touched by you," Cobie said, her voice low and raspy. "Where and how are secondary concerns."

Easing herself up, she covered as much of Cobie's body as she could with her own. She thrilled at the press and yield of her, skin and muscle, hot and sweet all at once. The fact that she'd never made love to a woman was immaterial, or at least secondary to the fact that she'd never made love to someone like Cobie. Someone open and beautiful, giving and patient, sexy and soothing. Maybe there wasn't anyone else like Cobie.

She kissed along her neck, her confidence growing as Cobie lifted her chin, giving access to the pulse point at the base of her throat. The move was more than surrender. It was an expression of trust. Lila marveled at Cobie's vulnerability, which only inspired more of her own. Completely stripped bare of so much more than her clothes, she kissed her way past the hollow of Cobie's throat and down across her chest. Taking one taut nipple in her mouth, she circled it with her tongue, eliciting a low hum of approval from Cobie. The sound was so primal, so evocative, it sent a shot of electricity through Lila, and she repeated the move just to hear it again.

Lila replaced her mouth with her fingers, not wanting to break the contact she craved as she painted a hot path with her tongue to Cobie's other breast. This one was already firm with anticipation, and she bit her lip, breath heavy as she savored the expectant tension. Cobie lifted up off the bed slightly, the small move a gentle request Lila had no desire to refuse. She answered with her lips, her tongue, her own desire.

Cobie drew her breath sharply, the sound adding melody to the bass beat of Lila's own pulse in her ears. She played each note, or maybe they played her, as their bodies became both the composers and the instruments of the symphony they were writing together.

Lila flattened her palm and slid it across the subtle ridges of Cobie's abs and over the soft rise and fall of her stomach. Pressing, caressing, fingertips and nails, the curve of her waist, the flare of her hips, Lila wanted to play every key. She closed her eyes and let her hands imprint every detail on her memory. Then easing lower, she followed the trail of heat to the center of Cobie's need.

Both of them gasped, a soulful, surprising duet inspired by the physical manifestation of everything they'd run from for so long.

"Yes," Cobie whispered as Lila sank into her more fully.

"Yes," she echoed, circling, stroking, relishing the liquid confirmation of their rightness. A visceral score played between them, the sheen of sweat, the rock of hips, the rush of breath all cresting in a harmony she'd never known, or had she? Her body knew. Maybe her heart had too. Is that why she'd fought this so hard. The idea seemed such folly now.

Lila pushed fully inside her, two into one, bass and treble, heart and soul. Cobie's arms wrapped around her back, skilled fingers playing their own urgent underscore.

"Stay here," Cobie whispered, her voice raw with need. "Stay beside me."

Was the request borne of immediate need or a more general desire? It didn't matter. The only words to this song were yes. Yes, a thousand times, no matter how high the melody soared.

"Lila," Cobie breathed in a rush, "please, Lila, don't stop."

She'd never heard such powerful lyrics. ==Cobie was both prophet and poet== as she lifted her voice, this time joining the refrain Lila had begun the moment she'd kissed her. "Yes, yes, yes."

They crested and fell. Cobie's body contracted beneath her, holding her tightly, pulling her deeper. Lila marveled at her unfiltered beauty, eyes closed in ecstasy, body twisted in pleasure. The sight ripped her open, raw, shuddering, shivering. They concluded the song in a throaty cry, on one final chord shared between them before collapsing, but Lila knew those final notes would reverberate through her heart long after silence fell over their bodies.

Chapter Twelve

"You knew we could be like that, didn't you?" Lila asked hours later as she nestled under Cobie's arm and rested her head on her shoulder. Cobie had no idea what time it was but suspected sunrise would find them soon and still sleepless.

"I didn't know exactly what we would be like," Cobie said, but she admitted, "I knew we could be good though."

"So good." Lila hummed contentedly and snuggled closer.

The scent of orchid and passion flower filled Cobie's senses and clung to her skin. "I think that's why I resisted so hard. I suspected you might be like heroin. One hit could kill me, but it would never be enough."

"I didn't know," Lila said dreamily. "I mean, I knew you held a sort of power over me, which was scary enough, but sex has never been like this for me. This was a first."

Cobie smiled. "You've been so far ahead of me in so many ways. I like the idea of being your first at something."

"That's why you kissed me on our first date?"

"Maybe a little bit, but mostly I wanted to do right by you. First times matter. They set the expectations for everything that comes afterward. I wanted you to understand that what happened on the bigger stage wasn't the sum total of you and me. I wanted you to look back at that moment and have at least one good, honest memory of your first kiss with a woman."

"Because someone gave you that?"

Cobie smiled. "I think you figured that out tonight."

"Talia," Lila said, without a hint of the jealousy that had filled her voice hours ago. "How did you meet?"

"She wrote the script for my third movie. Or she wrote the book the script was based on and consulted on the script, but the studio did a total hack job on the story. She denies it, but I know she only stayed with the project to protect me."

"Protect you?"

"I'd just turned eighteen. Finally street legal for all my male producers and directors and co-stars. What started as inappropriate jokes became uncomfortable conversations, which then turned into men twice my age pressing into my personal space and then worse, because suddenly without the law to protect me . . ." Cobie shuddered.

"You were fresh meat in a lion's den."

"But Talia became a lion tamer. Anytime someone got too close, she'd crack her whip and send them scattering. We spent so many nights in her trailer hanging out and talking. I told her about the boys and the bumbling and the shame of getting felt up on screen or off. She said it didn't have to be that way, then slowly, over time, she showed me."

"And you fell in love with her?"

"Yes," Cobie said, not having it in her to deny the charge even all these years later.

"Are you still in love with her?"

"No." The second answer came as fast and easy as the first. "But I'm indebted to her. She brought me out. She showed me who I am. She was kind and patient and caring. She saved me from more than just the skeezy Hollywood sharks. She saved me from years of pretending to be someone else or lying about myself and what I wanted. She saved me from thinking I had to compromise myself to fit someone else's ideal."

"I'm glad she was there for you."

"Me too, but she paid a heavy price," Cobie said sadly. "She's a brilliant writer and at such a young age. She's only a few years older than I am and was every bit as much a teen prodigy as you or I, but she made too many enemies trying to protect me. Because she kept some very powerful men from getting their hands on a body they felt entitled to, she got labeled hard to work with in the business. They called her a ballbuster and a dyke. Some of the men even defended themselves by accusing her of taking advantage of me. I think that hurt her more than anything. I think the strain of those allegations ultimately ran her away from Hollywood and everything associated with it."

"Including you?"

"Yeah." Cobie's jaw twitched at the memory of so many long lonely nights after she'd left. "The relationship lasted only a few months. She said we were better as friends, and as usual, she was right, but I think she worried the business had turned her into someone else."

"But where's she been for the last eight years?"

"Hiding away in the mountains at first. Then slowly starting to write again. *Vigilant* is her first book back," Cobie said, a hint of pride stirring in her chest again. "And it's a pretty spectacular reentry to the world."

"And you want a do-over, with you in the role of protector."

"I've never quite thought of it in those terms before, but yes. Our positions have changed. I want to usher her safely through the shark-infested waters this time. I want to give her the space and the confidence to shine and succeed without having to compromise again."

"And how does she feel about the sacrifices you're making?"

Cobie shook her head. "I think she appreciates the gesture but isn't really thrilled about the lengths I've gone to."

"And by lengths you've gone to, you mean she's not thrilled about me."

Cobie sighed. "She's not your biggest fan, but she doesn't know you, not the real you. Not many people do."

"No," Lila said. "I like it that way. Real is risky. Real is hard to control, which I think is why I got so upset about the first kiss.

It was too real. You were too real. I think I understood that from the very beginning. Even though I didn't want to. Real equals dangerous."

"See, I've always thought the opposite," Cobie said as she noticed the first glow of sunlight peeking in around the edges of the curtains. "It's the not knowing what's real that scares me most. Especially with people. None of my first times with men were real, but I didn't know that, so I was left confused, embarrassed, and unsteady. Then I started to expect embarrassment and confusion. I normalized all the wrong emotions. It wasn't until I experienced the real thing that I knew what I'd been missing. Which goes back to our first kiss."

Lila looked up at her and smiled playfully. "You wanted me to know what I'd been missing?"

Cobie laughed. "I wasn't nearly that sure of myself. I merely suspected you had gotten used to being shortchanged by the people you dated. I wanted you to know that I knew you deserved better than you'd been demanding for yourself."

Lila kissed her shoulder. "Most people think I'm already too demanding."

"Don't ever believe them," Cobie said seriously once more. "No matter what else happens, you've seen now how good things can be. Don't ever accept less."

"You're pretty smart, you know?" Lila said with a kiss to her cheek that sent Cobie's heart fluttering again. "I'm sorry I didn't realize that sooner too."

"I didn't give you a chance," Cobie admitted. "I haven't been very good at this charade. I'm sure I didn't inspire much confidence."

"Well you weren't exactly thrilled with the arrangement early on, but you have always been very good when the rubber hits the road. Too good, sometimes. Remember the night in the club in Vegas?"

"The time when you almost ditched me in the middle of a scene?"

Lila laughed. "Yes, that'd be the one, but I wasn't ditching you because you were bad. I ran because you were so good. If we'd stayed in the booth a second longer with your hands on me, I would have demanded you take me right then and there."

A shiver of excitement raced along Cobie's skin. "And if you'd have pushed a little harder in Toronto, I would've made love to you until the dawn burned all the darkness away."

"No," Lila protested. "I was a mess. You couldn't have possibly found me sexy with my puffy eyes and stuffy nose. God, I'm so sorry, Cobie. I hate that you saw me break down."

"Don't." Cobie kissed the top of her head. "I'm glad I was there."

"I freaked you out. You pulled away."

"Yes, but not for the reasons you think. I pulled away because of how much I felt for you. You cracked open my heart that night and crawled inside." Cobie held her a little tighter. "I didn't know what to do about that. I kept waiting for you to tell me what you needed, to give me some cues or a script, but you never did, and I floundered without you."

"I'm sorry I didn't talk to you. I didn't know how. It's not something many people know about. I wasn't sure I wanted you to be one of them."

The comment stung, even when delivered in a gently whispered tone, but she clamped her jaw shut against the urge to ask for more. This was more open than Lila had ever been with her, and she didn't want to undo the progress they'd made.

"I told Malik what happened," Lila said.

Cobie grimaced.

"It's not like that. It wasn't gossip."

"I can't imagine what he must have thought about me for bumbling through that."

"He wanted me to talk to you. He made some good points, but he also sort of scared me."

"How?"

Lila's shoulders tensed, as if the memory of the conversation still stressed her out. "Because he sort of suggested that if I'm ever going to let myself trust again, I'm going to have to deal with Selena."

"Your sister? Deal with her how?"

"I don't know," Lila said. "That's the scary part. I thought I already had. I haven't seen her in years. The only time I think about her is when I send her a monthly check so she'll stay out of the press."

"Wow." Lila paid off her sister to stay out of her life? "What did she do that was so bad?"

"Nothing," Lila said quickly, then added, "I'm not putting you off again. I mean it. She did nothing. When I needed her most, she walked away. She never answered calls or letters, just nothing."

"I don't understand."

"She's three years older than me, and we were poor. We shared a room. We shared homemade clothes and all our secrets. Our dad wasn't around, and our mom had a penchant for men and booze. We moved a lot. New rental houses, new schools, new stepdads or live-in boyfriends, but Selena was always there. And she promised she always would be. She taught me to cook and sew and dodge my mom's boyfriends. She said I could always count on her, no matter what. She said if we stuck together, things would get better eventually."

"But?"

"But things didn't get better. They kept getting worse. As years went on, my mom drank more, and the guys she dated got more violent. We started running out of food. There was so much yelling. Then came a boy with a fast motorcycle. He offered to take Selena away from it all, but you can't ride three on a bike."

"Oh, Lila." Cobie gave her a squeeze. "I'm so sorry."

"She just went with him one night. I cried and begged her not to leave me there alone in that awful trailer that reeked of cigarettes and desperation." Lila shook, and Cobie pulled up the blankets even though she knew they couldn't banish the chill in her now.

"Selena said she had to take care of herself, and she couldn't take care of me too. She peeled my hands off her and told me I had to learn to take care of myself. Then she walked out and left me in hell."

"And she never came back?"

"Not then, not when the boy left her, not when I moved out. Not even when our mother died. She never even tried to contact me until after I got famous. Even then, she only called because she needed some money. Shocking, right?"

"And you gave it to her?"

"I did. I was just getting started, and I'd worked hard to build my image as someone hot and exciting and, most importantly, uplifting. A trailer-trash sister talking to the press would've blown a major hole in my upbeat brand."

"Also, she's your sister."

Lila shrugged. "I waver back and forth on that. Most days it doesn't feel like I have a sister, but sometimes, I don't know, I just wish . . ."

"I get it," Cobie said softly, "and seeing me with Emma probably tripped some triggers for you."

"I think so. It hurt to see the contrast, but it was also good, you know?"

Cobie nodded, her chin rubbing the top of Lila's head. So many things made sense now. Lila's independence, the back and forth, the way her flippant attitude about relationships seemed to war with her passion about so many other things. But did understanding those connections actually change their situation in any way? Or did knowing what they were up against actually make their path harder than the less-than-blissful existence they'd shared before? She stared at the pale orange glow spreading slowly across the ceiling for a long time before she finally asked, "What are we going to do now?"

Lila sighed softly and shifted in her arm. "Try to get some sleep."

Cobie smiled. It wasn't the answer she'd hoped for, but it wasn't a bad idea either.

Lila placed a note on the table next to Cobie's bed. Part of her had wanted to talk before she left, but she didn't know how to say why, so it might be for the best that Cobie seemed dead to the world at eleven a.m. She hadn't woken when Lila got up or slipped away to her own room for a fresh change of clothes. She hadn't moved an inch in all the time it had taken Lila to shower and dress and sneak back in. Lila was a little jealous of her ability to succumb to physical oblivion so fully, but then again, if it weren't for the topics weighing so heavily on her mind, she might have slept the day away as well. Maybe if she just crawled back under the covers and snuggled into Cobie's protective embrace, she could lose all her troubles for a little while longer.

No. She'd put off her problems long enough, and after last night, she realized she'd paid a heavy price for doing so. She slipped quietly from the room.

Padding down the stairs, she pulled on ratty old tennis shoes and a ball cap, then, circumventing the press, headed out the side door where Malik waited with a rented car.

"You ready?" he asked.

"As much as I'll ever be."

They drove through the city in silence as images from the night before played through her mind. Cobie in her costume, dark eyes brooding with mystery. The moment when Cobie had pushed her, refusing to let her run, so strong, so fierce. The passion radiating off her as she lifted Lila to the bed, all raw strength and need. She shuddered as a little shot of arousal coursed through her again.

"You cold?" Malik asked.

Of course he would notice even the tiniest movement. "No, I'm fine."

She glanced around and realized she didn't recognize the neighborhood. It wasn't bad, or great, just nondescript. Lots of five- or six-story brick buildings lined with asphalt parking lots and covered bus stops. "Are we almost there?"

"It's the next block. I'll get out and sweep the stairway."

"No. You wait in the car."

"I'm sorry, but I can't let you go in until—"

"Malik, I have to do this," she said with a certainty she didn't feel. "You can guard the front door, but trust me, no one inside has the potential to hurt me more than they already have."

He pulled the car to a stop in front of a building that mirrored all the others and got out to open her door. "I want to go with you."

She hugged him as tightly as she could despite the fact that her arms didn't reach all the way around his massive torso. "I know. Me too."

He walked her to the door and stood with his arms folded across his chest. "I'll be right here."

She nodded. Knowing that did help a little as she climbed the stairs toward an address she'd written enough times to have memorized. Apartment 3A sounded so much less personal than this felt.

She raised a trembling hand, took a deep breath, and knocked three times.

She didn't get to wait and wonder, because the door swung open before she was ready to face the blue eyes so much like her own.

Selena took a step back as if shocked, but she managed to speak first. "It's you."

She nodded, still unable to form words as she processed all the similarities and differences: same eyes, same chin, but different hair, short and darker brown, like their mother's. Worry lines cut across her forehead, and parentheses etched deep around her lips, a smoker. Still, she hadn't lost her figure. She was nearly as slim and lithe as she'd been the day she'd ridden off into the north Florida sunset.

"It's never you," Selena mused. "I kept expecting you, but then so much time passed that I stopped."

"Can I come in?"

Selena nodded and opened the door wider to let her pass.

The place was nice enough. Clean, if not tidy. Lila hadn't known what she'd expected. She paid the bills, but she didn't know who Selena had become. Looking around now, she suspected their mother had colored her fears. At least Selena wasn't her. No one was her since she'd died nine years ago. Maybe she should ask Selena where she'd been then, but she couldn't bring herself to go back there.

"You want something to drink?" Selena asked, her voice firm, but the way she rubbed her palm gave away her nervousness. "I just have orange juice or water. If I'd known you were coming, I'd have gotten something else."

"I didn't know I was coming until about an hour ago," Lila said honestly.

"Why did you?"

"I don't know," Lila admitted. "I don't really have anything to say. Maybe I just wanted to see. I spent so many years wondering and worrying, afraid to go back, afraid to lose. I don't know. Maybe I just needed to face it. To face you."

"Well," Selena said slowly, "here I am."

Lila stared at her, waiting. Though for what, she couldn't say. She just felt like there should be more. An apology? An explanation? Some sort of emotional cue? Is this what Cobie felt each time Lila had stood there, stone faced amid her hurt and confusion?

"I'd ask if you were doing okay," Selena finally said, "but I see the news."

"The news rarely tells the full story."

Selena snorted. "No one ever does."

Lila shook her head. "What's that supposed to mean?"

"Just what you said, no story is ever a full story."

"I suppose you want me to ask for your story now?"

Selena shook her head. "There's not really much to tell, at least not much that would matter to you. I did some night school, waitressing, temping, there was man or two, none worth remembering. With your help I do fine, but all the interesting parts happened before we went our separate ways."

"Went our separate ways," Lila repeated. What a benign phrase for the worst tragedy of her life.

"If you're waiting for me to apologize, you should probably pull up a chair and make yourself at home because you'll be waiting awhile."

Lila sat but not to wait, to brace herself against the pain of the comment. "You don't regret any of it, do you?"

"Not a lick," Selena said, a hint of the old drawl tracing the edge of her voice. "Not because things turned out all that great for me, but every time I see you on TV or on stage somewhere, I know I did the right thing."

Lila blinked several times and even went so far as to open her mouth, but she couldn't form a response. Shouldn't it have been the other way around?

"You're a superstar, Lila. You're the poster girl for the strong, self-sufficient woman. Your whole career is like some how-to guide for independence."

"And?"

"And . . ." Selena drew out the word, then waited for Lila to fill in the blank before rolling her eyes. "Do you really think you'd be who you've become without the early lesson in independence?"

"Lesson in independence?" Lila exploded off the couch. "Is that how you justify it to yourself? Like some sort of tough love? Because your dumping me for the first guy with hot hands and fast wheels was some sort of selfless act that set me on the path to stardom? You don't get to take credit for who I am, not in any way. You didn't push me out of the nest to make me spread my wings. You walked out on me for a guy who turned around and walked out on you."

"Well, the last part is certainly true. He and I hadn't even been shacked up for six months before I woke up to find him and that pretty bike of his gone. I shouldn't have trusted him, but because I did, you didn't make the same mistake."

She couldn't believe Selena's logic.

"You never depended on anyone else. Hell, how many songs have you written on the subject. Never look to some man to save you, that's what you preach because you learned early to save yourself."

"You shattered me," Lila shouted.

"Obviously not." Selena shot back. "Your face is on a billboard that's twenty-five stories tall. You're a gazillionaire. You're one of the most powerful people under the age of thirty or something else some magazine ranked you as."

"I've never trusted anyone again." Lila practically choked on all the anguish gripping her throat.

"Good." Selena shot back. "That's my girl. No one can be trusted. Not our mother, not our friends, not any man I've ever met. They all get what they need and then they leave. That's what I tried to tell you the night I left."

"Oh, you did more than tell me. You showed me."

"And you took the lesson to heart. You were younger, but you were always smarter. It took me years to really get it, but you took off. You put your faith in you instead of depending on anyone else. If you came here today wanting to hear me say I was wrong, you wasted your time."

"Yeah," Lila said with a sigh. She wasn't sure what she'd come for, but it wasn't this. "I guess I did."

She pulled a check from her pocket and tossed it onto the coffee table. "How's your philosophy of not depending on people working out for you?"

Selena laughed. "Good dig, Lila. You always were a sassy kid. Always running around with that little gay boy and writing your weird poems on the cereal boxes. I know you don't believe me, but I'm glad you got out. I wanted it more for you than I did for me."

Lila shook her head again.

"I mean it," Selena said, catching her hand and giving it a tight squeeze. "Take care of yourself, always. You take care of you. You're the only one you can count on. Everyone else is only going to let you down eventually."

Lila pulled away. "Thanks for that again."

Then she walked out the door. She picked up her pace with each flight of stairs until she felt more like falling than running. She flew past Malik, who sprinted to keep up with her as people on the street stopped to stare.

"Ms. Wilder," he whispered. "Ms. Wilder, I have the car here. Ms. Wilder . . ."

She could hear him and see him, but she couldn't make sense of anything.

"Ms. Wilder." He finally stepped in front of her. "Lila, stop."

She did. Maybe it was his tone, or perhaps she was just lost enough to listen to a direct command.

"The car," he said firmly.

She blinked back tears and turned around in a slow circle. The sun shone overhead. Cars passed. People whispered. On the corner, a woman sat waiting for a bus, looking slowly from Lila to the gossip rag in her hand. On the cover, two photos shared side-by-side billing. The first one featured a perfectly framed and lit shot of Cobie kissing Lila at the party last night. The other was grainy and dark, but she knew the moment well enough to recognize the image of Cobie passing her phone back to Cordelia. Across the top of both photographs ran the headline "Date and Switch?"

The intersection spun, or maybe that was only her brain, but the lights whirred and the corners of her vision blurred until all the images blended together. Cobie, Selena, Cordelia.

"Lila," Malik said again softly, "let me take care of you."

"No," she said shakily. "I can take care of myself."

He regarded her seriously, his dark eyes full of concern.

She couldn't take his pity. The shame and embarrassment bore down heavily, but she would not buckle. She straightened her shoulders and blew out an exasperated breath. "I'm fine. Just get me a copy of all today's celebrity papers and meet me back at the car."

Then she turned and headed back to the car with her head held high.

Chapter Thirteen

"Good morning, Cobie. I had an important meeting I had to take this morning, and you were too beautiful to disturb, so you'll have to wait until I get home to hear all about it. —Lila." She smiled for the seventh time as she read the little note once more, then chuckled at the post script. "P.S. For future reference, this is how you leave a note for someone you've had amazing sex with."

She flopped back onto the bed. The sex had been amazing. She'd known at the time and every moment since then, but it still helped to know Lila recognized it too. It wasn't just sex though. She'd always suspected they'd be electric in bed, and they'd had plenty of previous experiences to bolster the belief, but last night offered something more. Last night hadn't been a lapse in judgment or some kind of emotional or physical breakdown. Maybe it started that way, but by the time morning had rolled around, they'd both been fully present and open in a way Cobie couldn't have imagined before. The emotional vulnerability surely equaled a game changer for them.

Neither she nor Lila could claim to be the people they'd pretended to be. They couldn't deny their connection went beyond work and play. Not anymore. The only question now was who would they become? And for the first time, Cobie was excited to find out.

She heard the front door open and fought the urge to bound down the stairs like a puppy. Then she heard it slam heavily, and her exuberance dimmed. Lila's footsteps fell heavy on the stairs but didn't stop on the second floor. The stomping continued up to the third story and only stopped when another slamming door echoed through the upper floor. Cobie's chest tightened, but she dared to hope Hurricane Lila had merely been sparked by a frustrating business meeting. Pulling on a pair of sweatpants and a Bramble College hoodie, she told herself to be brave. Dating a woman like Lila meant taking all of her, the talents and moods, the passion and the thunder. Besides, Lila had been angry the night before and that ended pretty well. She wouldn't mind a repeat performance.

With a cocky grin, she climbed the stairs, already picturing a fiery reunion. She paused outside the door long enough to note Lila wasn't playing any music before she knocked.

"I'm working," came a sharp retort.

"I've got some very important work to do too," Cobie called.

"Then go do it downstairs."

Cobie's smile faltered. She'd expected a little softer response when Lila heard her voice. "Actually, it's important work for both of us."

Lila sighed loud enough to be heard through the door before opening it. "Cobie, I've got a lot going—"

Cobie silenced her with a kiss. All the rigidity eased from Lila's shoulders as her hands came to rest on Cobie's hips. Cobie reveled in the brush of her softening lips and drank from the sweetness of their shared breath.

"Thank you," Lila said as they parted.

"Thank you," Cobie replied. "Now tell me about all the important work you have to do."

Lila's jaw twitched. "We need to go over today's press and start working out our break-up schedule."

Cobie's heart gave one painful thud. "What?"

Lila turned and walked into the studio where she'd spread out several newspapers and magazines on her glossy black piano. Cobie followed her slowly, all the skip gone from her step. Dread circled her like an icy wind.

Every one was open to a photo of Cobie and Cordelia Esme. Never mind that each was basically the same shot, either from a different angle or lit differently or cropped differently. A few of the stories had other photos of Cobie and Lila together or of Lila alone at the piano, but the sum total made it look like Cobie had spent most of her evening ensconced on the terrace with another woman while her girlfriend had sung her heart out inside.

"The event was covered by every major media outlet," Lila finally said.

"Cover or skewed?" Cobie asked, collecting the papers. "They make me look like a philanderer."

"They make you look dark, edgy, morally ambiguous, basically you're Vale."

"Yeah, well, Vale is single. I'm not."

"About that," Lila said as she walked around the piano, still inspecting the photographs. "I know we initially said we'd drag things out with a couple of big public fights, but that was before last night."

"Before we made love?" Cobie asked, her hope rebounding. "Before we slept in each other's arms?"

Lila winced. "Before you were photographed getting cozy with another pop star."

"The only pop star I got cozy with last night was you," Cobie said, "and you know that."

"Hmm." Lila made a noncommittal sound and pointed to a photo spread in the *Post*. "Did you see this one?"

Cobie glanced over her shoulder to inspect a shot of Cobie holding tightly to Lila's wrist as she tried to pull away.

"I wish more photographers had gotten that angle. Have you been online? Maybe there's video." She pulled out her phone while Cobie stared on in disbelief. "Look, one came up right away. *Access Hollywood* posted it two hours ago."

Cobie heard her voice coming from the phone. "You're all in my business all the time. I can't even talk to someone without you getting jealous and judgmental."

"Lila." Cobie tried to interrupt, but the video wouldn't pause itself.

"Oh sure, now you don't have anything to say?" Cobie continued through phone. "What, you don't want all your fancy friends to hear there's trouble in paradise? Wouldn't want anyone to see the cracks in your glittery armor."

"That was good," Lila said almost admiringly.

Cobie snatched the phone from her hand. "That was a play, fiction. It wasn't *real*."

"Real is what we make it." Lila grabbed the phone back. "And we can make a lot out of this. We could spin the story so you actually run off with Cordelia."

"Are you out of your fucking mind?"

"Yeah, she could never pull that off," Lila said quickly. "A little slow on the uptake, that one."

Cobie frowned. Cordelia hadn't seemed slow to her. She'd seemed kind and honest, but now didn't seem like the time to say so.

"I think the best option here is to paint me as jealous and dramatic and possessive. I could work with that. I could play the nightmare girlfriend driven crazy by her own suspicions."

"Are we still talking about acting, because that's actually what this feels like here."

"We've only ever been acting," Lila said quickly, but a little muscle in her jaw twitched, telling Cobie the lie hadn't exactly rolled off her tongue.

She pounced. "Bullshit, Lila. You don't believe that. I don't for a second believe you do. You can tell yourself whatever you want about what happened at the party. I don't care. But you cannot pretend like what happened between us didn't matter or didn't change anything for you, because I was there."

Lila rolled her eyes but seemed lost for an actual comeback. "What the hell happened between then and now?"

"I got back to work," Lila said coolly. "I suggest you do so too."

"No," Cobie said flatly.

"Excuse me?"

"If by going back to work you mean stop caring about you, about us, then I won't. If going back to work means I pretend everything I know to be fake is real and everything I know in my heart to be real is just some game, then I'm done."

"Done?" Lila asked incredulously. "Something doesn't go your way, so you just walk out?"

"Go my way?" Cobie looked around the room dramatically. "Are there cameras in here? Am I being punked? Are the paparazzi looking in the window? Why won't you acknowledge what happened last night?"

"We had sex last night," Lila said bluntly.

"We made love."

"If you want to call it that, fine. It was wonderful, Cobie." Lila's voice softened. "Truly. I will always cherish those memories, but they don't change anything. We both have dreams and plans. We both have careers, and we both have goals. That's why we got together, and that's why we have to go our separate ways. We can't let temporary feelings get in the way of what really matters."

"Oh," Cobie said stepping back. "Temporary feelings versus what really matters. Yeah, well, if that's what we're talking about here, I guess I can't blame you for, um, for dumping me, I guess."

"I'm not dumping you. We're following through on a business arrangement."

"Saying it that way actually makes it feel worse." Cobie tried to keep her voice steady despite finding it hard to draw a full breath. "I can handle being dumped. I've been rejected before. But last night, hell, the last few weeks, since I don't even know for sure when, it wasn't about business for me."

"Everything's about business for me," Lila said flatly. "It's all I've got."

"Did you ever think those two things might be related?" Cobie asked.

"Excuse me?"

"Maybe all you've got is business because that's all you ever let matter," Cobie said. "Maybe that's why you run through a string of fake relationships a mile long instead of making real human connections."

"I think it's time for you to leave the studio now."

"Why? I thought this was supposed to be an honest space, an open space, or is that something else that only applies to you? 'Cause you seem to have a lot of those spaces in your life." Cobie exploded. "You love rules when they're keeping everyone around you in check, but you don't care for them much when they bite you in the ass. Well, guess what? It's all going to come back and bite you in the ass."

"Cobie," Lila warned, but Cobie refused to heed her tone.

"You can micromanage your songs and your career and your marketing. You can hold stadiums in the palm of your hand." She had picked up steam now, and if she had to get thrown out, she intended to do so on her own terms. "You can line up a row full of pretty people to be seen on your arm wearing all the hippest trends. You can control your tight little empire."

"Oh, I intend to."

"But where will they be when you stumble, and you will stumble eventually, Lila. Everyone does. Late at night when the music fades and the lights are low, will you even recognize yourself in the mirror? What will you do when you've lied so much you don't remember what was real? When you've sold out everyone who cares about you? Will your limelight keep you warm? What about those trends you're always chasing? Will they hold you at night while you cry?"

"I mean it, Cobie. If you don't walk away right now—"

"You'll what? Break up with me? You'll say bad things about me in the press? How's that any different than what you're doing now? At least maybe then you'd be telling the truth. Maybe if I'm a jerk I could at least make an honest woman out of you."

"All right," Lila snapped. "That's enough. I wanted to do this the easy way. I was prepared to play the bad guy, the crazy girlfriend, the drama queen to your steady, stoic, upright self, because believe it or not, I actually do care about you."

Cobie snorted. "You've got a funny way of showing it."

"Maybe I do, but then again, maybe if you didn't have your head so far up your sanctimonious ass you could see something other than your own point of view. God, you're such a hypocrite."

"Me? A hypocrite? That's rich coming from someone who orchestrates fauxmances to score press points."

"And what exactly do you think you've been doing for the last few months?" Lila shot back. "Knitting hats for newborns? Working in a soup kitchen? Traveling the world with the Peace Corps? Oh wait, you've been right here beside me the whole time."

"That's different."

"Get off your moral high horse for a minute there, cowgirl, and tell me, did you or did you not agree to date me in the hopes of getting a movie deal?"

"I did, but—"

"And did you or did you not kiss me at a time when you felt anything but romantic because the press was watching?"

"Yes, but you—"

"And did you feel me up in a club when you knew the paparazzi would be given a full view?"

"Lila stop—"

"Have you been living here under my roof, going to my concerts, wearing my designs because you fell head over heels with me the first morning at Stan and Mimi's office, or did you do so because attaching yourself to me would help you get to make Talia's movie?"

Cobie opened her mouth, but she couldn't decide what to say. There were so many questions, and not just the ones Lila had asked.

"That's what I thought. You used me to get a career boost, the exact same way I used you. You knew the agreement going in, and you signed on the dotted line anyway."

"But I tried to be honest. I tried at every turn to be fair."

"You didn't," Lila said matter-of-factly. "Fair would have been accepting the terms at face value. Fair would have been not trying to change the agreement halfway through. Fair would have been taking responsibility for your own role in this. Just because you bitched and moaned about the details doesn't make you any better than me. If anything, it makes you more disingenuous."

"I'm not going to stand here and be lectured to about honesty by you, of all people."

"Why not?" Lila asked. "I'm the only one who was honest about what I wanted out of this relationship. I never pretended to be someone I'm not. You even lied to yourself. I've been painfully truthful about what I want from you, from my career, and from my life. I was also up front about what mattered to me and how I intended to protect it."

"Am I supposed to thank you for that? Pin a medal on your chest? Give you an award for being some cutthroat business shark who's willing to sell your own love life to make a few bucks. You've never done a selfless thing in your whole life. You've never lifted a finger for anything that doesn't serve your own interests. Owning that doesn't make you a hero. It makes you soulless."

"And what does it make you?" Lila asked. "Because the only difference between us right now is I can admit what I'm doing and why. Can you say the same, Cobie?"

Cobie stood there, eyes wide, face burning. She had so many emotions roiling inside her right now, but she couldn't give voice to them. Had Lila merely stunned her into submission, or was her silence born out of shame? Lila was right about a few things. She'd never misled Cobie about her intentions. She had never lied about her priorities or her goals. Cobie had gone into their relationship with her eyes wide open. She'd known exactly what she had signed on for, and she'd given the whole charade her signature of approval anyway. If she'd lied at any point about the nature of who they were or what they were doing together, it had only been to herself.

"Look," Lila finally said, more softly, "I'm not sorry for what we've done. I don't regret anything, but you and I both know that happily-ever-after is just some myth people like us help perpetuate with our songs and movies. That's the nature of the business, but in the end, it's all we really have to go on. Business."

Cobie's chest ached, but she couldn't argue with all the self-doubt whirling through her mind. She didn't know what she believed anymore. She wasn't even sure who she was.

When Cobie didn't reply, Lila nudged her again. "I have to get back to work now."

"Yeah," Cobie finally mumbled as she turned to go. "I guess you do."

The studio had no windows, which filled the dual purpose of enhancing sound quality and limiting distractions. It also helped the room function as a sort of de facto time deprivation chamber. Lila wasn't sure if she'd been inside for hours or days, but either way, she had little to show for her dedication. She'd written and scrapped no less than seven tunes and hadn't approached anything even resembling a cohesive lyric. Worst of all, she had no one but herself to blame, though that didn't stop her from yelling at Felipe when he knocked on the door.

"Doesn't anyone around here understand what it means when I go into the studio? Am I the only person here with a job to do? Do I follow any of you around interrupting your work time?"

"Yeah, all the time, Ms. Thang," Felipe said as he swung open the door.

"Felipe, get out. I'm not leaving here until I write a godforsaken love song."

"Sounds like you're coming right along, and I'll let you get back to your thrilling progress, but I wanted you to know Cobie's leaving."

"Fine. I don't need the car tonight. Tell Malik to drive her wherever she needs to go."

"No, girl," he said more slowly. "She's not going out. She's leaving. As in, like, taking her own car and all her suitcases."

"What?" Lila rose from the piano bench so quickly that several of her stiff muscles spasmed and she had to brace herself before forcing them to move again. "We never agreed to that. She never said a word about leaving. Tell her to come here."

"Yeah." He drew out the word to have multiple syllables. "Not going to happen."

"You're not going to tell her, or she's not going to listen?"

"Both, either, D, all of the above," Felipe said with a dramatic shake of his head. "This message was for informational purposes only. Need to know, just like you been keeping me lately."

She rolled her eyes. She'd have to deal with that little comment later. Right now, she had more pressing concerns. She strode purposefully across the room and thundered down the stairs in time to see Cobie fish her keys out of her pocket. She wore dark jeans and a black hoodie. Her black hair was spiked in its usual haphazard way, adding a chic edge, but she'd foregone the make-up she'd taken to using lately. She didn't need it anyway. The circles under her eyes more than compensated for the lack of eye shadow, even in profile.

"Where are you going?"

"Home." Cobie said the word as if it hurt.

"To the Catskills?"

"Yes."

"For how long?"

Cobie finally looked her square in the face. "We're done, Lila."

She gasped at the finality of the statement. "But we still have work—"

"No," Cobie said calmly. "You have work. I have work. You've got your story. I've got mine. *We* have run our course. *We* are over. You said so already. It's time to tie up the loose ends."

"You're just angry about earlier."

"I'm not," Cobie said, then seemed to think for a few seconds. "What I feel isn't anger, and even if it were, it's not aimed at you. You made valid points. You go after what you want, and you shouldn't have to apologize or feel guilty about that, but I need to get to that point too, and I can't do it here."

"You can't do it with me around, you mean."

"Yes. That too. I got in over my head with you, Lila. Again, my fault. I take responsibility. I played the willing fool, but I've been typecast before, and I don't want to make the same mistake again. I need to break out of that role before it becomes too natural for me."

"No discussion? You've made up your mind and there's nothing I can do to change it?"

Cobie shrugged. "I don't know. Is there?"

Lila pursed her lips. She knew what Cobie wanted her to say: that she hadn't meant anything she'd said earlier, she really did care about her, their time together hadn't all been a game. But what did any of that matter? Because it was the truth? The truth didn't solve anything. Truth was an abstract concept. The truth wouldn't save her from loneliness, from doubt, from grief. Nothing lasted forever. People always left when things got hard, a point Cobie was proving expertly right now. Things hadn't gone the way she'd wanted, so she was out. Lila should be glad for the reminder. It should have hardened her resolve. Instead, she said, "I really thought you were different."

"I am," Cobie said sadly, "but I forgot that for a while."

"So that's it?" Lila asked, a sense of helplessness rolling over her.

Cobie nodded. "I hope you get whatever you want with the new album, your career, everything. You deserve it."

Lila couldn't tell if the statement was meant to be a compliment or a cut-down, but all the fight had drained out of her, or maybe the sadness had merely pushed it aside.

"Hey, just to prove there's no hard feelings, I left you a peace offering upstairs." Cobie said it with a sad smile. "It's probably not good enough for you, but at least I'll be able to say I tried."

"Tried what?" Lila asked suspiciously.

"To live up to my end of the bargain. Maybe this will make up for some of the times I fell short."

Lila sighed. "You didn't fall short."

Cobie shook her head, "I did. In a lot of ways. But thank you for not bringing them all up right now." Then she leaned in to kiss her softly on the cheek.

"Cobie, please," Lila whispered.

"Just take care of yourself, okay?"

Lila nodded. That was the whole point, wasn't it? Everything she'd ever done was to take care of herself. She was the only person up for the job, so she stepped back when all she wanted to do was hold on. She kept silent when she wanted to call out, and she stayed still as Cobie walked out the door, no matter how badly she ached to go after her.

Then she forced herself to turn and walk up the stairs instead of watching out the window as Cobie drove away. She could handle only one thing at a time, and the stairs were all she had to focus on at the moment. Each one felt like her own personal Everest. Her limbs grew heavy and her breath shallow. By the time she reached the second story, she couldn't imagine climbing another flight, and even if she did, what good could come of sitting in the studio. Love songs weren't an option for her today. Maybe they never were.

She wandered down the hall, getting only as far as the living room before she could go no farther. She would have preferred to make it all the way to the soft ottoman, but the lethargy cemented her joints, forcing her to ease onto the closest surface. The piano bench was unforgiving, but at least she had to stay upright instead of sinking into full oblivion. She should probably be thankful for the reminder that music never let her down, but right now, music also served as a reminder of everything her career demanded of her.

She sighed heavily and placed her fingers on the keys, then let them go slack. She didn't even have the energy to tinker. But as she reached up to fold down the music stand, she noticed an envelope resting there. The front read "Lila" in bold, efficient script.

Remembering Cobie's mention of a peace offering, she slipped her finger under the loosely fastened flap and slowly pulled out the enclosed papers. The first page read,

"Dear Lila, I'm sorry I didn't always make your job easy. Maybe this will make up for that a little bit. Go ahead and tell people you wrote it about me. I'll play the bad guy, because believe it or not, I want only the best for you. Cobie."

Lila flipped to the next page, and her breath caught. She recognized the words as song lyrics even before she read them. The title simply said, "Miss Me."

You know all the moves,
You know all the right plays
You charm the whole word
With mysterious ways

You know what's cool
You embody what's hot
You like what's hip
And baby, I'm not

So go ahead and move on
Chase the next trend
Go on and see
What's around the next bend
But you're gonna miss me
Baby, you know
You're gonna miss me
After I go

You're flash and sizzle
You're sparkle and shine
You're a star in the sky
That was never really mine

But I'm not what you want
I'm just what you got
You're looking for chic
And baby, I'm not

So go ahead and move on
Chase the next trend
Go on and see
What's around that next bend
But you're gonna miss me
Baby, you know
You're gonna miss me
After I go

I could've fought beside you
Could've turned wrong into right
I could've held you forever
And stayed strong through the fight

But you're in fashion
You own every endeavor
And I'm just the one,
Who could've loved you forever

So go ahead and move on
Chase the next trend
Go on and see
What's around that next bend
But you're gonna miss me
Baby, you know
You're gonna miss me
After I go.

Lila's fingers fell on the keys once more. This time, not only did they have the energy to play, they also knew the notes. The melody flew out of her as if the words themselves set the tune. It only took three run-throughs to confirm her fears.

She had her love song.

She could record it. She could make it a hit and sell millions of copies the world over. But could she bring herself to perform it every night knowing full well the song was about her?

She recognized the truth there. She'd claimed to seek it. She'd said she told it, professed to live it in all the places that really mattered. Perhaps that was why she had to go forward. No matter what other choices she'd made in her life, she had always prided herself on always singing the truth. But never before had the truth hurt so badly.

Chapter Fourteen

"She what?" Stan leaned closer to the speaker on his phone in case he hadn't heard the information clearly the first time his receptionist had spoken the words.

"Cobie Galloway messaged to say her cell phone reception is spotty in the Catskills and if you have any time-sensitive offers, you should email her."

"Right." He dropped the paper he'd been holding as the implications of one seemingly innocuous statement sank in. "Can you please ask Ms. Levy to join me at her earliest convenience."

"I'm already here," Mimi declared as she pushed open the glass door with her shoulder, her arms full of tabloids and entertainment magazines.

Stan didn't smile. He merely leaned close to the speaker once more and said, "Hold my calls," before disconnecting.

"Cobie finally got in touch?" Mimi asked, dropping the stack of papers onto his desk.

"Barely. She texted my receptionist. Did Lila call you?"

"No, and Felipe isn't talking either, but he's not happy about something."

"That's so unlike her."

"Felipe? He's got a femme streak, but I think he still identifies as a *he*."

Stan rolled his eyes. "I meant Lila. It's not like Lila to be out of contact for days after a major press push."

"Oh." Mimi sighed and looked up at him for the first time. The dark circles under her eyes showed faintly through her concealer, and her frown lines etched even through the work of gifted technicians.

These little tells didn't make her any less beautiful, but they did make him wonder if she could see similar signs of strain in him. He shook his head. They both had enough to worry about without adding their vanity to the list. "Cobie's in the Catskills."

"She ran out on her?"

"Or Lila threw her out."

"It's too soon." Mimi leaned against his desk.

He sifted through a few of the gossip rags, noting that many of them had begun to suspect Cobie and Lila weren't living together anymore.

"But for them, for Cobie and Lila. They should have had more time."

"They should have fought for more time," he said, not sure if he felt disappointed in Cobie for not seeing that or disappointed in himself for caring enough to have an opinion on his client's romantic relationships beyond a publicity stance. "But at the end of the day, they both did their jobs."

"Maybe that's all either of them really know," Mimi said, sadness creeping into her voice. "Kids in this business, they are their jobs. I just thought maybe Cobie might be the one to show Lila something more."

"Maybe she did. Maybe Lila didn't like what she saw."

"Or maybe Cobie was too unyielding to give Lila the space she needed to—"

"Hey now." He cut in with a twinge of defensiveness. "I never saw Cobie doing any pushing. That was *your* girl in the driver's seat."

"Not the last time she was here. You saw her. She didn't make a single unreasonable demand."

"And that's the best compliment you can give her? No wonder Cobie's hiding in the mountains."

Mimi sighed. "Maybe she's hiding in the mountains because she got her heart broken."

The thought made his stomach clench. "And Lila hasn't called you because she's not ready to move on or make light of a break-up that feels too much like a break-up?"

Mimi didn't respond, but her eyes were hazy and unfocused.

"Hey," he whispered, reaching for her hand. "You can't do this for her."

"I know," she whispered.

"They're both adults, a fact they staked their careers and reputations on proving."

"I know."

"And they did their jobs." He lifted up one of the papers for emphasis. The headline read, "What's Next?" over a picture of Cobie and Lila. "They did what they set out to do from day one. Now all you and I can do is try to capitalize on the fall-out."

Mimi sighed, pushing off the desk and straightening the jacket of her red pantsuit. "I've already booked Lila in the Jungle Studios with a full team of techs and producers for the next two weeks."

"And I've got a meeting with Warner Brothers, Sony, and Paramount in the next two days to pitch *Vigilant* as a full package treatment."

"Good." Mimi nodded resolutely, then shifted from one three-inch heel to the other, undercutting her determined posture.

He wanted to soothe her, to tell her they'd done what they could, that they were good at their jobs. Both statements were true, and they'd always been more than enough. But for some reason, this time the words felt flat, even as they left his mouth. "We can't give them what they won't admit they need."

Her brightly painted lips curled up in a way that made his heart give one unexpectedly loud thud. "Why not? I do it with you all the time."

"Mimi, what are you going to do?"

"Nothing," she said breezily as she strolled toward the door, but as she pushed it open once more, he could have sworn he heard her add, "Yet."

"Cheers." Talia lifted her champagne flute and relaxed into her Adirondack chair on Cobie's back deck.

"Isn't it bad luck to toast a contract that hasn't been signed yet?" Cobie asked, even as she clinked the glass with her own.

"Hell if I know. It's been years since I've signed a movie contract."

Cobie had signed more than a few in that time, but somewhere along the way, she'd lost her excitement about doing so. *Vigilant* would be the first one to bring back some of that joy if the project went through.

Plenty of things could still go wrong in the next couple of weeks. Stan was working around the clock to hammer out the details, but it did seem as though all the major components were in place. Talia had been granted top billing in the screenwriting department, and the treatment had sold as a package deal with Cobie in the lead role. As far as she knew, no one had balked at the condition. She and Talia had also stipulated the importance of a female director, and each of the competing studios had agreed, though they'd made their own requests as to who that would be. The producers weighed in on that front as well, but so far, all the names being tossed around met with Cobie's approval.

"I'm still pulling for Sophia Coppola," Talia said as if reading her mind.

Cobie smiled as she stared off across the little valley. The vista had recently reached the tipping point from brown to green. Spring came later to the Catskills than it did to much of the country, but the mountains always made the wait worthwhile.

"Patty Jenkins would be good too."

Cobie nodded.

"And Jodie Foster rounds out my top three."

Cobie might have rearranged the order or made a few additions, but she didn't argue any of their merits. She hadn't had to argue about much of anything really. Everything came together much easier than she'd anticipated—if a multi-month dating charade that left her heart broken and her pride battered was considered easy. She'd been out of the city for nearly a month, and still the mountains had not fully healed her. She tried to pretend that fact didn't worry her, just like she pretended not to notice Lila hadn't called or released the song she'd written. But even with all the practice she'd had of late, she still hadn't perfected the art of lying to herself.

"Oh, and we have to get the designer who did your Vale costume for the party. What's her name?"

The question jarred her back into the moment, but once again, all trails of thought led back to Lila somehow. "Addie Hammels."

"Never heard of her. Where'd you find her?"

"Lila found her."

"Oh," Talia said. "Sorry."

"Why?"

"Didn't mean to bring up she-who-must-not-be-named."

"I'm fine. You can bring her up and say her name."

Talia made a face as if she'd eaten something sour and then shook her copper-topped head.

"Really, it's fine," Cobie said. "Lila, Lila, Lila."

"Don't turn around three times, or she might appear."

Cobie laughed in spite of a little twinge in her gut suggesting she wouldn't totally hate that option. "You were talking about the designer, though, right?"

"But do we want to use her if Lila owns her?"

"The costume was on point," Cobie said. "Besides, just because Lila collaborated with her doesn't mean she owns her."

"Fine, then who is she? What's she like? Who does she normally work with?"

Cobie shrugged. "I never met her."

"She didn't fit you?"

"No. Lila did all the sewing."

Talia arched one eyebrow so high it disappeared under her bangs.

"But this Addie woman did the design. Lila was adamant she get full credit."

"The great one shared credit with someone else? Who is Addie Hammels, and where did she learn the art of sorcery?"

Cobie wanted to argue, to defend Lila. She shared none of Talia's animosity, but she wasn't naïve either. For Lila to have a hand in something and not want her share of the headlines was highly suspect. "I'll admit, something never added up there. Lila insisted I give this Addie all the praise, despite the fact that Lila played a major part in the design production."

"Maybe they're lovers."

The idea made Cobie's stomach turn but didn't make sense either, not with the way Lila had kissed her that night. Then again, a lot of other things that had happened between them didn't fit with the way they'd made love either. "I don't pretend to understand why Lila does what she does, but I have a hard time imagining she'd take a backseat to a lover."

"If not love, then money? Fame?"

That seemed closer to realistic. "Lila doesn't ever do anything she can't sell, but I'm not sure how an unknown designer can offer Lila something she doesn't already have in spades."

"Let's Google her." Talia pushed up off the chair and pulled her phone from the pocket of her cardigan.

Cobie sat forward and watched her friend pace over the knotted pine floorboards. Talia was still beautiful even though the earliest signs of age had begun to show on her forehead and settle on her hips. She was attractive without needing to be made up, smart without being conceited, creative without being insecure, and loyal to a fault. Talia was genuine and trustworthy, and they'd had more than enough sexual chemistry in their day. Why had it been so easy to let go, or to remain friends? Why couldn't Cobie summon any of the feelings for her that still pulsed in her for Lila? Was there simply too much water under their bridge, or was it something more?

"I'm not finding anything," Talia finally said. "Not at any of the agencies or schools. The only hit for Addie Hammels and design is some teenager with an arts blog."

"That can't be right."

"No, this kid looks like she was in a cancer hospital."

Cobie's heart sank. "Let me see."

Talia handed her the phone. Sure enough, one of the first pictures was of a young girl in a bed, her head bald and a series of tubes and wires extending from her arm.

"That can't be her," Talia said. "Right?"

Cobie clicked on the photo gallery tab and thumbed through several pictures, each one growing increasingly dark. The figure in the drawing turned angrier, lonelier, more haunting. Her heart hammered with each swipe until suddenly she stilled. There was the drawing of Vale's costume in black and white and gray. She silently handed the phone back to Talia, who studied the screen for a second before sitting down again.

"What does it mean?" Talia asked.

Cobie shook her head.

"There's a number. I'm going to call."

Cobie waited as patiently as she could, trying not to jump to conclusions. Not that she had any conclusions. Nothing made sense. A teenage girl? Well that sort of made sense in that the demographic fit with Lila's appeal. But a cancer hospital? Where would they have even met? And why wouldn't Lila have just told her?"

"Hello, I am trying to get ahold of a representative for Ms. Addie Hammels," Talia said into the phone. "Oh, I see. May I ask who's representing her?"

Cobie waited, watching her green eyes widen.

"No. Thank you. I already know how to get ahold of them."

Talia hung up the phone and tossed it on the table before downing the last of her champagne. "So she's a minor, but she's got a legal guardian who doubles as her creative representation. That lawyer can be reached at the office of Levy and Levy."

Cobie sat very still for a long time as an idea began to form, only a loose connection on a complex timeline, but it nagged at her brain. "Can I see her website again?"

Talia handed her the phone, and Cobie scrolled through the blogs, back to about the time she and Lila had started their charade. From there it only took a couple entries to find what she was looking for. A post titled "Out of time" started with the line, "Looks like the cancer didn't kill me this time, so I'm off to conversion therapy. I don't know. I think I would have rather had another round of chemo."

"What?" Talia asked, hopping up again. "God, all the color just drained out of your face."

"She's the one," Cobie mumbled.

"The designer?"

"No. I mean yes, but also," Cobie shook her head, "she might be the kid who set Lila off about conversion therapy."

"Slow down. That's a major leap to make."

"It's not." She thumbed back up and read only enough to notice the shift in Addie's writings and in the drawings she shared over the next few weeks. "There's all this talk about parents and conversion therapy, and then there's not. All of a sudden, she has a lawyer and money and a design contract. Where does a kid come into those kinds of resources without support from her family?"

"Fairy Godmother?"

"Yeah," Cobie said, "or fairy pop star."

"You don't know that."

"One week the kid is living in a hospital under threat of anti-gay torture, and the next she's supporting herself and Lila Wilder is hand-producing her concepts?" Cobie's mind spun. "That's why Lila was so adamant I give Addie all the credit. She's trying to set the kid up quietly. She doesn't want to overshadow her. She wants her to make it on her merits, not because she's Lila's pet project."

"You're inferring a lot."

"And what about Lila's sudden interest in conversion therapy?

That just happens to pop up right around the time she buys the Vale design from a kid who's about to be shipped off to religious zealot camp?"

Talia finally shrugged. "Yeah, I guess that'd be a pretty big coincidence."

"It also means they go back months, even before Lila and I lived together," Cobie said as the full gravity of that statement hit her. "The costume, the kid, she took care of me and Addie at the same time and never asked for credit even when I accused her of being selfish and an attention-hog and flighty. She pulled this kid out of hell all by herself without so much as dropping an anonymous tip to the press about what a saint she was, and I called her self-centered."

"Hey, don't beat yourself up. You know what they say about broken clocks being right twice a day."

"Don't. I know you want to make her the bad guy here, but she's clearly not a villain. I was unfair to her. At the end, I was even kind of terrible." She dropped her head into her hands as echoes of their last fight roared around her skull. "I said she'd never done a selfless thing in her whole life and she'd never lifted a finger for anything that didn't serve her own interests. What kind of asshole says that to someone who went on a personal crusade to save gay kids?"

"Stop," Talia commanded. "You didn't know. You couldn't have known because she didn't want you to. It's not like you didn't ever give her a chance to open up to you. I know you would have crawled across hot coals for this woman if she'd asked nicely. She chose not to."

"Maybe if I'd given her more credit."

"No," Talia snapped. "You did everything but beg her to level with you. Even now she could pick up the phone and explain everything to you, but words don't mean anything until she starts making different choices."

"Maybe she would have if I'd put a little more trust in her instead of always assuming the worst."

"That's not how trust works. You can't keep giving it and giving it in the hopes that someday someone will be worthy of it." Talia put her hand on Cobie's shoulder and squeezed. "You had every right to question your trust in someone who consistently proved herself to be untrustworthy."

"Maybe," Cobie said, though she wasn't sure anymore. "I guess it doesn't really matter whether I should trust Lila or not. The bigger issue right now is that I don't trust myself."

"Cobe, you're one of the best, most honest, most caring people I've ever met."

"And yet, I made the same choices as Lila over the last few months and gave a lot less back. I lied. I cheated the system. I pretended to be someone I wasn't, and not for the greater good, for a movie deal."

"It wasn't just for a movie deal," Talia said quietly. "You did it for me. You weren't chasing your own fame. You were trying to put yourself in a position to right a wrong."

"Sure, I had my reasons, but apparently, Lila has hers too. Why do I get a pass and she gets condemnation? At least some of her motivations seem to justify her actions, right? At least some good can come of hers. Can the same be said for me? Or did I just sell my name and image to score a blockbuster for me and my best friend?"

"Do you regret it?"

"What does that matter?"

"It matters to me," Talia said sadly.

Cobie thought about her answer. She thought about all the frustration and the anger and the hurt feelings and the loss of her sense of right and wrong. "No. I don't regret it. And maybe that's what scares me the most. Even knowing what I know now about what I'd lose and what I'd gain, I'd make the same choice again."

"Because of me?" Talia asked.

Cobie shook her head. It would be easier to say yes, but it wouldn't be the truth, and she'd had enough of the lies.

"Then why?"

"Because of Lila."

⊠ ⊠ ⊠

"But you're gonna miss me, baby, you know," Lila sang soulfully into the studio mic, her voice lower and huskier than her usual register, but she was almost done, so she closed her eyes and sang-whispered one last time. "You're gonna miss me after I go."

The music faded slowly, and she exhaled some of the sadness she'd held at bay before opening her eyes. When she did, she met the astonished expressions of everyone on the other side of the recording booth window. Felipe's dark eyes were wide, and Mimi's jaw had gone slack. The producer looked from one tech to another before finally shrugging and turning back to Lila. "I got nothing. No notes."

Lila blinked a few times. "So again?"

He shook his head. "I think your first take was flawless, but if you want to go again—"

"I don't," Lila interrupted, quickly pulling her headphones off and throwing open the door of that stifling, little box of a room.

"Lila, girl, where did you, I mean, I could just . . . wow." Mimi pulled her into a hug. "I mean, you keep getting better with every release, but that was something else entirely."

She didn't feel like she was getting better. She should have by now. It had been almost a month since Cobie had left. Lila should have bounced back in half that time. She should be on someone else's arm by now. She shouldn't have any trouble getting through that song.

"It's going to be a hit," the producer agreed, giddily. "This song is going to make us all so much money."

"It's your first single, right?" one of the techs asked. "I can work through the night and have it layered and packaged by the end of the week."

"Yes," the producer answered for her. "God, the twenty-five to thirty-four market will eat this with a spoon. So much power, so much remorse."

Mimi squeezed her hand. "You've been so good at the young

girl anthems and the independent woman rock-your-face-off thing, but this is so raw. It's so introspective. There's real depth to the pain of those lyrics. "Miss Me" is the kind of song to stay with you forever. You'll still be singing it every night twenty years from now."

Lila winced. "Can you excuse me? I need to find the ladies room."

"Go, go, go." Mimi shooed her away. "We'll work on getting the nitty-gritty done quickly."

Lila fled down the hall and ducked into the bathroom. She locked the door behind her and nearly doubled over from grief. Her chest felt painfully tight and her throat too narrow for the amount of air she required. She hated feeling this way, but she wasn't surprised. Sadness had become a constant companion. It clung to her in all sorts of subtle ways. She rarely slept through the night, she hadn't had the desire to shop in weeks, and little things like Hallmark commercials and romantic comedy trailers made her eyes water. She'd learned to live with the little reminders, like a dull ache, but recording Cobie's song had felt closer to a stab wound.

She braced both hands on the cold porcelain sink and stared in the mirror. Why was this still happening? Because of the song? Did it keep dredging everything back up again? She couldn't avoid releasing it forever. She'd already waited weeks too long. She was losing momentum in the press. She really couldn't wait if she wanted to stay fresh, and yet fresh was exactly what the wound felt like every time she sang those lyrics. Each word served as a living reminder of the fact she'd worked so hard to ignore.

She missed Cobie.

She missed working with her, she missed sparring with her, she missed the feel of her strong arms and the brush of her lips. Most of all, she missed the quiet comfort of having her nearby.

Of course, none of those things mattered. It didn't matter what Lila felt. It didn't matter that Cobie was strong or good or kind while they'd been together. Lila had read the papers. She'd seen the reports of Cobie's big movie deal. It had happened fast and seemingly easy. And why shouldn't it? Cobie was a star. She'd gotten what she came for, and then she'd left, just like every other person in Lila's life. And she'd said her peace on the way out too. She thought Lila was cold and shallow and selfish. And Lila couldn't honestly argue with her. She'd pushed her away at every turn—she knew that. But she should have at least felt vindicated in knowing she was right, that no one was going to fight for her but her. Instead, she only felt sad, a bone-chilling, head-throbbing kind of sad.

"Knock knock," Felipe called, not daring to actually rap his soft hands and perfectly filed nails against the metal door.

"Just a minute," Lila called. "I'll be right out."

"No, pull up your pants 'cause I'm coming in."

She rolled her eyes as she unlocked the door and found him standing there with his hand over his eyes.

"Felipe, I'm fully dressed."

"Promise?" he squeaked in his highest vocal register.

"I promise."

He slowly lowered his hand and peeked through one eye. "Oh good. Now we can talk."

"We can talk at home."

"Nope." He flipped the lock on the door behind him. "This ends here."

"Felipe," she said, sternly, "I have appointments."

"Then your options are to talk fast or be late. I don't care."

"Mimi will come looking for me."

"I told her you had to take a very important phone call and not to interrupt. Also, Malik is standing guard at the end of the hall. This is happening now."

She tried to scoot past him and reach for the door, but he caught her wrist and held tight.

"Girl, do not try me. It's been a lot of time since I've had to fight for something, but you do not grow up a Latino queer in north Florida without having those lessons burned into you."

"I know. I was there," she snapped back.

"That's right. Every mumbled curse, every boy who played me and then punched me, every time a teacher looked the other way, you were there. You took care of me."

"And I can take care of myself too."

"I know, but just because you can doesn't mean you have to."

The comment tripped one of those invisible triggers that sent water rushing to her eyes, but before she had time to even process the breakdown, he had her wrapped in his arms. He smelled of coffee and lavender, and she sank into his soothing embrace.

"What did Selena say?" he whispered as he held her.

"She said she remembered that little gay kid I was always running around with."

"Of course she does. I'm fabulous, but you know that's not what I mean."

Lila wasn't going to get out of this. She wasn't even sure she wanted to. She'd carried the burden for so long, what difference would acknowledging it make? "She said she didn't regret leaving me. That it made me who I am."

"Wow, glad to see the years haven't broken that massive ego of hers."

"She had some points."

"On the toes of her shoes or the top of her black hat?"

Lila pushed him away. "She said I would've never gotten out if I had waited for someone to save me. She said I had to learn to save myself."

"What a great way for her to let herself off the hook."

"She said I became the poster girl for independent women."

"Well." He lifted a shoulder noncommittally. "Okay, that's the truth."

"And she said that only happened because she taught me to never put my trust in anyone else."

"And there's the bullshit again."

"Is it?" Lila asked as she started to pace.

"Yes," he said quickly. "No, wait. Let me think about it, um, just kidding, of course it's bullshit! Selena has been wrong about everything at every turn. She was wrong to abandon you, wrong to live off your money, and wrong to take credit for any part of who you've become."

"She wasn't wrong about my needing to trust myself instead of waiting for someone to save me."

"Right, but who's trying to save you?"

"No one. Now."

"Oh no, girl. You didn't." He snapped his fingers and pointed at her. "No, please tell me you didn't kick Cobie to the curb over Selena."

"We had run our course. I couldn't get too attached. She's got her movie. She was born to play Vale. Or maybe Vale was born to be played by Cobie. You don't even know, she's got a history with the screenwriter, and Cobie was flirting with Cordelia." The words all spilled out of Lila in a rush. "I have to count on me. I can't look to anyone else to save me."

"Save you from what?"

Lila stopped pacing. "Save me from what?"

"Yeah. You are railing about not needing someone to save you, but what was Cobie offering to save you from? What did she do to make you think she believed she was rescuing you somehow?"

"She didn't want to break up."

"So? Where's the savior complex there?"

"She got me to talk about Selena."

"And did she put on a cape at any point in the conversation?"

"No, but she said she didn't want to lie any more. She wanted to be a couple, for real."

"What is that supposed to save you from? She wanted to be honest about liking you. She didn't offer to take you on as a ward or hold a feed-the-children telethon in your honor."

"Okay, fine. I get it."

"Do you?" he asked. "Because I'm not sure you fully realize that where you are is not where you were. You're a fancy, gorgeous, white lady rock star gazillionaire who sings to cheering crowds for a living. There's nothing to save you from, except maybe yourself."

"What's that supposed to mean?"

"It means maybe Cobie just loved you. Maybe she wanted to spend time with you and get to know you and share your life with you, not as a savior, but as a partner."

"But Selena said—"

"Oh, my God. Fuck Selena. She's never done right by you, not once in fifteen years. Why can't you just admit she was wrong?"

Lila covered her eyes as the tears threatened to overtake her again. Cobie didn't want to leave her. Lila had made her.

"What?" Felipe asked. "What now?"

"It's just, if Selena was wrong about this, then I was wrong about something much worse. Oh God, Felipe, what am I going to do?"

"Um, well, I . . ." His facial expression was quickly nearing the grimace he'd worn when he worried she didn't have her pants on earlier. "I didn't think that far ahead. You're the independent superstar businesswoman. You'll figure it out."

"Business." She repeated the phrase, and for the first time noticed the acidic taste it left in her mouth. She couldn't stand any more bitterness. Something in her snapped, or maybe it snapped back into place as Cobie's voice rattled through her memory. *Maybe all you've got is business because that's all you ever let matter.* "Yeah, business. Let's take care of that first."

She stepped past him and swung open the door, but this time he made no move to block her. Instead, he practically jogged down the hall to keep up with her long, full strides. Malik, for his part, fell in beside her without so much as a questioning glance.

Mimi met her at the control room door. "Lila, honey, we were just talking about your new single, and—"

"Pull it," Lila said.

"What?" Mimi asked, her smile not faltering.

"Pull the song off the record."

Everyone froze.

"I mean it. That song is not getting released, not as a single, not on the album, not under my name."

"But, but, but," the producer stammered and turned to Mimi. "Handle her."

Mimi's eyes narrowed dangerously. "Excuse me?"

He took a step back and straightened his tie. "I'm sorry. I meant I want that song. Let's come to terms on a price."

"It's not for sale," Lila said firmly.

"Everything's for sale," he said, anger flashing though his voice once more.

Lila shook her head sadly. "I used to think so too. I was wrong, about so many things, but I think most of them came back to that one idea. Some things aren't for sale."

"Mimi," the guy pleaded. "Do something."

Mimi looked Lila in the eyes for a long, hard minute searching for something, and she must have found it, because her smile grew to wrinkle the corners of her eyes. Then she turned to the technicians. "You heard the woman. Pull the song off the record!"

"Yes ma'am," the young guy said with a look of astonishment.

Then with a flip of her wrist, she waved aside everyone else in the room, slipped her arm around Lila's waist, and marched them right out the door.

"Thank you," Lila said after they were out of earshot.

"I'm proud of you and who you've become," Mimi said. "I'll do whatever I can to help, which brings me to the next item at hand. Do you want to tell Cobie her song isn't going to be a top-forty hit or should I?"

Lila stopped short. "How did you know?"

"Because that song clearly wasn't you talking to her, so I figured it had to be the other way around."

Lila nodded. "I couldn't sing her words every night."

"Good," Mimi said resolutely. "I would've thought less of you if you did, but you still haven't told me what you intend to do now."

"I don't know," Lila said honestly. "I hadn't thought anything through yet."

"Well, I'm not telling you what to do with your business, but maybe you should start thinking faster, because Cobie and Talia have requested a meeting with Addie Hammels's legal representatives for Friday afternoon."

"What? Why?"

"Apparently, they want her on the design team for *Vigilant*."

"She remembered." For the first time in weeks, the little twinge in her chest didn't stem from sadness. Even with everything else that had happened between them, even when Cobie had got what she wanted, even with the awful way she'd left things between them, she'd not only remembered Addie, she was making good on her promises to Lila.

She covered her face with her hands. Cobie was still coming through for her. How could she have ever believed Selena over someone who had proven herself to be her polar opposite.

"What do you want to do about the meeting?" Felipe asked.

"I don't know," Lila said, suddenly unsure of herself once more. She couldn't just assume Cobie would take her back. She was clearly out of Lila's league in so many ways. What if Cobie realized that now? What if she was still mad? What if she didn't want to see her? What if she had already moved on? Just because Lila had come around to realizing the error of her ways didn't mean Cobie agreed with her. And Lila had barely survived the first rejection, even when she'd had work to fall behind. "Just give me some time to think about it, okay?"

Mimi's smile vanished, and Felipe and Malik shared one of their judgy, exasperated looks, but no one said anything to stop her. Once again, she was clearly on her own.

Chapter Fifteen

"Ladies, let me introduce Addie Hammels," Stan said, as he ushered a young woman into the conference room. "Addie, this is Cobie Galloway and Talia Stamos."

"Uh, yeah they are," Addie said in a teenager tone that made Cobie smile.

She extended her hand. "It's nice to meet you, Ms. Hammels."

"Um, I'm just Addie right now. My last name is, uh, in transition."

The comment made Cobie's chest ache, and she and Talia exchanged a look. "I understand you're in the process of emancipating yourself from your parents?"

"She is. That's why I'm representing her today," a woman said, entering the room clad in a business suit and carrying a manila folder. "Addie is in charge of all negotiations, but she'll run all legalities and contract terms through our office. Shall we get down to business?"

Cobie looked behind her to Stan and then to the door. "Are we expecting anyone else?"

"No, I guess not," he said as if the news disappointed him. She knew the feeling. It had hovered over her for weeks and had only amplified when she had returned to the city. She had hoped that by requesting this meeting a week early, she might have gotten a response from Lila. When no call or message had come, she let herself hold out some hope that she might just show up.

With those hopes dashed, Cobie struggled not to look too downtrodden.

Thankfully, Addie kept things moving by turning to Talia and saying, "I really like *Vigilant*. Like, I read it three times during chemo."

Talia smiled broadly and exclaimed, "You're hired!"

"Hired for what?" Addie asked, looking around the room. "I thought you just wanted to use the one drawing."

"Actually," Cobie said, "we're looking to assemble a team of artists to do some pre-production artwork for the film. Things like more outfits, some concepts for Vale's apartment, a sketch of secondary characters for us to send out to agents before auditions."

"And you want me?" She motioned up and down her own lanky form. "Even after you've seen who I am?"

Cobie sat forward. "Who are you, Addie?"

"I'm just . . ." She shook her head. "I'm just a kid, a bald, punky, lesbian teenager. I can't be what you came in here looking for."

Talia opened a folder and pulled out a few sketches she'd printed from Addie's website. "Are you the woman who drew these?"

Addie's eyes grew wide as she surveyed her work. She raised her hands to the dark stubble starting to grow unevenly along her scalp. Then she laughed, a loud shot of humor-laced disbelief.

The sound rolled over Cobie like a hot shower in the dead of winter, and she felt a part of her heart fall back into place.

"I'm going to take that as a yes," Talia said, her own voice light with amusement.

"Yeah," Addie finally said.

"Then I think a bald, punky, lesbian teenager is exactly what we're looking for on this project," Cobie said, quickly adding, "It's not going to be a cake-walk. You'll answer to a creative director who likely won't care that you're young. You'll have to work fast and withstand critique. And there's no guarantee anything you do will end up in the final version of the film. It's a long hard process."

"Holy shit, is this really happening?" Addie asked. Catching herself, she said, "Sorry, I mean yes. I can handle criticism. There's nothing a director could say to me that would be worse than— never mind. I mean, thank you."

"It's okay," Cobie said softly. "It's a lot to process on the spot, but you're right, nothing that will happen during the production will be worse than what you've experienced in other areas of your life. You have my word."

Addie's eyes narrowed. "Are you doing this just because Ms. Wilder told you about me? I didn't ask her to. I didn't even ask her to visit me at the hospital. She just did. You don't have to give me something just because of her."

"No," Cobie said quickly. "The truth is until a week ago, I didn't know anything other than your name. I'm sorry for that. I should've found you sooner. I should've done my research sooner. I let my own biases and assumptions get in the way of doing my job, and I'm here now because your drawings speak for themselves."

"But Ms. Wilder was your . . . or is . . ."

"Ms. Wilder is not here," Cobie finished for her, hoping she didn't sound as heartsick as she felt about that fact. "I can have some contracts drawn up for your attorney to look over, but you'll get paid scale for your work, the same as any other artist on the team, and you didn't hear this from me, but if you also asked for a hefty bonus on any piece that makes the final film, I would see to it no one balks."

Addie looked to her lawyer for the first time all meeting. The woman nodded, and the corner of her hardline mouth might have even twitched upward for a second.

"Yeah, that'd be lit," Addie said. "I mean, thank you, Ms. Galloway, Ms. Stamos."

"Please, we're going to be working together a lot. Call me Cobie." Then she fished a card from her pocket and slid it across the table. "And that's my personal number. If there's anything I can do for you in the meantime, in any way, please don't hesitate."

"Wow."

Talia scratched her number on the back of one of the drawing printouts and pushed it Addie's way. "There's mine too."

"Double wow." Addie grabbed both phone numbers and clutched them tightly to her chest. "I went from having, like, only two numbers in my phone to doubling that with two famous people. And, I mean, I didn't even used to like your movies." As soon as the words left her mouth, she raced to cover it with both her hands and her pale face flushed fire-engine red.

Cobie and Talia both roared with laughter.

"I think we're going to get along famously," Talia said.

"I'm so sorry," Addie said to Cobie.

"Don't be," Cobie said. "If we're being honest, I haven't really liked my movies for a long time either, but we're going to work together to make sure we're all proud of *Vigilant*."

"Yes, of course. Thank you," Addie said, standing as her lawyer did. "I appreciate this so much. I won't let you down."

Cobie walked around the table to meet her at the door. "I know. And I promise not to let you down either."

"Would it be totally horrible and uncool if I hugged you?"

Cobie smiled. "Maybe, but I'd really like it anyway. I promise not to tell if you don't."

Addie wrapped her long skinny arms around her neck, but it was Cobie who squeezed tighter and longer. The connection was good for her soul, more healing than all the time she'd spent in the mountains and more strengthening than any of the exercises she'd spent months doing.

"Okay, now go celebrate," Cobie said as she stood back. "Maybe your lawyer should take you somewhere fancy for lunch and bill the hours to Stan."

"Go ahead," Stan said when the lawyer looked over her shoulder. "It's on me, but be sure to ask if Mimi wants to join you. She's already called dibs on managing your career, something about girl-power and sisterhood."

"Thanks, Stan," Cobie said after Addie had left. "I appreciate your backing me with the studio about her."

"It's no problem. When they heard she did your costume, they didn't really put up much of a fight, but even if they had, your name carries a lot more weight than it used to."

Talia punched her on the shoulder. "Big shot."

"Are you suggesting I should turn into a more demanding diva?"

Stan smiled his big toothy grin. "Not with your manager of course, but if you wanted to do some more things like you just did there, it wouldn't be a bad thing."

Cobie nodded thoughtfully. She hadn't done enough of that sort of thing over her career. Perhaps doing her own thing and keeping to herself wasn't always the best answer. It sure hadn't been nearly as rewarding as seeing the exuberance on Addie's face. If getting into the game a little more meant more moments like those, she'd add it to the long list of life choices that needed to be reevaluated. "Point taken."

"Good." He clasped her on the shoulder. "Then I look forward to seeing more of you."

She wouldn't go quite that far, but her priorities clearly needed some rearranging as she went forward with the *Vigilant* project. This movie had to be different on so many levels. She couldn't just accept what she had come to consider the status quo, not for the work, not for the people she worked with, and not for herself.

She and Talia headed down the hall in silence until Talia suddenly stopped and gave her arm a squeeze. "Cobe, I really love that kid."

She nodded. "She's good."

"She's fantastic. She's talented and polite, but she's also kind of irreverent. She's not pretending to be someone she's not. She's not trying to sell anyone. And did you see her body, all wiry and scarred? She's been to hell and back."

"Yeah," Cobie agreed, a sense of protectiveness swelling in her. She didn't add that the kid would probably still be in hell if not for Lila.

"And she confirmed the no-parent thing and the queer status. What's wrong with people? What kind of parents abandon their kid? I sort of want to adopt her now."

"That's a good idea," Cobie said.

"Really?" Talia asked. "She's getting emancipated, so I was just kidding, but maybe she would like to stay with me instead of alone? Is that weird to ask?"

"Yeah."

"Oh, okay, then I won't, but wait a second." She punched Cobie's arm. "Are you even listening to me?"

"What?"

"That's what I thought." Talia rolled her eyes. "What's wrong?"

"Nothing," Cobie said, though the more appropriate answer might have been "everything." She had her movie deal and all the people she wanted on the cast and crew. Her manager told her she could ask for more, and she had just used her new star powers for good. She should be walking on air, but even her happiness felt off-kilter right now. She couldn't quite put her finger on why, or maybe she just didn't want to, because if she tried to find the source of her discontent, she'd be forced to admit nothing had felt right since her fight with Lila. Something about the moment hadn't just upset her, it had altered her core. No emotion had been clear or pure since that morning, and she suspected none would be until she went back and righted the wrong.

"Hey." Talia raised a hand in front of her face. "You're kind of scaring me. Come on, spill."

"I just thought maybe Lila would be at that meeting."

"I know, but—"

"I know you don't like her, but you don't really know her. I'm not even sure I really know her, and maybe that's because she didn't let me, or maybe it's because I didn't let me, but the fact of the matter is, I misjudged her."

Talia's eyes widened. "Cobe, she's—"

"She's a lot of things, I know. She's calculating and manipulative, but she's also smart and talented. She might be a bit of a fame hog at times, but she's also clearly capable of doing things under the radar too, things you and I never thought her capable of."

"Right, and she's also—"

"She's also made some mistakes and some poor choices, but so have I. Why do I get let off the hook for that when she has to pay? Basing an entire relationship on a lie isn't a good idea. But not everything between us was for show. Those moments when we were alone, when she had nothing to gain and still chose to give, those were real. And maybe they didn't mean the same thing to her that they did to me, but they meant something."

"Good, but—"

"It's really unfair to expect her to make compromises to her career and her life and her future without acknowledging that I need to make some changes too. I can't keep expecting this life to give me back anything I'm not willing to share. Lila gets that. She understands what it means to be part of something bigger, and I don't need to agree with all the ways she goes about that to understand she's always got her reasons. She's a role model to kids like Addie. What have I been to them?"

"Cobe, you have to stop right now."

"No. I'm just getting started. And maybe she doesn't want me. Maybe I'm going to have to live with that, but I'm not going back to being the person I was before. I want better. From her, and more importantly, from myself. I have to go to her house."

"You can't," Talia said firmly.

"I have to try to set things right," Cobie said passionately. "I have to go—"

Talia bopped the palm of her hand on Cobie's forehead and held it there, then leaning really close, said, "You cannot go to Lila's house right now because Lila is not home."

"What?"

Talia used her hand to physically turn Cobie's head toward another long hallway. "She's right behind you."

Cobie blinked a few times, but she still had a hard time clearing the rush of thoughts from her mind enough to process what she saw. There in the middle of the hallway stood Lila in a little sundress as red as her lips. Cobie's mouth went dry at the sight of her, a subtle sign that not all her reasons for desiring this meeting were altruistic.

"Yeah," Talia said as she finally released her. "Now that I see her in person, I sort of get why you let her get away with the things you did. Good luck with that going forward."

Then she did a little skip-jog back in the other direction, leaving the two of them alone.

Cobie sighed, and Lila smiled a slow, nervous grin. Cobie took a step, then Lila did the same until step-by-step they found themselves standing close enough to touch. This was their moment, the one she had waited and wished for. And as they closed the distance between them, she still had no idea what she intended to do with the opportunity. Should she open with an apology? Maybe she could beg for forgiveness for all the awful things she had thought and said, or try to open up with something lighter? One thing was clear, she should say something. Something smart, something charming, something heartfelt and true. I miss you, I'm sorry, I love you. All were valid options, and she had yet to settle on one when she parted her lips and Lila met them with a kiss.

The kiss was sweet and sad and powerful enough to zap any residual doubt right out of Lila's chest, but what it left in its place was something more powerful. Regret, remorse, the acute awareness that they were right and everything else was painfully wrong.

She wanted to drink from Cobie's lips as if she'd spent their entire separation lost in a desert, parched and alone, but she knew she had no rights to that well.

Pulling away slowly, she felt bolstered by the little whimper of protest that escaped Cobie's mouth.

"What was that for?" Cobie asked as she regained enough of her breath to speak.

"For everything you said to Talia, for everything you did for Addie, for everything you did for me that I never thanked you for and," she smiled shyly, "because I love you."

"I'm sorry, you what?"

Lila's face flamed. It wasn't quite the response she'd hoped for, but she couldn't take the words back any more than she could make them untrue. "Yeah, well, you don't have to say it, or feel it, or even acknowledge I said it, but I did it because I do. Love you."

Cobie looked around to see several people frozen at the other end of the hallway. "Oh, right. Is there a camera on?"

Lila rolled her eyes. She probably deserved that, but instead of falling on the easy excuse, she took Cobie's hand and pulled her into a conference room, slamming the door behind them. "No cameras, no mic, just me and you, Cobie. I'm sorry I didn't do this sooner, and I understand if it's too late, but I made a terrible mistake."

"We both made mistakes," Cobie said. "I don't blame you."

"I do," Lila said. "I went to see Selena the morning after we made love. I don't know why. I guess I felt like I had to make peace with her, but I was wrong. Or maybe I handled things the wrong way. I should have made peace with the fact that she wasn't there for me and never would be, and I needed to move on. Instead, I just stood there feeling like a helpless teenager all over again as she said I couldn't trust anyone. I should have woken up right there. I shouldn't have believed her. I don't know why I did, but I got scared."

"Of course you did." Cobie reached out to stroke her cheek.

"But I shouldn't have, because she kept talking about herself when I could only think of you. She railed on about saviors and rescuers. You were offering partnership. She ranted about things that had no bearing on my life anymore and no relationship to you."

"But she hurt you." Something hot and hard flashed in Cobie's dark eyes. "Someone you loved betrayed you again, and then all those pictures of me with Cordelia. Lila, I should've understood, especially after what you'd told me the night before. I'm so sorry."

"You don't have to apologize to me. I pushed you away. God, Cobie, I pushed you away so many times. My only experiences with relationships have been terrible, but you were different, and I refused to let myself believe that. You tried so hard to show me something better, and I scorned you."

"And I let you," Cobie admitted. "I should have fought, should have dug deeper, but I took the coward's way out. I knew we were more than we let people see on the surface, but I was just as complacent in accepting the tidy little narrative you wove. I was just as bad as the press about underestimating you or discounting your motives."

"I'm not even totally sure what my motives were, between Selena and my career and all the things you made me feel. I had controlled everything in my world for so long until you came along, then everything got jumbled. I panicked."

Cobie nodded. "We could never just be us. I feel like I don't even know who I am right now, or who I'm becoming. It's not who I was last month, and I don't even think it's who I was six months ago. It's going to take some time to figure it all out."

"Time," Lila repeated. "You deserve that, but does time have to mean time apart?"

Cobie shrugged. "I don't know."

"I'll try to give whatever you need, because I know I don't deserve a do-over, and I don't even want one."

"You don't?"

"No. I want a do-different. I want a fresh chance to do things right. I want to ask you out myself, no managers, no press. I want to kiss you with no one watching. I want to get to know who you are, not just what you can do for my career."

"But something like that would affect your career," Cobie said, suspicion in her voice. "You and I together long-term wouldn't mesh with your image."

"Then maybe I need a new image. The one I had doesn't fit anymore. And honestly, with or without you, the new record is on hold."

"Why? I thought you were done."

"I couldn't record the song."

Cobie frowned. "Because it wasn't good enough?"

"No." Lila took her hand. "Because the words were too good, too true."

"I thought you liked to sing the truth."

"I thought so too, but no truth has ever hurt the way losing you did," Lila said as she stared into those big dark eyes. "I couldn't live with the prospect of singing those lyrics every night knowing I was destined to miss you for the rest of my life."

"Lila," Cobie whispered, "I don't know what to say."

"Say you'll give me another chance," Lila pleaded, her heart throbbing against her rib cage. "Say we can start again from the beginning. I didn't show you before, but I'm strong and passionate, and I can bring those things to a partnership the same way I do in other areas of my life if you'll just let me have another shot."

Cobie's eyes watered, and she sighed heavily before saying, "No."

"No?" She nearly choked on the word.

"We can't undo what's been done. We can't just forget everything that's already happened between us," Cobie said softly. "I can't, anyway."

Lila nodded and fought hard to swallow the emotions threatening to explode out of her chest, but all she managed to say was, "If you feel that way ..." before the weight became too much and she started to cry.

"Hey," Cobie cupped Lila's face gently in her hands. "I said we couldn't go back, and I don't want to. I know we both made our fair share of mistakes, but I wouldn't trade them for anything, because they got us here."

Another tear fell. "You do know that 'here' is crying in a conference room, right?"

Cobie laughed. "But you said you loved me, and I love you, and even though I don't know where we are going to go from here, I think being in love is about as good a starting point as any."

"You love me?"

"Madly," Cobie said.

"Since when?"

"Probably since the first time you kissed me."

"You kissed me the first time."

"Nope," Cobie said, a hint of blush coloring her cheeks. "You stood right there in front of those windows, looped your arm through mine, and kissed me on the cheek. I melted for you right there. I let you talk me into your wild scheme and dress me up and parade me around like a show poodle, and I pretended it was all about my career because that seemed easier to face than admitting I was just another one of the many fools who had fallen for the beautiful and talented Lila Wilder."

Lila took Cobie's hands in her own and kissed her cheek. "Okay then, if we are starting this new stage of our life with a rousing bout of honesty, then I have to tell you I started to fall in love with you the minute you tripped over my shoes and offered to buy me new ones."

"No," Cobie protested. "I annoyed you."

Lila shook her head. "You were so damn beautiful and adorable and sincere and earnest, I couldn't believe someone like you could possibly exist in this world. Part of me didn't even really want someone like you to exist because of what it would mean for someone like me, who had compromised and neglected those parts of myself, but another part of me just wanted an excuse to be close to you. That's why I didn't bat an eye when Mimi suggested I come out as bisexual. All I could think was, 'I am open to any options so long as they come in the form of her.'"

Cobie kissed her again, full and fast, then broke away laughing. "Can you imagine what we would have been able to do if we'd just admitted those things on day one?"

Lila shook her head. "So many more days by your side, so many nights in your arms. No, I can't imagine, but I want to live it. You're right, again. I don't want to go back. I want to go forward, with you, starting right now."

Epilogue

"Cobie!"

"Lila?"

"Over here."

"Smile!"

Cobie heeded the last command, not because she felt any affinity for whatever member of the press had shouted the order, but because as she turned back to face the limo she'd just exited, she caught sight of one impossibly-high heel emerge, followed by a stunningly long leg.

Stifling the urge to hop back into the limo, she held out a hand and shivered as Lila's red-nailed fingertips slipped seductively across her palm. With a gentle tug, she helped her girlfriend to her feet, then wrapped an arm possessively around her waist.

Lila rewarded her with a little kiss on the cheek before whispering, "Look at the cameras."

"Why? They're all pointed at you."

"They're all pointed at us," Lila corrected as she lifted her chin and angled her face toward another barrage of flashbulbs.

Us. She did love that word. Using it for months on end had done nothing to dull the pleasure it sent through her core. Thankfully, the press hadn't seemed to grow tired of the concept either. If anything, their genuine union seemed to generate more buzz than their fauxmance had. Or maybe the union had just generated so many opportunities artistically that they were finally getting press for all the right reasons.

That thought made it infinitely easier to keep from rolling her eyes as they stopped every three feet along the red carpet outside the Lincoln Theater.

By the time they made it to the lobby, spots of white light were burned into her retinas, but she'd grown so used to the experience, she simply closed her eyes for the five or six seconds it took for her vision to return to normal. When she opened them again, she was met with another one of her favorite sights.

Talia and Addie walked toward her, with Addie's new girlfriend, Mazie, following behind in a star-struck stupor. The two of them had met on set, where Mazie had landed a summer internship as part of her art design program at NYU. "Cute as kittens" was how Talia described them together, and Cobie couldn't disagree, even though the term always made Addie scowl.

"Well, don't you look the part of dark and sultry superstar," Talia said, scanning Cobie's leather pants and tuxedo jacket.

"Lila dressed me."

"Duh," Addie said, as she ran her hand through her dark spiky hair, then turned to Mazie and said, "Lila will dress anyone who gets within a ten-foot radius."

Lila's blue eyes sparkled with mirth as she gave Mazie an exaggerated once over. "Six-foot, actually."

Everyone laughed as Mazie deliberately stepped closer.

Despite the excited buzz of press and producers, Cobie's heart warmed at the ease of the interaction. This moment, like the thousands of others that had taken place on sets and stages, spoke to none of their early encounters. The pace, and in some ways the pressures, had only grown as albums were launched and blockbusters filmed, but here, in their small circle, the reality always remained better than any performance. She gave the slender curve of Lila's hip a subtle squeeze.

Lila responded to the pressure by turning to face Cobie. Her red lips curled up and her long dark lashes fluttered. Everyone else faded from the room, and the contented pride that had filled Cobie's chest moments earlier was replaced by something more raw that registered lower in her body. The urge to kiss her was swift and strong, and she leaned into the impulse, but before she had the chance to muss up their make-up, someone thrust a microphone between them.

"There's the woman of the hour!" a young reporter in a navy-blue velvet suit exclaimed.

Cobie blinked away the haze of lust and looked over her shoulder, then back at him before realizing he was talking about her. Remembering that she was at work tonight, she quickly rolled her shoulders and flashed her camera-ready smile.

"Or should I say, the power couple of the year, because you've really both become so much bigger than any one moment." The reporter continued to ooze praise. "How does it feel to be just moments away from seeing yourself on the big screen as the character so many people now say you were born to play?"

"It feels pretty amazing to finally be in this moment when we can premiere *Vigilant* in the city that gave it life. This project was so much bigger than me though."

"But you're the one getting all the Oscar buzz," he said, giving her a little conspiratorial nudge with his elbow.

Cobie's natural urge to step back was counterbalanced by Lila's hand across the small of her back. She wouldn't shrink from the attention she'd earned from early screenings of *Vigilant*, but neither would she take the bait in that question. The awards would come later, or not at all. What mattered now was getting to share something she believed in with the people who mattered most. "I'm proud of the work that every member of our amazing team did to bring Talia Stamos's phenomenal book to the big screen."

"And rumor has it you personally oversaw the assembly of that team, going so far as to hand pick people even as far down the ladder as staff writers and costume designers."

Cobie glanced past to where some of her co-stars had gathered in the double doors leading to the theater, all bright, talented actors and actresses no doubt on the brink of stardom. Then she looked toward Talia and Addie, who had both taken several steps back, clearly trying to avoid the wide view of the camera lens. "And every one of those people played their parts to perfection, which I don't think of as being lower rungs on a ladder. They are artists every bit as much as I am, and they deserve to be celebrated just as much as I do."

She noticed Talia's shoulders tense at the mere possibility of being pulled onto center stage, and Cobie quickly turned back to face the camera. "I think when you watch the film tonight, you'll see how our team's shared vision for this project comes through in every detail."

"I suspect you also shared a vision with someone important on the soundtrack too," the interviewer said. The suggestiveness in his tone made Cobie return her focus to the woman making her heartbeat echo through her ears.

"Well..." she drew out the word playfully. "We may have had a few conversations on the subject, but Ms. Wilder doesn't need much help from me in the vision department. She composed a stunning instrumental score for the film entirely on her own and played several of the piano pieces herself during the studio recordings."

Lila gave an air of being bored with the compliment, but the hint of natural color peeking out from beneath her light blush gave her away. She was as proud of her work on *Vigilant* as Cobie was.

"Cobie is too generous," Lila cooed. "This is her night, and I'm proud of what she's brought together here."

"What *we've* brought together here," Cobie corrected. "Lila contributed so much to this artistic process. Aside from the score, she also had a hand in concepts for set design and costuming."

"And the first single from the soundtrack, 'Miss Me,' has been on the top of the charts for a record-setting fifteen weeks."

"But I have to give all the credit to Cobie on that one," Lila cut back in, wrapping a hand tightly around her biceps and pulling her a little closer, the way she so often did when memories of that song's inception flooded their memories.

"Right!" the reporter said excitedly. "Another joint project. Cobie wrote the lyrics to 'Miss Me.'"

"It's true. She has a way with words, but she did so much more than put them to paper for me." Lila turned now, committing the cardinal sin of taking her eyes off the camera to point that breathtaking gaze directly at Cobie. "Her biggest contribution to 'Miss Me' wasn't the lyrics. It was freeing me up to sing it by promising I'd never have to live its message."

Cobie sighed and smiled, and the reporter went away, or maybe he didn't and it simply didn't matter anymore. This time, no amount of microphones or cameras or mussed up make-up could keep her from kissing the woman she loved.

Also by Rachel Spangler

Learning Curve
Trails Merge
The Long Way Home
LoveLife
Spanish Heart
Does She Love You
Timeless
Heart Of The Game
Perfect Pairing
Close to Home
Edge of Glory

About the Author

Rachel Spangler never set out to be an award-winning author. She was just so poor and easily bored during her college years that she had to come up with creative ways to entertain herself, and her first novel, *Learning Curve*, was born out of one such attempt. She was sincerely surprised when it was accepted for publication and even more shocked when it won the Golden Crown Literary Award for Debut Author. She also won a Goldie for subsequent novels, *Trails Merge*, and *Perfect Pairings*. Since writing is more fun than a real job, and so much cheaper than therapy, Rachel continued to type away, leading to the publication of *The Long Way Home, LoveLife, Spanish Heart, Does She Love You, Timeless, Heart Of The Game, Perfect Pairing, Close to Home* and *Edge of Glory*. She is a three time Lambda Literary Award Finalist and the Alice B. Reader Award winner for 2018. Her thirteenth novel, *Love All* will be released in Fall of 2018 by Bywater Books. She plans to continue writing as long as anyone anywhere will keep reading.

Rachel and her partner, Susan, are raising their son in western New York, where during the winter they make the most of the lake effect snow on local ski slopes. In the summer, they love to travel and watch their beloved St. Louis Cardinals. Regardless of the season, she always makes time for a good romance, whether she's reading it, writing it, or living it.